BEYOND THE MASKS

A BEYOND SURRENDER SERIES NOVEL

NICKY F. GRANT

ISBN-13: 978-0-9995404-1-1 (paperback)

ISBN-13: 978-0-9995404-0-4 (eBook)

To Matthew:
My love, my king, and my hero.
The man that encourages my dreams
and the one who owns my heart.

And to the Goddesses…
This series title is for you.

"AGH!"

Shane Vaughn slammed the copy of *Rolling Stone* on her desk, nearly spilling her coffee all over the pristine white desktop.

David peeked into her office. "Did you read it?"

"Yes, I read it." Tossing the magazine aside, she ran her fingers through her hair.

"You didn't fail," he soothed, walking in. He unbuttoned the slim-fit, blue linen jacket before sitting in a cube-shaped visitors' chair.

They'd been through so much together since starting out in the music business while living in Austin, Texas. He had a special way of making her feel like a success even on her worst days. Working in a male-dominated field left no room for error, and he kept her grounded and focused.

She adored him. Loved the support he provided as she lived the dream and achieved success as a top executive for Omega Records in New York City.

He rested his right ankle over his left thigh, showing off his cropped jeans and gleaming brown, wing-tipped shoes. "You knew Jacob would try to sign Icarus Descending first. He always knows when you're close."

Jacob Andrews, her first relationship and music business partner in Austin, Texas. A man built to challenge her in every way possible. *"Only the best survive, Shane,"* he'd told her.

The mutual competition to rise to the top was appreciated. He'd pushed her hard, and she wouldn't be CEO of a major record company if not for him. He'd believed in her, even when they had differences.

"But how? The only other person who knew was Gavin and maybe his assistant." She drummed her fingers on the desktop. It would be industry suicide for the top talent director in the business to leak their intentions. "Shit. All the money spent on food and parties, not to mention the Rolexes and whatever else Omega flipped the bill for makes me feel like…"

"A three dollar whore?" He raised his eyebrows and smirked.

"Yeah, kind of. That contract was the biggest Omega has offered to date for any new artist. I just wish he'd find his own talent," she snapped. "He'll be the death of me." All this talk about contracts and business made her thirsty. A few steps to the mini fridge and she snagged a bottle of water. The chilled liquid soothed the heat in her chest.

She scanned the impressive collection of awards. Each had a spot on the shelf above the refreshment bar. These were her proudest accomplishments. Her hand grazed the gold phonograph award for Album of the Year. *Jacob doesn't have one of these.*

She returned to her desk and stared at the portrait on the cover. In the photo—flattering, but then, it was the cover of *Rolling Stone*—his shoulder-length, light brown hair glinted with blond hints. His tight, full beard framed his perfect face as his green eyes stared back. Mocking her.

Asshole. "I can't take the smug look on his face." She plopped down next to David in the adjoining visitor's chair.

"It is a nice face, doll. He's easy on the eyes."

"Don't remind me."

"Have you spoken to him?"

"Not since the *Billboard* gala last fall." She kicked off her shoes and curled into the chair.

She'd been discussing a new business venture with the CEO of *Billboard* when Jacob monopolized the conversation. Granted, he did drop a few desultory compliments to the CEO on her work ethic and beauty, but she knew better than to give in to Jacob's allure.

"Wow, that should go in the record books." He raised his hands as if displaying a headline. "I can see it now: *'Music Exec Shane Vaughn Makes It 365 Days Without Speaking To Her Long-Lost Love. Is It Really Over?'*"

She glared. "You read entirely too much *US Magazine*. And before you ask, I can't forgive him."

He tilted his head, the light from the window shining off his black-rimmed glasses. "Now, now. Shouldn't all gorgeous, successful men be forgiven sooner or later?" He swiped the magazine from the desk. "I mean, look at him. Man, I bet he's good in bed."

"Would you like to prove it?"

"Only if you hear he's batting for the other team."

"You'd never cheat on Sean."

Sean was the love of David's life and a production manager for a successful rock band.

"So true, but a guy can dream." He sighed. "Well, should we kick off the day?"

"Yes, and get Gavin Mayne on the phone and tell him to be in my office in five."

"Shane 'The Vicious' Vaughn is back, and she's already forgotten about Jakey," he mocked. "Are you firing him? Can I watch? I love it when you get all CEO."

"Watch it, or you're next."

"Nah." He tossed the magazine in the wastebasket before making his way to the door. "You've fired me a million times, and I'm still here. Besides, who's going to keep you looking fabulous?"

She lifted her shoes. "You're lucky I love these so much."

As he left, closing the door behind him, she dug the magazine out of the trash, gazing at Jacob's image.

What happened to us?

GAVIN ROLLED HIS NECK, all the muscles in his body stiff. Being called to the boss' office had put a damper on the morning. Shane was a nuisance, a constant irritation, poking and prodding his insides.

How the hell did she deserve a title as prestigious as Chief Executive Officer of a major record label? She had been promoted to right the ship, according to the board, but in his opinion, he didn't see the company improving.

He straightened his Canali suit jacket and yanked at his shirt cuffs. He was the number one sought-after talent director in the city, and if his artists didn't make it to number one on the charts, it was a personal failure. Not an option. Because of his natural ability to identify the next big thing, he'd pushed Omega Records to the forefront of the music industry. Not her.

Musicians beat down his door for a few minutes of his precious time in hopes he'd give them a shot. *He* was the face of Omega Records. Not Shane. She went around town riding his coattails, never once acknowledging his hard work. Taking all the credit for herself.

And now she had the nerve to summon him. Whatever she wanted, he would find it trivial, thus wasting his valuable time.

Not once in the last three years had she ever invited him to her office, let alone had a side conversation with him.

A few minutes later, he knocked and sauntered into Shane's office. "You wanted to see me?"

She stood at the windows, talking into her headset, and when she glanced at him, he could sense her irritation. "Yes, please sit," she said before continuing the call. *Such a power play*. Inviting him here to watch her work.

Brushing invisible lint from his suit, he sat and examined her office. Along the large windows sat her oversized white desk. Her taste was modern with mostly white features, something he found out of date. The large sitting area to his left was where she entertained vendors or the board of directors. A place to perform the work required to make this record company a success.

The awards encased in glass along the bar and rows of platinum records were strategically placed throughout the room, all from his connections and discoveries. She barked an order to whoever was on the other end of the call, and he casually looked her way. A crisp white shirt with black leather belt cinched her waist. His gaze drifted past the multi-hued pencil skirt to her long legs and blue peep-toe slingbacks. One thing he had to admit: The boss lady took care of herself. He leaned back into the chair. Waiting had its perks.

"Have Kelly pull out front at five o'clock…Yes… Not till later. Thank you." Shane tossed the headset aside and walked to the front of the desk. She leaned back against it, arms crossed.

"Is there something you would like to explain?"

The old game of cat and mouse. He preferred blunt and to the point.

"I'm not sure what you mean." When he steepled his fingers, his elbows rested on the arms of the chair.

Shane picked up the copy of *Rolling Stone* and tossed it in his lap. The headline read: *"Jacob Andrews of Avalon Music Group Signs Icarus Descending."*

The news had finally hit the stands, and now he knew what angle to play. "It was never going to happen anyway. No sweat, there will be others." He shrugged, throwing the magazine into the empty chair next to him.

"Last week, you said they were ready to sign." If looks could kill, her eyes would be the weapon.

"Things change." She wouldn't win this battle or the war ahead. He would go toe-to-toe with her until he wore her down and she had no choice but to bow out. His finger curled over his top lip. Anything to hide the smile that had formed.

"Things change?" She pointed to him. "I expect results, and when I'm told this is in the bag, it better happen."

"Don't get your panties in a twist, Shane. Icarus Descending played both sides."

"The only thing twisted is your understanding of the hierarchy in this company." She straightened and raised a finger. "One. You make assurances. Two." She held out another. "You deliver. And three. I pat you on the head and say good boy."

A laugh nearly choked him as he swallowed. Her imperious delivery almost seemed convincing. A thousand insults raced up his throat and settled on his tongue.

"Do you understand what this means to Omega? Their single received three million views on YouTube last month alone, for crissake. This is pure irresponsibility on your part. AMG has stolen what should have been ours—on your watch."

That's right, Shane. Maybe now you will keep an eye on your company.

Enough of this charade. He stood and stepped forward until he felt the heat radiating off her tight body. Staring down at her, he said, "And what are you going to do about it? Fire me?"

A force shifted between them. Shane inhaled sharply, the

sound a sudden tug to his dominant senses. Her gaze met his. That shut her up. He drew out the uncomfortable silence between them.

Finally, she said, "Consider this a warning."

He snorted. There was no way she could prove anything. He stared into her crystal blue eyes and allowed his gaze to travel to her full lips, then her long, light brown hair, which flowed in waves down to her perky tits. A dark thought stirred inside him. What would she be like bent her over her desk?

He gazed back up, slow and deliberate. "I'm too valuable to this label, and I'm the one who makes you look good. Remember that, sweetheart."

He turned to leave, striding toward the door.

"Which is why we are going to attack the new Ryan Digmore account together."

He stopped cold. Now she'd crossed the line. Interfering in his business affairs was off limits, even if she was the CEO. Ryan Digmore was poised to be the next up and coming indie artist. His sound fit into several categories of music, rounding out Omega's catalog of artists. Gavin had courted Ryan over the last several weeks and could almost taste the sweet victory of another deal closing on his behalf.

"No thanks, Shane." He pivoted to face her.

"It wasn't a request." She closed the gap between them, her spine ramrod straight as her chin jutted forward, arms crossed, pushing her breasts together. He could almost make out their shape. "Sources tell me AMG is going after him, and we can't have another unfortunate slip-up, now can we?" The corner of her lip curled in satisfaction. She'd done her homework. *Good girl.*

He matched her pose. Arms crossed. Feet shoulder wide. At six foot four to her five foot three, he could get used to this view. "Actually, he's close to signing with AMG."

Her face tilted to meet his. "They may be our biggest competitor, but aren't you the best in the industry? Change his mind,

Gavin. Or perhaps you can't live up to your overinflated potential."

He clenched his fists, and his heartbeat branded his rib cage as she artfully tested his connection to AMG while challenging his business savvy.

In a cool tone, he said, "Does the queen of the minnows think she can swim with the sharks?"

"Oh honey. You're mistaken. I've been swimming with you for a long time."

David's voice piped through the intercom. "Shane, your ten o'clock is here."

"One minute, David." She never flinched. "Well, Gavin?"

A small slip in her daily armor fell when he stepped forward. She straightened again. It was unguarded, even if for a moment. *What do we have here?* The reaction shot straight down to his groin.

He twitched a small smile. "Okay, Shane. I'll let you play with the big boys. But I have nothing to prove to you." He paused, allowing his gaze to flick over her face. "It appears you have everything to prove to me."

2

"HE SAID WHAT? I can't believe you didn't fire him!" David exclaimed, taking a dainty bite of his burrito.

"I know. I couldn't. When he left the room, I nearly fell to the floor, completely turned upside down. Besides, he's too valuable. The board would have my head." Shane pushed the carne asada around her plate, having suddenly lost her appetite after the sudden rush of heat and tingling nerves ran to her toes. Why him. Why now?

Since the day she hired him, he'd provoked a level of aggravation she couldn't overcome. The board had insisted he join the team, which, at the time, she'd thought was a great idea given his credentials and talent pool. But Gavin had proven to be a chauvinist with a separate agenda. He made his own rules, avoiding a unified front for the label. After several attempts at fostering collaboration, she'd given up, concluding avoidance was the only way they could work together.

"And something changed all of a sudden. He approached me and…it was strange. Like how I used to feel around Jacob." A warning bell sounded in her head as the fork clanged the plate. "Shit, now he knows he can get one over on me."

"Or get ON you," he laughed.

"Whatever."

But maybe this is something. A man she'd despised throughout their working relationship had changed in a moment. Did he notice? Or was she the only one to feel the shift in the air? His large body close. His scorching blue eyes searing her face. Tight, square jaw and Grecian nose cut from a sculptor's mold to meet wide sexy lips. And the aroma of anise and cloves...*Can't forget his smell. Holy hell.* The wave of attraction returned, sucking her in like a riptide. The gravitational pull had possessed her thoughts all day.

With an accusatory tone, she pointed her fork at David. "He's up to no good, and I need to keep an eye on him."

"How?"

She smiled. "We're working on the Ryan Digmore account together."

David's jaw dropped. "You think that's a good idea? He'll only camouflage whatever he's hiding."

"Probably, but my burning gut tells me he worked with AMG to secure Icarus Descending. I wasn't born yesterday, David, and there has to be a way to sway him off track. Catch him in the act. Something..." Her eyes went wide.

"What are you up to?" David leaned forward. A sly smile appeared.

She tapped a finger on the table. "He felt it too. I know it. There's no way he missed it. Men like him can pick up the scent of an aroused woman anywhere."

"How are you going to catch him?"

"Play to his charm. Become all starry eyed and bending. He'll be putty in my hands. The tougher the exterior of the man, the harder he falls."

Corporate domination roused her appetite, and she scooped a huge bite of meat into her mouth. The thrill of beating Gavin at his own game also provided the avenue toward discovering his motives behind cheating Omega.

"Sure. But have you considered how out of practice you are?" He blotted the corners of his mouth.

The comment wasn't rude but, rather, pragmatic. David not only understood her business life but also her dating life. Or lack thereof. She pushed her plate away.

"Maybe what you need is a night out. Brush off your old skills. It's been, what, a year?"

A year? No. Two years since she and Jacob were together. And the last time she felt the all-consuming, shoot-her-through-the-stratosphere amazing connection with someone. She shuddered.

"Two, but who's counting?" She waved her glass in the waiter's direction. "Two years and another margarita to wash that realization down."

"Doll, seriously, you need to get laid. Especially before conquering the man who invented the word sex." He removed a card from his wallet and slid it over to her. "Here."

Big red print blazed the words *The Resort* with a phone number. "What is it?"

"A pleasure club." He smiled.

"Where did you get this?" she asked in a skeptical tone. "Does Sean know you've been checking into these places again?"

He tilted his head, and his dark brown pompadour flopped to the side. "Have you forgotten he occasionally ventures into the dark side with me? You should go. It has a different crowd."

"How so?" Now her curiosity tipped the scale.

"They have a unique way of hiding your identity. With you being a bigwig in the music industry, you can't be too careful."

"Right. Keep going."

"For starters, you can wear a mask to conceal your face. Also, any tattoos or other features proving identification can be covered." Waving his hand over her wrists, he assured her. "So those tats will not be seen."

She covered the inked flesh, protecting them from view. When her dream of being a mega star failed, she'd gotten them. The colorful images of falling stars provided a constant reminder to continue pushing forward no matter the outcome.

"But what if I don't want to hide who I am?" Every day she suppressed who she was from the real world. She put on an invisible mask at work to make others believe she was a tough businesswoman. The façade wore thin, but it was the only way she knew how to remain successful and be taken seriously.

"You don't have to." He shrugged. "Whatever you're comfortable with."

She nodded with a sigh, rubbing her wrists to soothe her racing mind. "Okay. What else?"

"You get a stage name. Kind of like a stripper, but not the trashy type. Which is a bummer, because I could totally see you as a *Candy*."

"Shut up!" She playfully threw the napkin at him.

He caught it, sticking out his bottom lip. "Aw, that hurt. Maybe they could call you Goliath."

Shaking her head, she chuckled. What would her name be? It seemed silly, but on further consideration, she thought it best no one see the real her. At least for now. She glanced down at her tattoos.

"Star."

"Hmmm…Star." He mulled over her selection. "How apropos. I think it works."

"What's your Resort name?" she asked smirking at her friend.

"I never reveal my secrets," he said quickly, placing his hand across his chest in a dramatic gesture. "It's supposed to be anonymous."

"Come on. I told you mine. Besides, I need to know so I can avoid hitting on you or vice versa." She batted her eyelashes.

"Who said I would hit on you? You're hideous and a woman," he said deadpan. His lip twitched, sending them into laughter. "It's Delicious or D for short."

"And you said they avoid trashy names."

"Let's just say I'm special."

SLUMPING into the back seat of Omega Records' black SUV, she tapped the business card on her thigh. What would it be like to experience a D/s relationship again? There was no doubt she was out of practice. But she had never been with anyone other than Jacob in *that* way. Would she feel comfortable surrendering to another male?

She understood what it meant to be submissive in the purest form. Submission was instinctual to her. It was in her core. It was as necessary as breathing, yet she lacked a partner as skilled as Jacob to bring her back to center. Sure, she played the powerful role at work, but not having the escape from her daily guise made her hollow. Had she misplaced a piece of herself, or was Jacob holding it for ransom?

During the eight years they were together, he'd introduced her to submission. He'd discovered a pent up need to control her during sex to which she gave herself—body, mind, and soul—without question. She loved him and trusted he would never hurt her.

The sexual part of their journey brought them closer. He'd listened to things she enjoyed and things she didn't like, always adjusting their sexual play to meet each of their comfort levels. She would try anything Jacob asked, and he respected if she didn't care to do certain things again. All built on years of understanding and layers of trust.

The Resort, however, would be different. It would mean submitting to an unknown person. She'd be at the mercy of someone she hoped would have some experience picking up on non-verbal cues during sex. Blind trust. It was insane to even consider it. If she chose to visit The Resort, all her limits would be pushed.

But the compulsion to wake her submissive side from hibernation poked her insides. Placing herself in Gavin's world meant dusting off her submissive and sexual side to play *his* way in the boardroom. Or at least let him *believe* she was. Ryan Digmore was a big fish in a small pond, and she would be damned if she lost him to AMG. This was the only way.

The Resort would provide the tools essential to compete with Gavin. If she was honest, she couldn't deny the sweet anxiety rolling through her veins at the idea of jumping into a submissive state with a stranger. A wave of heat consumed her when she imagined the sinful pleasure of a man's hands, his mouth, and his commands. All while his face remained hidden behind a mask. She pressed her thighs together.

David was right. It was time to get back out there and experience something new. Giving over her body was the easy part. Separating her mind and not submitting her soul—with no interest in being with someone long-term—was another.

Would she enjoy it to the degree she had before? Would she fly?

JACOB HIT the gas of the silver Aston Martin on his way to congratulate his new band, Icarus Descending. The wind tousled his hair as he took to the streets of New York. His excitement and triumph thrummed through his veins, enhanced by the powerful engine as he bypassed a yellow taxi.

The familiar surge when he conquered the next up and coming band gave him a rush like a gambling addict beating the house. His job as CEO of Avalon Music Group inflated his ego, making him feel as powerful as a god. He always got his way, especially when it came to making his label the best in the industry.

But the surge wasn't as high this time. When he found out Omega Records was courting Icarus Descending, he assumed it would be easy. And when he won the bid, the surge felt underwhelming. Flat.

This would kill Shane. Visions of her flashed before him. Her blue eyes sad as her full lips parted in shock when she found out they had decided to sign with his label instead.

He shook off the guilt. This was business. Icarus Descending was the next generation of rock music, a sound AMG prided itself on. His record label could take them mainstream quicker and with more access and publicity to offer them. Omega Records was second rate to AMG as far as he was concerned. So he'd found a means to get them to sign.

Jacob stopped right in front of the restaurant and parked. With a casual toss of the keys to the valet, he entered the main doors. Ben, the lead guitar player and vocalist, tamed mohawk pushed to one side, and wearing torn jeans and black dress shirt, greeted him.

"Jacob. My man," Ben said as he put his hand out to shake. "How are ya?"

"I'm on cloud nine and thrilled to be celebrating this success with you. Your band will be at new levels in the coming year. We're happy to have you on the AMG team," Jacob replied, taking his hand.

Josh, the drummer, slapped him on the back. "There's the man that changed our lives!"

"I think this calls for a toast." Jacob waved down the bartender. "Five shots of Gran Patrón Burdeos Añejo. Neat." He slid his black American Express over the bar.

"First on the agenda, gentlemen, remastering your original album. I booked a studio for you to use for the next month. Make the most of it. Your new producer will be Michael Blaya. He's worked with other large acts in your genre and is the best in the music business right now. He will take your original work and make it something special."

"Special?" Ben chuckled. "I thought it already was. I mean you did sign us."

"Absolutely it is, but what the industry wants is extraordinary. Mike will polish your existing work, and while you're re-recording, we'll discuss your touring schedule."

He picked up the fine tequila and raised his glass in the air. "But before we get ahead of ourselves, let's toast." The band members grabbed their drinks and followed suit. "To an amazing partnership, lots of money…"

"And bitches!" Ben yelled.

"Only the best groupies for your band." They clinked glasses and swallowed.

Josh chimed in, "When do we start?"

"Next week. We'll pack your things and relocate you here to New York." He handed Ben a card. "You'll be staying at this location. The sooner the tracks can be laid on digital recordings, the faster we can push out your first single. From here on, consider yourselves true artists and put your energy into being just that. I will take care of the rest," he assured them.

Ben grinned at his comrades. "I guess we officially made it."

"First things first. Time to get you acclimated to the lifestyle of stardom."

THE LIMO SLOWED to a stop in front of Azotar, an exclusive night-club for New York's elite. Jacob relaxed into the vibe his new band created. Jovial back slaps, hoots, hollers, and give-no-fucks energy validated his decision to sign them. They were wild and what the industry craved. Rock was a dying genre, and his label pushed to keep it in the forefront. AMG was founded on rock, and he intended to keep it alive.

Icarus Descending had it all: music, talent, and sex appeal. This group would bring the next generation of chicks to their knees. There was no doubt they would prove to be his biggest moneymaker since taking over as CEO, leaving Omega Records in the dust. Shane's company had been edging forward to take the number one record label spot, but now AMG would remain the best.

A pink neon sign blazed over the main brick entrance. Lines of people crowded the sidewalk and stretched down the block, all waiting to lounge or dance as burlesque performers taunted the patrons with their bodies and evocative promises over the crowd.

Ben led the remaining band members to the end of the line. "No, gentleman. This way. We don't wait. Get used to it." Jacob slipped them through a side door.

A large bouncer rose from his stool. His meaty hand greeted Jacob with a handshake. "Welcome back, Mr. Andrews. They're ready for you upstairs."

"Thanks, Ivan."

Ivan was a beast and, when provoked, could lift a person by the back of the neck with one hand. Jacob had gained first-hand knowledge when his last musician got out of hand with one of the burlesque girls.

"Ivan, this is Icarus Descending, AMG's new rock band. Ben, Josh, John, and Carmen."

"Welcome to Azotar," he grunted, eyeing up Carmen, the band's bassist.

"What's up, man?" Carmen's lip piercing caught the light from above when he grinned.

Without amusement, Ivan called, "Miranda, can you show Mr. Andrews and his friends to their area?"

An alluring petite girl, wearing a short leather skirt, came out from behind a curtain. Her breasts spilled over the top of her corset as her light brown tendrils curled around them.

"Ivan, are you giving these gentlemen a hard time?" Her small hand squeezed his large bicep like a deactivation device. He sat, crossing his arms. "Much better. Mr. Andrews, so nice to see you again. It's been too long."

She batted her long lashes and blushed. Playing coy was her game, but deep down, Jacob knew the vixen living under the surface. A familiar desire awakened in him. Miranda had a way about her and satisfied him in ways no woman had since Shane. She possessed the right amount of kink to satisfy his needs without question. She was right; it had been too long.

He kissed her cheeks and rubbed his hands down the powder white skin of her arms. "Jacob, please. You are as striking as ever."

"You are too kind, sir. Please follow me this way." She turned on her heel, waving a delicate hand.

Miranda sauntered up the stairs in her five-inch, Louboutin black stilettos. The attempt to bait him didn't go unnoticed. The VIP section contained a couch, chairs, and several bottles of chilled Cristal set on the table's center. Perched on the furniture were the escorts he'd ordered for the band. One leggy blonde, a brunette, and two redheads.

"I only see four girls, Andrews," Ben observed.

"I will not be partaking in the rest of the festivities this evening. Consider this a gift to you."

Ben smirked as his band members made their selections.

"Thank you, fine sir." Miranda handed Jacob a glass of champagne.

"Thank you, beautiful," he said. He kissed the top of her hand, igniting a familiar spark between them.

After he'd abandoned Shane, he found himself at Azotar nearly every night, searching for someone to take away the pain. Miranda had helped him pick up the pieces and forget what a selfish bastard he had become.

Leaving Shane was no small feat although Jacob convinced himself it was the right thing to do. She'd become distant after the loss of her father, sinking her life into work. While caring for her and hoping she would come out of it, he also withdrew. When given the opportunity to become the youngest CEO of a major record label, he'd left Shane to pursue his lifelong goal. *Total selfish son of a bitch.*

"Anytime, sir." She began to walk away and turned back. "And don't be a stranger."

He clutched her elbow, hauling her toward him. Eyes sultry and inviting. The casual but intense connection they shared surged through him.

"What are you doing after your shift?" He inhaled her perfume, ripe peach and pure sin.

"What do you want me to do, Sir?"

A woman addressing him as *Sir,* coupled with asking what he wanted, spurred something dark in his gut. Being near her brought back a primal desire to fuck. No love and no feelings.

His guilt over signing Icarus Descending steeped below the surface. He'd done it to cut Shane out of his life, to achieve closure because he could never have her back. Their relationship was officially over, and Miranda was going to help him to forget it one more time.

"Stop by my place, like old times."

Her body heated through his fingertips. He sucked an earlobe, and his hand found her ass under the short leather skirt. A blooming flower of compliance to his touch. *Perfect.*

The consenting rasp in her wanton voice said everything.

"Yes, Sir."

"One hour."

3

THE NEXT MORNING, Shane clutched the phone as she called The Resort. Each ring brought her closer to the unknown. It was time to move forward. More than her demanding work schedule and craving an escape, this would be the only way to let Jacob go for good.

A small, nasally female voice answered. "Hello, and thank you for calling The Resort. This is Candy. How may I help you?"

Shane coughed, trying to disguise her laughter. Of course, her name would be Candy. *Did David know?*

"Um, ah, yes, I'm calling to discuss a membership."

"Absolutely. We will need to secure a background check prior to instating the membership. May I have your email to send along the forms to complete?"

After providing Candy her details, she was told the packet would arrive shortly. While she waited, she called David.

"Good morning, doll!" Heavy breathing muffled the receiver as she heard his feet hit the belt of a treadmill.

"Working up a sweat?" Music drifted in the background.

"Yeah, Sean's at work, so I decided to work out my sexual frustration with Enrique Iglesias and Adam Levine."

"Lucky you. Next time, invite me over, please." She laughed, spinning her chair toward the windows. "I had the most interesting phone conversation this morning."

"Oh, yeah? With whom?"

"The girl from The Resort."

"And why is that interesting?" She could feel his grin.

"Her name was…get this…Candy."

"Oh, holy hell!" He belly laughed, wheezing as she heard the treadmill stop. "You. Are. Kidding."

"Not at all. I suppose your name, Delicious, fits right in after all." A ping from her email sounded. "The background check forms came through. I have to go. I'm one step closer to the dark side again."

"Can hardly wait! Go get 'em. Shopping?"

"Yes, please. I'll call you when I'm done here." Ending the call, she opened the email. Scanning the attached documents, she exhaled to settle the butterflies having a party in her stomach.

"Now or never, Shane," she assured herself.

Blinking at the screen, she opened the documents, quickly completed the background check, and dove into the club policies and rules:

The Resort takes the privacy, safety, and consent of its members seriously. The following rules are enforced to create a safe, private, and mutually consensual environment and atmosphere. Any member acting inappropriately or found in violation of the rules will have their membership revoked immediately.

1. *Masks and other identity concealing aids may be worn in the common areas at the discretion of the member.*
2. *Masks and other identity concealing aids may only be removed when mutually agreed upon by all parties involved within a private scening area.*

3. *Protected sex must be adhered to at all times. This is for the safety of all members.*

4. *Medical history must be updated every three months. Failure to do so will result in membership suspension or termination.*

5. *Use of recreational drugs is prohibited. Drug screening must be completed every three months.*

6. *Any change in member's legal name, location, or other personal information must be reported to the club office at the time of change.*

7. *Dress code within common areas is strictly enforced.*

8. *Any member visibly intoxicated will be removed from the premises and their membership revoked.*

9. *Any member acting with force not consented to by another member will be removed from the premises and membership revoked.*

10. *Standard safe words must be used: Red, Yellow, and Green. No alternative safe words will be permitted.*

11. *Safe word usage is monitored at all times. Anyone not adhering to the safe word guidelines will be removed and membership revoked.*

12. *Fire, blood, needle, scat, breath play, and golden showers are strictly prohibited.*

13. *All members must adhere to the soft and hard limits of their play partner(s) upon receipt of such document. If these guidelines are not followed, immediate removal and revocation of membership will be upheld.*

14. *Sex toys, apparatuses, and other objects of erotic nature aiding in sexual pleasure or pain play will be inspected at arrival.*

The anxiety loosened in her chest as she read each line. The safety of their members was paramount. Meeting someone with his own set of rules and being harmed in some way was not an option. The protection the club provided gave her confidence in the members.

Next, she completed her medical history and order form.

Physical within the last three months and birth control. *Yes, and yes.*

Dominant, submissive, or switch. *Submissive.*

Concealment aids. *Satin gloves and mask.*

An overwhelming wave of unease flooded her as she gripped the mouse. The checklist for hard and soft limits spelled out all her fears and desires. *Were people always this specific?* Seeing the limits on paper made what she'd allowed Jacob to do so tangible. He knew her body so well she never worried about him pushing her into new realms of pleasure and pain.

She thought back on all the things they'd tried, concluding each act or scene had happened organically. Sure, they'd discussed exploring new ways to play, but she'd never hesitated because of the trust she'd placed in him.

What would it be like using these techniques and practices listed? Her mind spun as she read the details. *Arm binders, suspension, sleep sacks, anal fisting?* She shivered. "No way. Hard limits."

Riding crop, flogger, dildo, hair pulling, and orgasm denial. "Hell, yeah." She grinned, checking them off with confidence. She scanned the remaining list and stopped on voyeurism.

"Being watched or watching others. Hmmm."

What if…? A jolt of desire flooded between her thighs. Jacob was against sharing, which had stopped her from exploring it. Even if there was no contact, it still shared her pleasure with others. Something he considered a hard limit. A small side of her wanted to get back at him. "Maybe…"

Leaning back in her leather chair, she rubbed her eyes. Attempting to be submissive again was her good-bye to the

"Shane" she knew today. A glimmer of excitement promised hope. A journey in self-discovery and taking herself to a different place of power was what the doctor ordered. Reclaiming who she was on the inside, deep within her soul.

Determination set in. No more feeling scared to meet someone new. No longer would Jacob have any power over her. This was her choice. No approval from Jacob necessary.

Click. Swoosh.

Membership application complete.

She spun her chair and stared out at the New York City skyline. The beautiful sun peeked over the buildings, burning off the fog from Central Park. A new day. A new chapter in her life.

Rising from her chair, she proceeded to the master suite. She entered the white marble bathroom and moved to the clawfoot bathtub. As she turned the chrome handles, water flowed out of flat spouts and rolled into the tub like a waterfall. Steam soothed her face as she added a few crystals of wildflower bath salts.

She walked back to her cozy bedroom. Her retreat. A large sleigh bed filled the main space, and light filtered through the sheer curtains, giving her a sense of peace.

She peeled off her gray camisole and matching panties and tossed them on the bed. Standing naked in front of her dresser with mounted mirror, she placed a large clip into her mouth. She twisted her hair in a pile on top of her head and secured it. Her eyes traveled to the rest of her naked skin.

Gazing at her reflection, she admired the roundness of her breasts, slim body, and round ass. What would another man think about her? She blushed as a smile appeared on her lips.

What would her mystery Dom look like? Dark hair? Light eyes? *Yeah, totally different from Jacob.* A tinge of arousal trickled between her legs. The temptation to touch herself over-powered her will to ignore her desires. Her reflection peered back at her as she gently stroked her breasts. What if *he* were here now? Touching her.

She scraped her fingernails around her nipples. Her head fell back as she conjured up the man of her dreams. A delightful hum escaped her lips.

His lips kissing sensually down her exposed neck. His dark hair tickling her ear. His blue eyes absorbing her reaction in the mirror as she accepts his amorous advances.

As desire flared between her legs, her folds dampened. One hand drifted to her sex, massaging the outer lips. The delicate touch teased while the other tugged a nipple.

He continues kissing down her back, his lips meeting each shoulder blade and down her spine. Unhurried, priming her for what is to come. A path of heat from his touch runs down her sides, goosebumps left in its wake. As his hands approach her hips, he lowers to the floor. She moans as two fingers slide unhurriedly into her wet pussy.

"Yes…" She slipped her own fingers into the folds of her lips and down toward her opening, her melting core like silk to the touch.

He kneels, nibbling her round buttocks, caressing where his mouth has made contact. Slow fingers pump in and out of her sex like he has all the time in the world. Turning her toward him, he kisses and licks following a path from her hips to the crease where her thigh meets her sex.

Shane inserted two fingers, biting her bottom lip to stave off a simmering orgasm. Her knees buckled, causing her to lean the other hand on the dresser. Her labored breathing became synchronized with each thrust of her hand. In and out, she built a rhythm. The brilliant anguish from her movements tensed her core as she rubbed her clit.

When his tongue circles her swollen bundle of nerves, she blooms like a flower, inviting him in. He stops. Piercing blue eyes, laced with lust, gaze at her while still keeping a rhythm with his hand. He inhales her scent deeply.

"Fuck," she breathes out as her knees buckle, but his strong hands hold her upright. She is lost in him. Blue eyes and his commanding touch hypnotize her. Any past pain she held is stripped away as it slips into the sea of passion. She closes her eyes once more, unable to hold contact. It's too much. Her body aches for release, but he keeps her on the precipice. "Please..." she begs.

He flicks his tongue on her pulsing clit and nibbles with his teeth. Divine pleasure takes her up, up as he sucks the nub. She moans loudly, and the man's tongue circles her clit wickedly as his fingers thrust. Her core drips as sounds of her pleasure fill her ears. "Yes...yes!" she screams.

Her strokes quickened as she pushed harder on her clit with the heel of her hand. The mental images scrolled through her mind until she exploded into her hand. Her body shook violently until she withered to the floor. The orgasm quaked again and again, wracking her muscles and her body. *Damn, I needed this.*

As her body calmed, she rolled to her back and stared at the ceiling. Who would be the man at The Resort to take her on a sexual journey? Excited about the mystery, a final tremor moved through her.

Sliding upright, she carried herself to the bathroom on shaky legs. Sinking into the tub, she immersed herself in the warmth. She turned off the water and lounged back, allowing her body to relax as wildflower scents filled her nose. She exhaled, finally letting go of years surrounded by sadness and loneliness. It was time to take the plunge.

GAVIN BLINKED as the light crept in through the window of his

Brooklyn brownstone. *Morning already*, he thought, as his mind flashed back to the prior evening.

Ethan Pax, the new owner of The Resort, had done an excellent job reviving the exclusive club. The investment he'd made as a silent partner had been put to good use. Ethan and Gavin had frequented the club over the years, and when it went up for sale, they both saw a great deal of business potential for their hidden lifestyle.

The Resort was his retreat, and he was comforted by what it represented. The club allowed him to seek deep control, which complemented his overall life. The desire to bring a submissive to their knees as he artfully catered to their innermost fantasies became vital to the way he was wired. It was the foundation of his being.

He swung his feet to the floor and turned. A beautiful blonde slept soundly. *Blair.* The bedding had slipped to her waist exposing her full breasts.

He had grown tired of his last playmate and had decided it best to part ways to explore other interests. He was becoming a particular Dom. One only seeking a challenge. It meant struggle, which led to ultimate control—something his then playmate, lacked.

Last night, he'd met Blair. She merely filled the space between play partners, but she allowed him anything. Carte blanche. Blair was an experienced submissive with a short list of limits, was obedient, and ready to fuck. Good for now, but only temporary.

The chill in the air caused her dark nipples to purse, and thoughts of sucking them again hit his groin. *No repeats, remember?* That was their agreement.

He rose from the bed and dressed in running shorts and black t-shirt. She could rest a little while longer. Their marathon evening required it. He grinned. What a great show.

He jotted a quick note and left it by the bedside table along with her clothes neatly folded.

Thank you for last evening.
Please see yourself out.

No offense should be taken. Time limits had been clearly discussed. This was a one-time thing. Blair lacked what he ultimately craved—challenge.

As "Killing in the Name Of" piped through his ear buds, he ran down the steps and onto the sidewalk. The crisp air and hints of fall lingered as the breeze hit his face. Dodging walkers as he jogged, his mind turned.

Shane. The only thing standing in his way to becoming CEO. If not for him, Omega Records would've lost out on extraordinary talent and necessary revenues to put them on the map in today's market.

His breathing accelerated as he sprinted forward. But what was it about her in the office? Blood drained south. The small sway in power invigorated him. The hitch in her breath. The slight shift in her stance. So, what if he had been thrown at first? She'd surprised him.

Shane was always the intimidating, dominant businesswoman. She commanded the boardroom and never hesitated to remove dead weight. And now her mission was him. Inserting her presence into his deal with Ryan Digmore, she was on to him. Keeping enemies closer was a motto he lived by.

Was her dominance a façade? Leaning over in front of his home, he took deep breaths to slow his heart rate. *Male dominance was her weakness.*

The light bulb flickered in his brain. He wiped the sweat from his brow and smiled. Maybe working together on this deal wasn't so bad after all. Dominance could sway her off track. She was attractive, and he would have no issues reveling in her bliss to test his theories. Once she surrendered her mind, body, and soul, he would figure out a way to get her to relinquish her position. She wouldn't be able to resist him.

He bounced up the steps, lighter than before. He removed the ear buds and tossed the phone on the foyer table. As he rounded the corner into the kitchen, the ways he could manipulate Shane flipped through his mind.

"Good morning."

A cringe tightened his form. Blair...wearing his dress shirt from the night before with nothing else. He froze. Why was she still in his house? His gaze raked over her; she wore his garment so well, her lean, long legs on display, and her hair slightly disheveled from sleep and sex. There was a twinge of attraction for her.

Maybe one more time? No way.

She smiled. He gave nothing away of the sordid thoughts of her tied to his bed.

"Good morning," he said curtly.

She went to reach for his neck and he snatched her wrists. "No."

Confusion swept her features. "But why?"

"I have rules. I thought I was clear. Why are you still here?"

"Last night was nothing short of incredible, and I thought an encore was appropriate." She twirled her hair between her fingers.

"We had an agreement." The glimmer in her green eyes faded. "If you'll excuse me, I'm going to take a shower. I expect you will be gone when I'm finished." He was such a shit.

The smile faded from her red lips as he passed her on his way toward the stairs, leaving her to consider his order. He demanded one thing from his submissives: *Follow the damn rules*. She'd failed, and strangely, he wasn't even in the mood to punish her. His t-shirt thumped as it hit the hamper when he reached his room. He stopped to stare into the mirror, feeling like the bastard he was.

Boundaries were just as important to him as they were for the women he played with. Limits had been set long before he became a self-proclaimed Dominant. No relationships. No fucking feelings. No love. These were all things that would screw with the structured life he fought to maintain. One failed course and it could all end.

Seeing the longing in Blair's eyes told him he'd made the right decision to dismiss her. She would become a problem if he entertained her company. Blair would never understand his past, the darkness he kept inside. No one ever did.

Running his fingers along the edges of a fallen angel inked on his chest, it ached. When his palm smoothed over the inscribed name, nausea settled in the pit of his stomach. *Nicolette*. A constant reminder of why he needed distance.

4

"WHAT DO YOU THINK?" Shane twirled out of the dressing room.

David whistled.

"Perfect. No question about it. I mean, I did pick it out." He uncrossed his legs and stood. The champagne glass clinked on the marble tabletop. He tugged the skirt of the backless flared halter dress to rest perfectly on her hips. He leaned back, tapping two fingers to his lips. "Yep, this will do."

"You make this so easy. It will always amaze me."

"It's one of my many talents. Spin." He twirled his finger in the air.

She turned delicately, loving the way the dress fit her.

"Now, for shoes. Jessica, can you come here, please?" he called to the sales associate. Jessica appeared. "Giuseppe Zanotti's Cruel Summer. Size seven." She scurried off.

"Who's that?" She admired the low plunging neckline through her reflection in the lighted mirror.

"Only the best shoe designer in the world. If only I could stand walking in women's heels. My feet would be so happy."

Jessica returned with the shoes on a display tray, all five inches of sexy stared Shane in the face. Taking a seat on the settee, Shane allowed Jessica to place the shoes on her feet. The shiny metallic silver flames climbed her feet and buckled at the ankle.

"I will take them!" No denying this was the attire for her first night at The Resort.

She handed Jessica her credit card as David eyed his creation.

"You, my doll, could take down an army of men in that dress. May the Dominants fall at your decorated feet."

"Thank you." She gleamed in delight, hugging her dear friend.

"Now get your gorgeous butt out of this dress and let's eat. All this hard work has made me famished." He smacked her ass, and she yelped, running into the dressing room.

She dressed quickly in polka dotted rolled up jeans, sweater wrap, and tan wedges. With the dress draped over her arm, she found David scrolling through his phone. "Ready?"

"Yep. Sean messaged and wants to join us for lunch. Would you care, terribly?"

"I would love to see him. How's the little bistro on 7th ?"

"Great minds think alike." He held out an elbow, and she slid her hand into the crook of his arm.

The pair exited to the street and slid into the waiting SUV. As they pulled away, the buildings passed by as thoughts crowded her mind. So much time had been lost since the split with Jacob.

Her father's death had taken a toll on her. He'd been her savvy half. The man who'd taught her all she needed to know about survival in the business world. A hard-working union steel worker who'd fought for his beliefs and used his street smarts to get ahead, the lessons he'd taught never left her. Shrewd but honest was his mantra. She set herself up for success through observation, patience, and careful planning. One of the biggest things she'd learned was pivoting a negotiation on a dime, sending control back into her hand.

She'd identified with her father so much that, when he died, nothing else existed. Not family. Not friends. Not Jacob. Her job distracted her enough to keep going. A singular focus on success kept her from drowning in sadness. And what was the outcome? Losing the love of her life yet becoming the most successful woman to run a music label.

David's hand wrapped around hers, and he wiped a stray tear from her cheek.

"Now, honey, your makeup will run. We don't want to scare the waiter." He handed her a monogramed handkerchief he kept stowed away in his jeans pocket.

"I'm so silly. I don't even know why I'm crying," she choked out a laugh.

"It's okay, doll." He patted her thigh.

"Kelly, could you switch on the music?"

"Yes, Ms. Vaughn," the driver responded.

Bass sounded through the speakers as Anna Marie's new single filled the vehicle. The lyrics boomed through the bass, singing about Saturday nights and crazy parties. Omega Records had signed her last year, and she was destined to be the next Ariana Grande. Shane was sure of it.

"Is this your new protégé?" David asked.

She rolled her eyes. "As you know, her single dropped this week."

"Oh, right, right. Word on the street is she caused quite the scandal recently. Something about sleeping with some other musician's boyfriend."

"And where did you hear that?"

"You know, my girl, Celeb Deb."

"Who?" She laughed.

He whipped out his smart phone, and she glanced at the displayed gossip site. "Move over Perez. It's my job to keep you in the know, remember?"

"I guess knowing who's sleeping with whom could be a benefit. It'll help me gauge how good their next album will be."

"Shit does write itself."

They hopped out of the parked vehicle and entered the quaint bistro. A tall, broad man towered over her with a kind smile. He enveloped her in a bear hug, swinging her around.

"Sean!"

"How are you? It's been too long."

"Tell me about it. Wonderful to see you."

"Hi, babe," David reached to hug him as he set Shane on her feet.

"Hello, love," Sean said in a low baritone. He kissed David's cheek and led them to their table. "I already ordered the champagne."

"Special occasion?"

He slid into the booth and shifted the table to accommodate his size. "Nothing special. Only the first time we've been together in a while. And I figured David already had a few."

"He knows me so well." He fluttered his eyes at his beau.

Sean moved his arm to rest on the seatback behind David. He settled into the space comfortably even though his size said otherwise. His fingers lightly drifted over David's nape. It filled her soul to see them so happy and free to express their love.

"So, Shane, still conquering the industry one act at a time?"

"We're trying. We have some new things in the works, and award season is around the corner. A few artists will make the nominations list again."

"Oh, she's being modest," David chimed. "She's going to change the world."

"I bet she is." Sean winked. The waiter served a bottle of champagne and three glasses. His meaty mitt covered his glass, implying he had to return to work. "David tells me Jacob is still up to no good, signing one of your bands and all." Compassion shone from his chocolate brown eyes.

She sipped the bubbly liquid and rolled it around her tongue before swallowing. It still zinged her when anyone said his name.

"I'm taking it as a form of flattery. Now I need to figure out how he's tracking the talent we prospect. This isn't a coincidence."

"If I hear any talk going around, I'll be sure to let you and David know." The comment warmed her insides. He not only cared for David, but his friends too.

"Thanks. I'm taking a closer look at an internal employee as well."

"How so?"

"She thinks Omega's Talent Director may have given Jacob some inside information," David interjected.

Sean's eyebrows shot up. "No shit? And you think Jacob asked for it?"

"Maybe. Maybe not. I don't know. That's what I'm trying to figure out."

Sean's lips thinned in disappointment. He and Jacob had been close when the four of them were all together. "What's your plan with…?"

"Gavin Mayne?" she prompted.

"Yeah, him," Sean confirmed. Shane relaxed, thankful for the slight shift in the conversation.

"Not sure yet. But we'll be working on closing the Ryan Digmore deal together. Especially because AMG is entertaining him as well."

"Never a dull moment in the industry," Sean laughed.

"No kidding." She exhaled. "What about you, Sean? What has my favorite production manager so busy?"

"The usual. The current tour I'm on is pretty minimal as far as sets and coordination. My staff has things under control."

"He's lying. He's overworked and underpaid. We hardly see each other," David said, his gaze longing as he met Sean's. "I miss you."

"I miss you too." He placed his free hand in David's. "He's right. Who am I kidding? The travel is getting to me…us…and I need to think about settling down. I'm not getting any younger."

Fifteen years older than David, Sean had traveled his entire career. David had told her he was used to the grueling schedule, but she could tell it bothered him. Whenever Sean was on tour, David would stay with her. No hardship there. She loved having him. She hated being alone, and he was family and as much a brother to her as her own.

Her heart ached. She wanted what they had. She leaned her head in her hand. She was taking the right steps to get there and *he*, whoever that was, would come along in due time. Whenever the universe felt she was ready, he would appear and fill the void Jacob left behind.

CHATTER FILLED the open-air restaurant as Gavin patiently waited at a table. He typed an email to his team about giving Shane a debriefing on the Digmore deal when a shadow crossed over the table.

"Hello there, fine sir." Jacob held out a hand.

Gavin slid his phone into his pocket as he rose from his seat. "Sir," answering back with a curt nod and a hard handshake.

As they sat, the waiter arrived to deliver his beer. "Something for you, sir?"

"Yes, I'll have a Glenlivet. Neat," Jacob ordered.

"That kind of Saturday?"

"Long night. But let's get business out of the way first," Jacob insisted. Reaching for an envelope in his jacket pocket, he slid it over to Gavin. "You will find everything is in order according to our agreement."

Gavin peered inside the envelope. A royalty document and a sizable check made out to cash. "Thank you." He folded the contents and placed it in his pants pocket.

"No, thank you. It's been a pleasure working with you on this deal. I think all parties involved were compensated appropriately. Icarus Descending is pleased with their decision."

"I hope they feel they made the right choice." Gavin gritted his teeth. A twinge of guilt moved through him.

"Of course, they did." Jacob opened a menu. "Recording kicks off next week, and my team has them in front of a few promoters for next year's festival circuit. It's scoping out to be another profitable year for AMG." He smiled, folding his menu and laying it on the table.

The waiter returned with his drink and promptly took their orders. "Now with business out of the way, what's prompting the scotch?"

Jacob swallowed the amber liquid slowly. Hesitation?

"I dropped the band off at Azotar and made my way home shortly after."

"Who was the *after*?"

"Miranda. You know, that sexy little minx from the club? She'll allow pretty much anything." He seemed to puff out his chest.

"I've seen her there. Seems adventurous enough," Gavin agreed, although he found Azotar overrated. Jacob exuded power and elite status, like himself. He should be playing at The Resort.

"You haven't been around there much. Where've you been lately?"

"Around." Gavin shrugged.

Jacob leaned forward and tapped the side of his glass. "I'd be interested in knowing where *around* is."

He narrowed his gaze and fixed on Jacob's. A sly grin appeared. Jacob's confident composure and subtle hints regarding Miranda confirmed he did play in the scene.

"So, you *are* in the lifestyle. I figured as much. Didn't know we had so much in common."

"I did. We're cut from the same cloth, Gavin. Even when you don't realize it, you give bits and pieces away about yourself. I wouldn't have done business with you if I didn't think you were trustworthy. Which reminds me. When are you going to leave Omega and join AMG?"

He'd been waiting for Jacob to scout him. By working together, it kept Gavin's options open. The deal wasn't done in error. It was intentional in order to get a foothold at AMG, in case he needed it later. But what was Jacob's motivation in agreeing to it?

"I'm good at the moment. Thank you for the offer."

Currently, he had one goal, and it was to be the CEO of a record company. Gavin was ready now, and he would always be second in command if he moved labels. Getting there through Shane was the quickest route. Considering a move to AMG was Plan B.

"I think this last deal with Icarus Descending will square us up for a while, but if something changes, I'll let you know."

Jacob leaned back in his chair, examining him for more *bits and pieces*. Since there was history between him and Shane, Gavin couldn't risk showing he had a plan to steal her career.

The waiter set down their plates, and they ordered another round. "This is still open for discussion."

Another tense pause. Both vied for control of the table through their silences. Jacob dismissed it. "Back to the *around*. Where is this place?"

Gavin reached for his wallet and handed Jacob a business card.

"The Resort? Never heard of it."

"It's brand new. Heavy on the privacy and protection of the members. Nowadays you can never be too careful."

"Very true."

"I know the owner so if you want to try it out. Let me know," he offered.

"Thank you; I'll take you up on it." Jacob slipped the card into his pocket. "How's Shane?"

Gavin chomped a piece of steak. He considered Jacob's relationship—or lack thereof—with her. "Why do you ask?"

"We have history, so I tend to check in periodically."

Yeah, right. "I heard something about that." He swallowed the last of his beer. Placing the bottle down, he made eye contact with Jacob. Anger ticked like a time bomb in his chest. If Jacob thought he could get information about Shane through him, he was mistaken.

"Well?" Jacob pushed on with a tight jaw.

Stopping his interest in his meal, Gavin held his fork prongs to the plate. "Not sure I'd be the best person to ask. She's my boss, so I have no idea about her outside life and companions, if that's what you're getting at."

Jacob wiped his mouth with his linen napkin, placed it on his empty plate, and pushed it away. "Not why I was asking. I was more or less making sure you weren't too close given the underlying circumstances of our business relationship."

"I've proven myself to you. No need to test the waters," he confirmed. "But I think there was more to your question. Given your so-called past relationship, you have no interest in who she's sleeping with?"

"She can do what she wants, I have no claim on her. Even though we had differences in the past, I like to know she's doing well." The slight twitch in Jacob's grin said he was lying.

"It's obvious she's doing well, given her circumstances."

They stared at each other. Waiting. An underlying understanding was exchanged. This conversation was terminated.

Gavin stood, tossing cash on the table as Jacob followed suit, shaking his hand. A flare of adrenaline ignited in his bones. Things needed to be simple to meet his objective. If Jacob interceded, a reunion between the two could present itself, and Gavin's dream job would become be unreachable.

The race to win Shane's heart had begun.

5

"You can leave those in the hall closet. I'll put them away later," Shane said to Kelly as her apartment door swung open.

"Yes, Ms. Vaughn," she responded, professional as always. She never said much but what did Shane expect? She was only hired to drive and help with minimal tasks.

"Thank you for your help today."

Kelly set the garments and other bags inside the closet and nodded, exiting the apartment.

Shane walked to the kitchen and put her purse on the island. Kick-off for award season was around the corner, and submitting entries had become a top priority. Her meeting to review next year's forecast was also on the agenda. She smiled and rubbed her hands together. She loved her job, and this was the highlight of the year for her and her team. She started toward the office to prepare.

Ding!

She returned to her purse and whipped out her phone.

J: Are you home? We need to talk.

Now Jacob wanted to talk after stealing her artists?

"Asshole! What the hell needs to be said?"

Grinding her teeth, she paced back and forth. *How the hell does he still get a rise out of me?* Was it the anger from the past or his personal vendetta against Omega as industry competitors? Maybe it was both.

The muted light of the phone screen taunted her. Staring down at the text, she attempted to read between the lines. Guilt maybe? Perhaps he wanted to come clean.

Should she answer him? What would she say? Should she go for woman scorned or nonchalant? The thoughts were exhausting.

She went to the cabinet and plucked a bottle of red wine from the cooler. Twisting the cork, it popped like her mind erupting from his intrusion.

"Asshole."

The wine gurgled into a glass, matching her churning stomach. She downed the vino in one gulp.

S: *Mr. Andrews. To what do I owe the pleasure?*

With her hip against the island, she tapped her foot. *Yeah, cool and collected.*

J: *Very funny, Shane. Where are you?*

She rolled her eyes. This was so like him. She could hear the bite in his voice when she pushed his buttons. A twinge of satisfaction ran through her. He still thought he owned her. She still had it. A wry smile formed on her lips.

S: *Not that I feel the need to tell you, but if you must know, I'm at home. What's so urgent?*

J: *I'm coming over.*

"What could he possibly want to talk about?"

The last time he expressed this side of himself, they were still together. His quick response and words of confidence had made her skin tingle. Even through text, he still drew her in.

Shaking thumbs hovered over the keyboard, halting a natural impulse to yield. Could she be near him without wanting him?

She bit her bottom lip. Seeing him would put the past to rest.

Help her move on. Get the closure she'd been denied two years ago. But not here, not her apartment, it had to be somewhere neutral. Boundaries were necessary.

S: No. Your domination is no longer invited. Remember?
J: Where then?

She shook her head. Jacob and his highhanded attitude would never change.

S: The hotel bar around the corner from my place.
J: See you in 30.

There it was. Her Saturday night just got interesting. Her heart fluttered to counter the butterflies in her stomach. She was meeting the only man she'd loved and already doing a bang-up job of keeping it together. She could not let him see she was weak.

She poured another glass of wine. Getting through an evening with Jacob required liquid courage. Taking a deep breath, she grasped onto any anger from moments ago. *Remember, Shane, he's the enemy now.* Her confidence bounced back. This would be the one time Jacob Andrews wasn't taking control.

She grabbed her keys, purse, and dignity as she proudly walked out the door.

RIGHT ON TIME, Jacob's eyes darted across the hotel bar. There Shane sat, engaging with the bartender. She tucked her light brown hair behind her ear. Plump lips spread into a smile. Blue eyes blinked in delight. Fucking stunning.

His heart ticked a million paces. She still did it for him. Laughter escaped her mouth, a sound to behold. It nearly buckled his knees. The angelic sound floated into his ears and transported him back to their time together. He grimaced. *You really fucked up, Andrews.*

With one step toward the bar, her baby blues met his gaze like she'd felt him coming. The air suddenly charged, electricity sparked between two souls. An invisible string linked their hearts and reeled him closer with each step. He cleared his throat.

Remember why you're here. Gavin was a little too closed off at lunch compared to the open book he'd demonstrated at prior meetings. Jacob didn't trust him.

First, it was time to face the proverbial music. He'd handled the passing of her father poorly, and she deserved an apology.

The stool skidded across the floor when he moved it, their gazes never leaving one another. Her eyes became a stormy blue. A warning. *Did she know?*

He didn't sit, instead, propped his leg on the rung while the other remained planted on the floor. Towering over her gave him a familiar vantage point from their time together. Any lingering feelings of reconciliation diminished.

"Glenlivet," he said to the bartender, his gaze fixated on her beautiful face.

"Right away, sir."

When the bartender scurried off, Shane seemed to drink him in. Her lips parted slightly, and her chest rose and fell. She was probably trying to analyze his agenda but didn't say a word. *Good girl.*

"Shane."

"Jacob," she responded, short and strangely professional, like they were about to handle a business transaction. "What's this about?"

Amusement curled his lips. "That's my girl. Right to the point."

"I'm not your girl. Spill it, Andrews."

Narrowing his gaze, her pupils dilated, a strategic guise to hide the obvious reaction to his presence. It was adorable. But her hand stroked back and forth over the base of the glass.

Nerves. *Interesting.* Perhaps she still had a flame burning for him.

"One thing at a time, Shane. How about hello? How are you? It's good to see you."

"Good to see you," she repeated evenly. "Is that what *this* is?" Her finger acknowledged the two of them. "Good to see you? Humor me. Why is it good to see me?" A hard chin pushed forward.

"Oh, I don't know. It's been a year since the *Billboard* gala, and there's talk about great things surrounding your company. You're all grown up," he replied with a smile.

"Don't patronize me, Jacob. You called this meeting, so speak."

"I have to say, I didn't expect this approach. Is that how you talk to your employees? Now I know how things get done around your camp."

"You don't know anything about how I run my company. You left, remember? If you'd stuck around, you would know." Her smart mouth, full and pink, smirked in his direction. His hand twitched. He wanted to spank her and kiss the cocky expression off her face.

The telltale signs of anger reddened her neck. She was still hurt, which caused his heart to dip. But he knew what he'd walked into.

Yes, he was the asshole who'd left her in a lurch. He had to live with it, but she'd given him no choice. Callused by the loss of her father, she'd shut him out.

"There's the girl I knew, always reminding me of my faults. Your nose still flares a little when you're angry. It's very cute." He dotted the tip of her nose, and she retreated. "It could be possible I didn't do a good enough job at punishing you when I should have," he quipped.

"Maybe if you had, we'd still be together," she goaded, her

smile tight and eyebrows lifting in challenging amusement.

"Touché, Ms. Vaughn." Swallowing his entire glass of scotch, he enjoyed her feistiness. The air dissipated and the tension eased slightly from her comeback. "I'll make you a deal. We will discuss the matter at hand once we've achieved the proper exchange. In all seriousness, baby, how are you?" His hand rested on hers.

"Please don't call me that." She moved her hand to rest it on the foot of the wine glass.

He raised a brow, a signal to her. One he used as a warning to her to do as he asked. If she didn't listen, a spanking had resulted in the past. Thinking about her ass turning a rosy color hit him in all the wrong places.

"Ugh, you're such a difficult man. Fine. I won't tolerate this test of wills. The faster we get this done, the sooner I can leave." She exhaled. "And, Jacob, if you must know, I'm great. Fantastic. Couldn't be better."

"Why?"

"I have the career I've always wanted. I have money, friends, and family. Not a care in the world. You could say I've reached the highest level of power and success."

"Success, yes. But power isn't in your DNA."

Shane put the people in her life first, including him. By supporting his career and moving to New York, a question of loyalty and love had never arisen. She had always been there for him. Until her father died.

"Things change."

"Have they?"

"Yes. Now can you please move it along?"

"Patience," he said calmly.

She stared at him, narrowing her eyes. The discussion would move forward when he was ready, not because she asked.

The stool screeched across the hardwood when she stood.

"Thank you for the beverage. Now, if you'll please excuse me." One step and he snatched her arm. The connection shot through him, a natural state of command. He could turn on a dime. One minute playful, the next demanding. She'd tested his patience long enough.

He whispered in her ear, "I suggest you have a seat, Shane. I didn't give you permission to leave."

Frozen in place, she only stared at their connection point. After a beat, a sheen of confusion passed through her gaze. A whisper escaped, "No."

"Shane," he said between clenched teeth.

"This is a choice." The word *choice* stopped him. It meant something entirely different than what she'd known it to be. It threw him. She snapped to attention and glared. "Remove your hand, Jacob. You don't own me."

Without question, he released her, her words bringing him out of the scene in his head. *Choice. Own me.* What the hell did he think this was and why the instinctual response? He was supposed to be over her. The deal with Icarus Descending was his closure. Wasn't it?

"Please sit," he requested.

"I...I have to go." She walked toward the door. *Wake up, Andrews. She's leaving again because of you.*

In three long strides, he stepped in front of her. She stopped abruptly. "Move."

"Shit, Shane...I..." He glanced around the bar to make sure no one had noticed the confrontation. "I don't know what happened. Old habits die hard, Lovely." He ran a hand though his long hair.

She cringed at the slip of his pet name. "I can't do this. This was a mistake."

"Please, let me explain." She motioned to give him the floor. "Can we sit, please?"

The inner struggle rippled down her form. The stubborn girl still existed inside as she fought him and for good reason. He didn't own her, even though, deep down, a current traveled between them.

"I'll get to the point."

"Five." She held out her hand emphasizing the number of minutes he had left to explain. She returned to the stool and sat.

With feet glued to the floor, he rubbed his face. Touching her brought back the recognizable dynamic of the past. A cathartic wave of normality briefly passed through him followed by the familiar angst he'd carried with him, all of it taking residence in his stomach. The day he'd left his sub behind. The day he'd walked out on his life with Shane.

Fuck, he missed her. The way she yielded to his touch and his voice. All the things taken for granted. The plan to sever their hearts failed. He wanted her back. But how?

Eye-to-eye, he sat. "Thank you."

She nodded, swallowing her wine.

"I'm proud of you, Shane."

"For not putting up with your shit?" She laughed a little.

He smiled, relieving the last several minutes of tension. "Not what I was going to say, but yes. I'm proud of what you've become. Who would've thought the two of us would be holding such prestigious positions at competing labels?"

Her shoulders relaxed. "Thank you. It means so much to hear you say it." They stared at each other for too many moments. Something passed between them. Respect? Desire?

He cleared his throat. "Anyway, I wanted to say how sorry I am for how things ended between us. I understand my apology may not help, and you may not believe me, but know I'm truly sorry."

She gnawed on her bottom lip. Her eyes glassed over from tears. She was as stubborn as he remembered.

"Apology accepted. It was for the best anyway. Our lives have become so much more...fulfilled since the split." She drank her wine until the tears ceased.

"Perhaps." He sighed. "Your father was a good man, and if he could see you now, he would be so proud. He was an important part of my life too, you know. I guess seeing you go through your depression tortured me. I didn't know it at the time, but looking back, I realize I was grieving him too." He stood and turned her toward him. The soft sweater wrap caressed his palms as he rubbed her arms. "You believe me, right?"

Pain flitted over her features, the hard exterior disappearing, and only vulnerability remained. *His girl.*

"Yes. I believe you. It consumed me, and trying to take care of my mother through it all was difficult. I didn't think about how his death must have affected you too."

He swallowed the lump in his throat. The thousand-pound gorilla had finally been lifted from his chest only to climb onto his back. He needed to come clean.

"No apology needed. And you're right. We wouldn't be who we are today if not for me leaving."

A half smile appeared on her face. Wanting to tell her he wanted her, he searched her soul. *Did she want him?* Maybe he had a chance, but how could she ever love him again?

She tilted her head, reading his mind. "Is there more?"

He rolled his neck. He owed her a clean slate. "Yes. I've felt lately I'm finally over you after all this time. But..."

"Over me, huh? Finally, something we agree on." She half laughed. "It'd be too difficult to regain the trust we shared."

His heart cracked into a million pieces. How could she trust him again? Even if she did, when she found out he'd worked with Gavin to steal Omega's artists there would never be a *"them"* again.

It wouldn't even matter that AMG had been closing in when

he found out her label was too. Then it became a race to the finish line, an obsession to be the best. And if he was honest, subconsciously, he wanted to hit her where it hurt. Her job. The one thing that had come between them.

Backing away, he motioned for the bartender to get him another drink.

"You agree, right?"

"Yes, baby, I agree," he said, disgusted with his choices. Clean break. She deserved it. He threw back the entire drink, stood, and grabbed his wallet. Throwing cash on the bar, he kissed one cheek and the other. Her wildflower perfume filled his nose, and his heart sank further. "I'm happy for you and glad we were able to gather closure. Thank you for meeting with me."

She exhaled with a slight shudder. "Thank you for asking."

He pulled away. She smoothed her lips, and they parted then shut.

"What is it?"

"Nothing." She snatched her purse and stood. "It's silly."

"Tell me, please."

"I don't know. This whole thing... Would it be strange if I asked you to grab something to eat?"

He froze. "Now?"

"How about next week. Maybe we could turn a new leaf. Friendly competitors?"

"What did you have in mind?"

"A congratulations lunch for the new roster addition?" Her grateful smile killed him. After all this time, she still had the ability to be the bigger person.

"I can check and see if..."

"Please?" she asked hopeful. The relief in her eyes told him she'd buried the hatchet. Their conversation freeing her of something she'd been holding onto. *Him.*

"Sure, Shane. Let me know when."

THE BOOMING BASS from the dance floor was muffled in the back office of The Resort. Gavin tied the loose ends for the upcoming members appreciation night and glanced at Candy from his desk.

"How many guests are on the list?"

"Um, fifty-two," she confirmed in her sweet nasally voice.

"Fifty-two? I thought yesterday there were fifty-one."

"Nope, fifty-two. We had a new member submit her paperwork early this morning."

He walked over to her desk and leaned on the edge. "Who is it?"

Her fingers scrolled the mouse through the database and clicked the recent application. "Someone named Shane Vaughn."

Narrowing his eyes to focus on the name listed, a slow grin appeared on his face. "You don't say."

"Do you know her? Who is she?" She tapped the invitations on the desktop to straighten them.

"No one important." He covered a smile with his hand. "This got a hell of a lot easier."

Shane had unknowingly joined his establishment. His plan was coming full circle, effortlessly. All he had to do was get her in a compromising position and hold it over her head.

"Easier? How's adding one more, easier? Now we have to change the number of gift bags on order and who knows what else," she said excitedly.

"Don't worry, honey. It'll all get done." He assured her by patting her shoulders. She wasn't the brightest, but she was sweet, and the members adored her.

Ethan entered the room. "Hey, we need some help at the bar. Candy, would you mind?"

"Absolutely, Sir." She rose from the desk, mumbling the guest count as she left.

The men smirked at one another, and Gavin shook his head. Ethan closed the door behind her. "What were you two doing in here?"

"Reviewing the last minute items for the gathering."

Ethan glanced over his shoulder and focused on the application still visible on the screen. "Shane Vaughn. Isn't she your boss? Is she a Domme?"

He turned to read detail. "Nope, a sub." His insides jumped in satisfaction.

"No kidding. The way you talked about her, I would've guessed the other."

"No kidding, indeed. Anything else before the invitations go out tomorrow?"

"Nah, we should be good. You sticking around?" Ethan crooked a thumb toward the door. "Damien and Brit are about to start their scene. They asked if you were here. I think they need a third."

Damien and Brit, a married couple, heavily involved in the D/s community, had somehow made it last through the years. Brit's preferred kink involved two Doms, and she got off on Damien watching and commanding the other. Gavin enjoyed scening with them and had participated several times.

"Not tonight." He swiped his keys from the desk.

"Suit yourself. Have a good one."

"Thanks."

He proceeded down a low-lit hallway, passing a row of private rooms. The muted red lights above each door indicated most were occupied. Taking the back stairs leading to the street, he approached his Range Rover and got in. Shane Vaughn, a member of *his* club, would receive an invitation to the gathering.

The engine roared to life along with his inner desire to control his boss. "Ms. Vaughn, your worst nightmare is about to begin."

6

SHANE ROLLED her suitcase into her apartment alongside David after traveling to Los Angeles. Anna Marie's show and the after-party had kept the pair out till ungodly hours all weekend and into Monday.

She removed her sunglasses and squinted with the onslaught of daggers hitting her eyes from the light shining through the windows. *Never drinking again.*

David shed his cream suit jacket, still put together even though he'd partied just as hard. His white linen pants were pressed, and his blue scarf brought out the hazel in his still clear eyes. She snorted. She traveled more casually with her hair braided to the side, thigh-high flat boots, jeans, and a long-sleeved shirt.

They tossed their bags in the corner of the foyer and made their way to the living area.

"Anna Marie was a hot mess last night. What was she thinking?" David asked, kicking off his shoes before sitting on the couch.

Anna Marie, a typical young pop star, mistakenly thought she was invincible to any bad publicity. After being caught in a threesome in the back of her limo, the paparazzi flashes flickered around them as she ran down the photographers with a blinged out cane, said to be a necessary prop with her rainbow hair and blue fur coat. Shane and David caught it all firsthand leaving the party.

"I agree, sweetie, but she's the next best thing. I'll talk to Megan in PR about getting a press release out to smooth it over." She pointed to the kitchen. "Thirsty?"

"Yes. Sparkling water?" David continued as she headed for the fridge. "There's no way Megan can smooth over her outburst from the press. It's all over social media."

She stepped into the kitchen area and halted. In the center of the marble island, a red velvet box rested.

"Wonder what this is," she said to herself. Her fingertips grazed the soft velvet in apprehension and excitement. She picked it up and made her way back to the living room.

"Heelloo? Are you okay?" David called. She turned the corner. "Oh, honey, it came!" He clapped his hands.

"What is it? Did you send it?"

"Of course not." He waved his hand in disgust. "Red is not my color. That, my dear, is your Resort package. Come sit and open it up." He patted the spot next to him on the white curved couch.

She set it on the coffee table. It called to her as if it had made a come-hither motion. The intricate silver stitching in a swirling pattern hypnotized her. It was happening. Her welcome package to the unknown. She swallowed and spun the brushed nickel latch.

The lid contained a black envelope, marked *Shane*. Her skin tingled as her heart leapt. Smiling, she detached the envelope and removed the thick black cardstock. Silver embossed words leapt from the invitation.

You are cordially invited to
The Resort

A tab stuck out of the bottom. When she moved it, right to left, a flogger moved across the top of the invitation. "You have to see this."

"Nice touch."

She opened the card.

Members Appreciation Night
Saturday, the Twenty-Fourth of October
Eight O'clock in the Evening

"That's this Saturday."

"Looks like your dress will make its debut." He fanned his face.

Soft black silk lined each compartment. The right side resembled a jewelry box ring holder. One crease held condoms and the other a platinum key card. She inspected the mask nestled in silk from the top section. White lace intricately woven and interconnected with swirls and net-like patterns created the base. Real pearls decorated the upper edges, framing the eyes and nosepiece. A large pearl rested in the center of a stitched lotus flower at the middle of the forehead. She ran her fingers over the tails of thick silver ribbon. *Wow.*

David's jaw dropped as he snatched it from her hand. "You'll look like a goddess in this, doll! Mine is more masculine in the face. And no lace." He continued to inspect the mask. "They have three different colors. White for submissive, black for dominant, and red for switches."

"I guess that's a good way to maintain anonymity while letting the other members know who they can approach," she said simply.

"Exactly."

Removing the white satin gloves, she tried them on. Another layer of armor sparked awareness within her. Power rushed through her blood.

"You were made for those." And she couldn't agree more.

The platinum keycard, inscribed with *Star*, flashed in the light when she held it. Her alias. It held fire and promise. Her transformation had begun.

"What's this?"

"Your key into The Resort, but it also allows access to certain rooms. It's pretty fabulous. When you swipe your card to enter a room, your limits display on a flat screen monitor. This way each member can immediately understand each partner's boundaries." He shrugged. "A safety measure for the club, but I like to think it helps the members not lose the moment." He wiggled his eyebrows.

She giggled, removing the gloves and placing the items back in the box. "This is truly high end; seems like they thought of everything. Now I know where my costly membership fee went. Am I paying you too much?" She winked.

"Nonsense." He puckered his lips for a kiss.

She grabbed his face. "Muah! God, I love you. What would I do without you, huh?"

"Probably look like an average hag in terrible clothing."

"So not true."

His eyebrows lifted. "Seriously?"

"Whatever. What would you do without me?"

"Not possible. Wouldn't even think about it."

She shook the thought from her mind. "Okay. What's next?"

"How about food and bingeing on the *Real Housewives*?"

"Fine." She sighed rising from the couch. "But I get to pick the restaurant." Her phone pinged.

G: Dinner this week?

Confusion twisted her face. Discomfort shot down her spine as warning signals blared in her ears.

"Who is it, doll?"

"Gavin. He wants to get dinner."

"Oh boy." He rolled his eyes.

"What do you think it means?"

"Maybe he wants to talk about the Digmore deal. His assistant, Tasha, mentioned something about it last week. It's most likely nothing."

"You say it as if it could be something," she said with panic.

"Based on your last interaction with him, I mean, honestly, doll, he did come off a little strong. Don't you think?"

"Sure, but I think I'm twisting things in my head." She re-read the text.

"True, but *you* ordered the ball and chain. By the way, it came in the mail last Friday." He grinned. "Time to attach him to it." She laughed. "Don't look too much into it. He's most likely being proactive."

"I guess you're right. God, I need to get laid."

Gavin probably wanted to review the contract. *Proactive.* She was a professional and could push their interaction aside. Her nerves awakened, blood rushing south. A gorgeous male and the right amount of demanding. Maybe she was wrong about him being a misogynist. *Snap out of it, Shane!* Her longing to be with someone overpowered her need to stay in the game. It was making her crazy.

"You said it, not me," he said.

"Ha-ha."

S: Yes. Have Tasha set it up with David.

"When Tasha calls, book it at my usual place."

"Yes, ma'am." He saluted.

THE SUV MOVED through traffic on her way to Tribeca. As the vehicle passed each block toward the restaurant, Shane rang her hands together as palpitations swept her heart.

"You can do this. He's *your* employee. Not the other way around."

A meal with Gavin was out of character; however, she did require a debriefing of the Digmore account so they could come up with a plan to win him over. But why dinner? This could be handled in the office.

Unless... A wave of hot excitement drowned her nerves. Was he interested in her? She sank into the leather seat, ashamed her body had betrayed her. Attraction now brewed for her aggravating Talent Director. No denying the energy had shifted in her office. Her normal professional persona had evaporated. He'd stolen it from her. Or had she *given* it to him? She covered her face with her hands.

An automatic response had occurred. He'd triggered her submissive button. Dusted it off and—*pow!*—she didn't know what hit her. Maybe he hadn't noticed. Who was she kidding? He'd noticed all right. His final words rang in her head like a bell.

You have everything to prove to me.

The SUV stopped at her favorite sushi place in Tribeca. Shane smoothed on her lip-gloss and powdered her face. War paint. *Bring it on, Gavin.*

The hostess greeted her as she entered. "Ms. Vaughn, welcome. Let me take your coat."

"Thank you."

"Your guest has already arrived. Right this way."

She followed the hostess through a corridor and down a flight of stairs, stunned to learn Gavin had beaten her there. By arriving early, she had hoped to set the tone.

Thankful to be at her usual place, the calming décor centered her. Rich hues of gold, cream, and red surrounded the room. A several ton Buddhist bell hung from the ceiling. She narrowed her eyes as they passed by the Buddha ice sculpture. *You knew didn't you, O Enlightened One. What are you up to?*

They rounded the corner and Gavin sat in a channel-back booth with a drink in hand.

He observed her. She stumbled slightly at the intensity of his blue eyes.

"Hello, Shane. Thank you for agreeing to meet with me." He stood and guided her toward the booth, a hand at the small of her back, his touch so warm it scorched through the fabric of her dress, and her lady parts tingled. *Jesus.*

"Gavin." Sliding into the booth, regret edged her body. Requesting a regular table wouldn't have been so…intimate.

A dirty martini called to her from the table.

"I already ordered. This will allow for less distraction."

"Okay," she said slowly. The dominant advance wasn't lost on her. Jacob used to do the same thing when they dined, indicating a wicked promise to an evening well planned. She gripped the edge of the table as control slipped through her fingers. "Where are we with the Digmore signing? I read over the contract and have a few ideas."

He leaned back with a smirk. His eyes darted down her form and back up. "Do you?"

"Yes. First off—"

"Let's hold off on business, Shane," he interrupted smoothly. His baritone voice surged sensually through her blood.

She tasted her martini. The salty warmth of the vodka calmed the rising tide of desire. "Let's get it out of the way."

"The deal works as is."

"You're missing the sign-on bonus."

"We don't offer those any longer. It's not competitive and is a waste to our bottom line. Especially with an artist as green as Ryan."

Sharp confidence rolled from his tongue, but his body remained relaxed. Typically, if Gavin disagreed during business discussions, his body flexed in a tight mass of muscle as hard as stone. She'd observed the stance a million times during team meetings. It meant the negotiation was over. But his relaxed state presented an opening to contest his reasoning.

"I don't care if the market isn't doing it; Omega is."

"You're gripping the bat too tight."

"What's important to Ryan?" she asked. Even if she was gripping the bat, the handle wasn't splintering her palms.

"Not sure what that has to do with the bonus."

"It has *everything* to do with it." She struck a finger onto the tabletop. "Ryan comes from nothing. He's a traveling artist who's built a fan base performing the bonfire circuit at music festivals. If not for the girls at those concerts, he wouldn't have a following. He lived off selling his albums and bracelets made from broken guitar strings. The man has nothing to lose."

His jaw tightened. No musicians came through Omega without her knowing their histories and motivations. To win the best, you had to be the best. And how to achieve it? Through preparation and patience. And she lived it, every damn day.

"And?" He sipped his drink.

"And? He could use the cash. Without it, he's signing away his freedom and the copyrights of his albums to a money hungry corporation. And why would he?"

"Fame and stardom, Shane," he said plainly.

"Wrong. He takes care of his sister who's been disabled since birth. That money can help her."

"Bravo, Shane." He clapped twice. "Aren't you the saint?"

"Don't mistake the motives for sainthood. I play to win." She fished an olive from the martini, popping it into her mouth. His gaze traveled to her lips and back to her eyes.

"And so do I." A smile twitched at the side of his salacious mouth.

A flood of liquid pooled between her thighs. How did he do it? One phrase and she would abandon her CEO identity and get on her knees. A blush traveled up her neck.

"Are we on the same page? With the signing bonus, I mean," she reiterated.

He rested an arm over the back cushion and slid closer. The small space closed in further, the air thick with raw sensual tension.

Turning his body, his tan jacket fell open, exposing suspenders, and his blue oxford hugged his torso. Shadows underscored the ripped muscles hidden under the fabric. She bit her bottom lip then compressed them together.

"More or less." His patience stirred her. Where was the shark she knew? "I had time to think about this arrangement. Working side by side."

"I appreciate that."

"Wait." The thickness in his voice reverberated a million pin prickles under her skin. Her ears dialed into it. His assertive tone. His dominant authority crumbled her defenses.

"It wasn't ideal, but you showed me something."

"Really?" She sat back and crossed her arms.

"You understand business a different way. You don't attack your prey; you swim with them. You mentioned it in your office and demonstrated it now with Ryan. It appears you look at the benefit for all parties involved."

She turned, resting an elbow on the seat back. Perhaps he did understand her business and personal missions.

"A solid observation. But you sound uncertain."

He flicked his eyes back and forth, obviously dissecting her presence. "Not uncertain. Surprised. You're a good person."

Her cheeks heated. He'd discovered the layer she kept hidden from the industry.

"Not sure what you mean."

His gaze seared. Before he could dig deeper into her tough exterior, she snagged her beverage and downed the liquid.

He scooped the glass from her hands set it on the table. "Don't hide, Shane. Look at me."

Her oval-shaped hands fell into her lap. What happened? An instinctive reaction rooted itself inside her. She wanted to obey. Like a hairpin trigger on the gas, her mind veered toward a detour, missing the exit ramp to sanity and control.

His finger tapped the table unhurriedly. Each union with the tablecloth prodded her submissive button over and over again. The inner struggle to obey resembled a nerve on fire, an aching hunger to be satisfied.

She closed her eyes. He didn't command her, and damn him if he thought he could. She had a choice. Look at him or not. Do it with strength or wonder. What would she see? The curiosity compelled her chin upward.

There she met the face of desire beyond anything she'd seen from him. Straight nose and rigid jawline meant to tackle the world without apology. His generous lips used to speak with determination, yet designed to kiss each inch of a woman's body. Her lips parted. And were his eyes always that shade of blue? The stormy sky would be jealous of the fierceness brewing behind them. Slanted brows hovered with intent as his eyes penetrated her true identity.

A rumble came from his chest. An acknowledgement of a long-sought-after discovery confirmed. She rubbed her moist palms on her sheath dress. His dominant dance—deliberate or otherwise—made her imagine how he would fuck her and tell her how he wanted his dick sucked.

The waiter brought their order, and Gavin broke the silent

code passing between them. He pinched a piece of sashimi between two chopsticks. Placing it in his mouth, he chewed slowly, rolling it around his mouth, clearly appreciating the delicate flavor. God, it was sexy. With a mouth like his, he could savor more than his food.

"Would you excuse me for a minute?"

The dinnerware clanged when her knee hit the table. *Shit!* She needed air. Her office enemy had chipped away years of armor in a moment. He wouldn't make this working arrangement easy.

Her heels clacked on the metal stairs and down the hallway to the ladies' room. She threw her purse on the counter and turned on the cold water. Redness flushed her cheeks as she stared into the mirror. The cool water on her hands did nothing for her alarming desire.

"Keep it together, Vaughn. Nothing's changed. He's still the same smug prick."

She dried them and ran her cool fingers down her cheeks and around the back of her neck. *It's okay.* Years of no male contact had its consequences. She smoothed her emerald sheath dress, squared her shoulders, and headed back to the table.

She slid into her seat, armor replaced. "Sorry. You were saying?"

"Here try this." He selected a piece of sashimi. Cupping his hand underneath the fish to keep the sauce from dripping, he moved it to her mouth.

He offered a challenge for power, so she humored him. *Let's reel him in a little and see how far we can go.* Taking the salmon into her mouth, the texture rolled around her tongue. A sound of enjoyment escaped her. A smile capable of melting any woman who encountered it widened on his tempting lips. *Bingo.*

Clearing his throat, he set the utensils down. "Where were we?"

"Unity and benefits for all parties."

"Right, your way of handling the business." He paused to gesture her way. "The industry moves at a fast pace, and we're all working toward the same goal. Business can be done easier and without error when people work together. A unified front, if you will."

"What do you suggest?"

"I agree to partner with you, Shane."

She chuckled. "It wasn't a choice."

"It's always a choice." Her mouth opened, and he held a finger up to silence her. He continued, "In order for me to do that, I need to know you on a personal level. You're guarded and for good reason." His eyes softened. "By growing our bond outside of work, we can become a force professionally." His fingers lightly danced along her bare shoulder. Her body went from warm to boiling.

No telltale sign of attraction or deceit existed. The ministrations on her shoulder stopped; the loss jolted her to forge ahead. The vibrations of desire from hardly a touch begged the question: What would it be like if there was more? Maybe roping in her enemy would have its perks.

"Okay, Gavin. What are you like outside of work?"

He shook his head and smiled. "Tell me about your family, Shane."

She bit back the urge to control the conversation. "My mother lives outside the city near my brother, Evan, and sister, Melody."

"And your father?"

"He's gone. Died a few years ago." She popped the last olive from her empty glass into her mouth, the bitter flavor matching her response.

"I'm sorry. That must've been tough for you." Another sultry bite of sushi rolled in his mouth.

She snapped out of her trance. "Um, yes, it was hard on all of us. But life goes on." Shifting in her seat, she flipped the switch. "And you?"

He snickered. The chopsticks clinked on the plate. "I'm my own family."

The smooth, charming Gavin shut down, and his walls came up. Was he uncomfortable? Delight filled her. "Why?"

"It's not important," he dismissed, wiping his mouth with a linen napkin. "All you need to know is it doesn't affect my work."

Her eyebrows arched at the sting in his tone. She'd hit something dark and personal. "It's important if we are, as you say, to create a bond."

His chest rose and fell. Jaw rolling. "Tell me about your siblings."

His pawn moved forward in this chess match. A story existed there, and she vowed to find out more.

"Fine. Evan, is a blue-collar guy, like my father was. Owns his own body shop, fixing cars. And Melody is a teacher."

"You come from a struggling family unit?" he asked bluntly.

"Struggling? Quite the assumption. Just because my family worked for everything they achieved, doesn't mean we struggled," she said with disgust.

"I'm only saying, your life couldn't have been easy to get where you are now."

"Let's get something straight. I wouldn't change a thing about what got me here today. My parents showed me the value in hard work and how to love each other along the way." She glared at him. "And what about you, Mr. Mayne? By your reaction, I assume you came from wealth?"

A flash of anger swept his stormy blue irises. "I did. But it didn't shape me."

"Maybe not the wealth, but the family did. Everyone's past shapes them in some way."

He busied himself with the Kobe beef selection from the platter. It was clear he didn't like where this conversation was headed. She softened as her hand rested on his forearm.

"You show a great deal of accomplishment and pride. Like perhaps your family forced you to make it on your own."

His eyes focused on her hand. *Checkmate.* He swallowed down the last of his drink. Her hand fell back into her lap. For long moments, the only sound came from the passing waitstaff and the low murmur of guests seated around them.

"Am I close?"

"How do you do it?" The question was so low she thought she'd misheard it.

"I'm sorry?"

He slid closer. Their hips inches away. With an arm resting behind her, his body heat threatened to sear her skin as she allowed him to cocoon her. The blue of his eyes darkened as they caressed the peaks and valleys of her face. His tongue darted out to lick his bottom lip.

"How do you make a woman dressed in power undeniably attractive?"

"She becomes attractive when a man cloaked in adversarial self-righteousness finally pays attention." She smiled to lessen the tension wrapped in a cozy coil of sensual misgivings.

A hum sent an acknowledgment of a well-executed insult. "Self-satisfied much?"

She straightened, keeping her eyes on his. "Confident."

Both exuded strength and control yet held respect for the game. Two strong-willed people finding the challenge inviting and acceptable. A common ground of appreciation and regard exchanged. The moment eased the mental struggle she'd held for years.

He breathed out. "And it's stunning."

His lips parted, eyes softening, as if seeing her for the first time. Being this close allowed him a microscopic view of what made the woman heading up Omega. Did a woman in the driver's seat turn him on?

She managed a whisper. "Thank you."

Anise and cloves permeated the area, trapping her deep in sexual imagery. Thoughts of him taking over her body roared in her head. "I think we are…getting off track."

"From?"

Their lips were close. She wanted them all over her and wondered if this was real or a game. Should she take him on a wild ride or let him take her?

"Eating," she breathed out.

He laughed as his eyes glimmered with mischief, then he pushed away to hand a credit card to the passing waiter.

She chugged water like a thirsty man in a dessert and scooped a piece of Kobe beef into her mouth, stopping herself from an oncoming inappropriate discussion.

He stood and signed the bill, then snapped the black booklet shut before handing it back to the waiter. "Looking forward to working on the Digmore account, Shane. This should make our working relationship much more bearable." He spun on his heel and exited the restaurant.

Shane sat there in shock, her mouth full of beef as he walked away. Her body swarmed with anticipation and, finally, achievement. She smirked.

"He's totally interested."

7

HELL'S KITCHEN. A perfect area of New York to burn away the past and step into the future. Sometimes a person needed to walk through hell to come out the other side. Rejuvenation after seeing Jacob last week settled in Shane's stomach.

She settled into a bistro seat at a burger joint decorated with barn wood walls and a pictograph of a cartoon steer ready for slaughter. The area hummed with the Thursday lunch crowd.

She tapped the screen of her smart phone.

J: Running a little late. On my way.

Jacob was notorious for lateness but not at his fault. Work demanded a lot of his attention, and she related.

Tucking away precious moments used to be a priority for them. Every Thursday, much like today, a hotel not too far from their respective offices maintained a standing reservation under their names. Even though they lived together, their secret rendezvous from the chaos of their worlds gave them peace and a connection to always put each other first.

The last time they'd met on a Thursday occurred on their eight-year anniversary, over two years ago. The memory flooded her like it was yesterday. Her naked, perched on the bed in Sergio

Rossi gold stilettos with Swarovski crystals. The room covered in rose petals. The way he loved her like no man ever had or would. His touch. His kisses. His lovemaking. It always strengthened over time, and he acted as though every day could have been the last.

She shoved the phone in her purse.

"Shane?"

"Oh, hi." She forced a smile and stood to hug Jacob.

"Are you okay, Lovely?" He moved the chair as he unbuttoned his suit jacket. Green shirt. Chocolate brown suit. No tie. Matching pocket square. *The one he wore on their last day together.*

She waved him off, placing a napkin into her lap. "Yes. It's work." Did he call her *Lovely* like he used to?

He smiled, taking a well-worn paper menu from the ketchup caddy. "Something's up."

She took a menu, smoothing out the curled corners. "You're talking to me like you used to."

"It's hard not to. The other night was…"

"A relief," she breathed out.

He folded his hands in his lap, and his green eyes creased. "I was going to say eye opening."

The assumption they were on the same page wore heavy. "What do you mean?"

"What can I getcha?" Shane peeled her eyes from Jacob to the waitress with intrusive timing. Her black hair was buzzed short, and a sleeve tattoo extended down her arm as she tapped a pencil to her notepad.

"She'll have a cheeseburger with ketchup only. Medium. The tomato and lettuce on the side. And I will have the blackened bison burger with everything, hold the onion." Jacob perused the menu as if ordering for her was normal. "And a side of your loaded fries." He tucked the menu back into its holder. "That should do it."

"Anything to drink?"

His eyebrows motioned to Shane. "A chocolate shake and water, please."

"For you, sir?" He met Shane's eyes, and she could have sworn they smiled at her.

"Same."

They'd slipped into their old roles. Two years apart and the tension lifted. The waitress returned and plopped down their drinks, and Shane sucked on the straw to gather the thick creamy flavor of chocolate. Jacob watched intently. The coolness of the shake as she swallowed chilled the hot burst of lust blooming from his stare.

"Still have the appetite I see," he observed.

"Yeah. It's hard to find time to eat sometimes. Which reminds me: Congrats on signing Icarus Descending."

"Thanks, but I don't think congratulations are deserved."

She toyed with the straw, stirring the milkshake. "Why not?"

"It's what we do. We sign musicians."

"You make it sound like work."

Jacob loved the smell of wet ink on a contract. Lived for the thrill of pen scoring paper. He used to say it was his favorite sound next to her screaming his name. He never tired of competing in the industry to retain the best talent.

He sucked a long pull from the straw. "This one was."

"We had you for a second, didn't we?" She loved digging at him with competitive fun.

He leaned his elbows on the table. The table appeared dwarfed by his tall size. But he commanded it, and she loved it.

"I wouldn't go that far," he teased.

"You could never admit I could hang with you."

"Oh, you did more than hang, baby. Brought me to my fucking knees most of the time."

A wave of attraction and memories passed through her like an apparition stealing her breath. "Stop." Her hands slipped down the condensation of the glass and rested on the tabletop.

His fingers flexed. "Sorry. It's just hard sometimes."

She straightened. Did he think about her? "What is?"

"Nothing."

"You can be honest, Jacob. Maybe we needed the other night to get us to open up." She reached out for his hand. Her heart skipped a beat when, with a twitch of his fingers, he attempted to lace with hers. "We compete with each other every day out there. Let's cut through the awkwardness and lay down our swords, okay?"

He leaned back to allow the waitress to set his burger in front of him.

"Anything else?" the waitress asked.

"No, thanks." He shifted his plate to align the square edge to the wood grain of the table. When he was satisfied, his focus returned to Shane. "It's difficult seeing you here and not wanting things to be like we were. It was difficult at the hotel last week too. Trying to reconcile you as a competitive colleague versus my submissive lover crosses wires." He snagged a fry from the mountain of bier cheese, bacon, and chives sitting between them. He shoved it into his mouth.

She swallowed. Hearing him use the word submissive dinged her. They'd never used the term to describe what they had. Yes, it was what they were, but the designation made it sound arranged and impersonal.

"Is that what you thought?" She cut her burger down the middle, separating the two halves. *Dominant and submissive.*

"What?"

"I was your submissive lover?"

"You were. In addition to my girlfriend. Life partner. Whatever." He waved it off to swat away his word choices.

"It's strange hearing you say *submissive*. I mean I wouldn't have called you my Dominant."

He stopped mid bite into his enormous burger, then bit down and chewed to digest her statement. "Why not?"

She laughed. "You can't be serious, Jacob."

"I'm very serious. Why wouldn't you have considered me your Dominant? We did things falling into those buckets. I owned your sweet, beautiful body." He smiled, and her throat constricted. Dancing around memories wouldn't change their future.

"We were young. We didn't even know what it meant. It's not like we belonged to some local community and practiced the art of it with other people."

"Is that what you think a Dom/sub relationship is?"

"What do you mean?" She bit her burger, and the juice dripped down her fingers.

"Do you think it can only hold a label if people are in a group where they can outwardly identify with one another?"

He did have a point. Although she thought what they had was more. A Dom/sub relationship, to her, only meant a power exchange between two people playing a bedroom game. He said what he wanted and she did it. Both received sexual satisfaction and intimacy while building layers of trust. But outside the bedroom, they weren't in those roles. Or at least she didn't feel the labels existed any longer once they crossed the threshold.

"Well, no."

"What did you think we had? No. Let me rephrase. What is your definition of D/s?"

"Two people having a power exchange for sexual pleasure."

"And?"

"And, what? That's what it is." Wasn't it? It appeared so on the surface.

"Why did you kneel for me?"

"Jacob, let's not do this." She set her burger in its basket.

"No, let's. Maybe this is what we were missing. Because it sure as hell felt like more than a sexual connection." His voice became razor sharp with anxiety.

"It did for me too, but it won't change anything."

"Maybe not. But maybe it'll help clarify where we were as a couple." He steepled two fingers over his lips as though his food had suddenly become uninteresting. His sharp green gaze held anticipation and focus. Whenever Jacob was working through something, he gave it his entire attention. The friction of attraction against uneasiness rubbed like sandpaper in her throat as she tried to speak. Why did this matter to him? What was he exploring?

Her phone rang, and she went to grab it.

"Leave it."

His command left her hands hovering over her purse. Not because he said to, but because the last time they were together— at their last hotel rendezvous, on a Thursday afternoon—her phone had rung. A shrill sound she wouldn't forget. They had rules about letting anyone interrupt their time together, yet she had insisted on answering it. It was the phone call informing her of her father's death. It was the beginning of the end for Shane and Jacob. It was the butterfly effect, sending them on a downward spiral. Work had granted the only distraction to keep her from losing her soul, and in the midst of it all, Jacob had left.

She pivoted to face him head on, placing her hands in her lap. The phone wouldn't dictate their time together. This was important. Soon the incessant noise ceased, leaving them in peace.

"Thank you," he said. "Why did you kneel for me all those years ago?"

"Because you told me to."

"Is that the only reason?" He narrowed his eyes in curiosity.

"No." She smoothed her lips between her teeth. "Because it pleased you."

"And?"

"It pleased me to do it for you."

"Why?"

"Because I loved you."

Loved. A fucked up past tense word she wished could be struck from her vocabulary. But it wasn't worth exploring *love.* A pesky present tense word, which also didn't belong in her lexicon. It was over. But why did her heart thump from her chest?

He sighed, taking the arrow with her. When he scratched his bearded chin, the sound of friction scored her heart, a delicate glass shell now marked with disappointment and failure.

"We were connected in the mind and secured in the heart." His Adam's apple bobbed as though something was stuck, and he needed to force it out. "A D/s relationship is more than bedroom fanfare, Shane. It's where two souls defy all odds against a centrifuge of emotion, bonding characteristics of reality, fantasy, past, and futures to come out as one being."

Her eyes widened. How did he explain it so eloquently? So majestically?

"If you felt that way, why did you leave?"

"That's something I ask myself every day." Why not 'fess up? Was he protecting her feelings? Would the answer be the damaging encore to his beautiful soliloquy?

"You haven't been with anyone else in that way?" Her heart did the talking now, and jealousy waited in the wings to suffocate her.

"In a D/s arrangement, sure. But never in a relationship." He raised two fingers. "Two different things."

So what if he was with another woman as long as he didn't give his heart. And why did she care if he had? She was about to get into an arrangement too. At The Resort. And who knew if the masked man she chose would become something more.

But would there ever be a man worthy of a relationship with her? Or would Jacob always own her soul?

"Wow. Can I throw a congratulations lunch or what?"

"Lovely," he whispered.

She grimaced. "You can't call me that anymore, Jacob."

"I understand."

"How did we get here? To this conversation, I mean." The edges of the napkin in her hand shredded through her fingertips like their relationship.

He pushed his half eaten lunch away. "It was a long time coming."

"So now what?"

"Now? We go on our way."

He held out a hand across the table. She slipped hers into it. Yes, they would go on their way. Alone. Forging a two-pronged parallel journey apart.

8

PREPARATION for the members appreciation night at The Resort should have a rising tide of anticipation, yet a souring swell in the pit in Shane's stomach ruined the experience. What should have been an evening of enjoyment was now clouded by a final separation from Jacob and Gavin's implication of a personal relationship on the horizon.

On one hand, the Jacob separation provided a lighter bounce in her step. They would always have a past love, but their future was non-existent. They'd decided to move apart. Together. Not one side forcing the distance like before.

On the other hand, Gavin's advances could not be mistaken. He hit all her hot buttons. Shouldn't her normal reaction be anger? Fear? Anxiety? How dare he come on to his boss? And he didn't even like her. Or did he? But it was too late. She was in the game and whatever lay hidden would soon be out in the open.

Pinning back her hair, she shook her head. Tonight was about her. Her freedom. Her escape. Her mystery man.

She brushed charcoal eye shadow on her eyelids. Who would he be? Her skin warmed. If anything, it would be an unforgettable experience. Disrobing, Shane slipped on a black thong. It offered some layer of protection before the evening whisked her away. The dress spread out on her bed fell over her shoulders.

"You got this," she said aloud.

Each small movement toward getting ready amped the already pressing desire between her legs. The magnificent silver shoes David had picked out curled her toes.

"There." She stared at her reflection. The murmur of male voices traveled from the living room. Her escorts had arrived.

Practically skipping into the room, Shane beamed. Sean whistled, causing her to spin around. "You like?"

"Like? I love. You might not make it through the door before one of the Doms stakes their claim," he said.

"We were going for the seen-and-be-captured look." David laughed. "Ready?"

"Almost." She walked to the coffee table and lifted the lid of the velvet box, stopping to exhale. She smoothed on the gloves and put the key card, a condom, and the mask into her clutch. "Okay, now I'm ready."

THE GROUP ARRIVED at the club in a limousine David insisted they take to the event. Shane shook her arms to relieve the nerves, which had built on the ride over. "Here goes nothing." She tied her mask around her face.

David straightened Sean's mask. "You okay, doll?"

"I feel like its prom, and I'm about to lose my virginity."

Sean leaned forward on the bench seat and lifted her chin. "Shane, remember: You don't have to play. You can just enjoy the night. Okay?" His dark eyes were kind behind his red mask. His tux fit perfectly on his large frame.

"I know." Her shoulders rose and fell.

He dropped his hand to her lap, squeezing her thigh. "We're

here for you. If things get too intense, let us know and we'll leave. Got it?"

"I'll be fine once I get in there."

David opened the door and slid out with Sean in tow. She stepped onto the curb as Sean held her hand. Allowing her room to lead, they approached the entrance. An average gray door called to her, unassuming to anyone passing by it, but it was the gateway to dark fantasies.

Shane swiped the metal keycard. The red light beeped and flashed green. The sound of the lock opening shot her anxiety sky high. Before crossing the threshold, she allowed the last of her nerves and identity to fade into the city sidewalk.

"Welcome, Star!" A bubbly blonde came toward them from a podium. "My name is Candy. Please continue through the double doors at the end of the hallway. Let me know if there's anything you need tonight."

Her alternate name must have appeared on the monitor when she swiped her card.

"Hello D and S, welcome back!" she squealed, hugging Shane's strapping male company.

Shane struggled to contain a laugh. "D and S? Shouldn't it be the other way around?"

"Smart ass." With one hand on the handle of the doors and one on her elbow, David asked, "Are you ready, *Star*?"

"As ready as I'll ever be!" Excitement bubbled over, and desire bloomed in her stomach.

Trance music filled the air, and the lyrics from a male voice sang with salacious suggestion when they pushed through the main doors. The extreme beat pumped into her chest as goosebumps bubbled up on hyperaware skin. The room opened to a main dance floor as they hovered on the mezzanine level. An ornate chandelier, representing the heart of the room, hung over the dance floor. Its spherical shape caged smaller orbs as red and yellow lights pulsed to the cadence of the song, matching her racing heart.

LED lights along the ceiling surged to the beat and escaped through illuminated arteries until they faded into the walls. Gripping the railing from the sudden ardor in her veins, she cast her eyes down to the main floor. People danced as though participating in bacchanal festival disguised as a black-tie event. The room was alive and hungry, and they were the feast.

"The private rooms are back there," David yelled over the music. She followed his pointed finger.

"Oh." She creased her eyebrows.

"Honey, relax. Let's get you a cocktail before you run toward a life of celibacy." He laughed.

They approached the bar, and Sean waved over the bartender. "Champagne," he ordered holding up three fingers.

Leather couches surrounded the dance floor. A sea of people disguised by black, white, and red filled the room to capacity.

"Excuse me," a short bald man said.

"Oh, sorry." Shane sidestepped as he carried champagne to a neighboring booth.

"Why isn't he wearing a mask?" She pointed out.

"Usually they are in a relationship. They're not out to explore or invite other players," David explained, shifting his mask.

"And what about you and Sean?"

Sean chimed in. "Sometimes we go without when we want no distractions. But sometimes we wear them to see if someone would like to join us."

Taking the glass from his hand, her eyes widened. This was news. "You invite others into your partnership?"

"It's hard for me to give him everything he needs, doll." Sean wrapped an arm around David's waist. "Being a switch, he wants to be dominated too. I get it." David said it with understanding and love.

She blinked and shook her head. "Right. I'm sorry. None of my business, I was just surprised."

Sean smiled and a dimple appeared, unfazed by her abrupt question. "To an evening full of surprises." He held his glass in the air.

"You aren't kidding." She clinked and downed the bubbly in one swallow.

ONE LAST GLANCE around his private room made Gavin smirk. Shane would be arriving soon, and everything was in place.

A large bed, covered in silver satin sheets, dominated the center of the room. A black head and footboard discreetly hid eyehooks along each edge. Perfect for bondage play. The translucent glass panels embedded with lights and attached to the far wall, radiated a soft blue tone, which seemed to calm subs before a scene. In the corner sat a convertible spanking bench, and toys and implements for pain and pleasure adorned the opposite wall, all artfully set to complete the ambiance and encourage the desired effect.

Mental images of Shane at his mercy painted his mind. Tied up. Bent over. Ass red. She'd never know what hit her. Unless it was a flogger. He grinned. Enjoyment and sweet pleasure rolled through his veins.

He put on the tuxedo jacket, which had been on the padded chair, and retreated to the adjoining bathroom. After tying on his black mask, he smoothed his dark hair to the side and smiled at his reflection. A vibration cut through his pocket. A text from Candy. Shane had arrived.

The bass increased as he approached the mezzanine entrance. Confidence rumbled inside him. He leaned against the railing, scanning the dance floor. The heat coming off the members energized him as their scents intermingled. They were clearly enjoying themselves, making the evening a success.

A woman fitting the description Candy gave rose from the couch on the mezzanine, leading a submissive male behind her. David maybe? She never went anywhere without him. The third person in the party hung back, obviously eyeing up several dominant members in the corner.

Shane stepped down the metal stairs, her dress plunging low. Her voluptuous tits practically spilled from the edges. *Fuck.* What would they taste like? A surge of blood hit his groin.

Once on the dance floor, her body moved seductively as she rolled her hips side to side. She was a naturally sexual creature. How had he missed it before? Shane, a woman in power, he'd found her attractive and craved to be close to her. His competitive nature to dominate an equally assertive person came in a rush. Taking down his boss had its perks.

A man wearing a black mask approached her from behind, and she stiffened. Apprehension? Nerves? He narrowed his gaze. He assumed she and Jacob were in the scene together. This couldn't be her first time.

Master Damien approached with Brit on his arm. "Good evening." He held his hand out to shake.

Gavin returned it. "Thank you for coming tonight. I hope you're both enjoying yourselves."

"Yes, very much, sir." Brit batted her eyelashes through her mask. Petite, straight dark hair, her body cinched in a purple corset dress, and her pale skin a kaleidoscope of color from the club lighting, he didn't miss her attempt to proposition him with her brown doe eyes.

"Care to join us tonight, Gavin?" Damien inquired. "It's been a while."

Master Damien loved his wife and would go to great lengths

to satisfy her needs and desires, even if it meant inviting other Dominants into their scenes.

Gavin caught sight of Shane, resting her head on the man's chest as she ground her ass against him. Her eyes were closed, and she'd apparently lost herself in the music. He needed to get to her. "No, thank you. Not this evening."

Damien twisted over his shoulder. "Appears you have other plans tonight. We'll let you get on your way." He wrapped an arm around Brit as they disappeared through the door to the private rooms.

Gavin darted to the stairs and set his sights on Shane like the terminator. He swiped two champagne flutes from a passing waitress and weaved through the crowd.

"Sir, if you'll excuse us. She's with me," Gavin told the man who had his paws all over his conquest. Shane opened her crystal blue eyes. Her lips formed an "O" followed by a smile tugging the corner of her mouth. A jolt of electricity traveled to his cock as her eyes sealed her fate and his for the evening. She was interested.

"I don't think so, buddy." The man gripped her hips.

"I don't think you heard me," Gavin gritted, nearly shattering the glass of champagne in his hand.

"Gentlemen, please. The night is young." She turned toward her dance partner and whispered in his ear. Gavin kept a watchful glare.

"Thank you for the drink." She swiped the glass from Gavin's hand and strolled away.

"Seriously, man…"

"Here," Gavin barked. He handed the party guest the other a glass. What the hell was she doing?

With each step toward her, his possessiveness spiked. Shane wouldn't get away so easy. He reached the couch she occupied. His spine tensed as the electric charge became palpable. Perhaps being the captor was becoming a new kink for him. He never chased a woman. *Hard limit.* But she presented a real challenge. He committed himself to making her submit before the evening ended.

With calm authority, he asked, "Do you always treat men vying for your attention this way?"

"I figured it was best to let you two handle things. Looks like you won." She patted the seat next to her.

He glared. She was out of practice. *Let's get her in the right mindset.*

"Stand up." Her glass stopped before hitting her lips. "Now," he ordered.

The champagne flute clinked the tabletop, and she rose. She inspected his face until her eyes met his. A flash of fascination glazed over her baby blue irises. *Interesting.*

"Eyes to the floor. I'll tell you when you can look at me." Her pale skin flushed a rosy red along her neck when she did. "Turn around."

She pivoted and the club melted away. Only the two of them existed. He whispered in her ear from behind. "You're mine tonight. Do you understand?"

"Yes."

"Yes, what?" He nuzzled his nose into the soft skin of her neck and inhaled. A cloud of wildflower perfume spun him into a twisted web of possession and power. His erection stood at attention. She shivered. She was his…

She released a long, guttural exhale. "Yes, Sir."

"Better. I didn't want to spank you in front of all these people." Her thighs rubbed against his slacks when she pushed them together. Her head landed on his chest. *Good, dynamic understood.*

"Now that I have your full attention, go to the door at the end of the mezzanine and enter. Then wait. Do you understand?"

"Yes, Sir."

"Good girl. Now go."

SHANE HELD her clutch close to her body. Her pulse pounded against her chest. Wetness slickened her sex as she waited. Maybe she was out of practice, but holy hell, he was...beyond words. His voice had reverberated her skin, made her pussy clench, and sent her on a trip to the unknown, all within five minutes.

Party guests shuffled past Shane without a word. She supposed standing in the middle of a dark hallway was normal at The Resort. Could they hear her heartbeat?

She shook her head and propped her hands on the wall. *Breathe, Shane.* Since when did the men of fantasies become the real deal? *Seriously?* The immediate connection was almost too comfortable. Did she know him from somewhere?

She jumped as the man tickled her arms and peeled her hands from the wall.

"Shhh, it's okay," he soothed. "Come with me."

He led her down the hallway, cupping her hand. Her heels clicked, each step boosting her trepidation. At the end of the L-shaped corridor, a door awaited their entrance. He swiped a key card and, without a word, led her inside.

She blinked at the muted tones of soft blue lighting. Calm fell over her. The word *safe* resonated in her head and melted through her body. *Good, he wasn't a fan of the dungeon scenes.*

"Scan your keycard here." He pointed to a small box mounted under a monitor.

She shuffled through her clutch and removed her card. She swiped it, and her limits appeared next to his on the screen.

"Now stand before the bed." He separated the clutch from her sweaty hands. On wobbly legs, she stepped forward. He shifted

85

out of his coat and threw it on the chair by the entrance and moved to the far side of the room. A wall garnished with toys for any kink and fantasy awakened her insides. The chest of drawers scraped open, and he put something in his pocket, kicking her heart up a notch. What would he do to her?

From behind her, his warm hands stroked her bare arms. She jerked forward. "No need to be nervous. I won't push past your limits. If you call out your safe word, this all ends. Do you understand?"

"Yes, Sir." Liquid formed between her legs.

"Have you ever done anything like this?" His soft, controlled touch soothed her, dialing in to her anxious nature. It was obvious he was a master at his role, and she felt lucky he'd found her. A caressing squeeze to her shoulders brought her back.

"Two...um...years ago." She swallowed when his hands halted abruptly. The seconds ticked by without a word. She blurted out, "Is...is that okay? I mean I..." Did he change his mind? Disappointment hit her stomach.

He undid the button around her neck. She exhaled. *Okay, still interested.* She needed this, needed him in this moment to release her from Jacob. To forget her past love and bury it forever. This man could get her there.

"That's a long time."

Thanks for reminding me. Sure, it was a long time, but she couldn't bear to be taken by another man after Jacob had scarred her soul. How could she let this man know there was nothing he could do to hurt her? She didn't want to be treated like a porcelain doll. She wanted to be ravished and set free.

She opened her mouth when the dress slipped off her shoulders and puddled around her feet. Left standing in her thong, gloves, and mask, she was utterly exposed. As her arms went to wrap around her body, his strong hands stopped her.

"Keep these here." His low timbre coiled in her belly and vibrated her skin. "Who's been taking your pleasure?"

Generous lips danced down her neck to her bare shoulder, leaving a trail of fire behind. She closed her eyes. "I take my own, Sir."

A low growl caused her skin to prickle. "How do you take your pleasure?"

She swallowed, the room becoming dry and stifling as he coaxed the wanton woman from her den. Buzzing thoughts coated in lust swarmed her mind as he continued kissing her back and in between her shoulder blades. "I asked you a question," he prompted her.

Her voice shook. "Um, well, I start with my breasts and caress them."

"Like this?" Moving his arms under hers, soft caresses shot lightning bolts to her clit. Something as simple as a man's contact had her ready to climax with one touch. Her nipples pursed as his palms circled over each one.

"Yes, Sir."

"And then what?"

"I...god...I pinch them." Her head flew back at the sudden shock of pressure. She could feel his indrawn breath against her neck, then a click sounded right before the immediate rush of pain hit her right nipple.

"Ow!" she yelled. Two metallic balls magnetically clamped her swelling flesh. With a contorted face and heavy breaths, she labored through the pain.

"Continue," he instructed. His cock brushed against her bare ass through his pants while he continued to massage her breasts. *Screw fantasies when he exists in the world.*

"I take my hand...and touch myself."

"Show me." Cupping her small hand, he moved it toward her sex. He stopped right before they made contact. His tongue rimmed the outside of her ear and sucked the lobe. Her knees shook, and her eyes rolled back.

Traveling downward under her panties, their fingers stroked the outer layer of her sex. The silkiness of her gloves against naked flesh, mixed with his hum of approval, amplified her level of desire. Rubbing her bare folds, they traveled lower until their hands and fingers were covered in wetness.

"You like that? God, it's like velvet. Show me how you like it." He licked her neck.

She panted at his slow and methodical torture. Her nerves had left the building, and only the confident *Star* existed.

Wrapping her gloved hands around his, she pushed his wide, long fingers inside her slit, and they both moaned. She slowly drew them out to circle her clit until her knees wobbled. Her release was so close. Her ladylike persona was gone, and the wanton woman had come out as she dipped his fingers inside her again. Her pussy rippled around his digits as he ground his hips against her, both moving in unison to the ebbs and flows of passion.

"More," she insisted, but he stopped. "No, please."

"Patience. You will no longer take your own pleasure. It belongs to me now." He removed her panties and helped her step out of them. "Move to the side of the bed, face the wall, and remove your shoes."

She blinked from the loss of his touch but quickly complied. Bending over, she unstrapped her heels and moved them aside. Items being taken from the hooks on the wall ratcheted her aware-ness. He returned, holding a thick, black leather strap looped on each end.

"Step into each one."

She balanced on his shoulders and stepped into each loop. His pulse fluttered in his neck, his only tell of excitement, unless one counted the massive erection straining against his fly.

He was a man of few words, which heightened her focus on his voice when he did speak. She was oddly content being around him and fascinated by his patience. It drove her crazy. She wanted to kiss those lips, suck his tongue, and shift his large body on top of her. Addiction was settling in already.

"Move to the center of the bed and lie on your back with your head over the edge."

She followed his instructions. Her nipple throbbed as the metal balls continued to squeeze. Once in place, he stretched her left arm toward the headboard, buckling a soft leather cuff to her wrist.

"You're doing well," he praised. He clamped another restraint to her right wrist then to the footboard. "Raise your knees to your chest." As she complied, the center of the strap rested at the back of her neck. Her knees were forced up and out, exposing her completely, fully submersed in his control.

The man stared at her sex; fluid dripped out of her core and down her buttocks. Embarrassed by his gaze, she closed her eyes. The restraints allowed him access to her most secret places. She shuddered, yanking at the bindings.

Callused hands grazed her wet pussy. The strap prevented her from closing her legs, and his wicked chuckle of delight filled her ears. *Slap!* The sting from his hand ran from her pussy to her clit. She screamed. *Fuck, that was good.*

"You like that, my little whore? Tell me," he goaded.

Her eyes widened. While shocked by his filthy endearment she was even more surprised she liked it. She let go, traveling his dark path.

"I like it when you slap me there."

"Where?"

"My pussy, Sir."

"Whose?" he slapped again.

"Your pussy, Sir!"

The way his cock continued to tent his slacks, she would bet a sly smile had appeared on his face. He continued light slaps on her sex, raising her level of desire. Her body convulsed.

"Are you my little whore?"

"Yes, Sir," she cried out between contact. Tonight, she was.

"Tell me."

"I'm your little…whore," she moaned. Her body wiggled in place, begging for penetration, her mind lost in the abyss of desire essential to her freedom. Who was she right now? This man found the darkest places in her mind with ease.

Slapping the back of her thighs and ass with his palms, her skin prickled hot, each impact harder than the last. She screamed, moaned, and contorted her face as each sting of pain blended into warm pleasure as he alternated slaps with thrusting his fingers into her pussy.

"So good…" she whispered as he worked her body to bliss.

With the sound of a zipper, she jerked her eyes open. His glorious dick bobbed into view as his large hand stroked from root to tip. *Lucky me.*

"Look at me," he demanded. Her eyes darted away from his stunning manhood and met the feral irises behind the black mask. His tongue darted to lick his bottom lip. "Open your fucking mouth."

She did without question. The smooth crown slipped past her lips, and he held still. She swirled her tongue around the crease, the salty taste of his pre-ejaculate spurring her deeper. He grunted at her swift move before he continued pushing forward. It was so big she nearly choked, unsure if she would succeed. Relaxing her throat, she concentrated on breathing out of her nose. Tears beaded at the corners of her eyes behind her mask when her lips met the base.

"My little whore can take more than I thought." He spoke through his clenched teeth. Warm hands grasped her thighs, and his hot tongue licked her slit, she moaned. *Yes.* His hips shifted, pumping his dick in and out of her mouth. His lips sucked and licked her pussy. The sensation created a sexual charge as she drifted beyond the room and into a vortex of sexual sin.

When his dick trembled along her tongue, his balls flexed. She continued moaning and vibrating his thick column.

"Fuck."

Quickly removing himself, his hand met her cheek enough to alert her. She licked her lips to savor his masculine taste. "You're a temptress," he said, rewarding her with a compliment. "Your cunt is sweet like a fucking peach, and your mouth…"

"Thank you, Sir." She adjusted her jaw from the emptiness as the creeping heat crawled along her skin. She was revved and ready to explode.

The mattress dipped. She crooked her neck to see his immense body towering over her. He'd shed his pants, underwear, and button-down but was still dressed in a white t-shirt and mask. His muscular arms and chest flexed through the fabric as he climbed her body.

Mask-to-mask they stared at each other, a zip of lust connecting them. He visibly shuddered and moved to lean back on his heels. His cock jutted forward and he slowly rolled a condom on. Her breathing spiked. Had she ever seen a more erotic move? Slow. Deliberate. An animal capturing its prey. Lips curled. Eyes flaring. The wide crown notched her cleft, wetting the tip from her dripping juices.

"Ready for me?"

She nodded, and he pushed in without apology, grunting as her pussy enveloped him. She sucked in a gasp and held her breath. The sheer size of his cock expanded her more than she had ever been before. Jacob was no slouch in size but this man…holy mother...

"Take it all," he grunted.

Wincing in delicious agony, she squeezed her eyes shut. He cupped her ass and moved her hips up and down until his cock was fully inserted. Her gloved hands gripped the wrist restraints as she became accustomed to his size.

He moved in and out at a pace so fast she moaned loudly without inhibition. Drilling her, he cupped her breast and squeezed her clamped nipple, sending her deep into subspace. Pure ecstasy wrapped her in a cocoon of intense pleasure accompanied by pain. Her walls clenched as he found her special spot.

"Not yet, my whore," he gasped between thrusts. Sweat ran down his face and arms. Hot breath hit her face. She bit the inside of her mouth to hang on a little longer. Her mind flipped, and her body won the fight to pure pleasure.

"Now." His permission granted too late.

She screamed so loud it could have broken glass. Muscles contracted, rolling her orgasm over and over again. As her body convulsed, he bit down on her nipple and tore the balls off with his teeth, creating a burning throb of epic proportions as the feeling came back to the abused tissue. Her eyes rolled as another climax overcame her. *Oh my god...*

Limp and exhausted, the man didn't let up on his exquisite punishment until he came hard inside her. He crushed her when he fell over her bound body.

GAVIN BLINKED. Darkness. How long had he slept? He stretched, relaxing into the unwinding tension in his body. He rolled over to touch Shane. The bed was cold. He sprang up and grabbed the remote sitting on the side table. Lights filled the room. Disbelief sank in. She was gone. He smirked, rubbing his face. This was a first. Women typically begged to be taken again–which he would deny–while he pried their grasp from the still burning sheets.

He fell back onto the plush bed. Visions of Shane at his mercy brought his libido to life again as he teased his throbbing dick. The boss was a tart and easy to break from her otherwise aggressive persona. The base of his balls tightened. Her lush, shameless ways turned him on. It would only be a matter of time before he had her heart. Next step? Make her feel safe, push her limits, and get what he needed to execute his plan.

He made his way to the bathroom to clean up and dress. The rest of the evening would need attending to. The water he splashed on his face cooled his warm skin. He patted his face with a towel and halted at his reflection. Fear widened his eyes, and he moved swiftly toward the bed. There, on the floor, lay his mask.

9

"IN THE SADDLE, TEN SECONDS! GO!" the spin instructor yelled.

"Jeez, she is working us this morning," David gasped, out of breath.

Monday was their weekly spin class to rile her energy for the week. Today was no different except the underlying hum of satisfaction Shane still had from her weekend at the club.

"Get up! On those feet! Push, push, push. Squeeze those asses!"

Shane pedaled through the pain. Sweat dripping down her spine. "Sure is."

"So…you have said…all of two words to me…about your mystery man on Saturday," he spoke between squats on the bike.

"Nothing to tell." She sat back during the breakout. Shivers flooded her system even though the room was stifling.

"Liar! You disappeared out of nowhere. Sean and I waited as long as we could."

"Hey, you in the back, I must not be working this group hard enough with all the chitchat," the instructor called out. "Now push up your resistance and get ready to climb!"

"Now look what you did." Shane laughed, cranking the knob.

"This conversation is not over."

THE FALL BREEZE hit Shane's face with renewed vibrancy. The blue sky with cotton-like white clouds spanned over the high rises of New York. Honking horns and the sounds of passing people flooded her ears. The city was alive, and for the first time, she was a part of its kinetic energy. Awakened and revived, a long sigh was followed by dancing goosebumps on her skin. *Wow, what a weekend.*

"Okay, I can't take the suspense, doll. What happened?"

"Oh, you know, the usual." She smiled.

"The usual? There's nothing usual about my Shane hooking up with a random stranger. I didn't even get to see what he looked like! Come on, please? Don't make me beg." He stuck out his bottom lip.

Her smile widened until her cheeks hurt. "Get in the car."

He jumped in the air like a three-year-old and slid into the SUV. When they merged into morning traffic, she said, "For starters he was nice."

"Nice? You settled for *nice*? Please." He waved her off.

"And authoritative, patient and demanding. Blew. My. Mind." The masked mystery Dom, all tall, dark, and sexy, flashed before her field of vision. Goose pimples formed on her arms, and her toes curled in her boots.

"Now we're getting somewhere. What's his name?"

"Shit. I-I don't know."

"You don't know? How did you know what to scream, if you didn't know his name?" He laughed.

"Whatever. There wasn't a need for names. No connection whatsoever." Besides, the word *connection* would be an insult to what happened.

"You're blushing, which proves you are a horrific liar. There must have been something." He jerked off his glasses and cleaned them with a pocket square.

"I suppose."

"Shane, this game is boring me. What happened?"

She gazed out the window when the SUV slowed at a red light. Pedestrians moved toward the flashing walk sign across the street, one foot in front of the other, moving forward toward their destinations. Where was she heading? Her chest gripped. Admitting anything to David involved confessing the weekend meant more than sex and a physiological release. But getting it out would give her perspective.

She turned to him. "He was more than I imagined. He understood me, could read me. Took me places I never thought anyone but Jacob could reach."

A rough morning after left her sinking into regret. It was supposed to be about her getting back out there and having fun. Instead, a detour was taken before a final destination could be determined. She wanted to see the Dom again, craved what he'd done to her. It wasn't better than Jacob, just different, and the thrill of exploring it all again made it impossible to want to stay away.

"Now was that so hard?" He put his glasses on and patted her hand. "One problem. You don't know his name, so how will we ever find him again?"

"We?" she squealed in shock.

"If you're not going to track him down, I will. For you, of course. I haven't seen you this, this…" He stuttered, holding his hand out like he tried to grab the words from the air.

"Happy? Alive? Confused?" She spouted out the possibilities for him.

"Yes, doll. All of the above."

She was screwed. "Let's leave it for now. This was a long

time coming, and my brain is short-circuiting. I need time to separate the mystery man, Gavin, and Jacob all coming at me."

"Let me know if I can help."

"You listening helps." She kissed his cheek.

———

A LITTLE AFTER eight in the morning and Gavin sat at the helm of Omega Records in the cushy white leather chair from which Shane steered the proverbial ship. The city sprawled before him, full of promises while awaiting domination. The invisible radio waves of his soon-to-be empire crisscrossed the massive city. The music from his artists would be on the devices of every listener. The end game remained within his reach. Shane had slipped into his hand quicker than he'd thought possible.

A surge of power engulfed him in a fog of passion, lust, and control. The way she'd yielded to him, obeyed him, all without question. Fucking incredible. The boss lady had quite the list of sexual proclivities, all at his fingertips. Unless she recognized him. He rolled his lips between his teeth. *Fuck.* It could be over before it started.

Voices murmured from down the hall, and he left his eventual throne of power and sat in a visitor's chair.

"What the fu...?"

"Good morning, Shane. How was your weekend?" he asked nonchalantly.

"Holy hell, Gavin. What are you doing in here?"

"Waiting for you. I brought your coffee." He pointed to the latte sitting on her desk.

"Um, thanks, I guess." She cautiously made her way to the desk. She placed her purse and briefcase on the floor while maintaining eye contact when she sat.

"Are you okay? You seem off." He narrowed his eyes. Any sign of recognition from The Resort not present.

She crinkled her brow. "Is this how you make friends? Popping in on people without warning?"

"No, this is new for me. Usually I don't have to try so hard. Besides, I thought we were past friends." He winked. *So very 'past friends'.*

"Yeah. About dinner last week…"

"Are you denying there was something there?"

"No." She fumbled with her coffee, almost spilling its contents.

The chink in her armor had been exposed. His back-up plan was working in case she didn't proceed to push her limits at The Resort. But genuine curiosity about her good side filled him with wonder, lighting a dormant spot in his heart. The Shane she didn't show anyone. The person he glimpsed at dinner.

"Then what's the problem?"

She found her spot at the front of her desk. "The problem is I'm your boss, and you're an employee. We work together. That's it."

"That's it? As in all that's standing in my way or all we will be?"

She tried to hide her Mona Lisa smile. "All we will be."

He stood slowly. Her eyes followed his panther-like movements. Once he straightened, he had several inches on her. She confidently craned her neck so her chin jutted out a few inches. A dare initiated, not only between them, but within himself.

There comes a time in a man's life—*his* life—where hunting for survival rather than sport becomes paramount. His entire life, he'd played the angle, conquering his prey for game, but now his wires had crossed. Her slightly diminished alpha demeanor sent a shock to his heart. What was it about her?

Please, one night with the boss doesn't mean veering off

course. Stick to the plan.

One step closer and heat radiated from her small frame. She wanted more. He wanted more. Her plump, glossy lips parted, and he could kiss her. Tell her what he was. He licked his lips, the sensual tension so thick, a train could barrel through the office, and they wouldn't even notice.

A deep, shaky breath left her. "W-what's on the docket for today?"

His eyes deliberately danced over her face. Flushed cheeks. Breath hitched. Blue eyes dilated. "You tell me, Shane."

She swallowed as her hand pressed against his chest. He could take her if he wanted to. Her eyes did the bidding, but she had to say the word. And his dick thought it was a great idea. She blinked and shoved him back.

"Your boss," she reminded, moving to the other side of the desk.

He cleared his throat, rolling his neck.

"I have a lunch meeting with Don Miller to finalize the contract with Digmore. I thought you might want to come along."

"Trouble closing?" she joked.

He leaned on the desk. "Let's get something straight, I always close." She swallowed again. *That's right, baby. I always do.*

Her all-telling eyes glazed over for a second as the blush in her neck deepened.

She's totally interested.

"See you at noon."

"YOU'RE AWFULLY QUIET, Shane. You seem distracted," Gavin said as they waited at a table for Don Miller.

"Everything's fine. A lot going on right now."

"Like what?"

"Nothing of your concern." The top of her priority list didn't scream: *Share your weekend sexcapades with your employee.* "Where are we with Ryan signing since last week?"

He paused. Curiosity roused her insides. What was floating through his mind?

"We're close. The numbers are all outlined in the contract. This meeting is to clarify recording schedules and finalize payment to him." He nodded toward the door. "He's here."

Don approached the table. Wisps of silver feathered his temples and were peppered throughout his slicked back brown hair. When he smiled, the wrinkles creased near his kind eyes. "Don, welcome. This is Shane Vaughn, CEO of Omega Records."

"Wonderful to meet you, Ms. Vaughn," Don said, shaking her hand.

"Likewise, and call me Shane, please."

"I brought Shane so you could discuss any concerns with the contract. She's been anxious to meet the man behind Ryan's current success, so it made sense to get you together sooner rather than later." Gavin smiled in her direction.

Way to go, Gavin. Very smooth.

Don nodded. "It's a pleasure. Gavin has said wonderful things about your company, and we're excited to be considered for your impressive roster."

"Did he now?" She tilted her head toward Gavin. "I've listened to Ryan's first album, and for being self-produced, it's quite impressive."

"Thanks. Put in a lot of long hours to make it seem professionally recorded. I've never seen someone as invested in the output of his music as he is. And he wants to continue to be a part of the process."

"And rightfully so. Omega prides itself on being one of the last large record labels to encourage artist involvement. Hindering the creative process only puts roadblocks in the way," Gavin confirmed.

The waiter arrived, and they paused to place their order. Shane continued, "So Don, tell me about yourself."

Shane believed, in order to be the best, the CEO must understand the talent and the people behind the music. It helped avoid pitfalls and undervalued contracts in the industry. Every musician had a story. How they got there, why they pursued it. Each story contained a gem of motivation, and the contract was written to capitalize on it, making signing with her label more appealing than others.

Don leaned back in his chair and discussed his history with music going back twenty years. To get his feet wet, he had worked pro bono for a band touring the country. The lead singer decided to take Don on as their manager. Along the way, he met Ryan at a festival, playing his guitar around a bonfire, swooning a group of girls. He'd witnessed something special and brought him up the ranks, leaving his management position.

"Quite a risk on your part," she admired.

"Yeah, it was. But I believe in Ryan. If not for Gavin coming to one of his gigs, we wouldn't be here."

"It's my job."

"Maybe so. But you possess a certain manner in the way you interact with musicians. Ryan wants a label to treat him like a person. Other labels contacted us, but your approach made us feel at ease. Like you saw the same vision. The others pushed like vultures, ready to chew him up and spit him out," Don explained. "Ryan would like you to personally see him through this process including the album release."

She peered at Gavin, amazed to learn there might be a caring person inside. The arrogance he'd once exhibited, now relaxed listening to Don's request. Maybe he was more than a rough and abrasive exterior. Maybe the façades they showed in public paired with each other.

"Good to hear, Don," she said. "Tell us your concerns with the contract as it stands."

"As I mentioned, I believe in Ryan. The offer is low considering his talent and the rise of his last album."

"Everything in Ryan's contract is standard for any new artist." Gavin held his ground.

How was the offer too low? What about the signing bonus? She grabbed his arm, halting him. "Continue, Don." Gavin's glare cut her face. She didn't care.

"He sold about ten-thousand album downloads last year, all on his own through social media. His new album is almost complete, and Omega would make pure profit off the sales."

Gavin rested his elbows on the table. "The album will be remastered and refined for the airwaves. An unavoidable cost. Second, we don't know how his new album will sell. We're assuming some risk, which you can respect." He backed away to allow the waiter to serve his salmon. "Third, the benefits he and you will receive from our marketing team will make Ryan Digmore a household name. This offer is more than fair. We're only asking for a firm commitment of one album. The remainders are optional if we agree on future terms. If it fails, Ryan goes on his way after royalties are paid and the obligation for advances is met. We have the team to get him to the next level or you wouldn't have entertained my offer."

"Okay, let's talk about the next level." Don forked a piece of crab cake and chewed. "A ten percent royalty package is not enough. Other acts are signing for at least sixteen percent in initial album sales. The clause in the contact states the percentage is fixed through the first three albums. I would like to negotiate for twelve and a half percent at signing."

Gavin wiped his mouth with his linen and countered. "Ten

percent to start, twelve and a half after the second album, if it reaches three-hundred thousand copies sold."

"I will agree to the ten percent with sliding increases per album. But we would need twelve and a half percent with *two-hundred and fifty thousand* sold on the second and a renegotiation for more on the third album."

Shane's toes curled in her pumps. Masters at negotiation, she delighted in their exchange. Gavin's poker face, hard angular jaw, and laser focus on Don's counteroffer left her speechless. He provided a strong hand for Don to play against.

"I'll only agree to the renegotiation if there is to be a third album, based on the revenues of the first two. All other fine line offers in the contract stand as is." He set his fork down, waiting in silence. *Come on, Gavin. Offer the bonus.* Leaning back with an elbow propped on the armrest, his thumb casually rubbed the inside of his fingers.

She interjected, "Where are you with considering a contract with Avalon Music Group?"

"That's private," Don answered with arched brows.

"Now, Don. I know my competitors and understand their terms. But let me ask you this: How is Ryan going to support his sister through their contract?" They both knew AMG offered no signing bonus or any other incentives in trade for cash.

Gavin sat back, letting the conversation unfold.

"I'm not sure what you mean."

"I know Ryan's story. I saw the spot he did on AXS when his first album did marginally well. The whole up-and-comer-on-the-rise." She smiled. "It was a moving piece. Incredibly touching."

He softened. "Yeah. They insisted on putting the part in about why he pursued music for his sister. But he's pretty private about it."

Pride swelled her chest. "I'm glad he let it run. I'm a sucker for a story, especially with musicians." They laughed as Gavin forced a smile. Her hand cupped Don's arm. "What I'm getting at is, I value the people that make their music, and I want to be a part of it. How I do that is by signing them and allowing them to express themselves the way they want. I also see a good deal of business too."

"What are you saying?"

"Take the deal. Ten percent with an increase at three hundred thousand albums sold and throw in a signing bonus upwards of 80K. Not an advance, but a bonus Ryan can use however he wants."

Don wiped his mouth and pushed away the empty plate. She had him. Relate and sign. If people believed in their missions, any deal was possible.

"What do you say, Don?" Gavin chimed in. What resembled respect crossed between Shane and him.

"I'd say it's a pretty appealing deal." Don rose from his seat. "I will run these things past Ryan, but I'm very confident he will agree."

Gavin held out a hand after he stood. "The offer stands until the end of the week."

"Understood. I'll have an answer to you by then. Ms. Vaughn…" Don nodded before walking away from the table.

Taking their seats again, the excitement inside her bubbled over. Man, she missed this. "Wow," she blew out. "That was incredible."

"It was." He drummed his fingers on the table.

"You okay?"

"I thought we agreed on no signing bonus."

She laughed. "You said no bonus. I told you to put it in."

"I was under the assumption we were partners."

"We are, and what I say goes." Gavin's jaw tightened, preparing for a slingshot-like response. "And before you get your boxers in a twist, I liked that you didn't put the signing bonus in the contract."

A sarcastic chuckle sounded. "Really."

"Yes. Partners show each other when to make a move, when to hold back, and when to push each other's limits."

"I know about limits, Shane." His declaration hit her squarely in the chest. *Limits*... Were they talking about the same thing? Her thighs pushed together as she stared at the fury within his slate blue eyes. *Damn, he was sexy when he was riled up.*

"Anyway, you held back, and I made a move. Good cop, bad cop." She waved over the waiter. "A martini for me, and he will have a Blanton's, neat."

"Shane, it's one o'clock on a Monday."

"And? My schedule is clear until three." She snatched her phone and typed a message. The device made a swoosh sound. "So is yours. Any other objections?"

"What did you do?"

"David has Tasha clearing your schedule. If anyone has an issue she's to let them know you are with me."

SHANE'S FINGERS nearly tangoed off the keyboard. She was light and excited. Another part of her Gavin failed to witness previously. She was full of surprises. This woman had him wondering what the fuck was up or down and even if he cared.

Do I care? Yes. No. Maybe. What the fuck?

The waiter brought their drinks, and he gulped the tumbler of bourbon. Taking the edge off might require a little more than the burn of alcohol.

"Why are we staying?"

"To celebrate, *partner*."

Gavin lifted his drink. "To as good as closing Digmore."

"Indeed." She drank, leaving a pink glossy lip mark on the

rim of her glass. She smoothed her full lips. "Tell me something about you, Gavin."

Spilling his past wasn't part of the deal to get her job. He'd only feed her morsels to continue drawing Little Red Riding Hood into the wolf's den, not give the entire lot.

"Nothing to tell."

She leaned her head into her hand as if preparing to watch a scene in a movie. She blinked, and her blue eyes became clear, insisting he give her something.

"There is." She was relentless.

"There's nothing you need to know." Uncomfortable with the spotlight, his chest burned. A fine thread of control, ready to break.

"Please?"

He snapped. "Jesus, Shane, don't you have my employee file? Didn't you read it before I was hired? I'm sure you would find out more from my background check than anything I could tell you."

She blinked out of cadence, possibly stunned by his outburst or maybe embarrassed by the glances from neighboring tables. He ran a hand along the back of his neck. *Jesus, get it together.*

"Yes, I've read your employment jacket. Cover to cover, several times." She fished out an olive from the martini and chewed it.

He glared. Was she testing him?

"It's pretty interesting reading. So much so, John Talbot didn't want to hire you. Thought it was too risky."

John Talbot. The ruling Chairman of The Board for Omega Records with pockets so deep and secrets so long he might as well be running the entire music industry.

"And let me guess, you changed his mind. Your love of stories and all."

A smile threatened the corners of her mouth. Was he supposed to be grateful now? Feel some sort of ultimate loyalty to her?

"Perhaps." She shrugged. "But you know what those documents didn't tell me?"

"What, Shane?"

"The why behind it all. What you must have felt being in jail for months. The death of your daughter—"

"Enough." He couldn't bear to hear her name. *Nicolette.* Or what Shane thought about what he'd felt during that time. She wouldn't understand. No one did. He would continue to pay his penance alone. "Why the fucking interest all of a sudden?"

His fingers curled around the armrest to stop the room from spinning. Shane knew. Of course she did, yet she never mentioned it.

"Why not? We need to understand each other for this to work. Have you ever been honest with anyone? Honest with yourself?"

He snatched the tumbler of alcohol with such force he could have sworn it would shatter in his hand. She cupped his arm like she did Don's. He relaxed slightly, loosening the death grip on the glass. Her touch could open the gates to vulnerability and understanding. He shifted away.

"Knowing my past won't change a thing. What matters is today."

"What matters is letting go of the idea the world is out to get you."

Cynical laughter erupted from him. "That's what you think?"

"Very much." As calm as a summer breeze, Shane didn't lose her resolve.

His rage fought its way through clenched teeth as he lurched forward.

"Wrong. *I'm* out to get the world. And you want to know why? Do you want to understand all the details behind that night? Do you think you can handle it?"

He didn't recognize his own voice. His heart pounded with the rush of emotion and adrenaline. The man he'd been all those years ago threatened to make a reprieve. The one whose mother chose his father over him. The man whose father set expectations so high disappointment and failure could be the only results of his efforts.

"Yes, I can handle it." Shane remained steadfast. No fear. No running. No pity. Who the fuck was this woman? And why did he feel he could share his past? Her resolute and sobering tone cut through the chaos enough for him to speak evenly. He pressed the bridge of his nose and exhaled.

"Shane, only a few people in this world know my past, and I'd like to keep it that way."

"Anyone outside your family?" He shook his head. She sighed as she wrapped her fingers around a linen napkin on the table. "Not everyone is an enemy. Some can be allies. And if this partnership is to continue without tension, I suggest you start aligning."

SHANE MADE a beeline toward her office, relieved to find David at his desk. While leaning one hand on the desktop, she asked, "Sweetie? Can you call Tasha and get Gavin's schedule for the rest of the week?"

She'd cracked the outer shell over lunch. It was time to take matters into her own hands. If he wasn't talking, she'd dig.

"Oh, no. What are you up to?" He peered at her over the top of his black-rimmed glasses.

"Nothing." She smiled even though guilt laced her tone.

"Doll, you should know me better." He crossed his arms and pursed his lips. "No call until you 'fess up."

"You will because I'm your boss."

He lifted a perfectly shaped brow. That line never worked with him.

"Ah! Fine. There's a story, and I want to see"—she shrugged her shoulders—"...you know...what he's all about."

"You stalker!"

"Shhh. Not so loud." A few employees walked by the desk. "Let's call it research. He's holding something back and giving me no choice."

"Stalking is illegal in all fifty states, doll." He dialed the phone while grazing over her form. "Orange might be your color."

"Remember, you're an accomplice now."

"Shit...oh, hi Tash... Nothing, stubbed my toe." Shane giggled as his face wrinkled. "Can you send me Gavin's schedule for the rest of the week?...Yes...The boss wants it." He rolled his eyes. "I don't know, babycakes, she does...You know I don't ask questions." He laughed at something Tasha said. "Okay, thanks babe. Smooches." The receiver rattled on the cradle when he hung up.

"What'd she say?"

"She thinks you're up to something. Tasha's all about the gossip." He waved his hand to dismiss her. The email pinged. "There it is, I'll send it to you."

"Thanks, sweetie," she said skipping into her office.

She tore into his calendar. All typical meetings. A few scheduled with his staff, current artists and managers. Nothing crazy. This weekend, he was going to see a new musician at the Village Underground, and Wednesday he had six p.m. to eight p.m. blocked off at a restaurant in Chelsea. No name or invite sent out. Who was he meeting? Was it business or pleasure?

Perhaps she could accidently run into him.

"I'm not stalking." A little chuckle escaped.

THE NEW YORK sunset poured through the massive windows of Jacob's office. The warmth soothed him in an embrace, caressing each part of him. He relinquished a sigh as the solitary tranquil moment washed over him. The dark ache inside his chest hadn't dulled after seeing Shane. He wasn't getting her back.

He leaned a forearm on the window above his head and tapped his fingers on the glass. The last few days had been agony. Physical yearnings to reach out to her tested the restraint he'd nurtured over several years. One hour with her had unraveled him. The nights were hard. Flashbacks disguised as nightmares flooded his sleep, leaving him with cold sweats and the need for frigid showers.

He missed her. His errors plagued his hardened soul, ripping it open again. Their undeniable connection had never broken. And now he could never erase what he'd done to her and her company.

Breathing deep, he remembered her words—*because I loved you*—before the fading orb of bright light slipped past a neighboring high rise. Not *I still love you*. The sun had set on his chance to be with the one woman he cared for and should have loved forever.

"Mr. Andrews?" his assistant called.

He turned, taken from his moment of contemplation. She stood, leaning on the dark wood doorframe, her silky blonde hair in a tight ponytail. "Yes, Liza?"

"Is there anything else you need today, sir?"

He waved his hand in a gesture of dismissal as he approached his cherry wood desk. "No. You can go. Thank you."

She nodded before closing the door, and he sat, rubbing his face. Leaning back in the chair, the void in his chest deepened like a bottomless abyss, threatening to swallow his soul. She was over him, and he'd made sure they would never have another chance. He had been too naïve to think a rash business deal and seeing her would get him closure. Something he mistakenly thought he'd accomplished years ago. Not seeing her, smelling her, or touching her rehabbed his need to be with her.

He'd suffered physical and mental withdrawals, and he'd quickly learned to live without her submission and love. But seeing her changed it all, and like an addict's relapse, he craved her.

He sipped from the rocks glass on his desk and clicked on the internet browser. He typed *Shane Vaughn* into the search bar and sifted through the pictures Google had thoughtfully displayed for his viewing.

Many he'd seen but a new one appeared from an arbitrary website known for recycling stories from other mainstream celebrity gossip sites. She was leaving the airport with David following closely behind. She wore barely any make-up and dressed in tight jeans and a simple long-sleeved gray shirt. Gorgeous. She'd woven her hair into a messy braid, and large sunglasses hid her beautiful eyes. He squinted, wishing he could see them. They expressed so much, and he missed seeing the fascination they presented to the world. Simple things in life had always captivated her.

The caption under the picture read: *Omega Records CEO, Shane Vaughn, and friend arriving from L.A. amidst the Anna Marie scandal.* He chuckled. David would be pissed being labeled '*and friend*'.

He enlarged the photo and sat back. His mind traveled to her in his bed, memories so strong he could swear her perfume floated through his office. His cock awakened in his black pinstriped dress pants as he remembered touching her soft skin and hearing the way she'd groan his name.

Fingers teased the tip of his growing erection. Sharp pangs of desire gripped him. His breathing deepened as his hand rubbed root to tip. The friction from the fabric caused his dick to expand with each pass.

His elbows hit the desk, and he ran his hands through his hair. The self-inflicted routine occurred daily. Jerking off to her picture roiled his stomach. But who could he touch? Who would allow him to release his lascivious nature on them so he could forget Shane?

He lazily dialed the phone. "Where are you?" His voice snaked through the receiver in a sensual tone laced with sexual danger. He listened to the response. "Come to me."

A RAP on his office door stirred Jacob's insides. A petite woman peered in and smiled. Miranda strolled across the room wearing her signature black stilettos with a black trench coat wound tightly around her frame.

"Mr. Andrews, I came as soon as I could." She stopped before his desk, hands behind her back. Her small body swayed side to side. An innocent smile flashed across her round face. He chuckled inside.

When he rose, he rolled up his sleeves. Her eyes shifted to the bulge trying to escape the confines of his dress slacks.

"Miranda." The word slipped out like a prayer to forget the one he loved. He kissed her delicate red lips followed by each flushed cheek. "What are you hiding under here?"

He yanked the belt from her coat, and it opened, revealing nothing but a dainty buxom figure and a small landing strip barely covering her folds. An animal-like desire to fuck traveled to his already painful hard-on.

"I thought: Why waste time with clothes, Sir?" She giggled and blinked her mocha chocolate eyes.

"You thought right." The light and shadows highlighted her curvy frame perfectly. How would he have her? He snatched her hips like a vise, rubbing her cleft along his erection. A yelp escaped her. This would be quick.

Their eyes locked as she nodded her understanding. Loneliness was their calling card. Two friends who gave each other solace and comfort when the desolation became too much.

He slid the coat off her shoulders and stepped back. Were her clenched hands a sign of trepidation or anticipation? She liked when he stared. Her nipples tightened, and her large breasts swelled. She bit her lip, obviously waiting for him to strike.

He hated using her, but the primal impulse to fuck needed to be sated. This moment wouldn't fix his rapacious need for Shane. It wouldn't change his betrayal when he'd bought out Icarus Descending. It was a temporary Band-Aid for his self-inflicted wounds.

He gritted his teeth and scooped her up. Her legs wrapped around his waist. Lips smashed together. She removed the tie holding his hair and tugged at the roots, the tension burning his scalp. Sublime pain tingled along his spine. *That's it. Quick and dirty.*

He set her down on the arm of the couch, which partitioned

the large seating area in his office. Ripping his lips from the heated kiss, Jacob spun her around, shoulders slamming down over the armrest, the buzz in his body so intense he shook. He unzipped his slacks, whipped out his throbbing dick, and sheathed it with the condom from his pocket.

"This will be fast and rough," he groaned impatiently.

"Yes, Sir."

All the tension left his muscles. She understood her place.

Aiming the crown at her opening, he rubbed it against her cleft. The slickness of her cunt caused a frustrated groan as he thrust forward. Her muscles clenched, and he clutched her hips until she yelped.

"Fuck," he grunted.

It felt so good. So fucking good to touch someone.

The view was perfect as he moved. Her round ass cheeks created a peak to the valley of her crevice. Hourglass curves revived him as her hands held the cushions with her face pressed into them. *Thank God.* Shane was the only woman he met face to face in the throes of passion. And it would stay that way.

He nailed Miranda in haste, trying to drain any thoughts of Shane, even if for a short while. He closed his lids tightly. *Focus, Andrews. Just finish...* But the desired friction never came. Only numbness existed around his cock as he thrust into her channel. No electricity, no synergy like with Shane. A failed attempt at a quick fuck to reset him.

"Come on," he bit out.

Her pussy tightened, grabbing his attention. "Yes, more." He slapped her ass. A harder squeeze followed. *Fuck, yeah!*

She squealed like a porn star, cursing and yelling his name. Nerve endings were now in a frenzy, the pain in his mind released through each thrust.

"Move your foot to the armrest."

She did. With one foot on the floor and the other raised, her legs split wider, allowing him a deeper thrust into her pussy. He wrapped one hand around the arm of the couch and the other pulled her hair for leverage. He pushed forward, and the couch screeched across the floor.

"Fuck...right there," he grunted between breaths. Sweat dripped off his forehead and trickled down his spine. *So fucking close.* The sound of slapping skin filled the room. A high-pitched scream escaped her lips as her slick core contracted. She climaxed while he struggled to find his own. She did everything right, except she wasn't Shane.

A fantasy popped in his head while he continued to pummel Miranda's boneless body.

Shane is bare, sitting on his desk. Long legs spread wide. She waits for him with a wanton glare when he enters the room. She leans back. One hand grazes her glistening sex. Two fingers disappear into her pussy, and she removes them slowly. Gazing into his eyes, she licks her own juices from her fingers. "I'm ready, Jacob," she purrs.

Shane's voice echoed in his head as he thrust his hips forward. A shock of electricity climbed from the base of his balls to the top of his head. He collapsed over Miranda's limp body. "Fuck..." He emptied into the condom, and his body shook as, finally, calm fell over him.

Once their breathing slowed, he pulled out and sat. Bone tired and burning eyes. Guilt bloomed in his chest. Miranda didn't move, still splayed out over the armrest. This had to stop. It wasn't fair to her. He grimaced and ran his fingers through her silky hair, moving it to the side.

"Thank you," he murmured.

"Thank you, Sir."

He removed the condom and tied the end. Tucking his flaccid penis into his pants, he rose from the couch. He tossed the prophylactic into the receptacle under his desk before collapsing into the office chair.

Still in her heels, Miranda sauntered over to the black puddle of cloth on the floor. Her hips rolled with every step as the dim light from the office accentuated her curves. It was a shame he didn't see her as more than a friend. She had a way about her. She wrapped herself in her coat and smiled sweetly.

"Come here." He patted his lap. Kicking off her shoes, she curled into his lap and swung her bare feet over the armrest.

He held her. This was nice. Holding someone. She cooed as she nuzzled under his chin. He exhaled, letting it all go.

They sat in silence for a long while until her chin flicked toward the computer screen, which still displayed the picture of Shane.

"Is that her?"

"Uh-huh."

"She's beautiful." Her genuine compliment showed no animosity for Shane.

He hugged her closer, resting his cheek on the crown of her head. "Yes, she is."

Miranda straightened. Brown eyes filled with compassion. "If you still love her, you need to tell her."

His chest contracted, ready to smash his heart in two. He tucked her hair behind her ear. "It's not that easy, darling."

"Sure, it is." She played with the button on his shirt. "If the love of my life fought to have me back, I'd jump at giving him a second chance. Forgiveness is a gift I'm holding for him. He could have it, if he'd ask."

No amount of forgiveness would ever surmount the deceit he'd perpetuated. He'd made sure of it. And now the regret was eating him alive.

He wrapped her into his embrace and petted her hair.

"She may not feel the same."

SHANE PUSHED through the doors of the restaurant. Chatter flooded the room as the aroma of Spanish cuisine infused the air.

She planted her feet behind a glass and wooden partition, her eyes flickering through the crowds of diners in hopes Gavin would be finishing his meeting. Mahogany booths lined the narrow space, and the checkered floor made the area homey and comfortable. Yet it clashed with the black tied waiters buzzing by the tables covered in white linen.

Gavin's hard-to-miss large frame dwarfed a small ladder-back wooden chair. He wasn't alone. Cowering behind the partition, she stared. He leaned forward, obviously gritting his jaw in what resembled an attempt to keep from shouting at the brunette with shoulder-length hair seated across from him. An intense energy surrounded them in the midst of the bustle of the restaurant. Did he have a good relationship with any female? She doubted it based on the flexing of his fists on the table.

The brunette stood, snatched her purse, and pointed in his direction. Shane couldn't see the woman's face, but her body language told her he was getting an earful. He sat back, opening his mouth and closing it, taking whatever she laid into him. Why were they arguing, and who was she to him?

The woman pivoted toward the exit, tears streaming down her face. Shane's heart sank to her heels when she passed by. Natural curiosity had Shane wanting to go after her. The fleeting moment passed all too swiftly when the hairs on her nape prickled. An angry current had moved steadily across the space as the woman left. Now the ire was directed at her.

She swallowed, tucking a strand of hair behind her ear. Strengthening her resolve to continue as planned, she spun toward the table only to meet the harsh gaze of Gavin's cold blue eyes.

She offered an awkward smile and a wave. He, of course, did

not return the gesture. Eyes remained dark. Angular jaw tight, while he gripped the armrests. All used to conceal whatever emotions might have lain beneath the surface.

She squared her shoulders. "Hi there."

"Shane." He raised his glass and drank, turning his head away.

"Are you okay?"

"Why are you here?" he snapped.

"I was in the neighborhood and decided to stop for something to eat," she lied. "Mind if I join you?"

The chair thudded as he kicked it out from under the table. She supposed it was his way of inviting her to sit.

"Thanks." She set her coat and purse on the adjacent chair and smoothed her clammy palms along her gray sheath dress as she sat. "May I have a menu and a martini please?" she asked the waiter as he walked by. "How was your day, Gavin?" A little light conversation might steer her from addressing the elephant in the room.

"You must know. Tasha told me you asked for my calendar." The excessive rubbing of his thumb up and down the inside of his fingers ratcheted her insides. The fierce stare in his eyes shot warmth over her skin.

"I figured Tasha would have told you."

"Why are you here? This is outside of a work meeting." The bite in his tone expressed his dominant side. It tied her in knots. Denying him the truth wouldn't be wise.

The waiter set down a menu and her martini. The vodka did nothing to calm the rising heat in her veins. "I came to see you. Sorry if I caught you in the middle of something."

"Nothing I can't handle." He browsed the menu, waving a hand in the air to dismiss the teary-eyed brunette as if he'd finished up an ordinary business affair.

"Who was she?"

"No one important. Why did you ask for my calendar?" He peered over the edge of the leather bound bill of fare. A mask slid over his face, never letting his vulnerability be exposed to anyone. For her to learn anything of worth in order to keep him close, honesty was in order. And if she were honest, the game had ended a long time ago. She wanted acceptance. His trust.

"I want to know more about you." She averted her eyes, unable to handle his glare. She liked it. Too much.

"I see." He paused, making the air crackle around them. "You could have asked."

Her eyes widened. Was he toying with her? "I've tried, but you keep shutting me down."

"Because you keep asking me about my family. I was pretty clear that conversation was off limits. If you wanted to know about anything else, I would have told you."

She held the glass at the base, overlapping her fingertips. "Okay, then. What does Gavin do for fun?"

"Fun? There isn't time for *fun*."

"There has to be something you do to unwind, relieve stress, or something you look forward to."

A gleam twinkled in his eye followed by a gravelly hum. She squeezed her thighs, triggering something dark. "Yes, there are *things*, but…"

"But not up for discussion. Fine, why did you get into the music business? That query should be general enough for you." She glared at him from over the rim of the glass.

"David Grohl." He tossed back his drink and signaled to the waiter to bring another.

"David Grohl was the reason you pursued this industry?"

"Yes, but I didn't think I would become a talent director. I dreamt of being a rock star."

She laughed, imagining Gavin, all brooding male and cold to conversation, as an actual rock star.

"You find that funny, do you?" He smiled, showing his white teeth. It was brilliant. Joyful even.

"A little." She shrugged. "Why him?"

"He got a second chance. In many ways, I can relate." The waiter set down a fresh bourbon, and he nearly finished it in one swallow. How many had he consumed?

"In what way?"

"You pretty much know by my background check."

"Explain it to me."

His chest expanded and fell, eyes slightly glazed. The remaining liquid swirled in the tumbler as he spun the glass. "My life. A singular path toward destruction led me to one moment. I thought my life was over."

"From what?"

"I spent a lot of time alone as a child. Especially after my mother turned on me." The words were spat like venom as his lip curled. "She and I were close, and when she refused to leave my father, we stopped speaking."

"And your dad?"

His eyes darted to hers. "A gallivanting cheater who hardly came around. But when he did, I'd run to him like a goddamned puppy begging for scraps." He faded out as he swayed slightly and laughed. "They must have been meatier than he thought, because here I am." He raised his glass to celebrate a personal victory for surviving.

The bitterness in his voice punctured her chest. He leaned forward on the table, head bowed near his glass like it held his vacant life.

She moved a hand over his. "Are you happy, Gavin?"

He stroked his thumb over hers. The tender yet solemn touch provided an acceptance in itself.

"What's happiness? I have a scheduled life, money, and a job. That's all I need to survive."

"Don't talk like that. If something's missing, you can find it." Her heart fell deeper, hoping her words could help.

He retreated into his chair, and the gateway to his dark secrets slammed shut like an iron door. "You can't fix me, Shane," he bit out, finishing his drink. "What about you, Ms. Vaughn? What got you into the business?"

She grimaced. The real Gavin disappeared into the background.

"Britney."

"Britney Spears?" A husky laugh sent chills through her. "Really?"

She cleared her throat, holding a smile. "Not all of us have a story to back up our musical journey."

"But how?"

"When 'Hit Me Baby One More Time' came out, it looked…fun."

"And did the pop product make you want to become a CEO?"

"No. I ventured into the performer side a bit." She went for her martini.

"You? A performer?"

"Don't look so surprised. Ever heard of the small girl group, Club Divas?"

"Nope."

"Exactly. We had a small hit, and during tour rehearsals, we found out how much we disagreed on things." She smiled as the memories flooded her head. Although short-lived, she'd enjoyed the brief stint where she had made a record and prepared for a tour.

"I would have never thought…" The remark was lucid and alarming at the same time.

"What *exactly* did you think?" She leaned closer to him.

"I assumed you were always on the business side. It makes sense though, how you choose to run the business, I mean."

"In what way?"

"You take the time to groom Omega's artists and not make them a by-product of the industry. They're all"—he swayed and swallowed, his eyes hazy—"singer/songwriters. Sumptin' I can 'spect," His words slurred as he slumped in his chair. The bourbon had apparently achieved the desired effect.

"I think you should slow down. Have you eaten?"

He tried to straighten, and his eyes were glassed over like he was seeing two of her. "No, Shane, I haf'n eaten. I'm fine." His mood swung from relaxed to defensive.

"I think we should go."

"We? An' where would we's be goin'?"

"I'll get you home." She signaled to the waiter for the check and paid.

She held out her hand, and he smacked it out of the way. "I c'n help myself." He slipped, flopping back into the creaking chair.

"Let me help you."

"I don't need yours or anyone's help," he argued as the alcohol stole him away from reality.

She whispered in his ear. "No one will know about this. Trust me." She offered her hand again.

He paused, considering her statement. He put his hand in hers, and she hauled him to his unsteady feet. "Put your arm around me." Trying to hold his massive body while balancing on heels was a terrific feat in itself.

She walked out the front door to the SUV waiting at the curb. "Ms. Vaughn?" Kelly asked.

"Help me get him into the car." When Kelly anchored him from the other side, instant relief from his weight helped her regain strength.

"Come on, get in," she coaxed. Partly coherent, he propped himself into the car.

Sliding in next to him, she shut the door.

"Gavin, are you okay?"

He raised his head from against the window. Sadness dulled his irises. The lack of focus in his gaze made it feel as though she was transparent, and he was staring at something behind her.

"Nicolette?"

GAVIN'S BODY jackknifed off the bed, his heart trying to escape his chest as sweat dripped from his soaked hair. The nightmare was back. A speeding car. Pounding rain. And screams. *The goddamned screams.* He shuddered, rubbing his stinging eyes. He was unraveling. The visions only reared their ugly heads when things were off. When his schedule was off.

He peeled the damp sheets from his body and swung his feet to the floor. With his head in his hands, he breathed deep, attempting to snuff the blood-curdling sounds into silence. His head throbbed like a jackhammer. He'd overdone it. Let himself get too close to the edge again.

As he chased the calm, an eerie feeling came over him. Something wasn't right. He shuffled his feet along the floor and opened his eyes. Shifting his gaze down to the carpet, he realized he wasn't at home.

The dawn filtered softly through sheer white curtains. He turned to view the extravagantly decorated, female-influenced room. The bed with a padded cushion-like headboard and at the foot sat a tufted bench for dressing.

A sick feeling turned his gut. What had he done? Stinging eyes shifted down in terror. He exhaled in relief. He was still wearing his white t-shirt and black boxer briefs.

"What the fuck?" He groaned, lifted his head, and noticed his wallet and phone sitting on the round white nightstand next to fresh pink roses in a square vase. Swiping the phone, he pushed the button to illuminate the time. *6:48 a.m.*

"Fuck!" he yelled, scrambling to get moving. He'd never make the eight o'clock meeting with Don Miller and Ryan Digmore. The door creaked open, and he swung around. Shane peeked in. *Oh, shit.* What did he tell her?

"I thought I heard something."

"What the hell, Shane?" He searched for his clothes.

"Over there." She pointed to the vintage high back purple chair in the corner where his suit rested. "You passed out."

"But why am I *here*?" Infuriated, he stormed over to the chair, snatching his slacks.

"I thought you might not remember." He could feel her gaze on him as he tugged on a pant leg. "Kelly drove you home, but you fought us when we tried to get your keys. The only logical thing to do was bring you here and let you sleep it off in the guest room."

The zipper caught his finger when he glared at her. He pushed his arms through his shirtsleeves and grabbed his coat, tie, and shoes. He stormed past her and stomped down the long hall. When he found the living room, he sat on the couch.

She followed, her maroon pleated skirt swaying around her legs as she handed him his wallet and phone. "You forgot something." A hint of laughter twitched her lips.

His blood boiled with the desire to berate her for stepping over the line. She should have left him. He snatched the items from her hand and threw them on the table.

"Coffee?" She grinned.

"No." His stomach turned over at the thought.

"Aspirin?" She walked into the kitchen, returning with a bottle of pain relievers and water.

He swiped them and swallowed the pills. "How the hell did I get undressed?" Assembling pieces from the night before, he tightened the laces of his shoe.

"I may have..." His eyes grew as big as saucers as she continued poking the bear. "I thought you would like a freshly pressed suit for your meeting this morning."

"What? How did you...?"

Use your words, Gavin. He was all over the place. She'd thrown him off his game, and he needed to gain some semblance of control to put her back in her place.

"I have your calendar, remember?" She smiled again.

No humor existed within as he tucked in his shirt and stretched his suspenders over his shoulders. What could he say other than unleashing years of resentment on her?

He swiped up the last of his items and stormed toward the door of her apartment. Before he had a chance to exit, she said, "See ya at the office, dear."

A rush of obscenities halted behind gritted teeth before the door slammed behind him.

THE GLASS DOOR of Omega Records whooshed open when Shane bounced through on five-inch heels. Score one for Shane. Turning the tables on Gavin had never felt so sweet. A chipper David greeted her with a latte in hand. "Good morning, doll!"

"Hey, sweetie. Absolutely owning that suit today." She perused his dark purple suit with blue plaid designs and a vest to match. They walked the decorated corridor lined with platinum records and autographed pictures courtesy of Omega's musicians. Even after all her years of hard work, a flash of accomplishment still surfaced when she walked these halls. She straightened the last platinum record plaque outside her office door. *Yep, still amazing.* She sighed inwardly.

"Was there ever a doubt? So, how'd the stalker event go last night?"

"It was fine," she answered plainly. She set her portfolio and purse on the desk.

"I heard Gavin was upset this morning."

She removed her cream wool coat and scarf and hung both in the closet. "Really? I wouldn't know." Shielded by a poker face, she busied herself at the desk.

David sat in the visitor's chair, holding his coffee. Slowly, he put his hand down on the armrest. "Tasha received a frantic call from Mr. Compelling a little after seven, asking her to change his meeting time with Don Miller. The man never misses a meeting."

She leaned back in her chair. It killed her to not share the overwrought version of Gavin she witnessed this morning. "David, I have no idea why he would be upset. We had a couple drinks, and he left."

He scanned her face over his black-rimmed glasses. His lips formed a line. "Please tell me you didn't sleep with him."

"I did not sleep with him! What do you take me for?"

The corner of his mouth twitched. "Damn. I thought you would have. I would love to hear stories about how that man is in bed."

"You ain't kidding," she blurted out, reminiscing about Gavin dressing this morning. His underwear hugged all the right places. Hung like a freaking horse. And what was it about a man in a white t-shirt? She shivered as goosebumps rose on her arms.

"Mmmhmm. I thought so." He leaned forward in his chair. "You like him."

"No way. This is all part of the plan." A telltale blush crept up her neck. She couldn't even deny the effect he had on her. There was still so much to learn about his secrets and Nicolette.

"You're turning red. It may be part of your plan, but you're attracted to him." David smiled knowingly.

"I am not!" she exclaimed and paused to take a sip of her latte. "Okay, maybe I am. But seriously, he's hot. No denying it. Besides, I think we got somewhere last night."

"Somewhere how?" He got comfortable, resting his right ankle on his left knee.

"He opened up a little." A lingering jolt of warm energy shot up her arm when he'd brushed his thumb over her hand. It had been tender and electric. She inhaled, trying to catch her breath. "By the way. Could you find out when the Foo Fighters are coming to town?"

"Foo Fighters?"

"Yes, and order tickets for the pit, not the box or backstage."

"And what are these tickets for?" he probed.

"Research."

THE CAB DRIFTED through the night traffic of New York after a fresh rain. The streetlights through the window twinkled their invitation for those searching for escape. And Shane was on her way. The Resort provided the right environment to forget her interactions with Gavin and Jacob over the last week.

With Jacob peering through what should have been the closed door of their relationship, she did her best to avoid his gravitational pull. There was nothing left, even though her heart ached to rekindle something from long ago. Stubborn as she might be, perhaps forgiveness and a second chance shouldn't be ignored.

An incoming message pinged from her phone. Grabbing for it, she braced herself.

J: May I see you tonight?

She smiled. The streets blurred by as the vehicle kept moving toward her destination. Should she answer this time? He'd made several caring attempts to reach her. The messages started strong, confident, demanding, but as the week crept by, they'd become more inquisitive, almost gentlemanly. He was trying. But why? And why was it when people were ready to move forward did old skeletons come back to test their strength?

Seeing him opened a wound she'd thought long since healed. She appreciated his apology and insight to what their relationship meant. But it had stripped her to the core. A new understanding of what was acceptable broke free. Free to decide what choices aligned with her desires without him or anyone telling her different.

J: I miss you. We need to talk.

A shiver went through her. *I miss you, too.* But what was left? She had to move on and believe their recent meetings meant leaving the old Shane behind.

S: Can't. Maybe another time.

J: Dinner this week then? No more than that. I promise.

The desire to say *yes* ached through her thumbs hovering over the keyboard.

J: Please, Shane. I know you're there…

Biting her lip, she allowed her fingers to do the talking. His words sounded desperate. Needy. Curiosity coiled in her gut.

S: Okay.

She tucked the phone into her purse. *It's only dinner. That's it…just…dinner.* She swallowed her heart as it leaped into her throat.

The cab slowed to a stop at The Resort. She held her naked wrist. Rubbing her thumb over the falling star tattoo, she made herself a promise. *You will no longer fall. You will only fly.* Even Jacob couldn't take her promise away. Strength flooded her insides.

She abandoned the gloves as one small step to shedding the façade she hid behind to embrace her unknown future. Her eyes fixated on the door of the club. *Baby steps. Someday you will be whole again.*

She tied on the white beaded mask. A shield of protection. Whatever the evening and life presented, she would go without fear.

"WHAT CAN I GET YOU?"

"Water, please." She glanced around the room, taking residence on a stool. Patrons lounged in booths and lingered around the bar. A low hum of day-to-day conversation swarmed around her. They all appeared relaxed and ready to welcome their desires without fear. She had shaking hands and a quickening heart, a constant flutter of acute awareness prickling the hairs on her nape.

The bartender set the beverage on the bar. The ice-cold liquid calmed her temporarily.

How would she find the man from before? No name, no face... She might recognize his mask, but they were all similar. Perhaps by his extraordinary blue eyes, the ones which clouded her thoughts daily. And in a way, they'd been frighteningly familiar. The way they'd searched her dark desires and dragged out her submission from a deep sleep.

"Welcome back." She jolted. Or maybe his voice...

Gooseflesh traveled the length of her spine to her toes. She slowly spun in her seat. There he was. All blue eyes, dark and mysterious, giving nothing away. Her eyes drifted to take in the magnificent man before her. A flattering pinstriped suit and navy-blue shirt. His towering presence made her feel small in comparison yet strangely safe. His barrel chest moved slowly as he breathed, making him appear in control and determined. The open collar at his neck displayed a thrumming pulse, which matched her level of delightful trepidation.

She peeked through her lashes as a shiver ran the length of her body. "Hello, Sir."

The bartender set a down a beverage and scurried away. The man swallowed the amber colored liquid, keeping his plotting eyes marked on her. Or maybe questioning, she didn't know. She squirmed, pushing her thighs together.

"Do they always know what you drink?" she inquired nervously.

"Yes."

Setting the glass down, his arms caged her on the stool, the slate steel bar cool against her back. He traced a fingertip around the edges of her mask where it met her cheek and drifted to outline her lips. The light touch left a trail of fire in its wake as his finger skimmed her chin and the hollow of her throat.

"H-how did you know it was me?"

"Your beauty is unmistakable, and you're wearing the color of a siren."

His eyes traveled to the sweetheart neckline of her fire engine red mini dress followed by his touch along the contours of her breasts. They rose in response, the dress suddenly too tight.

"It was quite a show watching you walk down the stairs."

She blushed. He was good. Really good.

She panted to survive the cocoon of sexual desire he'd woven around them. He lifted her chin with his finger. A masked face with softening eyes left her sinking further into the stool.

"You must know. A woman who is confident in the bedroom always knows her power over men."

"I don't pay attention." She swallowed the dry lump in her throat. The air seemed to be his to command.

"Maybe that's the intrigue." The man lowered his head, lightly touching his lips to hers. Swept away, she closed her eyes to feel his commanding attention. His magnetism engulfed her. A strong but tender kiss conveyed hunger. She opened wider to feed his inner animal.

Tingles beaded along her lips as they swelled. She clutched the waistline of his pants, inviting him closer. He cupped her face. Expertly, he sucked her tongue as one hand wrapped around her nape.

He moaned, each tongue lashing coated in fire and greediness. The room faded away behind the *thump, thump* of her heartbeat. A promise of care and delectable sin rolled into one as the sensual attack on her mouth softened her body. A bite to her lower lip sent a kaleidoscope of butterflies fluttering in her stomach. If he gave the slightest indication he wanted to, he could fuck her right there on the bar.

But he stopped, bursts of hot breath hitting her lips.

She blinked out of cadence, and a flash of lust stared her down.

"Are you mine tonight?" he asked hoarsely.

"Yes," she whispered. "Yes, please."

The man let loose a growl as he released her. She caught herself along the bar, blinking rapidly as she tried to steady the shifting room.

Was this guy for real? Lucky me!

"Upstairs to my room. The same one from before. Your keycard will work on the lock. Get naked and kneel in front of the bed. Five minutes."

"*Your* room, Sir? Confident I'm a sure thing?" She joked till she could find her legs.

"Yes, *my* room. Don't address me with questions; do as you're told," he scolded. She shrank. The last thing she wanted was to disappoint him. She slid off the bar stool and made her way to his room, feeling his eyes on her.

1 2

SHANE DISAPPEARED BEHIND THE DOORWAY, shoulders slightly slumped. She truly wanted to impress him. She conveyed a deep desire to please a man through natural submission and direct obedience when corrected. Her commitment to submit matched his need to dominate. His cock pulsed painfully under his slacks, begging to be buried inside her tight, wet cunt. *Get a fucking grip. She's a job. Nothing else.*

But what the fuck was that kiss? Why did he surge beyond coherent thought? His body was doing the talking, leading him into unfamiliar territory.

He pressed the heels of his palms on the bar's edge. His mind had short-circuited. Tossed out all agendas and plans to become CEO. A complete shutdown and reboot. The idea of savoring her like a forbidden fruit trumped any need for a title. Was he falling for her? Was he capable of it?

Her beautiful and unexpected consent after his kiss caused fire to curl in his gut. The only present thought had become: *Lock her up and claim her as yours. Show her the real you.* Could he have more with Shane? Could she be an ally?

"Walk away," he said aloud, squeezing his eyes shut.

Stop this now before it's too late.
She will fail you like everyone else.
But she can save you. Give you happiness.

"Fuck," he whispered. The pain in his mind twisted between right and wrong on cloudy judgment. Happiness and loneliness. Power and domination.

White-knuckling the side of the bar, he refocused. Tonight, he would take out an insurance policy. Tomorrow, he would decide if he could cash it in.

ONE CAN LEARN many things about a person when limits are discussed, a necessary part of BDSM, so as not to exceed an area of darkness the sub wasn't willing to explore. Hard limits were sometimes tossed out the window to possibly be revisited if the Dom and sub continued their arrangement. But soft limits were another thing altogether. They presented the gateway to a fantasized or considered place for exploration.

Gavin tapped his chin. The monitor by the door displayed Shane's limits under the alias, *Star.* Some hard limits aligned with his while others didn't. But her soft limits painted a picture of her mind. Sent him deeper into his boss' unexplored areas of pleasure. He zeroed in on one in particular. A perfect puzzle piece to secure his insurance policy.

He removed his jacket and turned. Her back was to him where she knelt on the floor. The base of his balls throbbed. Obviously obedient and well trained.

When he unbuckled his belt, her posture straightened. Pure pleasure flooded him. He stripped to his t-shirt, boxer briefs, and mask, thinking of the wicked way he would incorporate her soft limit.

He moved in front of her and her obsequious grace floored

him. She was bare. Her soft creamy skin absorbed the blue light in the room as her nipples pebbled. Only her face was covered by a white-jeweled mask. *Perfect.*

"Eyes up."

Long lashes extended beyond the mask in a demure stare. A shockwave of warmth swarmed his body, causing him to ball his hands by his side. How had he been unaware of her submissive beauty in the past? His dick pulsed, standing at full mast, as synapses fired from his brain to his toes. Her eyes flicked to the bulge in his briefs. He twitched a small smile. *Yes, Shane, it will be yours as soon as I get what I want.*

He observed her, keeping his silence and hardened gaze. Her breasts swelled. "Gorgeous," he said. "Now stand."

She listened and her skin flushed from head to toe.

"Tonight, we push. Voyeurism is listed as 'possible' and I'd like to try something." Her eyes rounded in dismay. He narrowed his gaze, gauging her physical response to his request. "No. We won't be watched by anyone. It will be recorded."

She blurted, "Sir, please. I'm not ready. What if it gets out?"

His mouth tightened. "What did I say about questions? If you don't want this to continue, you can say your safe word. Understood?"

"Yes, Sir," she said, casting her eyes on the floor. Her body shook slightly. He stepped forward to stroke her chilled arms.

"What will it be?" he asked calmly. His fingers curled around a nipple and pinched.

Her mouth opened, eyes fluttered, but no response.

He needed her to be on board. If she spoke the safe word, it would be over, and his plan would be derailed.

He continued to assault the other nipple. It hardened and flushed a deep red. She gasped.

"Let me help you. The video remains with me; nothing will happen to it. I understand this is new, but given your experience, you're ready. In addition, I own the club. Your privacy is of the utmost importance to me."

A flash of relief passed through her eyes. She was getting it. The club owner who wrote the rules of anonymity would give a certain level of assurance to a member he played with.

"Yes, Sir. Continue."

"Good girl. You please me." He kissed her, and she softened into his touch. Comfort released his own anxiety. "Lie flat on your back on the bed."

She walked over as he selected a few items from the wall.

"Arms above your head." As she moved, he placed her palms together. He slipped a soft rope between her wrists and wrapped it around each one several times. A tight knot secured the ends through metal eyelets countersunk into the center of the headboard.

"Too tight?" He checked the restraints.

"No, Sir."

Moving to the foot of the bed, he spread her legs. A sheen of wetness seeped from her pussy. She enjoyed the anticipation, as did he. Preparing a sub for the scene set his focus in line, allowed any unnecessary tensions to dissipate. His muscles loosened. Nothing else existed. Not even his guilt.

Locking her legs to a spreader, he spun on his heel to the monitor by the door. The screen brightened at his touch. A few taps and music filled the room. The low bass set the mood with a sensual sound.

He dimmed the lights, and a flash of illumination appeared on the wall behind her. She fidgeted in discomfort, gasping as her breathing heightened, everything captured on the displayed image. The red *record* function burned like a stop sign on the monitor. Before he changed his mind, he set it in motion. She was his now.

"Do you see what you do to me?" She turned her face as he

stroked the tip of his cock through his underwear. "You, tied up in my rope"—he was fixated on the video—"your naked body projected on the wall behind you and mine to do with want I want."

He drank in her creamy skin as she writhed. She wiggled in her position on the bed through the projected image. He changed the view with the remote to a split screen showing all the camera angles mounted in various locations of the room. *Jesus, it was better than I imagined it to be.* His mind sank into his role, tapping into the zone of dominance he chased.

He held two items. "Do you know what these are?"

"Yes, Sir." She licked her lips.

Holding a butterfly vibrator and a flogger, he knelt on the bed, and put two fingers in her mouth.

"Suck." She rolled her tongue in sensual movements around his fingers. *Damn it, she will ruin me.*

He withdrew and inserted them into her cunt. She jumped as he moved in and out of her vagina to get her prepared. Her muscles contracted. The ascendance into Top space moved from head to fingertips to toes. He missed this arena of power and control. His sight alternated between the monitors and back to Shane as she writhed, moaning in pleasure.

"You're wet for me, aren't you?" Her juice coated his fingers, and he lifted them to his mouth and sucked. Her flavor, like tangy peaches, rolled through his rumbling body.

"Y-yes."

He wrapped the straps of the toy around her thighs and pushed it flush against her. He spread her folds open, and her hips rose from the satin covered bed. Acceptance. Uninhibited. He admired his boss splayed out and adorned with his toys. Confident of her trust in a man unworthy to hold it.

"You will feel a low vibration. If you make a sound, the level of vibration will increase. Don't come until I say."

He switched the toy on, and the feeling jolted her. She closed her lids tightly and bit her lip, holding back any noise threatening to slip. She tried to close her legs, but the bar made it impossible. Making a spectacle of her while in his control satisfied his ego and warmed his soul.

"Lie still," he instructed moving to the footboard.

He rubbed her feet, working his way to her calves and thighs. Noticeable goosebumps formed even though her body was scorching hot. His hands covered her belly, and he swirled his thumbs as they moved to her breasts. He pinched each nipple to test her will. A loud moan escaped, and he increased the pulsing toy.

He massaged her flesh, her body sinking into the bed. Her muscles relaxed, becoming pliable under his hands. Her breathing steadied. She was ready.

He stood and grabbed the flogger from the nightstand. Her eyes followed his movements as her body shook from the vibration against her clit.

"You're doing well."

The leather tails trailed over her naked form. A light flick of his wrist slapped her heavy breasts. Her pink nipples tightened as she bloomed right before him. It was a sight to behold. Her hips rose as he hit her again. Moans trickled from her lips, awakening the dark depths of his mind.

"Failing quicker than I thought." The vibration buzzed louder. Her body shook from all of the sensations, he warranted. She took long, deep breaths, probably to center her mind, as he waited. He snapped the flogger along her abdomen.

"Aaaaagh!" she yelled. One more notch on the vibrator.

"Keep it up and you won't be permitted to orgasm," he warned, his voice laced with amusement and demand.

Her focus snapped to attention, and she attempted to steady her breathing. She opened her eyes, and he could have sworn she dared him to hit harder. She had something to prove. A woman always in control, tackling this challenge like it was her job. Too bad, this time she wouldn't prevail under his hand.

Game on, Shane.

He swung the flogger with brutal force, making contact with her tits. No sound. Her face contorted at the sting then melted at the exact moment it turned to pleasure. She was there. Flying into subspace. His chest heaved, and his skin tingled as her scent filled the air, a pheromonal invitation to join her in the high.

As if the implement had become an extension of his hand, it struck her, never hitting the same place twice. He moved with precision up and down her body, leather slapping skin, as Shane remained focused.

Red slashes, *his marks*, came to the surface of her skin. The restraints went taut, and she was biting her lip. Still no sounds escaped. Determined, beautiful, and fucking amazing. Dedicated to her role and stubborn as hell, he was sure she would not fail. His heart had met its match.

She will not fail you...

He breathed past the thought in his head. "Are you with me?"

Her raspy voice begged, "Yes. More. Please!"

Fuck. His resolve slipped as the flogger struck her again and again. The request hit him like a freight train. They understood each other, and she was ceding him the power to push into new territory. Giving him permission to take her to ultimate ecstasy.

The sound of the leather falls hitting the floor made him aware he was on her. He needed to be inside her. No coherent thoughts of conquering a superior remained, only an urgency to fulfill their desires and his heart.

His hands shook as he unstrapped her feet and the vibrator. Stripping his boxers, he brushed along the throbbing crown of his hard on, pre-ejaculate spilling from the crevice. Sheathing himself with a condom, he settled between her thighs as his cock rubbed along her folds, only intensifying his need to claim her. She was soaked.

The sweetness of her kiss submerged his soul into hers. Thoughts of takeover diminished with each sweep of his tongue. Her thighs squeezed around his hips, urging him inside as she whimpered a plea.

He broke away, gasping for air, and her ocean blue eyes opened. Mask-to-mask she saw him behind the one he wore. An unfamiliar pang in his chest stung with warmth.

"Who are you?" he whispered. He stroked her face, knowing he was questioning himself. Why did he feel he could be with her?

"I'm Shane," she answered. The room shifted to an augmented space of reality. Her name sounded different. Alluring, sweet, and powerful.

"Shane," he repeated.

"Take it off. The mask," she whispered as the haze cleared from her eyes. "Please, Sir."

He slowly removed her disguise, revealing all of her, who she was to her core, stripping her of her daily façade. This was Shane, not the woman in the boardroom. She was more.

She sank into the mattress. The arm restraints went slack. "Please. Take me."

He wouldn't deny her any longer. He aimed his cock and pushed forward, inch-by-inch. Soft, wet tissues fluttered around him.

"Fuck," he moaned through clenched teeth. "You're so tight." A shock rippled down his spine. *Mine.*

He withdrew and pushed in again, soft moans filling the room. He rose and spread her thighs wider, gripping the skin. He couldn't hold back. He needed to possess her. Let her take him to the brink of orgasm. He pounded into her as he squeezed her thighs, surely bruising her white skin. Marking her.

His eyes darted to the monitors. Was this real? His erection swelled at the erotic sight of her losing her mind. As her head fell back with her mouth agape and eyes closed in ecstasy, they climaxed together.

SHANE SNUGGLED against the man in silence. Nothing was needed to fill the space as they came down together. He was warm against her back. One arm was wrapped around her chest, while the other petted her arm in lazy strokes. *So right.*

The only thought in her head was her identity being revealed and caught on video. But she didn't care. She'd shed her old skin and became her new self for the first time since Jacob. It felt right. It felt free.

She turned toward him. Dim light softly illuminated the room as she blinked to take in the man who'd made her fly. He was still dressed in a t-shirt and his mask. His blue eyes, almost lost or confused, searched hers. His touch continued in circles on her shoulder. A sigh came from his parted lips.

"Hello," she said, her voice strangely small.

He said nothing. He swiped the damp hair from her face. Then the moment slipped away. He swung his feet to the floor.

"There's a bathroom over there whenever you're ready." Reaching for his boxer briefs, he dressed.

She understood her role as a submissive even though she craved more.

"Yes, Sir."

He dressed near the door without a word or a glance in her direction. Sadness filled her chest. Was she the only one who'd felt the magnitude of what had occurred?

She rolled to her back and gazed at the ceiling. Sub-drop was a bitch; this was a temporary situation. And before she knew it, the door clicked, and he was gone.

13

THE SCENT of fried rice invaded Shane's nose as she entered the small and dingy restaurant. *This is where Jacob wanted to meet?* Slight mumbles from diners filled the room as she scanned the area. Metal chairs with torn leather and unbalanced tables lined the wall. This place was a dump but held so much appeal in her heart.

She stopped at the sight of Jacob, standing with his hands in his suit pockets while rocking on his heels. His boyish grin nearly crumbled her to the floor. She waved and clutched her shoulder bag as her heels clicked on the linoleum. The table had been dressed in linen, candles, and a bottle of wine. Extremely out of place for a fifteen-dollar meal.

"What's all this?" Her grip tightened in unease.

"Dinner." He scooted the chair out. She sat.

"This appears to be more than dinner. How...why did you do this?"

He smoothed his suit jacket as he sat. "This place always needed a tune up. But it was your favorite."

Her hand smoothed along the decorative ceramic chopsticks

wrapped in linen, perched on a stark white charger. "Still is…" she remarked.

Jacob poured two glasses of wine, and the waiter appeared with their food. He set down their plates, a huge difference from the normal origami cardboard boxes and packets of soy sauce.

Jacob spoke in Chinese to the waiter, and he responded with a laugh and a pat on the shoulder.

"Learning a new language?"

He fluffed the linen napkin and placed it on his lap. "Occupational hazard. Global talent reach and all."

He never ceased to amaze her. "How long have you been speaking Chinese?"

"Not long. Barely enough to get by."

"What did he say?" She pointed to the server.

"I think he said: *Your date is beautiful*."

She blushed. "This isn't a date."

"That's what I told him, but you can't deny the obvious." The heat in his eyes unraveled her. This was a mistake. She shouldn't be threading hope along the wounds in their hearts.

"You said *just* dinner."

The crisp white wine went down smooth. Jacob reached for the plate of fortune cookies resting between them. Three to be exact. He gave her one and kept the rest for himself. The cellophane wrapper crinkled as he opened one. Apparently, his tradition of "fortune first, eat later" still stood. He used to say it gave him something to contemplate over dinner.

"And I am holding that promise, Shane."

The cookie crunched in his hand, and the slip of paper slid out easily. He read it carefully. Too long. Her hackles went up.

"What does it say?"

"Nothing." He crumbled it and snagged a second one.

"Come on!" She went for his hand.

"Nope, you know the rules." He tucked it away.

She slouched in her chair, amused. How could she forget? If he didn't care for a particular fate he tossed it out; hence, the second cookie. His superstition revolved around sharing it out loud. He thought once it hit the universe it could never be taken back. "You're ridiculous."

He shrugged, and she snatched the second fortune from his hand as he released it from the cookie. *"Every exit is an entrance to a new experience."*

He chuckled, rubbing his beard, staring at her.

"Yes, I think that's accurate."

"What? I think…Oh, wait. Exit…new experience." She blushed. His laughter lifted her uneasiness.

"This reminds me of when we first moved to New York," she said.

"That apartment was so shitty. And we were making money then."

She shrugged, pinching an egg roll with chopsticks.

"It had its charm."

After years of living in Austin, they'd settled in the city to pursue new careers. He made love to her on the kitchen floor their first night and in every room thereafter. Shanghai Express was a step away from their old place and the first meal in their new apartment.

"And this." He rolled a chunk of spicy pork in soy sauce and popped it in his mouth.

And us…

"Right." She moved the lemon chicken around her plate. "How's your family?"

"Good. Dad is still representing the elite celebs in Los Angeles, and Mom…well, she's Mom."

She smiled. "I always liked your parents. Can't believe your dad still represents all those crazy people. And he loves your mother so much."

"He does. Always makes time for her." He swallowed back the vino. "One lesson I never learned."

Her heart lurched into her throat. "What do you mean?"

"All his business lessons; I took them to heart and made them into something. I became the youngest CEO of a record label and helped polish your acumen into what you are today." He winked.

"Can't say I hated it. Has served me well."

"Glad you see it that way." His lip twitched into an appreciative smile, then fell to a frown. "But I seem to have lost his personal lessons along the way. What made my father successful wasn't his business. It was his connection to family through whatever rise to power he achieved."

"What are you saying?"

"I took advantage of you, Shane. I always assumed you would follow me in my career because we loved each other." He sighed. "You always put me first."

"Stop. Let's not talk about this." Her chopsticks clipped her plate.

"Let me finish. The way I saw it, we were on our way to being king and queen of the music industry. And I never questioned your loyalty...still don't. We would've been unstoppable." He smiled, and it shot a dagger into her heart. "But when your dad died..."

Her hand cupped her mouth. "Please..."

"When your dad died, *I* was the selfish one. Somewhere inside, I had to keep moving forward or miss my chance at business success when my personal relationships were failing."

She blinked. A tear tickled her cheek as it fell. "Why are you telling me this?"

"Because you need to know how much I realized I fucked up. And I'm sorry."

She breathed. She wanted to believe him. Her heart tugged between anger and forgiveness. Conflicted by his newfound approach to their separation, she didn't know if she was coming or going anymore. The evening spent with her Dom set her in motion on a new path, but now…

"Jacob, can I ask you something?"

"Yes, of course."

"What's up with you? Why this need to…to…I don't know. Become friends?"

He wiped his mouth. "I don't want to be friends, Shane."

That was news. "Then what was our last meeting…at lunch? I thought we agreed to going our own ways."

"Look, I asked you here because I've been doing a lot of thinking and—"

"You said *just* dinner." She leaned forward, whispering through clenched teeth.

"And, again, I promise you nothing more will happen. But we've always been honest with each other even if it hurt."

She heated. His honesty always cut through her. That's why they worked…or didn't work…so well.

"As I was saying, I've been doing a lot of thinking, and I want to discuss a second chance."

Her eyebrows rounded as her heart hammered in her chest. "A second chance? At what? Aside from being competitors in business, we'd never survive another go 'round. Jesus, Jacob." Her hand pounded the table. "I'm not even sure I can trust you again after what happened. I don't even trust myself."

The world spun. Gavin, the mystery Dom, and now Jacob? A fork in the road taunted her. Where would they lead?

With a deep sigh and a clink from his chopsticks against the plate, his hand cupped hers, fisted on the table.

"Calm down." Her heart zeroed in on his voice. She shifted her hand into her lap as her gut swirled in angst. "I'm not saying let's jump right into things. Let's take it as it comes and see where it leads."

"But how? There's too much between us. I can't magically forget what happened."

"I know." His normally demanding focus appeared flawed. Hurt. His eyes creased and softened. "I miss you. I mean that. Seeing you uncovered so much emptiness I thought didn't exist. I have to explore it."

"I don't know…" Tears stung her eyes as the force to consider his proposal pierced her heart. She did miss him. Yes, they broke up. And yes, he left poorly. But she couldn't deny the need to have him fill the spot in her heart that still wore a bandage.

His chair screeched across the floor, and he crouched. His hand held hers. "Just think about it. If you choose not to, fine. But if you say yes, I want you in this with me. And I promise to do the same." His green eyes pleaded.

Her hand brushed the soft whiskers of his kempt beard. "But what if it doesn't work? What if I'm not ready?"

He forced a smile. "Then say the word, Shane, and I won't bother you again."

More tears flowed, dropping into her lap. He was giving her a choice, and even though she could tell it pained him, he still opened the door to the possibly it could be slammed shut.

"I'll think about it, Jacob."

"That's all I can ask."

14

SHANE STOOD AT A COCKTAIL TABLE, her team celebrating a banner year in music for Omega Records at the American Music Awards. Three of their artists had won, including Artist of The Year.

She raised a glass. "Here's to all of you. Without your hard work and dedication, Omega Records wouldn't exist. Thank you."

They cheered and drank. The group moved around the party, and she stood back, taking in the scene. She was still amazed at what she had become. If not for these people, she would not be a success.

"It is amazing, isn't it?" A familiar voice whispered in her ear.

She jumped, nearly choking on her champagne. "You scared me."

She turned and hugged Jacob. He kissed her cheek, holding her a moment too long. He was dressed in a traditional tuxedo, with a hint of sheen when it caught the light, and a white pocket square.

"And you've been avoiding me." He released her with a grin, the comment lingering in the air. A few weeks had passed since his proposal to try again, and she had avoided any contact, unsure of which direction to choose. "You received the flowers, I presume?"

A breathtaking bouquet of handmade flowers had been delivered to the office. Sheets of song lyrics had been spun into flower buds with vinyl record pieces used for stems and leaves.

"I did. They were beautiful and very creative."

"I thought you'd like them."

Silence deepened between them. He narrowed his eyes slightly, enough to let her know he waited for a reaction. She held still even though her stomach somersaulted. After all, he had taught her the best poker face in the business.

He cleared his throat. "Congratulations on your success this evening. And how lovely you look decorating it."

A sudden lightness rushed through her. She glanced down at her olive J. Mendel gown with pleated layers. They danced when she moved, exposing her black strappy heels. The plunging neckline was covered by fine lace with her waist cinched in a black sash.

"You know, David, I can't go anywhere without looking the part. And congrats to you too."

Avalon Music Group had won several awards, primarily in the rock sector. "Thanks. It's been an interesting year for sure."

He plucked the champagne flute from her hand and drank the remaining bubbly, setting the empty glass on the table. She narrowed her eyes and smirked. He was not referring to the awards ceremony.

He crooked his arm. An immediate hesitation jolted her then released. A few minutes with him couldn't hurt.

As he led them toward the outside balcony, she smiled at him, still enamored by his appearance. Every long, light brown hair in place, his beard tightly groomed, and his green eyes always flickering with heat, he still zinged her. It had to mean something... Stepping outside, the wind swirled, sending a chill through her.

"Here, take this." He offered his jacket and placed it on her shoulders.

"Thanks." She smoothed the stray strands escaping from her chignon.

As they walked to the edge of the terrace, he said, "Nice job on the Digmore deal. A signing bonus, huh?" His green eyes twinkled. "Should've seen it coming. You always felt for those starving musicians."

She laughed. "It's finally paying off."

"It has." His smile faded.

When she set her hand on his arm, a tense ripple of muscle expanded his shirt sleeve. "How are you outside of work?"

"Fine," he replied dryly. He leaned on the railing and gazed out over the twinkling city lights. His jaw tightened. She knew his tells, and nothing was *fine*.

"What've you been up to? I want to know." She giggled, pushing her index finger into his bicep.

"You could have called and asked."

She shrank inside his large coat. "I just needed time to think."

"Right." He gripped the railing and swallowed. "I've only had time for work. There's no one to go home to. Unless you've made a decision."

"I'm sure women are lining up for one of your D/s arrangements," she teased. She regretted the joke as soon as it left her mouth. Was she jealous?

"Ow. Harsh, Shane." He slammed a fist to his heart as his face crinkled in jest. "You have nothing to worry about. I'm still waiting for you."

He turned and grabbed her hands from under his coat. They were warm and inviting as they intertwined with hers. Her heart rate quickened. He still made her crazy. *Bastard.*

She removed them and quickly pulled the coat closed to add a layer of protection between them. She found the farthest building of the city skyline. "Jacob, don't."

He moved closer. Cologne wafted her nose, a familiar scent, melting her insides. He wrapped an arm around her waist and tried to tug her closer. She remained still, like stone, even though the temptation to fall against him called to her.

He leaned in so his mouth brushed her ear. "Don't fight us, Shane."

She moved back and blinked. She was fighting them, and she was exhausted over the distance she tried to achieve. Who was she kidding? The Dom at Resort was a fling. He'd made the temporary situation clear, and she accepted it. Maybe it wouldn't hurt to try again with Jacob.

Her skin heated, and her stomach fluttered. He inched closer, his eyes shifting to her lips. She wouldn't stop him.

"Shane. Jacob," Gavin said churlishly from behind them.

She squeezed her eyes closed, and the corners of her mouth pinched as if she had been caught doing something she shouldn't have. Jacob released her.

"Gavin." Jacob took the champagne glass Gavin was holding and offered his hand.

Gavin gave the other glass to Shane, ignoring Jacob's gesture. "Shane, may I have a word with you?"

"I'm in the middle of something. Can it wait?"

"No, it can't." His gaze hardened.

"I think it can, don't you?" Jacob smirked, rocking on his heels.

Gavin clenched his fists by his side as he stepped closer to him.

"Boys, please. Can we leave the theatrics at home?" She laughed, trying to ease the tension.

They glared at each other when Gavin said, "One minute, Shane."

"All right, fine. As long as this stops." She handed Jacob his jacket. "Hold your thought or whatever."

Shane and Gavin stepped past the threshold. The thick drapery hanging from the ceiling hid them from the balcony windows.

"What's gotten into you?" she whispered.

"You're walking into danger with him. You can't trust him," Gavin warned.

"A little dramatic, even for you. I've known him for years. Sure, he's tenacious, but never dangerous." She set the glass of champagne on the table next to them and crossed her arms. Her defensive hackles rose.

"I'm serious. You need to be careful."

"Careful? Seriously, what's going on with you?" She tilted her head. Gavin, the hard-brooding man in front of her, was kinda cute.

He rubbed his forehead, chest slightly heaving under his opened tuxedo jacket. The unease rolling off of him lifted the hairs on her nape.

"There's something I need to tell you."

"Okay, talk."

"Not here. Can we go somewhere?"

She glanced at the door to the terrace where Jacob waited. "I can't. I'm in the middle of something. Can we talk about this another time?"

His darkening irises met hers. "Okay. Fine. Another time."

She wrinkled her brow, a slight concern shifting through her. The man never refrained from bulldozing over her.

"Thanks. Now go celebrate and lighten up a little. It's a party."

He grunted and stormed away. Why the sudden protectiveness? Was he *jealous*? Appeared he was becoming fond of her. She smiled as she stepped out into the chilled air.

"Jacob?"

"Everything okay?" she heard him ask from the corner of the terrace.

She found him straightening from where he'd leaned on the railing. The wind delicately shifted his hair. A smile went wide like he understood her tone.

"Everything's wonderful. You wanna get out of here?" She motioned her head to the door.

"Where to?"

"Surprise me."

"MMM," Shane moaned. "It tastes so good. More please." Jacob scooped another bite of ice cream from the container and fed it to her. "Only you would keep my favorite flavor in your freezer after all this time."

"I thought maybe one day you'd be here to enjoy it again." He winked, scooping some for himself. "I have to say, you're on to something with this flavor."

Shane was in his penthouse, propped up on a stool by the breakfast bar with her shoes kicked off and perched next to her clutch. He had loosened his bow tie, and it hung around his neck with the first button of his shirt opened.

The spoon left his succulent mouth. Still one of the sexiest men she knew, even eating ice cream.

"Come here." She giggled and he leaned over to her. "You have some in your beard." Her thumb swiped the divot in his chin. He snatched her hand and sucked her finger, cleaning it of the remaining chocolate.

"Too good to waste."

Yanking her hand away, she blushed. "Now, now, you can stop with the charm. We're in a good place."

The container and spoon clunked on the marble island. "Is that your decision, Shane?"

"Can't we enjoy this without all the pressure? I mean, we're eating ice cream in your kitchen and enjoying each other's company."

He ran his fingers through his hair. She'd hurt him, but his eyes said something different.

"What?"

"Nothing." His voice came through anxious.

"It isn't *nothing*. You're doing your thing," she said, wrinkling her nose.

"What thing?" he half laughed.

She pointed, making circles around his face. "When your jaw gets tight and your eyes get all angry."

"I don't have a *thing*, Shane." She raised her eyebrows. He exhaled. "All I was going to say was maybe one more night together for good measure. A free pass. No decisions made until tomorrow."

His eyes flared a green-glowing fire when he leaned on the sides of her stool, trapping her. The mood shifted. Playful, upset, then fucking sexy as hell.

"Nothing good would come out of that, and you know it." She focused on the grooves along the hardwood floors. A tingling feeling in her gut spread like wildfire through her veins. *Oh, God.*

"You can't tell me you aren't the slightest bit interested."

She remained paralyzed. "I…"

"Tell me," he whispered. The energy seeping from his body made her stomach flip. The familiar demands from him never truly left her. Her body succumbed to his voice. It was torture to hold out, her courage to resist slipping. To revisit what they'd had —for one night—wouldn't be a hardship on her libido.

She gazed into his eyes, a calm control centering her. "I am interested." A sly smile appeared on his perfect face. "But I set the rules this time. I want it hard, and I want it deep. Tomorrow, we go back to how we are, decisions unmade. No expectations, no strings. Agreed?"

His eyes narrowed, trying to read her newfound confidence.

He nodded. An acceptance of her compromise. She kept her eyes locked with his. They battled with each other silently.

With agonizing movement, he removed the bow tie from his neck and tied it around her eyes. "We can't have you debating my every move with your sight, now can we?"

Shit. She swallowed and parted her lips.

The long black sash from her waist loosened before he shifted to the floor. He tied each leg to that of the stool. Divine intimacy sparked her heart. *Her Jacob.*

His hands skimmed her inner thighs, the dress moving with them. Her heart pounded when he reached the apex, exposing her to the chilled air. His index finger brushed the outside of her panties. Her clit pulsed.

"You won't be needing these." He ripped them in half.

Then she was alone. Exposed. The blood rushing in her ears was so loud she couldn't concentrate. This was a mistake. She flung her hands to cover her sex.

"Tsk, tsk, my Lovely." His voice came from the other side of the kitchen. "Am I going to have to tie your hands too?"

"No, not necessary. I'm sorry," she said quickly. *Just go with it, Shane. You can handle one night of ecstasy with him.* She allowed her hands to fall to her sides.

"Sorry, what?"

Sir. She rolled her eyes, thankful he wouldn't see with the blindfold. Pushing him to the breaking point of this mental game sent a thrill through her. Her rules. Her way.

"I asked you a question. Until I get an answer, you'll sit there," he said calmly.

She could wait him out. Eventually, he'd cave and continue. She straightened her posture defiantly.

"Let me be clear. I have the rest of the night. Every minute you make me wait, you'll be punished. Remember, Shane?" The floorboard squeaked as he moved. She could feel him before he spoke. He nudged her nose. Warm breath on her skin. "Each minute is equal to a punishment of my choosing with each lash becoming more intense. First, a spanking." He licked her neck, and she melted. "Second, a riding crop, and so on." He sucked her lobe. "It's your choice."

She shivered. The promise of pain moistened her sex. He was a master at play, and she should know better than to test him. But as much as she enjoyed it, she needed to set the tone. She had the power, and the choice was hers. Not his.

"One minute, Lovely," he taunted.

The angel on her shoulder squeaked, *Say it!* While the devil said, *No, let him wait.*

He moved behind her. "Two minutes. I did miss using the paddle on your ass."

"Okay! I am sorry, Sir!" she shouted.

His low chuckle reverberated her insides, turning them to mush. *Damn it.*

"Much better. Where was I?" A metal object scraped the marble island. "Let's see if we can officially make this my favorite flavor."

A cold spoon met her mouth. The chilled ice cream dripped as she sucked her bottom lip.

"Let me help you."

His warm mouth heated her lips as she held her breath. He licked the remnants of chocolate before his tongue entered her. God, Jacob was kissing her. It was as she remembered. Sensual. Firm. Arousing. He always made it seem like her lips were meant for his. Her hands made their way to his face demanding more of him. Her hands shook, taking on a life of their own, and brushed his face. He snatched them and secured them behind her back, not stopping his sultry assault on her mouth. Chills ravaged her body as he helped her remember her place. The old Shane flooded back. It had been too long since she'd had this privilege. It was heaven.

Flashbacks ran through her mind. Times when they were connected and strong. Her heart synced with his. The elastic band bonding them coiled them together. Forever present. She pushed deeper into his mouth. He moved away.

"Jacob, please."

"I plan on taking my time with you since this might be the only chance I get."

The spoon scraped the bottom of the container and droplets of cold liquid fell on her exposed sex. The back of the spoon followed. A surge of heat went through her, allowing a pool of her own liquid to drip between her legs.

"God." She threw her head back in agony.

He shifted lower, his beard tickling her thighs, adding to her rising senses. As the ice cream dripped down to her opening, a trail of prickling heat followed. She could feel his eyes on her sex, turning her on even more.

"Jacob," she breathed.

"Yes, Lovely?" His hot breath on her skin caused a tide of tremors to curl her toes.

"Please. Please, Sir."

"What do you want me to do?"

He loved this game. Liked when she told him what she wanted, loved making the anticipation last. Wringing out all the pleasure from her wanton body.

"Touch me, please. Lick my pussy."

A low rumble from his chest was followed by a wicked tongue lashing along her folds, lingering at her clit. His tongue swirled unhurried. Her legs bucked, pushing against the restraints, hands gripping the sides of the stool. She panted, unable to contain her shameless desire.

"More. Please, Sir."

He shifted her hips, placing her ass on the edge of the seat. His wet tongue lapped the creases of her folds toward her opening. Her arousal mixed with chocolate permeated the air.

"Mmmm, Chocolate Mocha Shane."

"God, yes."

Her hips and body shook as he fucked her with his tongue. The edge was near.

"I'm going to come," she rasped. He rose from his kneeling position on the floor. Frustration rippled from the loss as a grunt escaped her. Her abandoned clit throbbed.

"Not yet. You still need your punishment." She could feel his self-satisfied smirk.

"You're a cruel man."

"Cruel? I beg to differ." The straps around her feet unraveled, and she rolled her ankles. "Let's get you on the table, flat on your stomach, propping your beautiful ass in the air. Understood?"

"Yes," she responded and paused, knowing he would want her to call him Sir, so she refrained. It thrilled her to hold out.

He pinched her chin between his fingers. "Would you like to see the paddle tonight?"

She tried to shake her head. "I meant yes, Sir, I understand."

He praised her by taking her mouth in his, nibbling on her bottom lip. His strong hands caressed her back and down her front, and he slipped a finger into her wet folds, teasing her. She moaned, her head spun, and she gripped his muscular arms.

"Before we get too carried away, punishment first."

He lifted her to her feet. In one quick movement, her dress was discarded and hit the floor. He sucked air through his teeth. The cool air kissed her naked skin.

"Jesus, Shane. Is it possible you've gotten more beautiful?" Fingers slid down her face, neck, and breasts. "I've missed this."

"Me too." *So very much.* The admission slipped before her mind could stop her tongue.

"Oh, Lovely. You're making it hard for me to carry out your punishment."

He kissed her, wrapping his arms around her waist. Her hands threaded in his hair as he propelled her into the clouds. This was more than a free pass. The dance their tongues made ignited the dying ember of their relationship.

"W-we could skip the pain and go right to the good stuff."

He chuckled, biting her bottom lip. "You're not getting out of it that easy."

He led her to the table and pushed her shoulders flat. Her nipples pursed from the cool wooden tabletop.

"Don't move. I'll be right back."

She lay bent and sprawled on her belly, her earlier high beginning to fade as she waited for him to return. What did all this mean? Should she give him a second chance? Her mind reeled, and she buried the thoughts quickly. The man was a master sexually and always in tune with her. It was natural to feel something. Right?

"Lovely, are you with me?" he asked.

"Yes, I'm with you."

"Good. I want you to take this as a lesson and remember who's in charge." A warm hand rubbed her ass and squeezed. She jumped. "Relax. This will be over before you know it. One spank with my hand and twice with the crop." He dipped a finger inside her, her muscles squeezing at the invasion.

"Still fucking greedy. You're soaked. I'm beginning to wonder if this is a punishment for you."

Smack!

161

She yelped at the impact. The imprint of his hand seared like fire.

"There it is. Your ass is turning my favorite shade of pink. I never thought I would see this again."

The crop scraped the table. The leather keeper lazily caressed her behind. "I can't wait to be inside you. Your permission has made me the happiest man." He swatted once with such force, she bit the inside of her mouth.

"Darling, you're so quiet," he teased. "I want to hear you scream. Guess I'll have to try harder."

Fuck. He would always outwit her. She squeezed her eyes closed and gripped the side of the table, waiting for the last blow.

The crop smacked her on the pussy. "Jesus!" she screamed as she pointed her toes. She held her breath, allowing the sting to tingle until it turned to warmth. *Yes...there it is.*

"While Jesus is great, my name is still Jacob." He laughed, dropping the crop on the floor. "I need to see you fall apart." He took her wrist and pulled her to her feet. Fluid dripped down her leg as she stood. The pain still throbbed on her backside when he untied the blindfold. She blinked. "I want you to see me unravel. I want you to see what you do to me."

"I want to see it too." Her hands ran through his beard.

His lips bruised hers. His powerful touch swept her up, aching for him all over. Her body. Her mind. Her heart.

"God, Shane. You're so...oh god, I've missed you." Pain flashed through his eyes. Regret triggered her mind.

"Only tonight, Jacob," she reminded him.

He breathed out, chest heaving. "Undress me."

Her fingers stopped functioning as she fumbled to get through the buttons fast enough. Finally, she slid her hands under the shirt, allowing it to fall from his shoulders. She drank him in as she caressed the soft tuffs of hair on his chest. Her hands traveled over his ripped abs all the way to his defined vee.

He flexed at her touch, sucking air into his lungs as if she'd burned him.

The zipper of his pants sounded, heightening her awareness. She would see him again. All of him. Slipping her hands under his waistband as she undressed him fully, she kneeled, staring at the size of his penis and licked her lips, her eyes pleading.

"Yes, you may."

In one swift move, it hit the back of her throat. Soft skin, the tang of pre-cum, the fullness in her mouth, the smell of his manhood. She was starving. Ached in areas she'd forgotten.

He clenched his teeth. "Easy, Lovely, easy."

She held him in her mouth, enjoying the feeling of velvet and stone along her tongue. She savored each inch when she drew off. He fisted her hair and pushed her forward again, hips circled, taking control.

"Your mouth was made for me."

She yelped at the prickling of her scalp, her pussy pulsing as he thrust in and out.

He let go as she gasped for air. "On the table."

She rose, and he propped her on the edge. He narrowed his gaze. "This will be hard and deep, as you requested. Hold on."

Her fingers curled on the table's edge as he spread her legs wider. Eyes uniting, longing for the connection they had so long ago, he pushed in. They gasped in unison. Her body curled toward him as he stretched her insides. It was glorious. He fit perfectly. Tears bubbled to the surface as her heart expanded. Her love.

"Look at me, Jacob. Please." She lightly brushed the side of his face with one hand and pushed his damp hair back with the other.

He welcomed it and opened his eyes. A shudder released as she found the vast ocean of his soul. Playtime had ended.

"Shane," he muttered with a sexy smile. "You're perfect."

His thick, long cock withdrew to the tip until the crown

nestled in her cleft, and he thrust back in, making her close her eyes.

"Not so bad...*fuck...so good*...yourself."

"Keep them open," he said with a chuckle.

They fluttered open, meeting the green abyss. In and out, he pursued, his eyes never leaving hers. The stirring in her belly and the electricity in her pussy sent her down the path to her climax.

"I'm close," she said.

He grunted, trying to meet her there as the table screeched with each impact of his hips to her ass. "Come with me, Lovely."

The command tipped her over the edge into bliss. White appeared behind her eyes as they rolled back. Heat released from his cock, pumping into her, long streams going on forever. She floated through her orgasm as her muscles clenched, milking him. He groaned into her neck as he emptied. As a last tremor from his body released, she wrapped her legs and arms around him. Afraid to let go of the moment.

"Please, Shane. Be with me," he whispered in her ear.

The words hit her heart in all the right places.

She released him and stroked the hair from his eyes. "Give me time, Jacob. This...only this right now."

"Anything you need..."

He kissed her madly, his hair tickling her face. Drained of the last bit of energy she had, she ran her fingers through his long hair, enjoying this moment, kissing him like it was the first time. Lips and tongues meeting in urgency, his cock stirred as they continued embracing.

"Need you again," he murmured. He carried her to the couch, still connected. The soft couch cushions met her back and slow thrusts tingled each nerve ending of her core. It was loving this time around. Everything she remembered him to be. No more mental struggles of power.

Screw the past and forget the future.

This was now, and he was all she wanted.

A BLARING PHONE WOKE SHANE. She tried to collect her bearings as she rose from the bed, the sheet slid down her naked form to her hips. She rubbed her eyes and peered over to see Jacob on his stomach, fast asleep. It rang again as she padded out of the bedroom and into the kitchen.

"Hello?"

"Where in the hell are you?"

"Oh, David. Hi, sweetie." She was in trouble. How was she going to explain this to him? To herself?

"Doll, honestly. I've been worried sick. I've been trying to text you!"

"I'm sorry. I didn't hear my phone." Jacob was a complete distraction from the outside world.

"Are you okay? Are you home?"

"Well...not exactly."

"You little slut. I saw you with him. You ended up in bed together, didn't you?" he accused in a joking voice.

"Um..." She peered down the hall. "You could say that."

"Shane Marie. Am I going to have to pick up the pieces for you again?"

"One last romp won't kill anyone." She covered herself with his shirt from the floor. "We agreed there were no strings, no expectations."

"Agreeing and committing are two very different things, doll."

"I'm fine," she tried to admit to herself. "But can I tell you something?" She pulled the shirt closed and perched on the stool by the breakfast bar.

"Does the pope wear a funny hat?" He laughed.

"Depends on who you ask."

"Touché."

"I don't think I've felt that exhilarated with him. Ever. It was like we were two different people. Letting all the pressure and tension go allowed us to enjoy the sex. Like nothing I've ever experienced."

"Oh no." He paused. "You got it bad."

"What? No way!" Her belly did a flip thinking about last night. "It was a one-time thing. Well, maybe four times."

"Four times! Jesus, Shane!"

"We were making up for lost time." She absently made figure eights with her finger on the marble island. "But seriously, I'll be fine."

"Keep telling yourself that. Be careful, please. You've come so far from his train wreck years ago. I don't want to see you hurt again," he pleaded, concern dripping off every word.

"Don't worry. I have to go, though. I want to get out of here before he wakes up."

"Good plan, the walk of shame. Later, Coyote Ugly."

"Whatever," she said killing the call.

She rested her face in her hands. The entire evening burned in her memory. Him inside of her physically and emotionally. Sifting through her heart and capturing areas she'd closed off. *What was I doing?*

She peered down the hall as her body vibrated with the echoes of lovemaking in her head, prickling nerve endings blazing with want. *Maybe one more romp? No!*

Time to get out of his penthouse of pleasure and take time to decide what was the right path. She couldn't string him…or herself along.

She quickly ditched his shirt and shoved the wrinkled dress over her head. It would have to do. She turned, with clutch and shoes in hand, and walked straight into Jacob.

"Going somewhere, Shane?" A playful gaze danced in his eyes. A hand landed on his heaving chest as her eyes scoped out the drawstring pants hanging low on his narrow hips. Hair in disarray. Thoroughly fucked and gorgeous.

"Um, well..." *Get it together!* "Yes, Jacob. I have things to do. Thank you for a fun evening."

He moved until her back hit the breakfast bar, trapping her. Leaning over, he nudged her nose.

"Stay," he said softly.

She laughed. "I think we had enough, don't you?"

"Your body's telling me different." He kissed her lips. She responded, pushing against him. His kisses were her demise. He could get her to do anything with them. Hadn't changed one bit. She caught herself falling. *Not this time, buddy.*

"I have to go."

He paused for a moment before moving to the side. "Fine."

Strangely disappointed, she walked to the door, and when the knob turned, he called, "Consider this the first of many."

She smiled and turned. "You said this was a free pass."

He leaned back on the island with a smirk. "A free pass to our future."

She swallowed, unsure of where this would lead them. "Whatever. I'll call you."

J: Our night was beyond incredible. I know you felt it.

A zip of pleasure mixed with uncertainty ran through her. What the hell had she been thinking? She'd longed for Jacob to come back and now...? She shook her head. The unclear future of where she should be ached in her chest. Why couldn't things be easy?

"Are you okay?" David stood in the doorway.

"Oh yeah. These reports are about finished." She stacked them neatly in the corner of her desk.

"No, I mean you've been off since the Jacob incident."

"Is that what we're calling it now?" She snorted and walked over to grab her coat. "Yes, I'm fine. Your girl has this."

"Has he called?" He leaned against the doorjamb, arms crossed.

"Called, texted, emailed. I gracefully declined any invitation to see him."

Their night together was incredible, but one thing she knew for sure, seeing him would reawaken feelings she wasn't ready to face. She was too raw. Emotions clambered their way to the surface.

"Good idea. He lost you a long time ago, and it's natural to feel turned around. But you need to remember your boundaries."

"I will." She fell against him with a hug, a good cry coming to the surface.

He slowly released her and clapped his hands. "So now we drink."

"I'll pass. A hot bath and sleep are calling my name."

His hazel eyes narrowed behind his glasses. "You forgot, didn't you?"

"Forgot what?" Her mental calendar flipped through any upcoming events.

"Tasha's birthday! We're all heading to the karaoke bar on 35th."

"Oh, right..."

"Doll, you can't bail on her. She's turning the big two-five. Plus, it's always good when the big boss makes an appearance. Please? For me?" He stuck out his bottom lip. The attempt to persuade her with guilt worked every time.

"Okay, fine. But one drink."

"Sure, whatever you say."

THE QUAINT VINTAGE BAR, not far from the office, made Shane wonder if she'd stepped back in time. Old microphones were mounted on the walls. A retro jukebox with 45s stood in the corner. A small stage sat at the back of the room with a large monitor installed behind a lonely microphone. David scurried over to greet Tasha who was surrounded by other Omega employees.

Shane smiled as he jumped, yelling, "Happy Birthday!"

The pure enjoyment he got out of life impressed her. She

should take a cue from him and stop dwelling over Jacob and her self-inflicted worries with Gavin.

She approached the group and gave Tasha a hug. "Happy Birthday, Ms. Williams."

"Thank you, Ms. Vaughn. It's so nice to see you." Her dark brown hair with a hint of hot pink angled toward her face. Her light mocha skin and dark eyes beamed with excitement.

"Shane, please. And it's my pleasure. I wouldn't have missed it." She handed over her corporate card to the bartender. "Whatever they want is on me."

"Ms. Va— I mean Shane. You don't have to..."

David chimed in. "Tash, baby, if the boss lady wants to pay, you don't argue."

"Thank you," Tasha said right before David led her away.

"A martini and Blanton's, please."

She turned toward the deep male voice ordering her drink of choice.

Gavin stood tall, perched along the wooden bar, one leg propped on the brass footrest. He flashed a smile, stirring the resting butterflies in her stomach.

She sarcastically commented, "Mighty presumptuous of you, Mr. Mayne. Perhaps, I wanted a margarita."

"A margarita instead," he called to the bartender, a slanted brow lifted for approval. He didn't even make a fuss over it. He simply changed course. Maybe they'd moved into a solid understanding and respect for each other.

"Much better."

He handed her the drink the bartender left on the bar. She licked salt from the rim of the glass as his eyes followed the swipe of her tongue. He cleared his throat. Why the brief fascination with her margarita? Her lips twisted as her eyes met his, which darted away. *What's gotten into him?*

"I've been meaning to talk to you."

"About the 'dangerous' comment?" she snickered, raising a comedic eyebrow.

He straightened, towering over her. Placing his hands in his pockets, his resigned posture caused her to become alert. Something was off. A line formed between his lips, a pensive gaze flicking back and forth.

"Gavin?"

"There's something we need to discuss."

The hairs on her nape prickled. "Is it about the Digmore deal?"

"No. Not work related. Not really, at least." He paused, and his chest rose and fell. "It's about us."

The word sounded like it held weight. Were they an *us*? No. However, exploring the density of it did elicit a piercing curiosity.

"Us? You say it like we are—"

"Shane Vaughn, you are up!" the DJ shouted over the microphone, music piping out of the speaker system.

She cringed at the interruption. She faced David, giggling with the other Omega employees. She narrowed her eyes, immediately angered and embarrassed.

"Not now," she mouthed. David shrugged with his hands in the air.

"Shane Vaughn to the stage," the DJ called again.

"They're calling your name," Gavin said.

She faced him, closing her eyes as she put up a finger. "One minute…" She chugged her drink and finished off his bourbon to chase the tequila. His eyes widened in surprise.

"What are you doing?"

"Show time." She handed him an empty glass and smoothed out her high wasted pants. On her way to the stage, she tossed her purse at David. "You're in so much trouble."

She stepped on the small, elevated stage and stood in front of the Unidyne mic. An 80s bass line beat, and immediately, her skin flushed. *Of course, he would choose this song.*

"*You're dead,*" she mouthed as her shoulders rolled. *If David wants a show, he'll get a show.*

She grabbed the head of the microphone and hit the first set of lyrics. She pointed to the employee table swaying her hips, liquid courage taking her away.

David cheered, whistling loudly through his fingers. "Go girl!"

Tasha's hand cupped her mouth in shock as her CEO let loose. Shane made eye contact with Gavin across the room as he shuffled his stance. She affected him, and her confidence swelled when she hit the chorus of "Like a Virgin."

The sudden freedom to flirt and exchange hot glances made the word *us* become a possibility. It appeared her decision to be with Jacob had been decided. One night of passion didn't mean forever. He was a closed chapter, and she wanted to explore the lingering forceful attraction to her subordinate. *Screw it; Jacob had his chance.*

Gavin mouthed, "*What the fuck?*"

She smiled, removed the mic from the stand, and danced her way off stage to David sitting at the nearby table. Turning her back to him, she lifted one hand in the air and moved her body down, bending her knees. Gavin's scorching gaze was all over her as the hairs on her nape prickled in delight.

She slowly sauntered back to the stage, rolling her hips. She positioned the microphone and stared at him. Liquor swarmed her bloodstream like a truth serum, as the final words on the karaoke screen were more than lyrics.

As the music played out, the entire bar roared in applause, Gavin not relinquishing his gaze. His face was serious and stoic, unreadable at best, and all she could offer was a smile. The understanding of what she sang floated between them.

Another loud whistle caused her to snap her gaze to David. She bowed, walking to Tasha. "Happy Birthday."

"Oh, Ms. Shane, you're the best!" Shane hugged her as she snatched her purse before returning to the bar.

Shane shouted, "A shot of tequila, please!" Her nerves were meeting the reality of what she'd done. And the quick decision to eliminate Jacob from her life was firm. Maybe it was the alcohol pushing her over or Gavin's presence; she didn't care. It was something new. *Yeah, a fresh start.* Her face flushed hot from the wicked, but welcome, thoughts of Gavin taking her home. Making them an...us.

"Interesting show," he remarked, as the air became thick around them.

Fumbling to grab the shot glass, her brain scattered on sex and Gavin and...*oh my God, what did you do?*

"Yeah, yeah." She tossed the liquid back, closing her eyes as the burning sensation washed away raging thoughts. *Much better.* She exhaled and opened her eyes to see the grin on his face. "Something funny, Mayne?"

"Nope." He leaned closer with his hand resting on her thigh, reflexively moving of its own accord. Her heart leapt at the contact, and suddenly, she resembled a teenager on a first date.

"Let's go and talk somewhere."

Her phone rang, and she jumped to answer it. "The Foo Fighters are coming to town next weekend."

"Random." He retracted his arm, a mask sliding over his face.

"I need to get this. Meet me at the main entrance of Madison Square Garden at seven-thirty."

Before he could respond, she sped toward the hallway. *Real smooth, Shane.*

"Hello, this is Shane."

"Lovely," Jacob's voice snaked through the phone.

"I told you to stop calling me that." She cursed the butterflies in her stomach. *Make up your mind!*

"I'm not one to follow commands. You are," he teased.

"What can I do for you, Mr. Andrews?"

"Hmmm, *Mister* has a ring to it... Say it again," he requested with a low purr.

Her body responded instantly to his request, the hair on her arms standing at attention. She snorted in frustration. *What the hell?* "Jacob, please."

There was a brief pause on the other end of the line. "I know you got my text. You're running."

"No, I'm not."

"Then why haven't you told me you *don't* want to be with me?" He had her there. "Anyway, we can discuss it later."

"Is there a later?" She whipped a hand to her hip.

"I'm heading out and wanted to see if you were available."

"Available for what?" she asked, irritated. She peered out into the bar and saw Gavin talking with a tall blonde in a red dress. Her eyes narrowed with jealousy. *Who was she?*

"Slow down, Shane. This isn't a booty call, but if things present themselves, I wouldn't object." She could hear his grin through the receiver. "I was going to ask if you would meet me for dinner."

"I don't think it's a good idea. I don't trust myself, and this is too much right now." She set her purse on the chrome mounted pedestal sink in the bathroom.

"What happened wasn't by accident. Don't you see?"

"Jacob, I'm…I'm unsure about all of this." Her hip rested against the sink, and she pressed her tear ducts.

"Let's talk. I'll be at Asiate if you change your mind."

The phone went dark. *Enjoy your dinner for one, Mr. Andrews.* She tossed the device into her purse and stepped into a stall. The door creaked open followed by two voices.

"What a jerk," one woman said.

"Forget about him, Blair. He doesn't deserve you," the friend responded back. Shane smirked. This is what girlfriends did for a woman scorned over a guy.

"How did I get things wrong? One minute I'm *his* "little whore" and the next I'm treated like last night's lay. Just because he owns some sex club, doesn't give him the right to be an asshole." The woman's voice cracked, and Shane froze. Was the man from the club here? At this bar?

The stall creaked open as Shane approached the sink to wash her hands. As the friend rubbed the other woman's back, Shane noted the red dress she wore. It was the attractive blonde talking to Gavin. *This can't be. It has to be a coincidence.*

"Um, excuse me," Shane began. "I couldn't help but overhear. Are you talking about Gavin Mayne?"

"You know him?" Blair responded, crossing her arms over her large perky breasts. Shane's chest tightened in rage as Blair's inadvertent admission slammed her like a fist to the stomach. Gavin was her masked man. *That motherfucker.*

"I...work with him," she said, treading lightly as her face heated. She could have sworn smoke blew out of her ears as she washed her hands to keep her fists from balling. *How could he? Why would he?* Of course, he would know it was her, he owned the goddamned club!

Through the mirror's reflection, Blair examined her like the competition.

"Sounds like there's something more, or you wouldn't be asking," she huffed.

Drying her hands, Shane grabbed her purse. "No, nothing more than work. I'm sorry I asked." Tossing the paper towel in the receptacle she said, "Hope you ladies have a better evening."

Shane fled the bathroom, fuming inside. Her breathing accelerated. *How dare he!* She rounded the corner, and Gavin had his back to her, talking to Tasha and David. *Don't cause a scene. Your employees are here.* Fists formed at her sides, and blood pumped in her ears. She wanted to sock him in that beautiful face of his. David made eye contact, opening them widely. He sped over to her.

"Are you okay?" Her eyes remained fixed on Gavin. "Doll! Snap out of it!"

"I need to leave. Now."

"What happened? You look like Carrie ready to take down the prom."

"I'm leaving."

His smile faded to a frown. "Shane, you're shaking. What the hell happened? Is it Jacob?"

"C-call me tomorrow." Tears seeped from the corners of her eyes.

"I'm coming with you."

"No. Please stay. I don't need a scene."

His mouth tightened when his brows knotted. "Okay. But please be careful. Love you." He kissed her cheeks and hugged her.

"Thank you." She swallowed the lump in her throat. She'd been scammed, taken advantage of. Gavin fucked her and knew it. Her world was splintering around her as she reached the door.

The crisp winter air hit her face. She drew breath like it was the first time she'd inhaled since finding out. She slouched against the brick building, bile rising in her throat. What was she going to do? She walked aimlessly down the sidewalk holding her middle. She observed passersby, walking and laughing around her as Manhattan was coming alive for the evening. But she was alone and sought comfort.

She stepped onto the street, hailed a cab, and got in. "West 60th and Columbia."

16

"MAY I HELP YOU, MISS?"

"I'm looking for someone…" Shane's gaze frantically darted over the crowded restaurant until it rested on Jacob sitting in a corner booth. She blew out a breath, her chest loosening. "I see him."

The elaborate mauve and cream dining room soothed her as she approached his table. The large silver branches covering the ceiling loomed over the patrons as they dined. Floor to ceiling windows allowed the twinkling lights of New York to add to the ambiance.

Jacob ate by candlelight. The shadow of the flickering flame accentuated his bearded jaw as he chewed on his meal. He commanded the space even while alone. He had a certain air, and he was what she needed to escape Gavin's betrayal. Jacob was her comfort. He'd make the pain go away and make her feel she mattered.

He never missed a beat. His eyes flared, making her knees turn to jelly. He stood.

"You made it." He kissed her cheek. She pressed against him, drinking in his cologne, spicy and clean, causing her hormones to ratchet a few notches as the nostalgia swaddled her. *My Jacob.*

She drew back, stunned she could fall so quickly all over again.

Straightening she said, "I'm not staying."

He backed away coolly and sat, gesturing at the empty bench across from him. She paused for a moment. She didn't want to be wined and dined. She wanted one thing from him tonight.

"Sit," he said, emphasizing his command. She slid into the booth as he poured wine into an empty glass. "Drink."

The warm, red vino poured into her mouth, and she swallowed slowly. Her shoulders relaxed as the wine worked its magic.

"You've been upset." Her eyes met the linen dressed tabletop, a flush burning her cheeks. He leaned forward. "What happened?"

He wouldn't show her love if he knew she was there to erase Gavin's deception. Her heart squeezed at the thought of using him.

She blinked. "I want to fuck."

A humorous growl came from him. "Since when have you topped from the bottom?"

"I've changed since we were together." She slowly undid two buttons on her silk blouse. "Let me be clear, I want you buried deep inside me until I'm too exhausted to scream your name."

She tossed her hair behind her shoulders and lightly brushed the top of her breast. She absorbed his hot gaze as his green irises followed her movements.

He shifted in his seat, intersecting his fingers in a steeple under his nose. "You told me you were unsure about us when we spoke earlier. Have you changed your mind?"

"I'm sure about our arrangement."

"Is that what we have?" His brow furrowed.

"Yes. Friends with benefits. Fucking each other whenever we want."

"Shane, watch yourself," he warned with an authoritative bite, which caused her panties to dampen. "You have no idea what you're asking, and this wasn't part of the deal."

She poured another glass of wine. "Why have a deal when we can explore things another way? You want me, and I want you. Simple."

She swallowed the contents, not breaking eye contact. The room suddenly became too hot from the yearning of their two souls, the unspoken promises he made through his gaze, and she wondered if she would combust right there.

"That's what you want? Because I want you for more than just a fuck, Shane. It's complicated. Far from simple."

"Yes. I want you to take me." Regret surged through her veins.

The waiter approached the table. "Will there be anything else, sir?"

His gaze remained on hers as he removed a credit card from his inner coat pocket. "No."

ONCE THE ELEVATOR DOOR CLOSED, Jacob backed her into the corner until her spine hit the guide rail. His hand traveled the length of her nape and squeezed.

The heat radiating off his chest penetrated the air, kicking up her desire, his eyes a green blaze as they narrowed. "Don't think for a second I've ignored your brush-off. Something is up, but I'm giving you what you need. What you want. You can't hide from me. And if this is how I can prove how much you mean to me, so be it."

"But I…" she muttered, nearly suffocating from his sudden intensity.

"Shhh, Lovely. Listen." She gripped the cool steel railing.

His hand landed on her hip, pulling her closer, his erection meeting her sex. His words were smooth despite the obvious arousal between them. "Remember, Shane, this is on my terms. You're being given a privilege, and I want something in return."

"Oh?" she swallowed between labored breaths.

"I want this"—he pointed to her forehead—"free of any distraction. It's you and me tonight, no one else. No games, no play, just us."

Her lips parted to breathe as she drowned in guilt. He knew someone else existed, and she was using him. Her brow creased with worry and shame as he broke her down.

The way his eyes danced over her face to the way his thumb made lazy circles on her neck caused her blood to drop south to the ball of nerves throbbing between her legs.

"And I want this." A kiss landed on her breast right above her heart, and it scorched her insides.

She slid her fingers through his long hair and kissed him wildly as his beard grazed her face with delectable friction. He licked her mouth, his tongue plunging in and out while he moved her arms behind her back. He was in control. He sucked her neck, and she threw her head back, taking in his powerful stance and graceful dominance.

"Yes…"

She loved the way he commanded her, touched her. The way he explained what he needed was pure poetry, and she would obey his request. No Gavin. No distractions. Only them.

She wrapped one leg around his hip, and he squeezed her round buttocks. He ground his erection against her as liquid flooded her cleft from the impact. She was sure she would shoot into the stratosphere.

"Jacob," she whispered. "Please."

A smile spread against her neck as he nibbled the spot that always sent her into delirium. Goosebumps rose on her already hot skin. The elevator pinged and opened, allowing them to break.

"Are you sure?" She nodded. "Don't mess with me, Shane. I may be giving you what you ask but know it isn't without concern." His fingers traced her face. "I care about you, and even if I lose you, I won't regret this. I will ask again. Are you sure?"

She swallowed. His eyes fought to remain hard. But maybe this was what she needed—to feel him again. To capture his vulnerability.

"Yes, Jacob. I'm sure."

They hurried down the hallway as she scrambled for her keys, quickly opening the door then closing it behind them. He guided her into the bedroom as she attempted to shed her coat in a rush. She was in disarray, wanting nothing more than for him to be inside her. Filling her heart and soul. Making her forget the evening and uniting like they used to be.

He, on the other hand, radiated calm. Sliding his coat from his broad shoulders, he tossed it on the vanity chair. The only notice-able struggle to his control was the tight grip he had on the knot of his blue tie. He tugged it off and let it drop to the floor.

"Let me," he said, the sound coming out as though he had gravel in his throat.

He approached in two strides and undid each button of her blouse, then pushed it off her shoulders, revealing her see-through lace demi. He bent down and sucked each nipple through the lace, causing her back to arch toward him as the peaks hardened to a point in his mouth. Pleasure gathered in her belly as ripples trav-eled to her clit. He backed her against the bed, and she willingly fell onto the mattress. He stood over her, his eyes raking her exposed skin.

"God, you're fucking gorgeous," he said.

His body moved skillfully as he stripped. Each sinew of tight muscle flexed all the way to her favorite part, disappearing beyond his waistband. He unzipped her slacks and unhurriedly moved them from her hips. She fumbled with his belt buckle while she pushed the burning guilt from her mind.

She shoved his pants off, boxers and all, and his cock sprang forward. She stroked it, listening to the hums of pleasure that fell from his mouth. His lips caressed hers as she continued to gently stroke his thick, heavy column. It flexed in her hand as she sucked his bottom lip. A finger tickled her slit over her panties, causing her to purr.

"Spread your legs." Without objection, they fell open. "I need to taste you until you scream." His fingers moved her panties to the side while stroking the outside of her saturated cleft. "Always ready," he stated with a wicked grin.

"Yes." She closed her eyes, lifting her hips to his finger.

He could do anything he wanted as long as it was unabashed and raw. He groaned, lowering his mouth to her sex. In one long, leisurely lick, his tongue slid from her pussy to her clit. Bliss ravaged her body as she bloomed, opening fully to his commanding caress.

Her fingers threaded through his damp roots and pushed him closer. He sucked the swollen, hard nub of nerves. A fierce hum vibrated through hypersensitive tissues.

"Oh, god, Jacob. Right there." Her head slammed onto the mattress. Back bowing and hips undulating along his mouth. His warmth and skill leaving her skin feverishly hot.

Two fingers entered her. They rubbed around the inside walls of her core. Her hips involuntarily shifted to meet his thrusts. His wicked tongue licked her clitoris, circling it in a rhythm made to carry her into the clouds. The echoes of her screams bounced off the walls.

"Tell me what I want to hear," he demanded sinfully.

She managed to mutter through choppy breaths, "I like it...*ah*...when you eat me." He groaned and went in for more, eating her with precision, rubbing his fingers over the special spot inside as she was reaching orgasmic bliss. Her heart thundered in her chest, fists gripping the bedding.

"I'm...I'm coming!"

As she went over the edge, he pushed harder with his tongue as she came in his mouth. He lapped her come without shame, groaning at each contraction of her muscles. Her bones were rubber as she convulsed through the aftershocks. His fingers curled inside her, dragging along her clenching muscles. After he pulled them out, he licked them clean.

"Your sweet cunt was meant for me."

"Oh, god. You are filthy."

He stripped her fully, and her nipples pursed in the chilled air. He rolled them in his fingers.

"You like me filthy, remember?"

She gasped. "Yeah, I remember."

Gentle kisses peppered her stomach, breasts, and neck as he climbed her body. He kissed her mouth, and she tasted the tanginess of her arousal on his lips. As they rolled on their sides to face each other, their eyes met. She shuddered from the look of adoration he still held for her.

She closed her eyes, unable to take it. Seeing his face, his hope, stabbed her heart. She couldn't go forward with trying to forget the anger and pain Gavin caused by using him. She couldn't betray the love for Jacob still simmering below the surface. She pushed his chest away.

"Open your eyes," he said softly. "It's just me."

"I...I can't." A tear slipped down her cheek. Her mind ripped in two. She'd never wrestled so much with a choice until she decided to fall for two men. And all because she wanted to be loved.

"Shhh. It's okay." He swiped the wetness spilling down her cheek. "Shane, let me love you. Let me in."

She opened her eyes and creased her brow. "But, Jacob…"

He kissed her again. She saw it coming but didn't stop him. She needed love. The desire to feel more than an empty soul overcame any reason.

His fingertips stroked down her neck, breasts, and side. Her body rose as she responded naturally to his touch. Each pass of his tongue caused her sex to ache for him to satisfy her desire and seal the gaping hole in her heart.

"I want you to love me tonight," she whispered.

She threw her leg over his hip, opening herself fully. His control was absolute as he slid the wide crown of his cock teasingly over her entrance.

"I will give you whatever you need," he said.

She opened her eyes and saw a vast ocean of possibilities through clear eyes. He never hid from her. Her heart compressed like a metal vise. How could she do this to him? This was more than a quick and dirty fuck. He knew something lurked beneath her request, but he gave her what she needed, even if it might hurt him. He still loved her.

She traced the outline of his slanted brow, moving the hair clinging to his temple. She was the center of his world, and even though he'd wronged her in the past, he wanted to prove he deserved a second chance.

When she opened her mouth to speak, he pushed his cock in. Every thick, hard inch stretched her vagina, forcing her to relax to accommodate his size, their connection complete. Last time was all fun and games. This was love. He slid in and out. The divine friction of their connection was like an electrical storm around them.

He rolled on his back, allowing her to take the lead. She sat up, regarding the man who'd originally stolen her heart. She rolled her hips forward then back, and her body shook.

"Shane…fuck…amazing," he murmured.

He gripped her hips, guiding her ascent to orgasm. She circled in a figure eight, and he threw his head back onto the pillow. The veins strained along his neck in obvious ecstasy. There it was. She could still cause him to lose his mind, their sexual synergy unmatched by any other.

"I love it when you ride me, beautiful." His throaty voice spurred her on.

He caressed her breasts firmly as she leaned back with her hands on his thighs. His hips met her forward thrusts, hitting her spot over and over. *Their rhythm.*

"Ah, Jacob. Your cock…" she cried, gyrating harder. Her muscles rippled greedily around him. "Oh…right there…"

"Yes, baby…fuck…you're so wet. So good," he said in choppy breaths. Sweat glistened on the cut of his abs and chest. Spicy and sultry scents permeated the air.

She rode him, feeling him swell in her core. She tensed all over from the orgasms they tried holding back. His thumb circled her clit and her hips bucked forward, his breathing heavy, and sweat shimmered on his forehead. *He was ready.*

"Let go with me, Jake," she whispered.

And he did, both leaping off the edge in a storm of passion. Rapid expletives fell from his lips as his body tensed. Hot spurts of semen filled her, muscles pulsing relentlessly as wave after wave of ecstasy tightened her body to extreme pleasure. When her body weakened, she fell on top of him, tremors overtaking their muscles in unison. His hands soothed down her back aimlessly. She could feel his heart rate slow against her cheek. He wrapped his arms around her and squeezed.

"My Lovely." He kissed the crown of her head. The warm

embrace stopped time. She didn't want anything to break the bubble. She slid off his chest and nuzzled into the crook of his arm, running her fingers lightly through the soft smattering of hair on his chest.

"Do you remember Austin?" he asked.

"Of course." She propped her head on her hand, meeting the relaxed mossy gaze of her past love. "Which part?"

"The night we met."

She rolled her eyes. "Yes. I was a complete mess over you."

"Over me?" His sexy arrogance slipped through the sound of laughter.

"Yeah, you were all hot in your ridiculous Ramones t-shirt, acting too cool with your boys. I thought there is no way you would want someone like me. But there you were. Standing in front of me. I couldn't even speak."

The memory washed over her. His chin length hair and a soul patch on his face. He had been dressed in cargo shorts and said shirt, which she later claimed as her own.

He tucked a hair behind her ear. "I happened to love that shirt."

She pushed his shoulder. "You would get that from what I said."

"Do you remember our first date?"

She narrowed her eyes. A trek down memory lane could only lead to problems. "Let's see…" She tapped her chin. "I remember Billy."

He flipped her on her back so fast the room spun. "My friend who tried to steal you from me?" His lips twitched, and a gleam of amusement flickered behind his eyes. Billy didn't stand a chance; she'd only had eyes for him.

"Oh, yeah. He had the tall, dark, and handsome thing going for him."

Tickling her, she laughed. "Stop!"

"Only if you take it back." He dug his fingers into her ribs, her laughter taking the air from her lungs.

"Fine! Fine…I take it back!" she squealed.

"You better." He kissed her neck, a smile lingering there. His warm lips sucked delicately as her hands came around his neck. The rush of joy from laugher relaxed her. He felt like home. A shiver ran through her as his mouth landed on a nipple.

"I've missed this, Shane." He moved to nibble her collarbone, and she sank into the mattress. His face met hers, and he placed a lingering kiss on her lips. "I missed *you*." Lacing their fingers, he stared into her soul. Something he could always do. "You made me so happy."

"Why did you leave?" she asked. "The truth this time."

He frowned, moving to lie beside her. "At the time, I thought you needed space to heal…"

"I'm sorry. I was lost in grief. It was my fault."

"No, baby. It wasn't. I couldn't see past my own career and ego to help you." He cupped her hand and kissed each finger. "Seeing you in pain for months was too much for me. Anything I tried didn't work. We stopped having sex. You shut me out. I couldn't even touch you without you cringing. And I thought…" He exhaled, swallowing.

"What did you think?" Her anxiety ticked up.

"I thought you'd fallen out of love with me."

Her mouth dropped open, and a tear tracked from her eye to the pillow. The pain covered his features from the burden he'd carried around for years. Her heart broke, and she covered her face. She had recoiled at his touch. Not because she loved him any less, but because the depression had overcome any other emotion.

"Don't hide."

"Why are you here now? Why did you agree to come?"

His fingers traced a path from her cheek to her mouth.

"Before we officially met in Austin, I'd watched you for weeks."

"Where?" She'd assumed their meeting was by chance.

"Different concerts where you did the promotional gig for a while." He smiled, causing her skin to warm as he twirled her hair in his fingers. "But the night we officially met, I had to know who you were. I was the mess." He lay on his back and stared at the ceiling.

"You?" Someone as cool and collected as Jacob Andrews? She found it hard to believe he even knew the meaning of the word nervous.

"Yes." His chest rose and fell. "And I still am. I can't help it. I'm here to prove to you I will be there no matter what."

"But…"

He faced her. "Shhh. I get it. This is troubled water. I need to earn your trust again." The words came in a rush, slight desperation backed by determination. "But you need to know, I think I still love you."

"Oh, Jacob. There are things you don't know." He abruptly stopped his casual touches and his Adam's apple bobbed.

"What?"

"Nothing I can discuss with you."

"Be honest with me." He tensed.

"There's more outside of this arrangement." Her eyebrows creased as she bit her bottom lip.

The room suddenly went from hot to freezing. "Is there someone else, Shane? As in *someone else?*"

The question sent dread through her bones. A special moment broken by her selfishness.

She stared blankly, hoping the silence would hold enough truth.

"Okay, there *is* someone else." Rolling on his back, he slung his arm over his face. "I should've known." He groaned in agony.

"I'm sorry. I never meant for this to happen." She reached to touch his forearm.

He jerked away. "It's okay, believe me. I fucking get it. We're not in a relationship, and *you* can do whatever *you* want."

He whipped the comforter aside, anger contracting the muscles in his back as he dressed his sculpted body in the dim light.

"It's not like that," she whispered.

He glared as he tugged his pants around his hips. "How is it then?" he asked, raising his voice. "You get upset over whatever happened with *him* and find *me* to bury your fantasies in? What the fuck, Shane? I admitted... Fuck it. Never mind."

She drew her knees to her chest, not knowing what to say. That was *exactly* what it was like.

"I...I thought you knew," she said between shaking breaths. "What you said..." Her clogged throat made words difficult to labor through.

He flexed his hands at his sides. "Knowing and wondering are too very different things." He sat on the edge of the bed and bent forward, elbows meeting knees, his fingers running through his hair. "You threw me off when you called me Jake. Fuck." He breathed out.

He put on his shoes. *He was leaving. Again.* And this time it *was* her fault.

"I'm sorry."

He snatched his jacket from the chair. Tears streamed down her face as she willed him to yell. She would rather see him release his frustration than hold the look of disappointment on his face.

"When you figure this all out, Shane, let me know."

"Jacob, I'm sorry I hurt you."

He turned to her. "Now I know how it feels."

17

Isolation and emptiness darkened Shane's soul, curling her shoulders over her chest, a headache pounding her brain. Her shaking hand rang the doorbell at David's home the next morning. She only had enough strength to toss her hair in a messy bun and put on yoga pants, a large sweater, and boots. The overcast morning was still too bright for her puffy eyes as she moved the sunglasses from her head to shield them. Her blood ran cold as she tightened her coat around her even though it was unseasonably warm for December. Tears blurred her vision at Gavin's betrayal and how it had driven her to hurt Jacob.

Jacob didn't deserve her selfishness. Even though she'd dreamed of causing him pain in the past, she no longer held those feelings. One thing she was sure of: He would never have been so crass and insensitive. She'd become someone she didn't know, and she was no better than Gavin at the moment.

A little dog yipped at the door. A few minutes later, the door swung open, and David stood in designer sweats with his hair tousled. All handsome in his black-rimmed glasses and tight gray t-shirt.

"Doll!" He grabbed her. "Are you okay?"

The dog barked, jumping and scratching at her legs. He picked up the Chihuahua. "Dickens, hush." He patted his head as the dog licked his owner's face.

She leaned over to pet him. "Pretty fucking far from okay."

"From *Carrie* to *Pulp Fiction,* huh? Aw, shit, doll. Get in here."

She walked into his house. Contemporary lines designed with a homey feel put her immediately at ease. Sean was the handyman of the couple, and the finer details he had created aligned with David's vision. She removed her coat, tossed the phone on the coffee table, and threw herself on the fluffy beige couch as he disappeared into the kitchen. Moments later, he returned, holding two steaming cups of coffee with Dickens on his heels.

He handed her one and allowed the dog to snuggle into his seated lap. "Lay it on me, Marsellus Wallace."

Perhaps her soul was gone, kidnapped and held in a briefcase somewhere in the world. Removing her sunglasses, she tucked her knees to her chest. "I saw Jacob last night."

He sipped the hot java, and his lips thinned. "I figured as much."

"I hurt him." She rested her forehead in her palm. Tears threatened even though she was sure she didn't have any left. She'd cried herself to sleep and even through the morning. Her chest tightened as the evening flashed before her. The hope on Jacob's face—before she stomped whatever optimism he had of them being together—had evaporated like a candle extinguished in a breeze.

David's eyebrows lifted over his black frames. "Is that even possible? Something happen at the bar? What did he do?" He was ready to call in the troops.

"Jacob didn't do anything. In fact, he was perfect. He was the innocent in all this," she said, exhaling. She set the coffee down on the table. "It's Gavin. He lied to me."

"Here we go. What did Mr. Compelling do this time?"

She played with an imaginary piece of lint on the couch cushion. "He, um… He's the mystery Dom from The Resort."

He choked on his coffee. "What!? No. Fucking. Way. Are you sure?"

"Pretty sure. This woman, in the bathroom, was talking about a club owner who called her "his little whore" and—"

"Wait, wait. How in the world did you put two and two together?" She gave him a half smile. "Oh, my. You dirty girl."

"Stop trying to make me laugh." She blushed. "This is serious." She shrugged in disappointment. "But I guess he uses the term of endearment loosely." A tinge of jealousy flooded her veins.

"But she could've been talking about any guy in the bar."

"Right, but I asked her if she was talking about Gavin Mayne."

He covered his mouth to hold in a laugh. "You do realize you admitted you slept with him?"

"Not at the time I didn't! Not until she eyed me up and confirmed she *was* talking about him. I didn't know what to do. I saw red and got out of there. What the hell am I supposed to do with this?" She slapped her hands against her thighs.

"Okay, okay," he said calmly as the dog barked from the shift of emotion in the room. "So where does Jacob play into all this?"

"He knows there's another guy." Hearing herself say the words out loud made her sick. How could she have been so stupid?

"And you used him." She nodded. "Doll, he probably has some hot ass on the side. You aren't a couple, so why does it matter?"

"He doesn't. He wants me back."

"No shit."

"Yeah. No shit. And I can't stop thinking about it. Something happened between us. It was like I was going home."

"How's the no-strings-attached thing working out for you?"

She moved her head slightly side to side, her lips forming a frown. "It's not."

"You're not capable of separating sex and love with him. I *knew* this would happen."

"Tell me about it." Wetness spilled down her cheeks as she tried to make heads or tails out of this entire saga. Not only had she dug up repressed feelings for Jacob, it was obvious he had too. And undeniable attraction to Gavin, even though he wasn't honest about being the Dom at the Resort, still burned her loins. Was it possible to fall for two men at the same time? Was she really that fucked up?

"Gavin knows about my lifestyle. What about work? How long has he known? And there's Jacob, someone I've come to respect again, and I pull the rug out from under him."

"Come here." She fell against his chest. "It's okay. It's not your fault. You had no idea. What did Gavin say when you told him you knew?"

She sniffed, wiping her nose with her sleeve. She rose, brows furrowed.

"Doll..."

"What?"

"The Shane I know would have called him out, clocked him in the face, fired him, or all of the above."

"I couldn't with half of Omega's staff there. And I can't fire him. Gavin has to see Ryan Digmore through to his release date. Don had us put it in the contract."

"You're choosing work over what's morally right," he said slowly.

"If John Talbot finds out we lost the Digmore account because of personal shit, he'll have my head. He's practically breathing down my neck after Icarus Descending fell through."

"But this is serious, Shane. This crosses all lines."

"Maybe. I mean, I don't know." She twisted her hands in her lap.

"Okay, let's take a step back. Do you love Jacob?"

"Loaded question. I'll always love him to some degree. I don't know if there's anything left long-term."

"But there is with Gavin?"

"Not what I said."

"But you're using some stupid contract as an excuse. You can take care of Digmore without him. You told me the other day how much you bonded with his manager over lunch."

She stalled as her insides twisted against her emotions. Right and wrong. Deceit and desire. Curiosity and choice.

"Gavin *deceived* you. He took advantage in your most vulnerable state and chose to lie about it." His words were delivered harshly to help break through her fog.

"I think he's misguided. The more I talk to him, the more I know he struggles with…"

"Being normal?" He leapt to his feet, waking Dickens from his slumber. The dog jumped from the couch with a yelp before running to the bed in the corner of the room.

David paced the length of the living room, hands flailing. She shrank into a ball. "It's about human decency, Shane." His hands moved in her direction, emphasizing each word. "He manipulated you."

"You're making assumptions." Guilt roiled at her defensive words. David didn't know the worst of all. *The video.* She slammed her mouth shut. If she told him, he'd insist she end it or worse, probably kill Gavin for making it and her for agreeing to it. She was seriously losing it.

"Oh. My. God. You're falling for him!" He searched the heavens, probably hoping a lightning bolt would strike her.

She threw her body back on the couch. "I don't know what I am right now. Gavin is the most intriguing creature I've ever met, fucked up mind and all! The sex…" She dropped her voice to a throaty sound of angst. "Oh my god, the *sex*…beyond anything I've ever experienced. And my brain is trying to compute that the Dom and Gavin are the same person. I'm out of control, and I'm dying to find out more."

"Despite his indiscretions?"

She pounded the back of the couch. "He made me fly, David. If he didn't care, why would he try so hard? He could have done the minimal to prove a point. Besides, I can't let him win. I have to stick to the original plan. Get *him* to fall."

"You're a lost cause." He plopped down next to her. "And for all we know, he could be out to get *you* to fall. And not in love."

Her job.

Her hands covered her face. "Look, I know I'm looking for justification behind what Gavin did but there's so much leading me to believe he's changing. I want to fix him."

"It's nothing but classic sub frenzy. Haven't seen anyone in this state in a long time, doll. Why him? Other than the sex, 'cause lord knows you've won the golden ticket to sexual sin. Not to mention with two men. Lucky bitch." She lifted her head to encounter the smirk on his face. She laughed. "What? Seriously though. Who's better?"

"Let's not get into that, please."

"Fine. Why Gavin?"

She gnawed her bottom lip. "He's demanding and takes charge of situations. He's focused and knows what he wants. Going toe-to-toe with someone like him daily makes me want surrender sometimes. Reminds me of my relationship with Jacob, only more intense. More on the line. Ya know? And of course, there's the…"

"Mystery," he finished. "We all love the intrigue and excitement of something new. But for all we know, his lies could be damaging all parties involved. He struggles with sharing who he truly is with anyone, including himself. Honestly, he's not ready for something like this."

She straightened. "Something like what?"

He rested his arm on the back of the couch and tilted his head. "Something long-term. Sharing his life with someone else without judgment. *Unconditional love*. You deserve unconditional love from someone. He doesn't like who he is at his core, and it shows. He's incapable of giving you more."

"How do you know?"

He lifted a shoulder and let it fall. "Someone keeping secrets like he does is afraid of someone finding out who he is deep down."

He had a point. Gavin's background check for Omega Records revealed only the surface of his secrets, but what else was he hiding? What could've been so bad he was afraid to share simple things like his family or what he was like as a kid?

Her mind spun. Did she need to know, when he hid the biggest secret of all? Knowing he fucked her in *his* club.

"And whether you choose Jacob, Gavin, or someone else, don't discount yourself for the mystery." She dialed back from her thoughts when he gave a comforting squeeze on her arm. "There are too many questions surrounding Gavin's reason for lying. He's got to go."

Too many questions. And ones her heart desperately wanted answers to. Curiosity had gotten her this far in life, so why not pursue it a little further?

"I need to ask him why. Give him the chance to explain."

His eyebrows shot up. "You're not serious. Don't be ridiculous."

"There's a good person in there. I've seen it, David. In the last few months, I've seen a change in him. In the way we are together." A thought crossed her mind. "And he came to me."

"When?"

"At the award show and again last night." She rubbed her forehead as her voice faded. Gavin had appeared unsure. Upset.

"What did he say?"

"Something about..." A possible path to reasoning hit her as the pieces fell into place. "He was going to admit it. I know it."

"Now you're making assumptions."

"No. No, I'm not. He said there was something we needed to discuss—about 'us'." She made air quotes.

"I don't see how this makes it better."

She shrugged, twisting her fingers until they ached. "I know there's a story there. And I want to understand his past and what makes him this way."

As they fell silent each part of their conversation broke down, the rising tide swept her deeper into confusion.

A conversation about us...

Toe to toe with him in the workplace...

Getting her to fall...

Surrendering herself...

He was after her job...

Her head lifted as she gasped. David nearly choked on his coffee. "Jesus, doll. What the hell?" He wiped the spilled liquid from his chin and shook out his hand.

She smiled as elation released the pain deep in her chest. Gavin might think this was about taking her job, but it was something more. She tapped two fingers on her lips.

"The concert's coming up."

"I know that look. What are you thinking?"

"Not sure yet, but we'll see come next weekend."

"You're setting yourself up for something bad. You *have* to play it straight. The game is over." His hand landed on her knee. "Look, I know you want to fix him, but you can't."

David wouldn't understand the dynamic she and Gavin shared at The Resort. The way his dominance rooted in her submissive bones and the pure joy he had from release. Subordinate or not, Gavin was wired that way. And she'd given him what he craved. Control over her. Something he couldn't have in their daily lives.

"I know it seems like I have one foot in the insane asylum, but like with all business deals, sometimes the highest risk yields the best reward."

He sighed, angrily rising from the couch. "This is not a business deal. This is your life, your heart. You're making a huge mistake."

18

MADISON SQUARE GARDEN bustled with concertgoers. The anxiety swarming her thoughts muted Shane's normal anticipation of the band's performance. A week had passed since finding out, and with a travel schedule and perpetual work demands, she was able to avoid Gavin until a plan came to mind.

By dissecting their time in the workplace and at The Resort, things had become clearer. Once the playing field and solid time-line had been established, the obvious changes in Gavin emerged.

His patience in the club after learning about her two-year absence from submission.

The way he prepared her for each scene.

The masterful blend of pain meeting unimaginable pleasure.

The respect she'd earned over the Digmore deal.

The way he showed jealousy toward Jacob at the award show.

All of it, put together, showed an interesting evolution of the one she should call enemy but desired to call Sir.

She tugged her white knitted hat down to cover her ears. Standing among the crowd, the dark sky filled her vision. The winter breeze cooled her hot skin. A few light snowflakes fell as she breathed in the chilled air.

"This is it," she said aloud.

"What is?"

She froze. *Gavin.* "Ah, nothing. How are you?"

"Cold." He smiled while his gaze raked over her. She hoped he couldn't see her restlessness.

"Shall we?" She moved to the line. "So, how was your week?"

"It was fine. You're acting strange." He raised one eyebrow.

"I am? Sorry, long week."

Once inside, he removed his coat and slung it over his arm. He wore dark jeans and an untucked black dress shirt. Sleeves rolled to his elbows exposed a gunmetal gray watch and muscular forearms. *Damn.*

"What?"

"I've never seen you in normal clothes." She removed her cape and hat.

"Normal clothes?" He laughed, rumbling her insides. "Whatever you say, Flashdance." He plucked the hem of the oversized, torn graphic-tee falling from her shoulder.

"Hey! I happen to love this shirt. It's a rock concert after all. Beer?"

"If you say so." She wasn't sure if he'd made another joke about her shirt or agreed to the beer. She chose the latter.

She turned quickly to take the entrance leading to the floor while he walked straight ahead. "Gavin," she called. He stopped and pivoted to face her.

"Our box is this way, Shane." He pointed down the corridor.

"We're not going to the box." She nudged her head to the stairs. "Follow me."

Gripping the handrail, she could feel his stare. She sauntered down the stairs, swaying her ass, hoping he would like the view in her tight jeans.

They approached the floor, and she squealed excitedly, "Come on! Over here." The energy of the stadium took her back to why she'd fallen in love with the music industry. Listening to the crowd banter, nostalgia bloomed in her chest.

"Did you hear their new album?"

"Heard their last show was epic."

Over her shoulder, she caught sight of a small but noticeable twitch on his lips. It showed amusement, shooting tingles through her.

"The box would have been more comfortable." He sat placing his coat on the back of the chair.

She set her things down. "Come on, Gavin. Learn to live a little." She raised her arms. "This is where the magic happens."

"Magic, huh? A bunch of screaming fans crowded on a floor. Sounds great." His hard passive expression made him difficult to read.

Her smile fell, and he laughed, the low, throaty sound smothering any previous lingering tension.

"Think you're funny, Mr. Mayne? Seriously, don't you remember experiencing the music? Being in the crowd and taking in the atmosphere?"

"There's no time." He sipped his beer avoiding her question.

"Sure, there is. You just don't remember how."

He rolled his jaw. "Is that why we're here? For you to help me remember? Why the curiosity to know my personal life?"

Because you manipulated me as Gavin.

Because you cared for me as a Dom.

Because I'm fucked up and want to give you what you crave.

Saved by the dimming lights and cheering fans, she jumped out of her chair. "Show time!"

GAVIN REMAINED IN HIS SEAT. What was she doing? And why would she bring him to *this* show?

"Stand up!"

He reluctantly stood. She continued chanting the band's name. Like a little kid seeing her favorite band for the first time, her smile lit the room. It resonated within him.

She didn't give a fuck what people thought. He, on the other hand, was out of his element. With his left hand shoved in his jeans pocket, his eyes bounced across the stage as the band grabbed their instruments.

A low, steady strum sounded from the guitar. Screams over-powered the intro as the crowd instantly responded to the first chords. Shane whistled between two fingers as he swallowed a long pull of beer. His foot lightly tapped along to the beat.

Her warm hand snatched his and held it in the air as she sang the first few lines to "Everlong."

The lyrics echoed in the deep cavern of memories he'd buried. He'd heard the song a million times over, but tonight it sounded different. Could he feel something real? Could he cross his own boundaries?

After the last time she gave her submission to him at The Resort, he'd been unable to reconcile his once loathing response to the present burning desire. She'd crossed a barrier he'd let slip, and she continued breaking the walls down. As much as there was fear, he also had hope. In the forefront of his mind, Shane existed, not his quest to becoming CEO. And telling her the truth weighed on him. Kept him awake at night and distracted during the day. He wanted nothing more than to explain what he'd done. He'd tried and, both times, stalled like a coward.

Thankful for her absence from the office this past week, he'd attempted to process a course of action. Yet nothing had come except the same scenario where he lost her and his job. And right now, losing her would hurt more.

Swiping his forehead, uneasiness ran rampant. As she swayed to the music, her eyes closed as she took each moment for what it was. Perhaps he could learn from her. Live each moment tonight and see where it would take them.

He closed his eyes. Each note teleported him to his younger years. Lying on his bed with his earphones in, he would clutch their album against his chest. He liked to imagine being on stage with the band. A fantasy of a different life. A life where he'd escaped his father's will and his mother's neglect for one on the road toward happiness. The souring thought turned his stomach. He opened his eyes to find Shane his reality. He was his father's son, and she was his victim. Telling her was the only option.

SHANE'S KNEE bounced as she bit her thumbnail. The energy was too high. The hope of Gavin showing his true colors and letting go frayed her nerves.

With two beers in hand, Gavin returned, flashing a panty-dropping smile from ear-to-ear. *God, it was beautiful.* "Did I miss anything?"

She laughed at his boyish tone. "No, they're setting up for the acoustic set." They stared at each other for a moment.

"Ga—" she started.

"Sha—" he began.

"Go ahead."

"I was going to say thank you."

"Thank you? Wow, Gavin Mayne, the gentleman. Who knew?" she joked. "No need to thank me."

"Why'd you do this?" His eyes—a smoky blue-gray—narrowed under the dim house lights. His tone was warm and genuine.

She ran a thumbnail along the edge of the plastic cup. "I don't know."

"Shane," he said sternly, causing her to meet his gaze.

"You mentioned you liked them, so I thought…"

"Thank you. I mean it."

"Well…" She faded out as Grohl sang.

Removing her cup, he set it on the floor with his, and stood. He held out his hand. A hot rush flooded her body as his eyes exposed the storm brewing behind his irises.

Her heartbeat drowned out the music as she slowly lifted her hand and placed it in his. He wrapped his arms around her waist as he swayed to the music. Her nerves soothed into thrumming electricity, his hard figure enveloping her small frame from behind.

She closed her eyes as he sang into her ear. She imagined the words were his to tell, and for the first time, he wanted to let his past go and learn to live for himself. For her. For them.

His warm lips kissed her neck in slow pecks to her bare shoulder. Her body temperature soared from hot to boiling. She reached back to grip his jeans for fear she'd lose her balance. She turned to face him, and his hooded gaze captured hers.

His knuckles stroked her cheeks. In lustful anguish, he asked, "What are you doing to me?"

"Kiss me," she whispered.

He moved closer until she could feel the spark of his lips hovering over hers, his labored breath on her skin, and the noticeable thread of control leaving him. His lips grazed hers. She opened, and her body rose for more. He sank into his kiss, becoming urgent as each swipe of his tongue found hers.

The two of them continued their embrace through the ebb and flow of the music. The final set of lyrics hit a little too close to home. Divided by the truth and her emotions, could she stay with him or should she leave?

THE CAB STOPPED in the front of Gavin's brownstone. It had been a quiet ride from the venue as Shane contemplated telling him she knew about his deceit. His hand came to rest on her thigh.

Her hand fell naturally to lace their fingers. She met his penetrating gaze. His expression seemed to be searching for reassurance. Was he nervous?

"Do you want to come in?" he asked.

He issued an invitation, didn't demand her company. She smiled, tickled by his question.

"Yes."

"Good," he breathed out and paid the cabbie. Climbing out of the car, he linked his hand in hers and helped her to the sidewalk, then led her to the front door.

Once inside, he removed their coats and hung them in the closet. She followed him upstairs and into his bedroom. He made his way to the restored fireplace and turned it on.

Gavin had dissimilar tastes when it came to his bedroom versus the room at The Resort. This space held a quiet confidence. Distressed hardwood floors ran the length of the bedroom with the furniture a dark cherry shade. Rich, earthy colors of chocolate and deep greens swept the room. Hints of copper accents from the mantle and the side lamps resting on the nightstands twinkled with the reflected light of the burning fire. The terracotta accent wall behind the bed brought out the robust virile feel to his sanctuary.

A massive timber headboard had been mounted to the bed. It anchored the room, giving the space a commanding focal point. The wood appeared flawed, exuding a warrior image. Her hand covered her mouth. This was *him*.

He stood from his crouched position, his blue eyes fierce and large body tight as he approached her. She rested her hand on his chest, and his strong heartbeat raced.

They searched each other. Two people strangely linked through their unspoken deceptions. She found herself shy and hesitant, unlike before. No masks. No hiding. Both embarking on a singular moment meant to change their relationship forever.

He licked her parted lips and drove his tongue into her mouth, fisting her hair at the roots. The pleasure radiated as her hands reflexively pulsed around his waist. He peppered kisses down her neck, and her heart pounded in her ears. A raging want throbbed between her legs.

He inhaled against her neck. "Fucking wildflowers. Drives me crazy." He gritted through his teeth as his steel-like erection pushed against her. Her breathing hitched, weakening her patience.

"Just fuck me," she said eagerly.

His lips unexpectedly stopped at her neck. Anxiety overcame her anticipation. *Isn't this what he wanted?* He lifted his head, eyes narrowing as the corners of his etched lips curved.

"No." His fingers teased the skin along the curve of her neck. "Tonight, you deserve tenderness..." He kissed her lips. "...and romance..." His tongue seared the hollow in her throat as he licked the perspiration forming there. "...a slow seduction. Tonight, I take my time. Tomorrow, we fuck."

And with a wicked promise for more, she shivered even though the fire heated the room.

"I want to ravish every inch of your skin, Shane." He inserted a finger into her mouth and pulled out slowly. She sucked as his hooded eyes dilated with desire. "We have all night," he purred.

Lifting her shirt over her head, he walked her backward until her legs hit the oversized chair in the corner of the room. His lips danced along the tops of her breasts, which spilled over the edges of a blue lace corset. He nuzzled her cleavage and licked leisurely, wrapping his arms around her middle and taking time to savor each section of her body.

Dexterous fingers found each clasp until the corset fell to the floor. He massaged her breasts gently as he continued the erotic assault on her mouth. She ran her fingers through his dark hair to share in the tantalizing touches.

He dipped her back. Sucking sounds and sweet torment to her nipple with his mouth had her writhing against his leg for relief as his large frame hovered over her. Her head fell back as his tongue circled her nipple, nibbling lightly.

Sharp pangs of pleasure rippled down to her neglected clit. She needed him. He gently placed her into the chair, leaving a trail of kisses down her abdomen, dipping his tongue in her belly button. Such sweet seduction raised goosebumps on her scorching skin. His eyes flickered like blue flames when he unzipped each boot and set them aside.

"When we first met, I wanted you like this." He caressed each foot and ran a thumbnail over the arches; a thrill of pleasure zipped her spine.

"What?" she gasped, taken by his touch and trying to formulate a thought. "When?"

He slipped the denim and panties from her hips. "I will never forget my first day at Omega. The way you commanded the boardroom. The way you demanded answers from your employees without a care to their feelings."

The jeans slipped off her heels, and she lay bared to him. His scorching gaze inspected each inch. He licked his bottom lip as if preparing his mouth for a meal. He coaxed her hips to the end of the chair.

"I wanted my cock buried inside you. This." He leaned over her mound and inhaled. "You." He spread her open and licked her thigh, teasing toward her sex. The delicious friction from his stubble grazed the inside of her thigh as he ascended. "Fucking divine."

"Oh, god…but you hated me." The words were a breathless whisper and a feeble attempt at understanding his reasoning.

He lifted each leg over the armrests to spread her open.

"Not hate, Shane. I wanted to teach you a lesson. Your smart mouth…" He teased her entrance with a finger, and her core clenched. "…left me wondering if you had ever been dominated. Had you ever served? It became my goal." He inserted a finger, and her pussy squeezed at the invasion. *To dominate me…*

"Wet and greedy, baby."

"Is this what you're doing? Dominating…god…" Her body soared as he pushed in. "…me?"

"Yes." He licked her opening and rimmed her clit, melting her core to oblivion. "You're as stunning and desirable as a diamond, Shane. Everyone is drawn to you, and seeing you this way, under my control…God, you're beautiful when you let go."

Her body shook uncontrollably with his declarations, his touch.

"Do you like that?"

"Yes, very much," she whispered.

He hummed. "But you are a diamond encased in glass. You keep people at bay." His lips closed around her pulsing clit and sucked.

A deep *"ah"* escaped her lips. "That's what you think?" She rolled her eyes back as he leisurely licked her nub.

"You fear letting someone in. Even me. Understandably so. Open for me, baby. Let me see you." He thrust to his knuckle, rubbing the walls meticulously until her muscles gave her no choice. Her core melted and spasmed.

"I want to know each magnificent facet of your diamond. I want to touch parts no one ever has." When he inserted another finger, she gripped the cushion of the chair. "Yes, Shane. Let go for me." She writhed on his hand, wetness spilling from her opening. "So beautiful."

A million sparkles of light crossed her vision, cracking the façade she used as her disguise. She was scared. Frightened another person could take her heart and not return it in one piece. Like Jacob…only worse.

"You're meant to be loved, Shane." He removed his fingers and spread her legs wider, licking and sucking. "Loved and cherished. You taste so fucking sweet." She groaned through the spikes of pleasure. Of truth.

She wanted nothing more than to be loved. Is this what he was doing? Loving her? Her hands grasped his hair and urged him forward as she undulated on his tongue. Her boldness and unabashed nature carried her into the clouds. "Gavin…"

"Just feel. Let me bring you pleasure. I want you to know what you do to me. I want to show how you've changed me. I want you to love me." His tongue swirled as she tipped over the edge, screaming his name. Heat suffused her body, and her breath ceased from the impact of her orgasm, sending her into free fall. *Love him…*

The electric current from her sex as it met his mouth brought her back as she crested. He lapped her juices, the tender flesh swelling with each pass. She sank into the chair, unable to move. He kissed up her body until he reached her mouth.

"You're so beautiful when you come." She tasted her essence on his tongue. The musky scent of sex surrounded them before he picked her up and carried her to the bed.

He shed his shirt and remaining clothing. Her eyes widened. She lost her breath at the sight of his body. His well-defined broad shoulders and biceps flowed to his chest all the way to his abs. Following the lines to his cock, her need spiked so high, the atmosphere in the room altered. Hadn't he blown her mind a moment ago? Her gaze became fixated at his right shoulder and down his chest. A tattoo in tribal designs marked his skin, blending into one focal point.

"Gavin." She sat upright and held out a hand to touch the word inked on his pectoral. *Nicolette*. His daughter. The name was nestled in the arms of a fallen angel expressing sadness.

He held her hand flat on Nicolette's name. He grimaced slightly but allowed her to feel his soul.

"Lie back," he said gently.

The questions could be saved for later. He rolled a condom over his thick cock. He leaned his fists on the bed, one on each side of her.

She cupped his face. "It's okay. It's just me."

"I know. And it scares me."

"Me too," she admitted. All of it was insane yet undeniable.

His arms wrapped under hers, and he curved his fingers over her shoulders. The crown of his penis notched at her slick opening.

"Could you love someone like me, Shane?"

Her heart sank. Had he ever been loved before? She never thought tonight would open a world of possibilities and deep-seated fears. Her heart pounded in her throat, wanting to confess everything.

"Yes, I could."

His back muscles tightened against her hand. "But what if there are things you may not be able to live with? Things I've done?" Exhaustion appeared to coat his irises from the turmoil brewing inside.

She wrinkled her brow. How could she when she didn't know anything about him? Especially with what he did. It was unexplainable. "And what if I can live with them? I want to understand you, Gavin. I want to know everything, even the things you don't want to say. Trust me to understand."

"I do trust you." He bent down to kiss her. Gently at first.

Then he slid his cock into her with delicate strength until fully seated. "Yes, Shane. Feels so fucking good," he breathed out.

His hot breath against her lips made her seal her promise in a kiss. Long licks and tongues tangled. Hips meeting in desire. Over and over as her orgasm built gradually with each penetration, giving everything they had in a sensual dance. Taking them both over the edge together.

"I need this, Shane. Always."

1 9

SHANE BLINKED. Had she been asleep long? She stretched her muscles, smiling at what had transpired. She shivered in delight under the duvet and rolled over to find the bed empty and cold.

"Gavin?" she whispered. She sat up, her eyes adjusting to the darkness.

Something shifted in the chair by the fireplace, making her jolt. She squinted. "Oh, Gavin. You scared me."

His bare chest lifted and fell. Arms curved over the contours of the armrests and his face remained hidden by shadows.

"Hey." A chill layered her naked skin as she got up and went to him. "Are you okay?"

"Fine, Shane."

She knelt between his legs. He tensed when she settled her hands on his thighs.

"You sure? You look upset." Uneasiness settled in the pit of her stomach when he shifted his hand up, rubbing the inside of his palm with his thumb.

The coarse hairs tickled her palms as her hands smoothed the length of his thighs. His jaw tightened as stone cold blue irises flickered over her face, any desire from before extinguished. Even his most intense dominant stare at the club could bring on arousal. This was anything but. It was frigid and distant.

"It's time to go."

"What?" Her hands halted at the hem of his boxer briefs.

"You heard me." The calmness in his tone set off an alarm.

"Yeah, I heard you."

"Then what's the problem?"

"I'm trying…Did something happen?" She replayed the last thing she remembered. He'd held her as the fire burned. She'd fallen asleep. Did she say something while dreaming?

"No. Nothing happened." He shoved her hands away.

"Something did, so tell me what the hell's going on."

He narrowed his gaze. "We fucked. You slept. Now, you leave."

A wave of nausea and suffocation threatened her as he sucked the wind from her euphoric sails. "You can't be serious."

"Your clothes are on the nightstand. And there's the door." He gestured to the doorway with his chin. He was evading her. Avoiding what happened between them.

"I'm sorry. Did I miss—"

"It was a great time, and now it's over."

Tears welled behind her eyes. The burn approached rapidly as her throat constricted. *Keep it together.*

"Okay, I witnessed someone totally different earlier, and here you are"—she rose to her knees—"acting as though I'm some chick you banged in a bar who's worn out her welcome."

"I have better taste," he said sharply.

"What the fuck has gotten into you? You asked me if I could love you."

He tilted his head, and a wry smile appeared. "It was a game, Shane."

Yeah, a fucking game. A game I set out to win for us both. The bitterness and triumph in his voice echoed in her ears. Had he been playing with her the entire time? Or was he changing course?

"What was? Screwing me and explaining how you want to know the facets of me, of a goddammed diamond?" She pointed a finger. "You meant every word."

She'd seen the expression in his eyes. The clarity before he pushed her over the edge. She'd seen it at the club when he reached vulnerability and peace. The inevitable tears escaped to their destination, dripping one by one down her cheeks and onto the floor.

Unfazed, he leaned forward. "It's like this, Shane. I tell you what you want to hear, I get what I want. You want romance? I give it. In return, I use your body."

She slapped him, a sting reverberating on her palm. Her sticky throat caught. "You're a liar. You care."

"You need to go."

He started to stand but she pushed him down. The chair skidded. "Fuck you, Gavin."

The heels of her hands met the steel of his chest. He swiped them, restraining her against him. Rapid heartbeats thumped against her cheek. He felt something. His heart was screaming with nerves, not the calmness he tried to convey.

"You're only delaying the inevitable," he said between clenched teeth.

"Where you break my heart and yours too?"

His grip tightened for an instant until he stood. "No, where you leave after you lose control. Look at you." A flick of his wrist and a face full of disgust, rippled shame from head to toe. Empty and debased.

"There's nothing you can say to get me to leave. You care about me."

He shook his head. "You're wrong."

The bitterness in his words cut through her. She rose up. Chest out, dropping her hands to the side. Showing herself. Proof she wasn't running. Any artillery of malicious intent he threw wouldn't chase her away.

"You're bluffing."

He smirked, and in a low, venomous tone, he said, "I fucked you at The Resort. Knew it was you." Her chin trembled when her lips parted. Why would he admit it? She swallowed as her heart cracked open. "And I did it to take your job."

"Screw you!"

"It's true. And let me say, you're a good fuck. To your credit, it was one of the best I've had."

A bolt of energy burned from her shoulders to her hands. They shot forward to push him square in the chest. He remained unmoved. She sat back on her feet and cried into her hands. Why was he being this way?

The hurt flooded her soul. She was confused. As she tried to think clearly, he stood. What was her plan? Her eyes followed him. Dilated pupils. Hard jaw. Rigid muscles. Clenched fists. A bulge evident in his boxers. He was turned on seeing her humiliated and weak. Then it hit her.

Submit.

The tears stopped, and she fell into a place of power. She cast her eyes to the floor and spread her kneeling thighs as she straightened her back. She placed her hands on parted legs, palms to the ceiling. An eerie calm soothed her.

"Thank you, Sir."

His toes in her view apparently rooted to the floor. "What did you say?"

"Thank you, Sir. I'm happy I pleased you." She'd certifiably lost her mind but had to test her theories. This version of Gavin didn't add up. The Gavin she knew, the one beyond the mask, existed. She needed to draw him out. Let him take her body and control every facet he desired.

"Get up."

She folded forward extending her arms, crossing her hands at the wrists. Her forehead met the cold floor.

"I said, get up."

"Please, Sir. Take me. Let me please you again." The floorboards creaked as he shifted.

"This is over, Shane."

"It's only the beginning, Sir," she said against the hardwood, clenching her eyes as the throbbing between her legs engaged.

"Stop calling me that," he whispered as though it was an unacceptable title.

It held power and status, something he knew he hadn't earned. To call a Dominant Sir, meant she'd yielded trust. She believed he'd underestimated the reason behind the initial deceit.

"Leave!" He scooped under her arms. She shook loose, her knees hitting the floor, falling back into the offering position.

"You want this. Take it. It's yours!" she yelled.

He knelt. His mouth against her ear, so close, burning with so much anger and hunger, a tidal wave of desire coursed through her. He yanked her to her feet by her hair. A soft yelp escaped her swollen lips. She loved it as wetness flowed from her core. Sweat glistened on his chest. His eyes were almost black as coal as his erection jutted forward from his underwear. She had him. He was there. He wanted it.

***

HER HAIR WAS in his hands before he could register what had happened. Her swollen lips quivered in anticipation. Dark red with arousal. Mascara streaked down her face, the sight gorgeous and shameful at the same time. Two reactions eliciting the same response. It turned him on. He'd caused her pain. When she cringed in his grasp and a breathy yelp escaped, something broke inside.

Her immediate submission after he admitted the truth about The Resort confused him. Why would she gift it to him? Why wouldn't she leave before it was too late?

"Why are you doing this?"

"You..."—he grasped her throat, and she gasped—"didn't want my job, Sir."

"Stop fucking calling me that!" She recoiled. *Sir.* He hadn't earned the name. Not with what he'd done to her...continued doing to her. But this was the only way. Push her away so he couldn't bring her deeper into his world.

"Of course, I wanted your job."

"You didn't. You said it yourself."

His fingers constricted on her throat enough to transmit warning. She swallowed, and his dick pulsed. Her body fought for him to continue. Challenging him.

"You wanted dominance," she choked out. She inhaled as his fingers loosened. "And when you finally had it, it struck a nerve."

He gripped her jaw, drawing her face closer. She'd twisted the truth in her mind. This *was* about her job. It always had been. Now he had to set her free. "You have no idea what I felt."

The dried tears from her mascara-streaked face set a deep desire thrumming through his body. She closed her eyes when he loosened the grip on her hair. Goosebumps appeared along her flesh as the pleasure release hit.

"My God."

She liked this. Her arousal was sharp and aware.

"It was in your eyes." Her piercing crystal blue gaze, against the darkness, provided the only light in the room. "They soften with resilient focus right before you hit the precipice of control. You took me there, and we dropped together. I was with you the entire time."

What the fuck? How did she read him when she was beyond the clouds when her mask was removed? But she was present. It was her invitation to take them over, together. The moment had changed his trajectory. His dominance over her made the world right.

He tossed her to the floor. She broke her fall and bounced back to her knees. "Admit it, Gavin. You felt the release. I gave you submission. It was what we were missing. It's why you pursued me."

He pushed her, the tension in his muscles rippling to his feet. She kneeled higher and tugged at the waistband of his boxers. "What are you doing?" he snapped.

"Take my mouth, Gavin. Take it and see. You need this. *We* need this."

An internal rage brewed at the pain he would continue causing and the pleasure of taking control. He wanted both. Could she be right? Did he find complete peace? Impossible.

He snatched her hands, and she lunged forward, rubbing her lips on the fabric separating her submission from his truth. A low moan escaped him at the faint touch. He would explode as soon as he forced her mouth. He held her wrists with one hand and drew out his cock with the other. Pre-ejaculate trickled from the opening.

"You want to prove something, Shane? You can't. Now, I'm going to take what I want and dispose of you. Is that what you want?"

"Yes." She licked her lips. Her arousal speaking through a raspy voice.

His internal denial would become her revelation as well as a baptism by fire and desire.

"This isn't a scene. This is reality. Open," he growled, and she complied. She stuck out her tongue and offered her mouth to fuck as he saw fit. *Good fucking girl.*

He rubbed the tip around her mouth and hissed. The bead of rich creamy liquid spread above her lip as he marked his area. "Wider."

She did oh-so-obediently, and his balls tightened into his body. *Jesus.* He shoved his cock deep without testing her reflex. She gagged, and he shoved farther until she couldn't breathe.

"Eyes."

Her eyes opened, pupils dilated. Her hands went limp at her sides as spit flowed from her mouth and onto her chest. Complete submission and it was everything to him.

The base of his balls throbbed, and his thighs tightened as semen jetted down her throat. Her throat flexed along his length as more filled her mouth, spilling out the sides. "Fucking swallow."

She did, like the good girl she was, and went to wipe her lip. "Leave it." Her hand fell to her knee. No question. No fight. He blinked in surprise. *Keep pushing. She needs to go.*

"Get up and bend the fuck over. I'm not done."

He said it as though he needed to convince himself, pursuing what she offered without failing. She listened and spread her cheeks.

"You think this is a game?" *Smack!* His hand came down so hard on her ass it stung his palm.

"Sh...Shit." She exhaled, rising on her tiptoes.

His fingers tested her cunt. Soaked. "You think you fooled me? You think this is something you can fight?" From the nightstand, he snatched a condom. As the foil packet ripped, she held still as he prepared himself. *Smack, smack!* "Answer me."

"Yes, Sir."

"Fuck you, Shane. This is nothing," he bit out. His emotions crossed from rage into dominant pleasure.

He gripped her wrists behind her back, tugging hair back with the other hand as he pinned her between the bed and his body. The length of his throbbing cock rested in the crease of her ass.

"You don't get me," he seethed into her ear. "You think you have it all figured out." He slid his hips back, and the crown of his penis notched her pussy. "But you are nothing but a conquest."

"Please," she cried out. "Please fuck me."

He smacked her again, and she grunted. "I say when. But if you need satisfaction, my dominance is what pushed me to pursue your job, so be it." He pushed in an inch, and a low moan escaped her lips, soft tissues fluttered around him.

"More, please," she said breathlessly.

"This isn't for you." He pushed in another inch. "This is for me." Another. "Your cunt is mine to use and mine to get rid of."

"Yes, Sir. My cunt is yours."

"Now you're getting it." He slammed the last of his thick cock to the hilt. A rough *"uh"* left her from the impact. He moved in and out, gripping her hair, holding her taut against the bed. Unmovable and his object to claim. "Why are you doing this?"

"Fuck…you…" she spat.

He slammed back into her again, all air leaving her body. "Why, Shane?"

"It doesn't matter!"

He slapped her ass, and her core tightened around him. He was so hard it hurt. He bent forward and yanked her face to meet his.

"It does!" he boomed, and her face contorted as he slammed into her again and held still. "Is it so you can say you were right? So you can say your pet project was a success?" He didn't know what he was saying. Any present insecurity gathered around them. A sliver of dominance held on as they fell deeper into their roles.

"I'm going...to..."

"No, you don't. You are not allowed to come."

"Please!" Her muscles tightened and sticky breath caught her throat. He wouldn't last long.

"Not until you answer." *Thrust, thrust.*

"Fuck," she growled. "I-I knew it was you!" As the last syllable left her mouth, Shane's body shook from orgasm so hard he went over with her, filling the condom. Her admission shuddering out of his muscles like an exorcism toward the truth. *She knew. She fucking knew.*

He fell over her, trying to find the words through heavy breaths. He whispered in her ear. "What?" Any aggression left at her admission. When had she found out? And why had she stayed?

"In the club. I figured it out."

He separated and lay next to her. Their faces met. "How?"

"Blair. At the karaoke bar...I confronted her."

He blinked. "Shane...I...Why are you still here?"

"I saw you in the club. I felt you at the concert. You were there. The real you. You deserve someone who can forgive you without reservation."

The pain in his heart burned outward to his hands and feet. "Oh, Shane. No, I don't. You can't..." He brushed the hair from her face. Confusion and doubt rumbling inside. "Hasn't what happened been enough for you to stay away? I will *hurt* you. You need to understand, I'm no good."

"No." She almost smiled. So sure of her answer. "You won't hurt me."

"But I have."

"Not anymore." She cupped his face.

"How can you know?" It came out as a whisper as he searched her eyes.

"I just do."

She believed it. His hand smoothed down her face and around her neck. He tilted her chin, and his eyes softened.

"I don't deserve you."

"I DON'T CARE what you have to do, Kev," Jacob boomed into the Bluetooth headset as he rolled his sleeves. He turned to see the city sprawl from his office windows. "Our whole year is riding on this album and I don't care what the band did. If the they ask you to suck their dicks, you fucking do it."

Kevin, the A&R Director of AMG, droned on regarding the current rock project with Icarus Descending.

The office door opened in the reflection. Liza peered around the doors while she gripped the handle. He motioned with his chin for her to speak.

"The fabulous Mr. David is here to see you." Shrugging her thin arms in the air, she gritted her teeth, spreading her normally plump lips taut.

He smiled wide and nodded. "Kev, don't call me again unless it's to tell me Michael Blaya is finishing this record." Killing the call, he tossed the headset on the desk. David skipped cheerfully into his office.

"Jakey!"

"The fabulous Mr. David?" He laughed again, grabbing

David's hand and bringing him in for a hug. "Good to see you, man. Please, sit." He grabbed two waters from the mini fridge, tossing one to him.

David whistled as he gaped over the space. The modern design encompassed dark wood features accentuated with silver and green palettes throughout the room.

"Shane would be jealous; you scored the bigger office."

He propped his feet on the coffee table. "Yeah, she would. So, what's up? Looking to get out?"

"She'd have your balls on a platter. Again, might I remind you." He waved him off like a prima donna.

He loosened his tie. "Don't remind me. How is she?"

David's lips thinned. Jacob's chest brewed a possessive fire at whomever would be the cause of her having difficulty.

"Ah, the question of the year. Shane is"—he tilted his face to the side and narrowed his eyes—"good."

"You sure?" He leaned forward, setting the water on the table.

"How do I say this without breaking the girl code?"

He snickered, missing the witty banter David offered. Rising from his chair, he gazed out into the city. "I know she's seeing someone."

"Yeeeaah, she did mention you knew." He had a pained expression as his chest rose and fell through his fashion t-shirt and sport coat.

Something *was* wrong. "Talk," Jacob demanded, maybe a little too eager.

"She is…well, she's confused."

"Is that a question? Give it to me straight."

"Do you still love her?" he asked hesitantly.

"What does it matter?"

"Because it does. She would kill me if she knew I was here. I'm literally risking my life." David motioned across his neck with his finger.

Snorting out of his nose, Jacob's eyes remained fixed on the towering sky-rise outside the office window. "Yes. I still love her."

"Then fight for her!" he cried out, making Jacob jump.

"Whoa, David. Calm down. What's this all about?"

"I can't say. But know if you care for my doll, you need to be the carnal man you are and fight for her!" His voice could break glass.

Jacob exhaled and sat. There was nothing more in the world he would rather do. But Shane had made her choice, and he'd promised to leave her alone once she did.

"This someone else…is she interested in him?"

"Sure, but she doesn't *love* him." David's eyes rolled as he confirmed his darkest fear to be untrue. His heart leapt. Did he still have a chance?

"How does she feel about me? She moved on. And she proved it by being with me the other night. Which I'm sure you know about too."

David winced. "Yeah, she feels real bad about that. But I can't say any more. I'm tied to her." He crossed his fingers. "But you *need* to find out on your own."

Jacob rubbed his face, smoothing his fingers through his hair. David wouldn't come here and tell him idle gossip unless there was major concern. Even though Shane wasn't upfront about being with the other guy, Jacob had his own secret. A secret, waiting for the hatchet to chop any chance of being together in half.

"I will see what I can do." David's grin widened. "I'm not promising anything. And I hope you'll keep this conversation between us. I don't need to complicate things for her any more than they already appear to be. Got it?"

"You're the best." He rested his hands on Jacob's shoulders when they stood, eyes sincere. "You have my word."

With David on his way back to Shane, Jacob sank into the leather desk chair. The pit of his stomach churned.

Sliding open the drawer of his desk, he removed a ring box. Dust floated to the floor like the past remnants of their relationship. He snatched it in his fist, infuriated by where life had taken them. Aggression burned deep. Who the fuck was she confused over? He texted her.

J: I need to see you.

He waited for a response as the velvet tickled his thumb with each pass.

S: OK

J: My place?

S: Yes

J: 1 hour

S: C u soon :)

The chair rolled away as he shot up. "What the hell...?" She wanted to see him. *Smiley face.*

Tucking the ring box back into its drawer, he grabbed his coat, leaving the office in a rush. Perhaps he would get his second chance.

THE KEYS CLANKED in the glass bowl on the foyer table as Jacob tossed them with a renewed sense of vigor. He would fight for Shane even if it meant telling her the truth. It wasn't a mistake they'd rekindled their passion, and he would do it with a clean slate.

The elevator pinged. *Time's up.* The doors opened as he set glasses and wine on the kitchen island. Desire surged within as her flared skirt swayed around her long legs. Her form-fitted blouse hugged her luscious breasts, wakening his insides. She was sexy as hell.

"Shane…" He drank in the sight of her like a weary desert traveler seeing water for the first time.

She fell into his arms, her purse and coat thudding on the floor. He held her, inhaling the crown of her hair. *Flowers.* Her body shook as the unmistakable sound of sobs flowed.

"Are you okay?" he asked softly.

"Yes. I'm overwhelmed."

"Come here; talk to me." He put his arm around her, leading them to the sofa in the living area. She sat next to him. "What is it?"

A restless laugh escaped her. "I'm sorry. It's silly. I tried to hold it in, but when I saw you…it came flooding out."

"Why?"

"I'm relieved you texted." Her hands twisted in her lap. "I'm so sorry. I didn't mean to hurt you."

He stroked her cheek with a thumb. He'd lost the ability to be angry with her. Especially given the things he had to tell her.

"It's okay."

"Really?" Her brow creased, and her pale blue eyes questioned him.

"I can't say it didn't hurt, but I get it." He dropped his hand. "I wish you would've told me you were with someone else."

She nodded slowly, glancing back at her hands. "I'm sorry. I would've wanted the same thing."

He tucked a lock of hair behind her ear. *Honesty.* Here he was requesting it as his guilt sat like a rock in his gut.

"Come here." He hugged her against his chest. She sniffled as her body tensed. "Relax, Lovely."

"Why are you so good to me?"

"Because I—" He swallowed. The word *love* lodged in his throat. "I care about you." It required all he had not to tell her everything. Take her on the couch and make her remember how good they were together. Could still be together.

She backed away, searching his eyes, no doubt reading him. They were always in sync, having never lost the ability to communicate without words. But she said nothing, only smiled. Plump, pink lips shone behind her gloss. Blood plummeted to his stomach. He could kiss her and make it right. *Just one kiss...*

"Wine?" He sprang from the couch.

"Ah...sure." Following him into the kitchen, her fingers linked with his, and a jolt of electricity flew up his arm. He dropped her hand to pop the cork on the bottle of wine. He raked his fingers through his hair as her blue eyes caught the light over the island. She was something. Watching as though she worshiped him. His heart swelled as she settled on a barstool.

"It's not polite to stare," he teased.

She blushed. "I wasn't staring."

"Mmmhmm." He slid a glass over to her. "What do you call it?" And like a shmuck, he'd give whatever she asked.

"Memorizing."

That came out of the fucking blue. A sledgehammer hit him square in the chest as the wine glass stopped at his lips. She planned on moving forward with the other guy. The thought shattered him, taking the wind from his sails.

"Interesting response." He frowned. The glass clinked the island. He held onto the island's curving edge until his knuckles whitened. "What's going on, Shane? Why did you agree to come here?"

Wetness glazed her irises. "I-I don't know."

"Bullshit," he gritted out, blood rising to his ears. "You came here to say good-bye."

The stool screeched on the hardwood floor, and she met him on the other side. His heart sank. This was it for them. No reprieve. The end of their story.

He could feel her soft skin even through his beard when she cupped his chin. Her perfume filled his nose, and time stopped.

Savoring every last moment, his arms wrapped around her. She shuddered, the desire still simmering. She ran her fingers through his hair, prickling the nerve endings of his scalp. His chest swelled as it became too much. Too real. It was for the best anyway. He didn't deserve her, and perhaps this other guy—whoever he was—could treat her the way she deserved.

"Jacob..." she whispered.

He opened his eyes. The truth in her gaze told him what he needed to know. He kissed her anyway, swept her lips with a haunting desire as sadness enveloped his being. This was the last time he'd ever kiss her beautiful face. His eyes shut, and he hoped the tears would stop as he licked her lips. She opened in response. He almost expected to feel passion and heat. Hear the guttural moans of pleasure she always responded with. It never came.

This was her farewell.

Her *I'm sorry.*

The final *I love you.*

He forged on, hoping his kisses told her he was sorry for leaving. Sorry for betraying her. And wishing he could be the man she deserved. A man strong enough to never hurt her. Her lips answered back. She understood.

They broke away, touching foreheads, breathing heavily, until her hands fell to his chest.

"This isn't why I asked you over," he said in anguish.

"It's not why I came, either. I needed to tell you I was sorry. I will always love you." Her head fell against his beating heart. Could she hear it breaking?

"I'll wait for you."

"Oh, Jake." Sobs shuddered her body as he rocked her side-to-side, kissing the crown of her head. He would wait. He'd let her go and maybe she'd come back. He would find a way to prove to her they belonged together.

"I should go." Her voice cracked.

Reluctantly, he released her, moving toward the dining room windows. As he leaned on the glass, snow, adrift in the chilled December breeze, swirled around the buildings.

Just like him.

A FLASH DRIVE spun between Gavin's forefinger and thumb. *Flip, flip.* The initials, *S.V.*, inscribed on the outside, caught the light. A small device intended to create an atom bomb of pain and fear, now lighter in his hand.

His goal toward corporate power didn't hold the appeal like the power exchange shared with Shane. A deeper bond burned his loins and filled his heart.

Love, maybe?

A new light existed. A flame of promise he didn't know he was worthy of capturing. Worthy of receiving. Her ability to walk blindly into trust moved him. It also scared the shit out of him. The desire to know more behind the mystery of Shane demanded his attention. He wanted her, nothing else.

As he popped the flash drive into the computer, a thrill ran along his spine. With a few clicks of the mouse, he enlarged the image and hit *play.*

Her consent to voyeurism spurred him on as the video played with her lying on the bed. A biting lip and reddening skin told him she enjoyed obeying him. Moved by her submission, his chest swelled with pride. It was an act of selflessness he'd never appreciated with prior subs.

Skipping to the end, he focused in on her eyes. She'd let all inhibitions go, something he'd never truly witnessed in her daily life. Something he was able to give her with his dominance. His body heated as his blood pumped south. His cock strained against his zipper as she writhed in pleasure.

She'd effortlessly given her trust to him, someone she thought she'd met only a few times. It perplexed him. How did she do it? Why did she do it?

Pausing the video, he narrowed his eyes at the moment he removed her mask. Submerged in subspace, she didn't flinch. She floated, feeling what he gave, and she did it shamelessly. But there was a glint in her eye. A moment she described as seeing him on the precipice of control and he was. *Damn.* It was simply breathtaking.

The door to the office opened, and he minimized the screen quickly.

"Oh. Hey, man," Ethan said, closing the door behind him. "Didn't know you were still here." He brushed the back of his short blond hair.

Gavin raised an eyebrow, trying to let his erection calm under the desk. "Yeah. I'm still here. What's up?"

"Uh, nothing." The uniquely placed dimple appeared directly under Ethan's hazel eye when he grinned. "You heading out?"

A prickling awareness ran down his arms. "What are you up to, Ethan?"

A deeply playful Dom, Ethan lacked total self-control when it came to the opposite sex. His dick and hormones did the talking whenever he was about to get lucky. Although luck wasn't a factor. His carefree nature and easy charm swept women off their feet. Not to mention one glimpse of his dimple and different color eyes, they fell for him. But his ego always got the best of him, giving him a false sense of control.

"Nothing."

Groaning, Gavin swiped his keys from the desk. "Whatever. Just don't do it in here."

He nodded with his hands in his dark jean pockets, rocking on his heels. "Later, man."

"I mean it."

"Go. Get some sleep. You look like hell."

Gavin agreed with a grunt, exiting into the vacant hallway. Ethan was up to no good, but he didn't have time to find out who it was with.

WHEN HE ENTERED HIS HOME, he trudged up the stairs as a message pinged from his phone. He eyed it carefully.

J: Does your offer still stand to get me into The Resort?

Could Jacob be back on the prowl? Pleasure shot through him, no more competition.

G: Yes. When?

J: Tomorrow

He typed the address and told him to keep an eye out for Candy's email for the necessary paperwork to complete and a temporary passcode for visitor's access to the club.

Exhaustion overcame his body as he fell onto the mattress. Too tired to undress, he drifted asleep. A wave of unease swept over him. He lifted his head from the pillow and wiped his face.

"Fuck." He put his feet on the floor and dragged the phone from his pocket.

G: Are you still there?

E: Just left. Why?

G: Never mind

AN EERIE FEELING swept Gavin as he walked the dim, quiet halls of The Resort. The lock clicked with his key, and he flicked on the office light, making his way to the computer. A quick grab of the flash drive and he could get home to sleep. A cold shiver ran down his back at the empty USB slot on the tower. Where was it? He retraced his steps, and without panicking, he called Ethan.

"This better be good," Ethan said irritated. Female giggling filtered through the phone and what sounded like him shuffling out of bed.

"Did you move the USB drive from the computer?"

"What? Hold on." He muffled the receiver so Gavin couldn't make out the words. "Okay, sorry, man. What's this again?"

"When you were in the office, did you take the flash drive from the computer?"

"I didn't notice one. Why?"

"No reason," he barked. Shuffling papers on the desktop, he hoped the device would fall out from between them.

"What was on it?"

"It's private," he bit out.

"Okay, okay. Get a grip, Gav. Are you sure you left it there?"

"Yes." He rubbed his face and plopped into the chair. Glancing into the garbage, he noticed a used condom. "Jesus! What did I say about doing it in the office!"

"Dude, calm down."

"Ethan, there's private information stored in here. Fuck, when will you start thinking?"

"Asks the guy with a missing flash drive," he quipped. "Are we done here? I have things waiting for me."

"Fine." He killed the call. The phone thudded on the desk. He leaned over, burying his face in his hands and rubbing his temples. A migraine was now inevitable.

It's here somewhere; it has to be. He scoured the room. Maybe it fell out while Ethan got off. The floor, desk, and all the drawers searched. He ripped the entire office apart only to find nothing. His temper soared as his face heated. Cursing under his breath, he halted mid-stride to the desk.

"Who the *fuck* was in here with him?" He dialed Ethan again.

"You know the drill." Beep.

"FUCK!"

A wave of nausea came over him. If the video got out, it would ruin Shane's career and life. She'd never forgive him. Immediate regret from his tarnished ways hit him like a wrecking ball. He'd been too blinded by his goal to see she was the one to make him a better man and now it might be too late.

He wiggled the mouse. The monitor woke. A few clicks and the video feeds, used for security measures, opened. As the hall camera feed loaded and played, Ethan walked hand in hand with a tall blonde. When he opened the office door, their grip fell, and Ethan went in without her.

Gavin narrowed his eyes on the blonde. An aqua halter dress loosely scooped past the cleavage of her surgically sculpted breasts. Her hair was pulled tight, accentuating her long neck and a mask covered her face. After a few minutes of waiting, she left.

Fast-forwarding the feed showed Ethan leaving the office shortly after Gavin to find his conquest of the night. A few minutes later, they returned. Her identity was still hidden.

"Damn it," he muttered.

When she entered the office, a small tattoo marked the back of her neck. He enlarged the image and froze.

"Blair."

SHANE STRETCHED, surrounded by a cloud of blankets. A ridiculous smile appeared at the sound of her alarm. She was aroused from the dream of Gavin's godly male figure on top of her. In the dream, every inch of his skin was pure perfection. As her hands skimmed his back, her nails dug into his firm ass while he plunged into her. A sigh escaped her. She could hardly wait to see him today.

She opened the drawer of her nightstand and grabbed a vibrator. She stared at it and a shiver rushed down her spine. The clock read six o'clock. Was Gavin awake? She snuggled back in place and grabbed her phone.

S: Are you awake?

Patience, a virtue lacking at the moment as anticipation for a response ached in her sex. What if he didn't reply? Even if the fever had broken between them, she was still unsure about his feelings. Suddenly, a ping caused her to jump.

G: Yes

She bit her bottom lip as her thumbs hovered over the keyboard. Nothing but a simple *yes.* Was he mad? Or busy? She tensed. The ellipsis appeared in the left hand corner of the screen.

G: A little early for work, don't you think?

S: Not too early for other things…

She snapped a picture of her bare breasts followed by a swoosh sound.

G: I see. Show me more and I'll consider it.

The air went out of her, and she curled her toes. She removed the comforter, exposing her naked body and positioned the camera at her sex with her legs open. *Swoosh.*

G: Is that for me?

S: Yes

G: Touch your cunt. Tell me how wet you are.

All desire coiled in her stomach, causing her skin to heat and her core to clench. The purr in his voice, even through text, sent a wave of warmth to her clit. She dipped her fingers into her pussy and gasped, reeling from images of him inside her.

S: Dripping. Are you hard?

Ding. She clutched her phone against her chest and breathed deep. Lifting it, she yelped. He was on display, all male and beautiful and hers. His massive erection spanned root to tip up to his navel. *Jesus.*

S: Fuck, you're so hot. Let me suck you.

G: Your sexy mouth is hot and wet. Your sweet tongue swirling the tip of my cock, tasting my juices. I want to fuck your pretty little mouth.

The illicit details sent her into a tailspin. She rubbed her clit as she read each filthy word. Her hand smoothed the slick arousal over her folds. She whimpered. Building her climax with a rush as her fingers circled her throbbing bundle of nerves.

G: Don't come.

Holy Fuck! How does he know?

S: Can't help it. Put it in.

G: I say when. Tell me what you are doing.

S: I'm squeezing my nipple, imagining it is your mouth biting it. My fingers are pushing deep inside me.

She hit *send* and, moments later, the phone rang. Hitting the speaker button, she said in a low raspy voice, "Hello there."

"You're a dirty girl, Ms. Vaughn. Tell me how you want it."

"I want it slow." She gasped as her hand circled her hot button. "I want to feel your dick touch every part of my pussy as you enter me."

"Fuck, Shane..." he hissed. She could hear the bed shift. Fantasies of her grinding on his hand surged her forward. Animal noises filtered through the phone, making her thrust her hips against her hand. Heels digging into the mattress.

"Gavin..." she whined in a breathy whisper. "I want...you..."

"Steady, baby. Not until I say."

She tensed to slow the racing climb to the top. A frustrated sound escaped, and she slowed her movements. "What would you do to me?"

"I would lick you. Starting with your neck to your fuck-me tits. I would suck your nipples until you begged me to stop. Once I reached your pink cunt…"

"Yes," she whispered. "Then what?"

"I'd watch your body writhe as I teased you. Make you beg for my mouth. You're hungry and greedy. Waiting for me."

She gasped, sweat glistening off her body, teetering on the edge with every mention of his description. "Please."

"Are you grinding on your hand?"

"Yes…" She threw her head into her pillow, her eyes closed to concentrate on the dark sensual tone of his voice and the feel of her hand.

He groaned. "My dick is so hard it hurts, baby. I'm pumping into my hand while cupping my balls. Would you like my sack in your mouth?"

"Ah…yes, please."

"I bet you do." He snickered devilishly. "They're falling into your mouth. Are you sucking them?"

"Mmmm." She pushed two fingers inside her sex.

"Yes…your fucking mouth." He gritted through his teeth. "Do you have a vibrator?"

"Yes."

"Turn it on and place it on your clit. Tell me how it feels."

She switched it on. The buzzing vibrated between her thighs.

"It's so good."

"Good girl. I want to hear you breathe. I want your smart mouth to call my name while you tell me how good my cock feels thrusting into you. I'll go with you, baby."

Their panting matched a unison staccato rhythm. "Feels good, Gavin. Too good."

"Yes."

"Fuck, it's too much. Your cock is so big. It's stretching me. Ah, god...I'm, I'm…"

"Yes. Tell me."

She held her breath as she crested her release, screaming out his name. Her back bowed. The spasms clenched around her fingers. Come dripped down her buttocks and onto the bed.

"You make me come so hard," he roared. She imagined semen spurting over his tensing six-pack.

They lay there, listening to each other breathe for who knew how long, her body too weak to say a word, her mind calm.

"A great way to wake up," he said finally.

She smiled. "You're welcome. See you at the office."

"Can't wait."

SHANE PRACTICALLY SKIPPED through the main doors of Omega Records. Nothing could ruin her day.

"Good morning, sweetie." She kissed David's cheek as he handed her a latte.

"Good morning, doll. You're awfully happy."

"What? It's a beautiful day."

He glanced out of the reception area window at the gray sky threatening snow. "Only if you live in Mordor."

"A couple of clouds never hurt."

Gavin entered the reception area in a tailored black suit, his top button undone and his coat slung over his arm. She caught his eye and blushed. He remained calm, his exterior tough as usual, except for the mischievous glimmer in his eyes that sparked devious thoughts.

"David. Shane," he greeted in a curt voice. He strode past them as she checked out his ass in his suit pants.

"Um, doll? What the hell was that?"

"What?"

"The force field I walked into? Seriously, some major heat there." He fanned himself as they walked to her office.

"Yeah."

She hung her coat and pulled the hem of her red form fitted sweater dress. David sat in the usual visitor's chair for their morning chat, eyeing her for an explanation.

"I talked to Jacob last night." She sank into the desk chair.

"And?" He straightened.

"And I decided to close the chapter for good. I want to pursue things with Gavin."

"What? Seriously?"

"Don't look at me like that. I know you don't agree, but I feel this is the right avenue for now."

"And how did Jacob take it? I assume he's on the same page?"

She narrowed her eyes at him, suspiciously. Why the sudden interest in Jacob? "He understands. He's broken up, and it was truly the hardest thing I've done. All I ever wanted was for him to be there, and now he is, and I can't do it."

"Did he…" he trailed off.

"What?"

"You know."

"Say he loved me?" She exhaled. "No. But he said he'd wait for me." She picked at the thermal sleeve hugging her coffee cup.

"He will."

"Even though he shouldn't. It isn't fair."

"But he'll do what he feels is right."

Why waste time when he could find someone else? Her chest panged with jealousy. What if he did? She buried the thoughts and cleared her throat. She was fine. Made her choice. Moving on…

"Stubborn male." Stinging tears threatened to come through. With David, confidence was a must or he'd jump all over her. She set her drink on the desktop and shuffled a few papers around. "I've made my decision."

22

"WHO WERE you with last night, Ethan?" Gavin paced his office. His gut tightened at the thought of Shane's sex tape being in the wrong hands.

He removed his jacket, tossing it on the back of his chair. He rubbed his neck, reeling with anger over his own ignorance.

"I told you, I don't know."

"How can you not know?" How could his business partner be so careless? How could *he* be so careless?

"Uh, because we own an anonymous sex club." He chuckled. "Why's this so important?"

"The USB is what's important. It's missing, and she was the only other person in the office besides you."

It was his lifeline. He turned when his office door creaked opened. Shane peeked her head inside. Panic filled him, but he remained stoic, careful not to give anything away.

He went back to the window, a squall coming through the city. Even as the fear of outing her identity crippled his insides, the sight of her jolted his cock awake.

"Must be something good to get you this riled up. I'm heading over there and will take another look around. If she comes into the club tonight, I'll spot her. Sorry, I can't be any more help," Ethan said.

Shane's reflection drifted across the windows. She inspected every detail of his office. She sauntered past the rows of dark bookshelves arranged in square cubbies, which held hundreds of vinyl records. She examined his father's turntable—the only good thing about the man. Her mouth parted in awe at his collection.

"Call me if you do. Have to go," he murmured.

"Later, man."

"Can I help you?" he asked gruffly as he sat in his chair.

"Nice to see you too." She spun the lock on the door.

"What are you doing?"

She perched her ass on the edge of his desk, close enough for him to see the sultry look in her eyes. She pushed his emotional limits, like he had done physically to her.

"I wanted to say thank you for this morning."

"No need."

She stood and walked along the bookshelves, her fingers flicking along the vinyl. She inhaled the vintage flare they gave off and slid one out. Examining the cover, she raised her eyebrows at him.

"Whitney?"

"It was my sister's."

"You have a sister, do you?" Her smile could light an entire city.

He rose from the chair. "And a brother." Information poured out of him. This is what Shane did. Made him want to share his life. "His name is Liam."

"And your sister?"

"Riley. Lives in Europe. A kept wife of a millionaire." Her lips opened and shut. "Go ahead," he coaxed.

She bit her lip, inspecting the album. "Are you close with your siblings?"

He plucked it from her hands and carefully placed it back in its spot. "Not particularly. Liam and I have an understanding. He stays out of my business, but if he needs something, he can call on me. And with Riley consumed with her husband and kids, we rarely speak." Her brows creased. "You think it's strange."

She shrugged. "No. All families are different."

He brushed his hand down her cheek, unable to not touch her. "True. I will get there, Shane." A small promise they would move forward in time.

"I want to believe you. And this is a start." She kissed his thumb as it grazed her lips. The acceptance and touch panged through his chest and reverberated south. The air thickened as his chest heaved. A devilish grin appeared across her flawless yet rosy face. She felt it too. She walked the length of the wall.

"An impressive collection you have."

He leaned an elbow on the shelf, amused by her strategy to draw out the tension thrumming between them.

"I like to think so." He stared unabashedly at her rolling hips and playful ways.

She pivoted. "Have you listened to all of these, Mr. Mayne?" She flicked her wrist to the albums.

"Yes. At one time or another." His lips quirked, and their eyes met, heat growing between them.

"I would like to hear them." She closed the gap between their bodies. Wrapping her hands around his suspenders. He wanted her bent over the desk and calling his name.

"Which one should we start with?" He linked his hands at the small of her back and moved her against his growing erection. A small gasp escaped her pouty lips, and a wicked gleam flashed in her blue eyes.

"Do you have 'Nine Inch Nails' "Closer"?" she rasped.

He lowered his mouth to her ear. "You want to be fucked like an animal, Shane?"

"If it pleases you."

Fuck. He'd met his match.

He nipped her earlobe, her warm breath hitting his cheek. He gently savored her mouth. Her hands released the suspenders and shoved through his hair. She tugged the roots, driving him to deepen the kiss as her back hit the shelves. The albums skewed from the impact.

She made him lose control, and he liked it. He squeezed her breast as her leg wrapped around his hip. His cock ground against her cleft, and she whimpered into his mouth.

"Pull up your dress and bend over the desk." Her eyes widened as she panted. "Now."

As she approached the desk, she lifted the hem of her sweater dress until her ass was perfectly on display. Black thigh-high stockings were held by red garters, which matched her panties. He raged inside to give her what she wanted. Dominating her did sate his need for control in the office. A required balance for them to work. He splayed a hand over her round, smooth ass and squeezed. A purr of approval fell from his lips.

"You are in so much trouble, Ms. Vaughn."

Power and confidence rolled through his body. His hands skimmed her sex and snapped the garter.

"Ow!"

"If we're going to do this, I need you quiet." He pushed the rolled tie sitting on the desktop into her mouth. "There, much better. What am I going to do with you?"

He slid the top drawer of his desk open and snatched the scissors. He pulled the crotch of her panties out and cut them in half, exposing her as he inserted two fingers. She bucked, and he pushed her shoulders against the desk. He cupped her sex as she squirmed, pushing toward him and moaning into the muffled tie.

He laughed. "Oh, I intend to."

"Mr. Mayne?" the phone intercom buzzed. Shane jumped, and

a muffled squeak came through the fabric. He pushed her back onto the desk without skipping a beat. He continued thrusting his fingers in and out of her soaking wet pussy. He loved an audience even if they didn't know they were one.

"Yes, Tasha."

"There's a Miss Blair Grayson at security to see you."

He halted, sliding his fingers out as Shane shot up from her position. She tossed the material from her mouth onto the desk and shimmied her dress back into place, eyes wide and mouth tight.

He looked at her. "Tell her I'm out."

"She said it's urgent. Something about a—"

"Five minutes, Tasha," he barked.

"Sure thing, sir." The phone clicked.

"Why's she here?"

His head tilted in surprise at her heated tone. "Are you jealous?"

Her crystal irises turned an aquamarine shade, and one side of her upper lip curled. She was ready to pounce.

"No...yes," she huffed. It warmed him. Women had appeared jealous in the past, but he never reacted. *They* didn't own him. Shane did.

"Shane, listen. It's nothing," he lied. It was everything.

"Then what could be so urgent? And when was the last time you fucked her?" she blurted out.

"Before you, baby. And it was one time." He uncrossed her arms. She tapped her foot. "Hey, I swear. I don't divide subs. And you know I haven't done relationships in the past."

She flinched. "You combine them. Ménage."

"I have. Yes." He dropped her wrists.

She sighed, rubbing her lips together. "I have a lot to learn about you, Gavin Mayne."

He tugged her arm, and she fell against his chest. He smelled her hair. *Wildflowers.*

"Five minutes is all I'm giving her."

"Fine. And no sharing. Hard limit." She smiled sarcastically.

He touched her face and cupped her chin. "Good. Because I won't share you."

She snorted. "I meant you."

"Aahhh." He kissed her lips. "You don't have to worry. I'm all yours."

As Shane left, his anger bubbled over. He exhaled, rolling his neck. This meeting required a gentler approach to get what he wanted—the video and peace of mind that Shane would be safe.

Blair entered. At first glance, she fit the mold of the typical blonde men grew up idolizing through obscene magazines. Or those viewed as eye candy strolling through town with men of particular power. Her long golden hair was always in place with a slim, toned body. A set of man-made tits completed her look. They could claim any man like Medusa if caught staring too long.

"Blair." He gestured to the visitor's chair and closed the door.

She smoothed the back of her purple pencil skirt.

"What do you want?" He sat on the edge of his desk.

"We needed to talk."

"About?" Would she admit she'd taken his device?

"I know you were pretty clear you didn't want to see me again," she said, referring to the night Shane left the karaoke bar without a trace. A smile that didn't reach her eyes appeared.

"Yes."

A red painted fingernail tapped the armrest as she leaned back. "Do you still feel that way?" Hopeful eyes blinked at him.

Where did he go wrong with this one? Clear on his motives when they met, she'd agreed. He wouldn't have fucked her had she not fully understood the original arrangement.

"Yes." The smile slid away from her face. "But I want to know about your relationship with Ethan."

Her thin eyebrows arched. "Ethan? Wow, Gavin. Keeping tabs on me wouldn't have been on my list of things you would be concerned about." She laughed.

As anger rippled through his body, he straightened and pointed at her. "Don't fuck with me. We both know why you're here."

"So sure?"

"You were with Ethan last night. At the club. I know you have the video."

She uncrossed and crossed her legs. "Were you with Shane?"

The mere mention of her name on Blair's lips pissed him off. He leaned over her with both hands on the armrests. "It's not your concern."

"Not yet." She brushed his cheek with her hand. A sick feeling crawled over his skin as her vanilla perfume soured his stomach. He backed away. She opened the clutch nestled on her lap. The flash drive became visible in her hand. "Interesting stuff on there. Didn't know you had it in you."

He swiped it from her fingers and put it into his pocket. "Get out."

"It played as your friend fucked me from behind. I wasn't sure what I was seeing at first until her mask was removed." Her gaze seared him, and he matched it. "Not really your type."

"Shut up," he gritted.

An evil smile appeared, pushing the last button of his control. His body heated as a vein pulsed in his neck.

"Some position you got your boss into, don't you think? I mean"—she laughed with a sigh—"that little video could ruin everything for her."

He clenched his fists to keep from shaking her. "I'm warning you…"

She tilted her head. "Aw. You care about her. How cute. Does she know you recorded her?"

"Yes. I only deal with consent. You know this."

"Yes, yes, you and your *rules*." She air quoted. "Like the rule you laid out during our night together." She tapped her chin. "How did it go? Oh, yeah. Some bullshit about how you don't sleep with women twice, and I was to leave promptly in the morning. Did you ever think for a minute how I would feel?"

"Feel? When? *After* it happened? Come on, I know you're not naïve. We had a deal. You knew where I stood."

"But something changed."

"You're only hurting yourself."

A finger brushed the device in his pocket, and a wave of disgust for Blair and himself washed over him.

That"—she indicated his hand—"is only the original. What I want in exchange for the copy is thirty days to prove we should be together."

He paced the office. "I can't." Visions of a month with Blair and the hurt it would cause Shane shattered him.

"You're giving me no alternative."

"What do you have against her?"

A smug smile appeared. "She's taking what's mine. You. Your choice, Gavin. Me or the fall of Shane's empire."

His heart broke. What had he done? "I'm not yours. You don't know what you're doing."

"Don't I?" she quipped, standing with her coat slung over her arm. Conquest beamed from her body. "I know *exactly* what I'm doing."

"Please, don't." His feet froze to the floor as he tried to form a solution.

"Huh, begging. A good start."

"Surely you wouldn't think of ruining another woman's career by exploiting her. You know how hard it is to live in a man's world." His voice sounded like gravel; it was obvious he was grasping for straws.

She smiled, her hand resting on the doorknob. "You don't get it. She's competition, and you need to be taught a lesson. Think about it. I'll call you tomorrow."

SIPPING ON A GLASS OF SCOTCH, Jacob stretched an arm along the backrest in the corner booth of the main floor of The Resort. He absorbed the entire picture of the understated yet erotic vibe of the club.

Members danced with heat and desire as the bass pumped through their veins, heightening their sexual awareness. Masks hid their identities, but did they hide something more?

They disguised who they were to the masses during their everyday lives. Many of them could be found on the high society pages. Rich moguls and famous celebrities found hobnobbing at charity events. And here they were, still suppressing who they were to their core even with those who shared their darkest sexual kinks and interests. It was a shame even though he understood it.

While lost in his musings, his attention shifted to a tall, dark brunette approaching his area. Her silky black hair was parted in the center, creating a curtain down to her waist. Her face was sculpted in sharp edges with a narrow nose and bee-stung lips. As beautiful as a supermodel.

"May I join you?" she asked with a South American-accented voice.

"Yes," he said coolly, noticing she chose not to wear a mask. He raked in her curvy figure in a one shoulder, long sleeved violet dress made to call attention to her flawless bronze skin.

Sitting, she held out a hand. "Giovanna." The word trickled easily off her tongue. Her eyes, black as coal, stared mysteriously into him with a hint of mischief.

He kissed the top of her knuckles. "Jacob."

She set the champagne flute she had been holding on the table. She propped one elbow on the back cushion, and her hand fell gracefully, revealing a large oval amethyst the color of her garment.

"So, Jacob. I noticed you sitting alone," she remarked.

"I'm here to take in the evening, Giovanna."

Her full lips curved, showing her perfectly straight teeth. "Handsome man like yourself must have someone, no?"

He was flattered. In a few short seconds, he could tell she owned men and possessed all life offered. Any person who dealt with Giovanna, would feel as though they were on the winning end of the deal, but she would know different.

"No, I'm not with anyone."

Black eyes inspected every movement, taking in the details of his space. The way he breathed, his eye contact, and his body language registered in her eyes. Only one type of person examined with such intent.

A slow smile teased her mouth. "Ah, but you are not a truth teller. There is someone." She moved her right hand in a circle, her ring catching the light above. "Is she here?"

Had he lost his ability to bullshit even with his actions? She was good. It had been a while since he sparred with an equal of the opposite sex.

"No. She's not here."

"I see your struggle. You are deep and wounded. The type of

hurt of a Dom losing his sub, no?" She stated her assumption with ease, like she had known him in a past life.

He smiled. "You're good, Giovanna."

"Vanna, please."

"Vanna, it is. You must be a Domme."

"*Si, Dominadora*," she said in her native tongue in a matter-of-fact way. "You go to her."

"She's finding her way."

"It's your job to show her the way. To protect her. You must know. Show her she is yours. The love is not lost on you. Only... misdirected. Whatever you did, fix it. Letting her go is not an option."

He rolled his neck, the uneasiness of her intrusion not sitting well. What did she know? "I appreciate your concern. But you don't know what you're talking about."

"Oh, but I do. I've been there." She placed her hand on her heart. "Lost my way as the protector for my sub and he fell away. I could not let go of my idle, how you say, bullshit to submit to him."

"Submit to your sub?" He leaned forward and set the rocks glass on the table.

She nodded carefully, taking in his sudden interest. "Experienced Dominants realize their faults. They learn to achieve absolute Dominance through personal submission."

"How so?" Her insight into the lifestyle woke something deep within him.

"To love as a Dominant, one will surrender their heart. Remember, Jacob, the submissive holds the power, and the Dominant yields to the trust. Which is the ultimate gift."

His cowardly departure years ago and today meant nothing in the grand scheme of things. Shane had lost confidence in him. *In them*. She didn't feel, in her heart, he would protect her. Leaving her devalued the trust she'd bestowed in him. His mind cleared. He'd never surrendered his heart, and still, to this day, he hadn't.

He ran a hand through his hair. The thought of putting himself out there and meeting rejection shocked him to the core. Keeping it in was the cocky approach, so his ego wouldn't take a bruising. It was how he did business. But Shane wasn't a business. She was the love of his life.

"They are symbiotic. One does not survive without the other."

She smiled and nodded. "Now you get it."

He looked at her raptly, wondering why the Universe would present her to him. His chest ached. Time to come clean, submit his lies and his life, even if it meant losing her.

SHANE ENTERED the main doors to the club and scanned the dance floor from the mezzanine. Gavin was nowhere to be found. She checked her texts to see if, by chance, he'd texted about dinner. *Of course, he hadn't.*

The afternoon had sped by, but she'd noticed Gavin had shut down after his meeting with Blair. He said he was knee-deep in contract negotiations and otherwise distracted. When she asked how his meeting went, he'd waved her off with some excuse about a last-ditch effort to get him back. But before Shane could pursue their conversation further, a falling out with Anna Marie and the new producer on her next album had diverted her. Since Anna Marie only liked to deal with Shane, she had to tackle the issue.

Blair had wreaked havoc on her day. Jealousy boiled over, distracting her from the simplest tasks, and she wanted to clear the air.

As she walked down the stairs, the entire room came into focus, everything clearer without her mask. With truths laid out about being Dom and sub, she refused to hide behind cover. She wanted him to see her. Let the world see her for who she was at least within these walls.

Perched on the stool, she crossed her thigh-high boot-clad legs. She opened her clutch and the club lighting shone across the members only keycard. *Star*. She would never be her. Starting something new with Gavin, she would be herself. Butterflies flickered in her belly, and she tapped the corner of the card against her chin. A thought hit her in the gut. She smiled inwardly, snapped her purse closed, and found her feet, moving quickly toward his room.

"I CAN'T BELIEVE you know Billy!" Jacob exclaimed. A weight-lessness had come over him since arriving at the club.

Billy had been the bartender at the restaurant where he'd taken Shane. He'd teased her, insisting Jacob got to her first before he had a chance to sweep her off her feet.

"Yes. He is doing well."

Giovanna was a real estate mogul in New York, Las Vegas, and Miami. She owned a dozen hotels, and Billy managed the restaurants and cuisine. He spearheaded the designs, selected the chefs, and organized the openings for each boutique location. She had an eye for reviving otherwise fleabag hotels, giving them a new spin by restoring them to their original beauty with a flare of modern taste.

"Tell him to find me the next time he's in New York." Jacob handed her a business card.

"Will do, Mr. Jacob." A mischievous smile appeared. "And we should discuss collaborating on your record release parties."

She had won this deal, like she knew she would. Giovanna was the type of woman who always saw an angle for business and seized it. Before he could agree, he caught a glimpse of Shane walking briskly from the bar to the mezzanine stairs. Adrenaline stiffened his body.

Giovanna followed his gaze. "Ah, she *is* here."

"Yes, she is." Her sexy long legs landed on each step to the top. Now was his chance. He stood. "Vanna, it has been a pleasure. Thank you."

She took his hand, knowing his appreciation meant more than her company. "Submit to her."

He kissed her hand. "Until next time."

She nodded as he headed toward the stairs. Shane would not get away.

PASSING A FEW MEMBERS, Shane drifted down the hall of private rooms, anticipation growing with each step as she wiped her clammy hands on her dress, her stomach bound in knotted rope. Taking a deep breath and shaking her arms, she rushed forward before the determination fled.

"Shane!" Jacob shouted.

She stopped and turned as he closed the gap between them. "Jacob? Wh-what are you doing here?" Her eyes shifted to Gavin's room.

He exhaled nervously. "I should ask you the same question." He stepped closer and smoothed her arms. "Shane, I need..."

She stepped back. "Why are you here?"

"Lovely..."

"No. Stop." She put a hand between them. "Don't call me that," she whispered. Her heart quickened. She thought they were done, but seeing his hardened, determined gaze floored her.

The gusto left his body. "Listen."

"We said everything we needed to."

The last time they kissed, the passion no longer existed. She had emotionally separated. Moved on. But seeing him infuriated her. Caused her heart to rip in two. If she were over him, she'd feel nothing, right?

He gripped her arms gently. "I thought the same thing, but there was something I didn't say."

"No. Please stop. I can't…" Tears spilled down her cheeks. She could not keep doing this with him. To him. *To herself.* She stopped her lip from quivering and jutted out her chin. "There's nothing anymore."

"But there can be," he frowned.

"We had our chance. I've moved on."

"Moved on to him, you mean."

"Don't do this here."

"Don't tell me how to be, Shane," he said in a low voice. His green eyes flared as fury poured from his body, jealousy flashing across his face.

His forceful words triggered something deep and familiar. He had been her first in a lot of ways. The control and the desire to obey swept her under his spell. She blinked and shook off the dazed state.

"It's over."

He pushed her against the wall. Gripping her wrists, he restrained them behind her back and laid a smoldering, wet kiss on her lips. Without warning, she fell into it. Heat surged in her loins, flooding arousal between her thighs. His tongue commanded her mouth, in absolute control, so much so she faltered. There he was. The all-encompassing Jacob she knew and hadn't seen since before her father died, and he fragmented her resolve.

Her eyes closed. His hard body pushed against her. A masculine, spicy scent enveloped her senses. This level of devotion and rapture hadn't been there since they were together. The hallway seemed to be engulfed in the inferno of their lust. She whimpered into his mouth. Her brain met her desire when she broke away from his grip.

"I said, stop!" she said, panting from his kiss. She held her hand out in front of her when he tried to surge forward. "This isn't right. This isn't how things should be."

"Shane, I lo–"

"Fucking *stop*, Jacob!" She couldn't bear to hear the word lingering on his lips. She glanced down the hall to her destination. The door leading to her future with Gavin. "It's too late. It's too fucking late."

He deflated. Looked out of his element. Unsure. Unknowing. A flash of comprehension flickered in his eyes. An understanding she held a different fire, and the flame was meant for someone he knew. He straightened his jacket and cleared his throat.

"You're here for Gavin," he declared. "He's dangerous, Shane. You need to watch out for him."

Her brow wrinkled, and a laugh escaped her. "Funny. He said the same about you."

He swallowed, not denying it. "And you believed him?"

Her hands lifted and slapped against her thighs. "I don't know what to believe anymore. Except this is over."

He ran his hands through his hair and placed them on his hips. She could see his struggle. His denial. His apprehension, protection, and anger separating within a vortex of emotion, and this time, there was no putting it back together.

He advanced toward her and in a low voice, spoke words she would never forget. "When things go south, don't come running to me."

"Resorting to threats? How dare you. I waited for you for *two years*. Two fucking years and not so much as a phone call. Even after everything we had together!" She boiled, disgusted by his last ditch effort. Hot tears spilled down her face. "Don't you see?

I couldn't wait any longer for you to man up. I cried for you, wasted the last two years of my life on *you*. Now you change your mind, and I'm supposed to change my direction? Fuck. You. Don't put your shit on me," she snarled.

He straightened, eyes narrowing in pain. "Don't act like the other night meant nothing. We both know I came clean for what happened." His eyes raked over her. "Unlike you." The hatefulness in his words burned. He'd never acted this way. He stared and left.

She wiped her tears, rubbing the smeared mascara she assumed was running down her face. She never wanted it to come to this with Jacob. She took a deep breath as she leaned against the wall until she gathered the strength to walk to Gavin's room.

S: Can we meet for dinner?

A deep exhale escaped Gavin. He hadn't answered, contemplating whether a public place would be wise to reveal the deceitfulness he'd inflicted on her. He'd gone over scenarios in his head from giving Blair her thirty days to denying her and staying with Shane. Including the one in which he told Shane the entire truth. All forks in the road ended with losing her.

He rubbed his face. Whatever Blair had in mind, he would do. He could contain the aftermath at least and perhaps have a chance with Shane in the future. Blair was a loose cannon, and understanding the depths of her insanity and how far she would go to take down Shane had to be dealt with first.

His phone rang. "Hello."

"Sir? Shane has arrived," Candy said. She had standing orders to alert him whenever she checked into The Resort.

"Thank you."

He stood, taking the black mask from the desk. Grazing his

thumbs over the raised pattern, they reminded him of scars. Permanent markings of a man hiding behind his past. He tossed it on the desk. Shane wouldn't understand his motives at first when he left, but she would later on.

Telling her it was over meant seeing disgust and betrayal on her face. A look he was used to with his family and friends after Nicolette died. These were the wounds he carried. A man always searching for ulterior motives to propel him forward, and what had he lost?

Shane.

JACOB STOMPED DOWN THE HALL, fury burning him all over. *Fucking Gavin?* Could she not see past the veil he'd placed over her eyes? He ran his fingers through his hair as Gavin appeared from a doorway.

"Mr. Andrews. Enjoying your evening?"

Jacob snatched the lapels of Gavin's suit coat and pushed him against the wall. "How long, Gavin?"

In a calm state, Gavin's brows twitched. "How long, what?"

"Shane, asshole. How long have you been messing with her?" Spit flew from his mouth.

"I suggest you contain yourself. I'm not messing with Shane. We are together." Jacob's grip loosened. "She doesn't love you anymore. Hasn't for long time from what I can tell. Never mentioned you, actually. It's not my fault she fell for someone who can take care of her."

"Fuck you."

"What do you want with her anyway? Guilt? Wasn't your side deal a way to forget her?"

"*Our* side deal, asshole. I assume you haven't told her or she wouldn't be here."

Gavin smirked. "Assumptions don't seem like your game."

He slammed Gavin against the wall. "She's worth so much more than a conniving prick only around to take advantage. You don't even know her. What she is and what she means."

His brows mocked Jacob. Gavin peeled his fingers from his lapel. "And you do? Funny. Maybe this was never about her. Maybe it was about you getting ahead."

"And what about you?"

He shrugged and straightened his jacket. "Did it ever occur to you, Jacob, there is more to life than business? Shane is life. And yes, I fucked up, but at least I'm willing to admit my wrongdoings in order to prove to her she's worth it. When I approached you about Icarus Descending, I knew nothing about Shane personally. I had an image in my head as to what she was. Wrong, yes. But now I see her. Given your long-time relationship with her, what's your excuse?"

"What does that have to do with anything?"

"It has everything to do with it. Don't you see? People change. And Shane changed me. And you appear to be the same guy from all those years ago, still putting yourself first."

Jacob curled his hands into fists as the blood thumped in his ears. "Fuck you. You know nothing about change."

"Who did she choose?"

The question penetrated past the rage in Jacob's head. Shane didn't choose him even when he propositioned her months ago. Her hesitation. Her agreement to nothing but an *arrangement* should have set off bells in his head. Yet his fucking ego stood in the way.

"How does it feel to lose at something?"

He tapped a finger against Gavin's chest. "She is not a prize."

"Your words...and you're right, she isn't. She's meant to be treasured. Yes, I'm a bad person. *Was* a bad person. But she touched something inside. I want to be a better man. For her. Not me. Can you say the same?"

Jacob swallowed. As much as his gut told him to pummel Gavin, he wasn't incorrect with his statement. Being a better man meant more than understanding the meaning of it; it meant showing it. The last few months had swarmed around winning her back. *Winning.* Not earning her trust or love. His own needs were still put ahead of hers. Again. Suddenly, his entire life with Shane flashed before him. The shadows of his ego had prevented her from being in the light. Becoming *his* light.

"I didn't think so," Gavin said as he walked away to find the woman Jacob lost to a man no better than himself. The wrong man. No, the wrong *men*. Neither was worthy of earning her trust.

As GAVIN SWUNG the door open, he half expected Shane to be kneeling out of habit. But there she was. Standing. All the magnificent beauty in her bared face was surreal.

"Gavin…"

Striving to be a better man for her was the only way. And shedding the physical mask was the first step. He approached her. The room felt like a vacuum, sucking the air from his lungs. He wanted to tell her how he felt, a feeling he'd never shared with anyone.

"Hey," he finally said, breathing out.

Her eyes flickered over his face. "It's…" She put her hand out and he closed his eyes, her soft skin touching him. "…it's weird seeing you here without your mask."

He cupped her hand and kissed her palm. "Yeah. It is." He hugged her tightly, and she let him. He didn't want to let go. "Are you okay?"

"Just happy to see you."

He grimaced, tightening his grip at the small of her back. "You're lying."

"I *am* happy to see you."

"Nice try. There's more." He narrowed his gaze.

"How did you know?"

"You rub your lips together when there's something up."

The corner of her lip curled as her fingers grazed his jaw. Tingles shot down his body. "Watching me closely, huh?"

"Always. Tell me what's wrong."

She sighed and nuzzled into his shoulder. "It's Jacob. He's here and..." They separated. "It's hard seeing him."

He could break steel with the tension squeezing his muscles. Had she changed her mind? "What way?"

"What's going on with you two?"

"I don't like him." He clenched his jaw as he tightened his grip around her. Shane was his.

"The feeling is mutual, apparently."

"You're the one thing we have in common. I don't want you near him. You're with me now."

Her mouth dropped open as she pushed away. "We have history and work in the same industry. We're bound to run into each other."

"Exactly the reason. History. Stay away from him." He ran a hand through his hair. He'd crossed the line, but he couldn't afford for his side deals with AMG to become a news release too. One thing at a time. Video first.

"Jesus." Her hands went to her hips. "And what about Blair?"

"What about her? I told you I sent her away."

There was her lip rubbing again. Guilt slashed his insides to pieces. "I don't want to fight, please. Can we let it rest?" His voice cracked. It felt like days since he'd slept, with only hours having passed since Blair's ultimatum.

"Gavin, what's wrong?"

"We lost so much, and time is working against us."

She softened and smiled. A thumb smoothed over his eyebrow to relax the permanent crease he'd created. "We have so much of it."

If only that were true. They had less than twenty-four hours together. And he had to show her something. One thing, he hoped, would bring her back after he broke her heart. It would lay the pathway to a possible future after Blair. She deserved it even if the future didn't exist.

"There's so much to tell you. But it's hard to know where to start."

"How about the beginning," she offered.

He swallowed, the pain of revealing his past faults shutting down his heart. "Okay. Let me show you." He held out his hand.

"Where are we going?"

"To my past."

SHANE'S EYES fluttered opened as her hair moved past her shoulder. Strong fingers brushed her cheek.

"Shane, wake up."

"What time is it?" She stretched her cramped muscles.

"After one."

"How long was I out?"

"About an hour. Come."

She rubbed the sleep from her eyes and slipped her hand into his. The winter chill had picked up, and he wrapped a large coat around her. Anise and cloves crept into her nose, and any apprehension faded to calm.

"Where are we?"

A mansion spanned her sight. Several chimneys decorated the

steepled rooftop. The outside was quaint, but given the size, she knew it was anything but.

His large hand covered hers as he led her behind the house that overlooked a harbor. The inlet had frozen over, and the full moon lit the sky enough to show the vast waters creeping along the border of the property. In the dark glow of the moon, an ominous feeling slithered along her spine. Cold and empty. She tugged the coat panels tighter.

"What is this place?"

He guided them to a pier leading over the water. Once they reached the end, he leaned on the railing, letting go of her hand. A long exhale turned his breath into a mist before disappearing.

"I grew up here."

"In this house?" She gaped over the grounds of the massive estate. She placed her hand in the crook of his arm.

"I always thought Nicolette would too." His voice was weak.

"Tell me about her."

"She was my world." He stopped as his eyes glistened in the moonlight. "She was my…everything."

She only knew the elements of his past referenced in his background report, which had been laid out in black and white; she knew there was color behind his story.

Rapid heartbeats thumped through his chest when he hugged her. He was afraid. She wrapped her arms around his waist under his suit jacket.

"Her laugh. God. Her laugh was so innocent and could cut through me." Tears pooled in her eyes. "Even on the worst days, she brought me light. She loved me unconditionally. Something no one ever did."

Remaining quiet for fear he would stop, she waited. Silent support given through her stroking hands along his back.

"Nicolette," he breathed out. "She was my daughter, and I killed her."

2 4

SHANE'S BODY STIFFENED. The admission echoed in her head. *I killed her.* She flinched, ready to run, but Gavin held her close, his heart thumping through his chest as his body shook to its core.

"Please, don't run." Droplets of wetness hit the crown of her head. "Please," he begged.

"Okay...okay," she whispered. Was he capable of intentional harm?

"I was fucked up, Shane. This life you see, the house, the family, and the money. I thought"—he swallowed—"I was invincible. I had it all."

She licked her lips, tasting the salt from her tears.

"Nicolette's mother and I..." He stopped. "That was Sarah you saw at the restaurant."

"Oh..." She remembered the way Sarah's eyes had spilled tears as she shuffled to the exit.

"I didn't pick up Nicolette from her friend's house like I said I would. What kind of father forgets his own child?" he asked himself as his body shuddered involuntarily.

His eyes projected the emotions of a tortured soul. "Go on," she encouraged.

He turned to the water and gripped the railings. "I was angry with Sarah for blaming me for our problems. She was right. I wasn't ready to be a father and resented her for it. I wanted to live my life and she...*they* were holding me back. Nicolette was the only thing keeping us together."

The moonlight glittered off his damp cheeks. She could feel his pain, reliving the last time he saw his daughter. A time he'd buried away to never be spoken of.

"I was driving too fast as we fought and took a turn too quickly. The car fishtailed, and a truck came from the opposite direction and hit the back end of the car." He wailed, leaning over the iron rails. His fingers fisted the roots of his hair as if the physical pain would alleviate the emotional demons. "They said she didn't suffer. They said it was fast. And I want to believe them, I do...but my child, my baby..."

The tears became unstoppable. She cried with him as they crumpled to the ground. Her fingers glided through his silky hair as he fell against her chest. His weakened arms wrapped around her waist.

As his sobs slowed, she said, "Gavin, you can't keep beating yourself up. You've paid your penance."

He lifted his head, his eyes reflecting a gray desolation in the moonlight. "I haven't, and she would want it that way."

"No, she wouldn't. She would want you to live your life. For her. While embracing the wonderful things that bonded you, not clinging to the nightmare that ripped you apart."

"Why are you...?" His question was a whisper through quivering lips.

"What?"

"Not running away." He closed his eyes.

"Look at me. You didn't kill her. It was an accident. I can't begin to understand the magnitude of your loss. And I know you need to deal with this in your own time. But what I can do is help you see the person I see. It made you stronger and in control. You are successful and determined. Your life could have taken a different spin." His eyes softened. "And had it not been for your past..." She paused. "I might not have met you."

Her heart squeezed at the thought. What if she'd never met him? Even though he still had secrets, she would view them as discoveries meant to understand a person, not condemn them.

The cold concrete dug into her knees, the discomfort insignificant when compared to the torment he was going through. She grabbed his face and wiped the wet tears. Tenderly, her chilled lips grazed his, still stiff and unyielding. She coaxed him, and he melted into the gentle slant of her mouth.

She could feel the moment he let go. A sweet connection bound them together. This man was broken, and she would heal him. She showed him acceptance with each swipe of her tongue, telling him he would survive this with her help.

As he slid her into his lap, his hand fisted her hair. Finally, he broke the kiss and settled his face against her neck.

"Thank you," he whispered an exhalation of peace.

THE BUZZING of an alarm woke Shane, and she quickly silenced it. As the light filtered through the curtains, she found Gavin still sleeping, his arm slung over his tortured, beautiful face while the other hand lightly fisted the sheet. His brow furrowed, twitching at whatever dream had him.

She removed the comforter and padded out of the bedroom with her phone. The display read nine o'clock. A later time than usual, but time much needed to settle down from the evening prior. She dialed David's number.

"Doll. Where are you?" he asked. Steady typing on his computer continued through the receiver.

"I'm home. Long night." She yawned.

"Right. Sure." His business-like tone forced her to cut to the chase.

"What's going on?"

The keystrokes stopped. She winced. "Nothing, Shane."

"Okay, I was *doll* a minute ago, and now I am my formal first name. You're mad." She scooped grounds into the coffee maker and removed two mugs from the cabinet.

"Of course, I'm mad. And worried. Is he with you?"

"Yes," she sighed. "And if it makes you feel any better, he told me about his past."

He let out a whistle. "Okay, so what did he say?"

"I can't tell you."

"What? Seriously?"

"You need to understand, it's not my story to tell. I can't share it. Not yet."

A frustrated sound escaped him. "Jacob called for you."

"God, what did he want?"

"Don't sound so disappointed. He said to call him. Something happen? You never take a tone with him."

"He overstepped last night." She pinched the bridge of her nose as she leaned back against the counter. "If he calls again, tell him I don't want to speak to him. He'll know why."

"Will do, boss," he said shortly.

"Excuse me?"

"You've changed, Shane. What is it with you? It's like you've lost your ever-loving mind. But whatever, you know where I stand with all of this," he chirped.

Her chest tightened. The last thing she wanted was a lecture. Slamming down the carton of creamer, she said, "Look, David. I love you more than anything, and *if* I could share this, I would. Give me time, okay?"

A long pause. "Fine. What are you doing today?"

"Thank you. Please rearrange my meetings. If it can wait till Monday or Tuesday, make it happen."

The clicking of his mouse indicated he was searching her agenda. "Doesn't look like anything is pressing. What about Mr. Compelling?" The smart-ass comment didn't escape her.

"I'll wake him and have him call Tasha to figure it out." She poured the coffee over the creamer. "I love you."

"Put the pouty lip away. I can feel it over the phone."

She smiled. "Come over tonight after work?"

"Only if you promise to drop the crazy act and tell me what the hell is going on."

"Okay. I promise."

She killed the call and flipped through her missed messages. Three from Jacob this morning. She groaned, tossed the phone onto the counter, snatched the coffee, and headed to the bedroom.

She stood over Gavin as his breathing remained slow and deep. He'd shifted to his stomach, exposing his wide, muscular back. An arm was slung around her pillow as he dozed soundly. Handsome and peaceful. A rare moment.

She set the steaming cups on the nightstand and climbed back into bed. She knew she should wake him, but given the hard evening, she waited a little longer. They had driven back in near silence, and she invited him to stay. He didn't protest.

They had simply fallen into a deep sleep as he held her tightly as if he feared she would slip away in the night. It felt wonderful to be needed, something she hadn't experienced in a long time. It was wonderful to finally be there for someone.

Her pulse quickened. She'd fallen for him. Hard. But did she love him?

Her fingers swept along his furrowed brow and tears threatened as she relived the story of Nicolette. She couldn't imagine the feeling of losing a child, especially because of one's own mistakes.

As she smoothed her palm down the side of his torso, he lazily opened his bloodshot eyes. But his gaze gave way to his innermost vulnerability, something she knew no other woman had ever witnessed.

He rolled to his back, took her hand, and pulled her on top of him, not saying a word or breaking eye contact. She straddled him. His fingers brushed along the side of her face.

"You are so beautiful. I can't explain how you make me feel," he whispered, pulling her forehead to meet his. "I've never..."

"Shhh. It's okay. I'm here."

"Kiss me, Shane. I need to taste you. I want to feel it all." She met his lips. His hands stroked her back as his tongue licked the inside of her mouth, each pass becoming stronger with need.

Desire percolated in her veins. He moved his hands under the silk chemise. Light touches made her shudder in delight as her core melted with anticipation. His erection grew along her cleft with each pained kiss. Stripping her chemise, he wrapped her in his embrace. Warm skin to warm skin. Her back arched, and his hot mouth covered a nipple. The heat scorched the tender tip.

"More, please." Her eyes rolled back from his unapologetic torture on her flesh.

His other hand pinched the other nipple, sending lightning to her sex. Her hips undulated and her sex rubbed against his long, thick shaft, the friction causing pleasure to shoot through her.

"Take me."

He flipped her onto her back, positioning his broad body between her thighs. He ran his knuckles down her cheeks, causing her eyes to flutter open. His blue eyes were soft, like an ocean breeze, revealing a calm she'd never witnessed.

"I need you. All of you. Don't leave me." He squeezed his eyes shut.

"I won't."

His kiss became harder, and he pushed his tongue into her

mouth, licking, tasting, and swallowing her whole. His hand slid up her inner thigh, stopping where she needed him to ease her ache. He broke the kiss and secured her wrists above her head with his free hand. His eyes turned from calm breeze to carnal want, causing her skin to tingle. Gavin the Dominant appeared ready to claim what was his.

"Tell me you're mine," he gritted, slowly inserting two fingers into her wet slit.

Her mouth opened as he rubbed her inner walls with delicate precision and pressure. "I-I…"

"Tell me, Shane." The urgency in his voice betrayed his otherwise controlled appearance. The sinful torture to her bundle of nerves promised bliss as his thumb pushed her clitoris and circled.

"Gavin…I…uh…" She closed her eyes as he inserted another finger, stretching her wider. She moved her hips to meet his hand, losing thought as he moaned his appreciation of her body. One thrust. Two. Climbing to the heights of orgasm with each stroke until he stopped.

He removed his boxers with his free hand while still gripping her wrists. Their need built more as his eyes pierced into hers. He aimed the crown of his cock at her opening and waited.

"Yes, please."

"I need to know. Tell me."

"Take me, please," She twisted out of his hold and grabbed for his hips. He reestablished her wrists over her head.

"Do you want this?" He pushed in an inch. Perspiration glistened on his chest.

Pure, agonizing bliss flushed her body. "So much."

"Do you want *me*?" He slid out, leaving a void desperately needing to be filled. He ran his large palm along her neck, holding it firmly in place, sending a lightning bolt to her stomach. "Open your damn eyes."

He applied the slightest pressure around her neck. Catching

her breath, she opened her eyes as he slowly pushed in an inch. Her pussy clenched with her need to feel the fullness of his cock.

"Yes, Gavin. I want *you*."

"Then fucking tell me." He left her empty again.

Sweat beaded on his forehead, a sign he hung on by a thread. She controlled the switch. All she had to do was obey. His gaze, harsh and powerful, claimed her mind.

Her body trembled as she attempted to push her hips against him, but he held her still. His implacable determination, his mere presence, and his unbelievably hard body made her want to submit it all to him. The trust he'd bestowed in her last evening was a gift she wouldn't take for granted.

She tore her wrists from his grasp to touch his face. "I want it all. I want your love, your life, your trust. I am yours," she breathed out in a rush.

He thrust in to the hilt with such force she screamed while he groaned from the relief of being wrapped by her wet core.

"God, Shane." He rolled his hips as the air continued to leave her body. Letting go of her throat, he spread her thighs wider. "Fuck...So. Fucking. Deep. Say it again," he growled.

"I'm yours."

He pummeled her over and over. Any shred of restraint gone. "You. Are. Mine." He spoke through clenched teeth, claiming her, his balls slapping her buttocks with each hard plunge of his glorious cock.

At his words, she let herself go. *You are mine.* Her stomach knotted from the pleasure of his cock rubbing the bundle of nerves he hit with each thrust. She tensed around the sweet invasion. Her vision blurred as the fog rolled in. The white behind her eyes took her from the reality of what surrounded them.

"You want to come for me, baby?"

He found her clit and pushed, sending her into oblivion. She screamed his name as he continued to chase his release. Groaning, his body stiffened, hands squeezing her thighs so tight they would surely mark her. Hot jets of come filled her endlessly, searing her insides as though he'd branded her. Claiming her as his.

He shuddered and toppled over her, perspiration from his neck and face mixing with hers, both breathing heavily as he nudged her nose with his. He moved a strand of sweat-soaked hair from her brow as he gazed into her eyes.

"I love you, Shane. No matter what, please know I love you."

SHANE PUSHED a brush through her hair, and thoughts swarmed as she sat at the vanity in her room. Gavin had come so far overnight, revealing the dark past haunting him. And she loved him for telling her. He'd finally brought something to the table they could build upon. However, she was haunted by his caveat: *No matter what.*

The room chilled, and she closed the robe around her. Maybe he had more secrets, things he felt she couldn't live with. There was no doubt it would be a complicated relationship at first, and she wanted to believe they could get through it.

Gavin's voice echoed from the home office as she padded across the living room. She followed the deep timbre of his voice.

"Yes, it's done…where tonight…?"

She leaned on the doorjamb. As he faced the windows, his body flexed taut beneath a white collared shirt and dark gray pants. His face was in his hand, until he ran his fingers through his hair.

"Fine. I'll see you there." He ended the call and turned. Placing the phone in his pocket, he met her halfway. His knuckles grazed her cheeks as he set a hard, chaste kiss on her lips.

"Are you okay?" she asked.

He backed away, hands falling to his sides. Blue eyes

searched hers, and his jaw tightened. She could swear a glimmer of fear flashed quickly across his eyes. "Yeah."

"Who was that?"

A line formed between his wide lips. His eyes creased with worry. Hesitation thick around them. She grabbed her middle to ward off the spinning gut, waiting for his answer. "It was Blair."

Her heart fell to her stomach to be met by boiling heat. "What? You're going to see her?"

"Can you sit?" He touched her arm, and she flinched.

"Why the fuck are you going to see her?"

"I'll explain if you sit."

"No. You better 'fess up before...before..." She curled her hands, fingernails cutting half-moons into her palms.

"The video, Shane. She has it."

"W-what...*our* video?! The one you promised would be safe?"

He caught her as dizziness set in, leading her to the office chair. He knelt, eyes bloodshot and filled with worry. "Yes. And I'm going to get it back. I promise."

"Is this some sick game? How did she...?"

"I fucked up. I was careless, and I'm sorry."

She slapped him, and his neck twisted. A defined red mark blushed along his cheek.

He swallowed and paused. "I need you to listen. I love you, and I will protect you. She stole it from my office at The Resort. She's asking for thirty days and—"

"Thirty days? For what?" His brows knotted, and his mouth opened. "You're fucking kidding me." She pushed up and spanned the room, shaking in anger. "You're not seriously considering this."

"I have no choice. I'm doing this for you. I can't let this get out. It'll ruin you."

Trembling hands met her face. Hot tears fell from her eyes.

He was serious. "It's that easy, huh? What kind of power does she have over you? And you promised this video would be safe."

He gripped her shoulders. "I know. Shane, you know I'm fucked up. I ju—"

"Don't touch me." His hands went up in surrender, and all she could see was red. The color of war and personal protection surrounding her heart. A fever poured over her like lava, burning away the façade she'd been living in. He stood there, a worn version of the strong man she thought he was. Everything was clear for the first time.

"Fucked up doesn't even begin to explain it. That video was supposed to be private. You swore it would be. And I denied my gut because I wanted to *trust* you. I gave that to you." He flinched, but she held her ground. She straightened to a height of power she'd lost a few months ago. Strength backed her voice as she said, "That recording better be in my hands today. Do you understand? Today. And this..."—she stepped forward—"...is fucking over."

25

GAVIN IMPATIENTLY TAPPED his fingers on the bar as he looked at his watch. 5:37. She was late.

Seeing Shane's face today, the hurt he'd caused, shattered him. She deserved better, and he was a fucking coward. Now he'd never have her. But at least he could still save her.

A spicy vanilla scent wafted through the air. A seductive scent used to draw in men and suffocate them with her power. *Blair.*

"Gavin," she whispered in his ear.

He closed his eyes to keep his stomach from tossing his lunch. "Blair."

She removed her coat and hung it on the back of the stool.

"Don't look so happy to see me. I'll have a red wine, please," she ordered from the bartender.

"Let's get to it."

"Always so brooding. Do you ever smile?" The bartender set her wine down and she sipped the blood colored liquid.

For him to win her over, he needed to seduce her. Make her feel charmed and light on her feet. He did a once-over, seeing her in a low cut, see-through top and mini skirt. His insides crawled. He could do this. "It's over. With Shane."

She leaned back on her stool, and her red painted fingernails tapped lightly on her crossed arms.

"What is it about her?"

"There's nothing about her. She's temporary. *Was* temporary." He cringed.

"I was temporary. You've been spotted all around town with her. Seems a little more than a short-lived fuck."

"We work together. Of course, we'd be seen together."

"Perhaps. But the way you demanded to have the evidence back was a different kind of fire than your normal animalistic vibe I've seen. You love her."

Love. Her use of the word belittled its meaning. Her tone crawled all over him like an allergic reaction.

"We can't have that, now can we?"

"Get to your point, Blair."

"So, you say it's over..." She reached out, and he took her wrists.

"I'm sorry for what happened."

She scoffed. "Since when did apologies become part of your repertoire?"

"Since Shane."

Her upper lip curled. "I thought you said it was done."

In reality it was, but in his heart, he couldn't let go. "Is this what you want? A man who loves someone else? Thirty days will only draw out the inevitable." Her green eyes flicked over him, and a moment of softness crossed over them. "I understand what I did was wrong. Even if we had an agreement, I didn't consider how your limits might have changed."

"Stop." She closed her eyes.

"I'm telling you I'm sorry."

An actual tear slipped out of one eye. He was shocked to see she was capable of one.

"Where's the video? Let's walk away from this unscathed and

move on. You're an attractive woman. There are plenty of men who will treat you better than I will."

She grabbed his face. Muscles tensed throughout his body. She looked as though she would agree.

"Just one…"

"One wh–?"

She moved in and placed her lips on his. He remained stock still as his stomach turned. He pushed her shoulders.

"It's over…"

The calmness in Blair sent tingles down his spine as she rose quietly from the stool, flung her coat over her arm and snatched the phone from her clutch. "You want the video back?"

A sigh of relief pushed out of his nose. "Yes. Thank you."

She sighed with an oomph sound. "I get it, Gavin. I'm like you, only female."

"What?"

"You were right. Thirty days would've never worked." She tapped the screen then tossed the device in her purse.

"You'll see; it's better this way."

Her venomous smile returned. "We are so much alike. The way we still fight even when things don't go our way. You're right; it feels better already."

His phone dinged, and he viewed the incoming text. It was from her. "What did you do?"

"Cut my losses. Have a nice life." She blew him a kiss on her way out.

He opened the message and clicked the link. A webpage opened, and the video of Shane and him at The Resort played.

THE SCREEN of Jacob's phone lit up when he checked his notifications. No answer from Shane. Three messages and several hours later, he'd zoned in and out of the meeting. Rex Peyton, a global super star, having achieved number one chart status twenty-one times, was about to sign his entire catalog and future albums to AMG.

"What's the contingency plan if Rex doesn't sign?"

Jacob blinked. The chairman of the board and several other AMG executives stared from their conference chairs.

"He'll sign," Jacob said.

"Not what I asked," the chairman went on. "What is plan B? I'll remind you, this deal is in your annual forecast and will either keep us ahead or Omega will pass us."

The name of Shane's company stung. *Maybe her company should pass us for a change.* Well, that thought had never crossed his mind before.

He cleared his throat. "He will sign."

"So, no contingency?" one of the executives asked. Gray-haired and balding with a wiry comb-over, the man was so old he could have started AMG.

"No," Jacob said.

What was the point of this discussion? And what did he care if this deal went through at all? It was the biggest of his career, and it had involved several years of grooming to get Rex Peyton to take the offer. He should he elated. But the hole in his chest could never be filled by business. Not anymore. Could it ever? It had been the fuel toward some unattainable goal. When would the obsession to be the best end?

Jacob scanned the room as the chairman conducted the remaining business. The smell of leather chairs and stale coffee used to push him to a non-existent finish line. All this success meant nothing if personal relationships failed. He couldn't live this lie anymore. Not after violating Shane's trust in him. A lie she had no idea about.

He stood and walked out of the meeting. The conversation died before he could get to the glass doors.

"Mr. Andrews," the chairman called.

Jacob didn't halt. He pushed through the doors on his way to a fresh start.

JACOB'S ASTON MARTIN squealed to a halt in front of Shane's sky-rise. Shane spun out of the revolving doors, body wrapped in a red cape, and light brown waves blowing in the breeze from under a white knitted cap.

He hopped out the car. "Shane!"

She looked up from her phone, saw him, and then walked in the opposite direction.

"Shane, wait." He sprinted forward.

"We have nothing to say." The heels of her shoes stopped clicking, and she turned to him. "Don't you get it?"

That stung. "There are things you need to know before you move on this."

Her hand went to her hip. "Move on this? Please leave me alone." She turned, and his hand touched her shoulder.

"Hear me out, please." He held his breath as her lips rubbed together.

"Fine. But this is the last time."

Her heels clicked next to him as they walked to the car. Once inside, he turned to her as his heart raced. Her blue eyes held irritation as her arms crossed.

"I'll make this quick." He gripped the steering wheel. "I get you are with Gavin. I fucking hate it, but I understand why you didn't choose me."

"You do?"

"I'm a fucking ego-chasing businessman, Shane. Made my

life the priority instead of you. It finally sank in why I lost you. I get it. You should have been first and the thought of me being without you fucking kills me. But I can't let you be with a man choosing to hide behind his deceit."

"Who? Gavin?" She tensed.

"And me…" His fingers ran through his hair as his throat dried. His hands became damp, and even with the winter chill seeping through the car, the windows fogged from the heat of his body.

"What are you talking about?" She blinked.

"I'm telling you this because I want you to make the right choice even when this will sever us forever. I will lose you, but I won't lose you to another man piling rocks over his bed of lies."

"It's over, Jacob."

"I know—"

"With Gavin. You got your wish."

He rubbed his face. The air in his lungs squeezed to escape, yet halted at her statement. "I don't understand. You left him?"

She shrugged and narrowed her eyes. "Doesn't matter. Tell me what *you* did."

The stubborn breath finally left his lungs. He'd come back to Gavin in a minute. This was about telling Shane the truth. His heart lurched to his throat. No turning back.

"I purchased Icarus Descending from Omega Records." He swallowed.

"Purchased?" she repeated evenly. "As in paid off Omega to bow out of the signing? Why the hell would you do that?"

"I became obsessed with winning them. We were so close, until your label stepped in. I found myself channeling my fucking anger and went for the jugular."

Her brows rose. "For a fucking *band*? For your bottom line?"

"Yes." Tears glistened Shane's eyes as her chin jutted out. She was trying to be strong. "I still blamed you for us being apart when, deep down, it was me. The whole time. My fucking pride ruined us."

She swiped the falling tears with a gloved hand. Her face fell with her heart. "And what does Gavin have to do with this?" she whispered.

"He's the one I paid off."

A long breath escaped from Shane's mouth, fogging the windows. "Wow. I know how to pick 'em."

Jacob's phone dinged, and he fished it out of his pocket. Rapid texts from colleagues barraged through, the sounds filling the small space. He muted it and tucked it away. It could wait.

"Don't blame yourself. You are wonderf—"

Springing forward, she unloaded. "Don't tell me how wonderful I am. If you believed your words, our business relationship would have had boundaries like our fucking relationship did. Don't you see, Jacob? Boundaries are made to protect people. And it's apparent I gave you none. I trusted you. Even when we weren't together, I *trusted* you. Thought you were an upstanding man who would never do anything to hurt me even though we were apart."

Every word hit like a hammer to his chest. The warranted verbal attack shredded his armor, piece by piece, leaving him vulnerable to feel her words cut.

Her phone rang, and she dug it from her clutch. She silenced the incessant ringing. "I have to go."

His breast pocket vibrated, and he fished the phone out again. *Ten missed calls.* He flicked the text string, stopping on one. The blood drained from his face. The door clicked open, and he grabbed her arm. "Shane, wait."

She shrugged out of his grasp. "Get off. I have *business* to take care of. Ethical business. And stay the hell out of my life." Her heel hit the pavement, and the door slammed in his face. He clicked the link inside the text from his assistant, Liza. An internet site opened, and what he saw lit the fire in his heart. *That son of a bitch!*

He leapt from the car and hollered, "Shane, stop!" She was on her phone and halted a few yards away.

Jogging to her, he heard, "What, David? Slow down...the video is what...?" The phone crashed to the ground, and Jacob caught her.

"Shane!"

EACH BLINK CREATED a fine sand paper scrape over Shane's dry eyes. She stared blankly at the ignored texts and voicemails from Gavin.

G: Shane, call me, please.

G: I am so sorry.

G: This wasn't supposed to happen. Please answer my calls.

Her hand swirled the clear liquid inside a rocks glass. *Over, over, over.* It was all over. Her work, her heart, her reputation. And for what? One night in a club, getting off with a traitor? One goddammed decade of trusting a lying asshole? A lifetime of hard work? *Over.*

The warm liquid drowned her spinning thoughts. Mumbles from the kitchen struck like a knife in her heart. Why was Jacob here? David came from around the corner and sat.

"How you holding up, doll?" She raised her glass. He filled it. "Yeah. Stupid question."

She slouched against him. "I'm so sorry, David."

"There is nothing to be sorry about."

"You told me to be careful. And now...if I had listened." Tears formed in her eyes. A blurry image of Jacob appeared in front of her. Exhaustion replaced by burning rage thrummed in her veins. "Get. Out." The grunt came out so vicious Shane swore she would spit venom.

"I can't," he said.

"What's going on?" David asked.

"You don't belong here, Jacob. Fucking leave." She shoved the glass against David's chest and stood.

"I won't."

Stubborn fucking mule. When she needed him, he was gone. Now she wanted him gone, and he stayed. Time to draw the boundaries. Shane never understood what people meant by seeing red. Now she did. A spark of heat spread from chest to fingers. A jolt of energy at the sound of his support so furious, she lunged forward. Arms swinging, she made contact with his chest. He shuffled back.

"Get out! Get the fuck out!"

"Shane!" David yelled.

"No, let her," Jacob responded, pushing forward to close the gap. "Hit me, please. I deserve it."

Her hand flew across her body and landed on his cheek, the force of the blow resonating from her hand all the way to her shoulder. The crack of the contact was drowned in the sound of her voice.

"Shut up! Get out! I can't…I fucking can't…You did this. You made this happen!" Her voice became hoarse on her last words and Jacob gripped her wrists and turned her body, hugging her close. She strained and wailed loudly as her sobs overtook her panicked breaths. Heart hammering thuds against her chest pained her. "Stop… let…go…" She fought as Jacob squeezed harder. She tried to kick behind her, and he lifted her off the ground.

"Stop, Shane. Stop…I'm so sorry." Her boneless knees gave out, and she crumbled to the floor.

"Jacob…" David said, kneeling next to her.

"Can you give us a minute?"

"But..."

"Please." Jacob must have made a face because David nodded and left.

Shane fought to release her wrists, but his hands gripped harder. "Leave...me...alone..."

"I'm not leaving you."

"I don't want your help. Why are you here?" She shuddered in his arms.

"I won't walk away this time. You had no support when your father died. And I refuse to let you deal with this alone. I left you once; I'm not doing it again."

"Helping won't make me forgive you. You did this, all of it. Had the deal never occurred, I would have never pursued Gavin to get information and maybe..."

His chest expanded and fell. His cheek pressed against the wetness of hers. Her heart shattered as if the world crumbled around them on the floor. "And if I hadn't left you all those years ago, the video wouldn't have been made. Maybe you would still have an unbroken heart. I would go back and change it all. Every last bit." He squeezed and rocked her exhausted body for long moments. "I'm not looking for anything in return. Let me handle everything for right now, okay?"

Too exhausted to argue, she sank into his hold, sleep taking her under. But it wasn't relief at his help that she felt as she closed her eyes. It was the bottom of an abyss with no way out.

26

"DOLL…" Shane heard David as the side lamp clicked on. She squinted as the harsh light met her burning eyes. She rolled away. The bed shifted as his hand cupped her shoulder. "Honey?"

"Mmm," she managed. Was it all a bad dream?

"I made you some tea."

"I'm good." She pulled the comforter over her face, not wanting to face the day let alone the rest of the year.

"Please?"

She blinked as he moved the blanket away, too weak to stop him. His handsome face was full of sorrow and pity. Not a dream. The video had gone viral, hitting all the major news outlets and social media sites in the world.

Her life was over, her career gone, everything she'd worked for taken by a man who blurred reality and fantasy. Was anything Gavin said sincere? She shifted to sit. The hot cup warmed her palms. At least she could still feel something.

"Is Jacob still here?"

"Yes." Falling onto his back, he put his arm behind his head and crossed his ankles. "He's bound and determined, that man. He'll make it right."

She set the cup on the nightstand and held her head in her hands. The dull headache refused to leave.

What the hell happened? A fog flooded her mind. She removed the comforter and made her way to the adjoining bathroom, trying to come to grips with her unraveling life.

She winced at her gray reflection. Yanking her hair up with a hair tie, she splashed water on her face as David appeared in the doorframe.

"How bad is it?" She patted her face with a towel. The tears started again when his mouth tightened. "So my life is over," she said matter-of-fact.

She returned to her living grave, face-planting into the pillows. Her chest tightened as the magnitude of the scandal sank in. She'd spent a lifetime becoming a successful and respected businesswoman. Now she might be viewed as a slut by all her associates. He rubbed her back, silently giving support. She wiped her nose on the sheet.

"What do we know?"

"That's what we're trying to figure out. Jacob's been relentless, trying to find out how this got out and how to stop it. He hasn't slept all night, calling in all kinds of favors." She cringed at his name. "What's up with you two? I've never seen you unleash like that before."

"He and Gavin paired up to take Icarus Descending from Omega."

"They *what*?"

"Jacob paid Gavin off so he would bow out. What is it with him?" Hot tears welled again.

"I'm gonna fucking kill him." David started to spring out of bed, but Shane snagged the sleeve of his magenta sweater.

"No don't. Let him do…whatever he is doing."

"But Shane. What the fuck?" The mattress bowed when he settled back down.

"I don't know. Strangely enough, it's the least of my worries." Humiliation washed over her. "Did Jacob see the video?"

He nodded. "Not sure how much of it, but he did. He wants to kill Gavin. He better watch his back."

Jacob's protectiveness didn't surprise her, but the humiliation ran deep. No lover should ever see someone with another person, especially the way she'd been with Gavin.

"He knows it was him. Jacob found out at the club."

"Yeah, I figured as much when I told him and he didn't seem taken aback by it." He rolled to his side. "Fucking coward. Of course, Gavin would be protected in all of this with his mask still on in the video. Why would he do this?"

"My job," she said confidently. Anger swept through her like a wildfire. All the things she tried to deny before were now coming to the surface. She should've listened to her gut. She buried her face in her pillow. "Fucking asshole! He took it all!" She screamed until her throat burned.

"Shhh, doll. Let it out."

───────────

"A LIE MAY TAKE care of the present, but it has no future."

Jacob stared aimlessly at the blue and white paper he had collected from the fortune cookie when he and Shane had dinner. He should have taken it as a sign to be honest before asking her to consider a second chance. Hell, he should have never agreed to the fucking Icarus deal in the first place. He tossed it aside and rubbed his tired eyes.

A light rap on the door caused him to stand. "Come in."

David entered with a fresh cup of coffee. "Thought you could use some fuel."

"Thanks." He took it and they sat, him at the helm and David on the couch against the wall.

"So, how does it feel to betray the one you love? I thought you were different."

"I'm not," he said. He buried his face in his hand, the chair creaking when he leaned back.

"No, you're not. But what are you going to do about it?"

He sighed, setting the cup on the desk. "I don't know. All I can do is help the current catastrophe. The video's out there, and the media's all over it. My IT guy at AMG has a team scouring the internet to rip it from any sites. I should've protected her. Now and back then. Things would be different now. She would have her reputation and her job."

"And you."

"If it hadn't happened this way, I would've found a way to lose her anyway. God, how could I be so stupid?"

"Stupidity has nothing to do with it. Ignorance might be a better word."

The glare over David's glasses cut through him.

"Yeah. And selfishness. The list goes on for miles. But I can't sit here and roll in my self-pity. She needs help cleaning this up, or at least minimizing it."

"Will she lose her job?"

He slouched back. "I know John Talbot, and he doesn't take well to personal scandal in the workplace. He won't let this action affect his reputation or the label's, even though it wasn't Shane's fault."

"Could you talk to him?" David's eyes glittered with hope.

"I'm trying. Left several messages to reach him. I would bet until he goes through the entire investigation, he's unsure what the board's action will be."

"Investigation? She's not a criminal!" David screeched.

Jacob stood to pace the room. "I know, but this is how things are done. It's business. Shane could...*will* lose everything she built."

"And Gavin? There's no way to prove it was he in the video. He gets off scot-free? What the hell?"

"As it stands, it's his word against hers. If the decision was made today, yes, he would walk away unscathed. Probably be appointed as the interim CEO given his industry track record and involvement in the business."

"Jacob, please. She won't be able to handle this. What can we do?"

He sat next to David and placed a hand on his shoulder. "All we can do is be there for her. Help her through it."

"Shane said he did it to get her job."

"Seems about right." He sat back, laying an arm across the seat back. Their time working together on the Icarus Descending deal floated through his mind. It all made sense why Gavin was so eager. "And he would do anything as a means to get it. Where is she?"

He tilted his cup to finish the last drop of java. "She's in the shower. Trying to scrub off the last twenty-four hours." He stood to leave and faced Jacob. "I hate what you did to her, but I hate what Gavin did more."

"Yeah, but the lesser crime isn't any more bearable for her."

"I know." David pursed his lips. "Whatever you're doing… keep doing it. She needs you even if she doesn't think so."

"Thanks." Jacob's phone rang, and he glanced at the screen. His gut twisted. "I need to take this."

David nodded solemnly and shut the door behind him.

"John."

"Mr. Andrews," John Talbot said. "My assistant said you were anxious to get a hold of me."

"Yes, sir. Thank you for your call."

"Is this concerning the recent news about Shane Vaughn?" John was known for cutting to the chase.

"Yes." Jacob plopped in the chair. "I'll get to the point. Are you considering letting her go?"

"Confidential information cannot be shared with our main competitor, Jacob."

"Indeed. But off the record, John, you and I have known each other for a long time. This conversation will remain between us."

"Why are you so interested in what happens other than finding an angle to play for AMG?"

"Because…" His mind tugged apart. Admitting he was still in love with the Omega's CEO would ruin his career and was bound to end Shane's. "The recording showed her in a very private moment."

"It did. I don't like personal scandal in the workplace. You know this. The last CEO was let go because of his sexual involvement with top musicians and employees. I won't stand for it again."

"But the release of the video happened to Shane *unknowingly*. For all we know, it could have been used as revenge porn. What happened to showing support to an employee and top executive? You wouldn't want to ruin Omega's reputation of standing behind their employees and musicians by letting her go."

A chair creaked and silence fell on the line. "How do you know she wasn't aware?" A small waiver of concern swaddled John's words.

"Because I know her. She would never let that happen…" He paused as his heart hammered against his ribs. The fortune stared at him from where he'd left it. *Tell the truth.* The truth would end it all even though his intentions were meant to help Shane's career. "I love her, John. And we have…"

"Been together? Fraternizing with the competition is grounds for removal, Mr. Andrews. Perhaps Icarus Descending wasn't an accident."

Sweaty palms left a hand mark on the desktop as he stood to

pace the room. "I understand what it looks like, sir. But Icarus wasn't her doing. Trust me."

"You know more than you are sharing. Give me one good reason why I shouldn't have her ejected from my organization purely on the grounds she is sleeping with you."

A sickening thought flashed before him. It was the only way. He cleared his throat. "John, Shane is innocent. I'm the one involved in the Icarus Descending deal with another one of your employees."

"Who?"

"You'll find out soon enough. This about Shane right now."

"This is about the integrity of my company," he said harshly.

"I agree, sir. But the important piece for survival is holding onto Shane. She has sacrificed her life for your business and will continue to if you stand behind her."

"Humor me, Mr. Andrews. Why? Because your attempt at saving her is making my decision pretty clear. This is a serious corruption of business."

Exhaustion ran rampant through Jacob's body. His hand shook as he held the phone. "In exchange for keeping her, I will leave my position at AMG." Sweat rolled down his back as he stared out into the city. As much it pained him to leave AMG, she deserved her job more.

"You are the most successful CEO in the industry. Shane is close behind, yet could never overcome your chart-topping deals."

"She could have with the Icarus deal." The assumed revenue numbers flashed in his head. Omega would have edged by, especially with landing Ryan Digmore as well. "Without me at AMG, Omega will take the top spot. With your talent pool, it will continue to grow. Unless you lose the best thing you have... Shane. You know this is a solid trade, John."

The silence was deafening. His legs weakened, and he leaned against the window.

"Do you know how long I've been married to my wife, Jacob?"

His brows twitched at the softening in John's question. "Uh, no, sir."

"Forty-three years. Do you know how long I've been in this business?"

"About the same?"

"Longer. My entire life. My wife and I had our struggles, marrying young, creating a family, all while I climbed the ladder. There were some scary moments where I allowed my business life to overshadow my personal one. She always kept me in check." He paused. "It wasn't until I almost lost her that I woke up. You see, Jacob, dominating the industry was my first love. Being the best. My wife always took the back seat. It was almost too late before I realized my priorities were misaligned. You are ahead of your time."

He swallowed the lump in his throat. "Why are you telling me this?"

"I've never witnessed sacrifice like this. Especially in this grueling industry. I can't make any promises, but you've given me a lot to consider."

Unease mixed with relief fled his veins as he nearly crumbled to the floor. "Thank you, John."

"I'll be in touch."

Jacob leaned his forehead on the cool window, tamping down the heat radiating from him. Maybe Shane had a chance. He breathed deep to stop the nausea. His decision to tell John of his involvement could end up earning Shane a spot on the unemployment line with him. He wiped the tears falling from his eyes. But it was worth it. She was worth it.

SHANE ROLLED OVER, curled up in her bed, the sheer curtains shading the darkness. What time was it? She'd received a phone call from John Talbot letting her know she was officially on leave from the company with instructions to report tomorrow for a discussion with the board. He called it a leave of absence, but firing her was inevitable.

She gripped her pillow as tears flowed. How could she produce anymore? Sorrow pained her body as though someone had died. Wiping her nose on the fisted sheet, she shriveled from the shame she'd caused herself, her family, and her colleagues. Her career was dead, and putting back the pieces was not an option.

Her phone pinged, and she snaked an arm from the covers.

AM: You crazy bitch. Call me! xx

Anna Marie's British accent played in her head as she read the words on the screen. Surely, she meant to send it to another Shane. She could never face her musicians again. Even the drama-filled crazy ones like Anna Marie.

She threw on a robe and dragged the zombie-like version of herself to the kitchen. She flicked on the burner and set up some tea. Floral chamomile scents wafted to her nose as the bag settled into a cup.

The quiet apartment helped her thoughts to wind down to a whisper. *You can do this. Think of it as a new beginning.* Her phone pinged in her robe.

G: I'll never be able to fix this. But know I am so sorry.

Gavin. Even his attempt at an apology made her nerves jump. Why continue barraging her with texts and phone calls when he got what he wanted? A whistle startled her. The water was ready, and she poured it. She shuffled to the couch, covering her chilled body with a blanket. The opened curtains allowed her to drift into the pin dot taillights of the cabs below. She had become a part of the never sleeping city.

She clicked her phone screen to brave the outside world. How bad was it? Knowing how large the scandal went would only help her prepare for tomorrow's meeting. A few swipes and taps and Google presented her with the news.

Who is the masked man?

How could a successful woman allow abuse?

Shane Vaughn, an example of what men in power will do to a woman.

She's a sham.

Abuse? A sham? Nausea was her new friend as she emotionally cut through the opinions of others. But maybe they saw something she didn't. Her entire life was driven by other people. Her success came only from the circumstances propelling her. Somewhere along the way, when she left Austin, Texas, she lost her purpose.

Flicking through the other search pages a headline appeared:

Jacob Andrews Silently Leaves AMG.

"What?" Her body went ramrod straight, hot tea slipped down the sides of her cup. "Ow, shit!"

While the rest of the music world has been wrapped up in the Omega Records scandal, a spokesperson from AMG recently confirmed Jacob Andrews' departure from the world renowned rock label. There was no clarification behind the reason for the resignation other than it was 'sudden and unexpected.'

The spokesperson said, "We value the work Jacob

Andrews has put forth for AMG and are sad to learn of his departure."

She frantically scrolled through other articles, all reporting the same thing. A warmth spread in her heart followed by stabbing hurt from his betrayal. The phone slipped into her lap as she revisited the early morning world outside her windows. Making plans for her future came first for a change.

JACOB GLANCED AT HIS WATCH. The two o'clock hour was a stand-still in time. His former employees at AMG insisted they would continue scouring the internet and remove any remaining links to Shane's sex tape. There was nothing left to do. Shane would suffer the backlash at her upcoming meeting, and the only thing he could do was pray she would be okay. John had assured him he'd take appropriate action per Jacob's confession. Jacob immediately resigned from his post and hoped it would be enough to save her.

Rolling his shoulders, he rose from the desk. As he rounded the corner into the kitchen, sniffles and a deep breath startled him. Two more steps and he found Shane on the couch huddled in a blanket, overlooking the city.

"Shane?"

She jumped and wiped her nose on a tissue with one hand. A teacup was perched on her bent knees. "Shit, Jacob. I thought you were gone."

"I was just leaving. Sorry for scaring you. Are you—" Stopping his words, he stepped toward the door, an ache growing in his heart. He wanted to run to her.

"Why did you quit your job?" He heard her before his hand touched the knob. He swallowed.

"It doesn't matter."

"If it doesn't matter, then tell me why."

He spun on his heel. Tired, swollen blue eyes pleaded. Even with her hair piled high in a messy bun, no make-up, and a reddened nose, she still stunned him.

"It's late and you need rest."

"Jacob." She exhaled. "This is really hard because I hate you right now, but David's gone home and...can you sit for a minute?" Shoving his hands in his pockets, Jacob shuffled over and sat. "Tell me why you left AMG."

"It was time."

"Bullshit. It would never be time," she scoffed.

He leaned forward and rubbed his palms. "I was CEO for all the wrong reasons."

She skeptically peered over the rim of her cup as she sipped. "Please. It's everything you've always wanted. You told me so the night we first met in Austin."

"A young punk kid will always believe success, money, and fame will get you everything in life. Here I am, mid-thirties, and it turns out that punk kid was wrong."

"How?"

"Wanting to be the best never ends, Shane. Ever. There's always another mountain to climb, another competitor to beat; it's sprinting toward no finish line. And look what it made me do. I fucked with your business. And for what?"

She looked down into her tea, rubbing her lips together. "When you set your mind to something, it can't be stopped. Always number one."

"No kidding." He leaned back and gazed at the ceiling. He rubbed his temples. *Always number one, all right. An A1 asshole.*

"But... I finally came out on top. Literally. Your news came in second on the most viral topics of the week." She waved her phone with a sad chuckle.

"Well, there's that."

"So, what will you do now?"

"No fucking clue. What about you?"

"I could sell my tape and make enough to retire."

"Silver lining." The joke fell silent as she scanned the city, the dim lighting framing her beauty.

"Who am I, Jacob?"

"What do you mean?"

"My whole identity has been through other people. Achieving things to prove something. My career was for my dad, and after you left, I fought to prove I could make it...alone. And where did it get me? A sex tape in a club for one night of ecstasy and a lifetime of humiliation."

"No, Shane. What I saw..." He faded out, thinking about her bliss in Gavin's arms. He gripped his jeans.

"What did you see? Not that I want to discuss my sexual activities with you, but maybe... I don't know what I'm asking." She waved it off.

"Freedom, Shane. You enjoying yourself. You, well past getting over me. These last few months, I was trying to win you over when you'd already moved on."

"I wasn't..." Her lip quivered.

"What?"

"Over you. And now I don't know what I am. What I'm searching for. I feel like when I cling to something, whether you, Gavin, or my job, I become a different version of myself."

"I'm so sorry..."

"I've been running from something, and all this set me to ground zero. A place I can start over, on my terms." His heart sank and eyes stung. "What made you do it? Why go to such lengths with buying the band out?"

"Love makes us do stupid things. There are two sides to it—the festering darkness from hurt and the brilliant light of joy and vulnerability. There is no in-between. It either exists with both halves or not at all."

"Do you still love me?" Her eyes glimmered with hope. He wasn't worthy of such things.

"What? No, I..."

"Be honest. If you felt nothing, you wouldn't be here."

"Shane, what does it matter?"

She shrugged. "Maybe it doesn't, but I'm lost. Flailing into emptiness and... Forget I asked."

"Love or no love, I respect you. Knowing which one will only hold you back from finding what you're searching for. And I've proven I'm not the man to help you find it. Trust...trusting someone means trusting yourself. Do you at least have that?"

"Not anymore. I thought I did but..."

"Find a way to trust yourself, Shane, and all the other things will fall into place. And promise me you will do it without influence. Stay true to the woman inside."

"What woman? The slut who caved her empire?"

He winced. "You are not a slut. You are brilliant, smart, and fucking gorgeous. And you will come out of—"

"Rock bottom."

"Yeah."

"But what if I need someone to lead me?" She straightened, tears tracking down her cheeks. The teacup sounded on the coffee table when she set it aside. "Otherwise, I make fucked up choices and become the laughingstock of the industry. Don't you see? Only someone like you can guide me toward sound decisions. And that's why I hate you more than the lies. With one decision, you altered my world. Even from afar, your presence controlled me and now..." She sniffed. "I'm lost, and I have no idea what path is right." She covered her face and sobbed into her hands.

He went to her, drawing her to his chest. "You *can* do this. You are resilient."

"No. I'm not. I'm a shell without someone to guide me."

His body ached as her heart poured out around him into a puddle of despair. Regret racked his insides for even leading her into the lifestyle. To make her feel un-whole and unworthy of herself.

"Do you remember when you took the Promotions Director job at Omega? You were scared then, but you owned it. Brought the label into the forefront."

"You told me not to take it," she recalled.

"Yes, I did. Omega was a small rate label, buried in debt. Too much risk. But you didn't listen. You went anyway, and man, did you prove my sorry ass wrong."

She pulled away. "I took it to be with you. I knew you were primed to move to New York with AMG. It was going to happen, so I had no choice."

His heart plummeted to his feet. She'd always thought about him first. Always.

"You had a choice." He cupped her ruddy cheeks, her swollen eyes shedding waterfalls of tears.

"The only other choice was to stay in Austin and let you go."

His jaw went slack as her words entered his ears and clutched his heart. The remaining love she held, flashed in her eyes. "Jesus, Shane. Why didn't you tell me this?"

"Would it have changed things for you? Would you have put your dream on hold to be with me?"

His eyes flicked back and forth over her grieving ones. A hammer beat the walls of his chest as the question took on a life of its own. Would he have stayed? Would he have gone away without her? When she told him she'd scored the job, he never thought twice about their future. But she had. And she made the choice because his career was important to him. "I…"

"You don't have to answer. I'm not trying to put you on the spot. I need you to understand why this is so hard."

Tears constricted his throat. "I do. I really do."

He held her until his arms ached, rocking back and forth until sleep swept her under. He scooped her in his arms and carried her to bed. Laying her gently on the mattress, he covered her with blankets. She seemed peaceful, although her sleep was most likely racked with fits of stress. As though with a will of its own, his hand touched her. Soft skin pulsed under each fingertip as it ran the length of her face.

"I'm so sorry, Shane."

His lips met her hair and a bouquet of wildflowers bloomed in his nostrils.

"Find yourself, Lovely. She's in there. Even when it seemed like I wasn't looking, I saw you. And I do love you. I always will." A piercing ache stabbed in his chest. *Let her go.*

And he did. For her. A woman meant for brilliance. Someone he always cherished. She lived in his blood. And now, from afar, he would watch her become the strong person she had yet to discover.

27

SHANE PULLED her worn *Austin City Limits* sweatshirt over her head and shimmied on black leggings. Dawn had pierced the horizon when she woke. Jacob's last words continued to ring in her ears. *I do love you. I always will.*

As she tossed her wet hair in a messy bun, her phone rang.

"Hello, this is Shane."

"Have ye fallen off the face of the earth?"

She winced. "Anna Marie. Hello."

"Oi! Chaps! I'm on the phone," she yelled. A funky beat played in the background. She was in the studio recording in Los Angeles. It stopped. "Sorry, love. Ye got my messages, aye?"

"Yes. I did."

"I knew I liked you, and with this"—she whistled—"you upped your cool points." The distinct sound of her smoking a cigarette came through the receiver.

"Not sure *cool* would be the word. So you watched it."

"Aye! It was the best thing I've seen in celebrity scandals. You are on another level. I may have met my match."

Strangely, her embarrassment simmered down at Anna Marie's interesting reference to a sex scandal.

"I should mention I'm on a leave of absence from Omega, as you can imagine. So I shouldn't be talking to you."

"Oh, bloody hell. I'll talk to whoever I want. Ye need to come to LA."

"To visit? I don't think—"

"Visit? No, to stay. Live with me in my flat."

She chuckled nervously, taken aback by her invitation. Sure, they'd worked together on her albums and best PR moments, but to say they were close would be an overstatement.

"I appreciate the offer, but I live in New York. I have a life here."

A cackle sounded on the line. Apparently, Shane was clueless about her life. "Oh, darling. I'm offering ye a fresh start. Come work for me."

"Work for you?" Shane's new reputation would ruin her career.

"Come be my manager. Ye get me. And I admire your lady balls. You're a tough bird, aren't ye?"

"I suppose," she laughed. "But you *are* signed with Omega, remember? Even if I'm removed from the company, it would be a conflict of interest."

"If you leave, I leave."

"You can't be serious? Your contract is for another two albums and the advance and lost royalties alone would cost you millions."

"Listen. It'll take care of itself; Daddy has great solicitors. They can eat the effing contract."

Shane had witnessed first hand the capabilities of Anna Marie's father's legal team. They beat Omega up so bad on her contract, she'd often wondered if the label even made money.

"I don't know what to say."

Voices filtered in the background. "What? Aye, all right, I'm coming," she yelled to her band mates. "Gotta run, lovey. Think about it."

Before she could answer, the line went dead. She smiled. Anna Marie had a way about her. It strangely sparked joy to know she could fall back on something. She tossed the phone on the bed. Who was she kidding? Manhattan was her home even if it existed behind four walls.

A SNAIL MOVED FASTER than the elevator at Omega Records. She sighed, bracing her body against the brass rails. The car slowed and revealed the glass doors of her office. Once a place of pride and success. She smoothed her long ponytail through her fingers, digging deep for any residual strength to get through the board meeting...or funeral. The sandblasted engraving on the door read, Omega Records, permanently memorialized in glass and in her heart. *Yeah, definitely a funeral.*

A blast of cold air pushed over her when she entered the reception area. It was after eight p.m. A vacuum in the distance calmed her to know only the cleaning crew remained.

As she walked the otherwise quiet halls, dark and dull tones surrounded her, unlike the days, months, and years prior. She stroked the framed platinum record next to her office door. A shiver ran through her, and a deep pain struck her chest. They tormented her, haunting melodies of past hit records ringing in her ears. All gone. But not all for nothing.

Dropping her hand, she entered her office. She clicked on the light and squinted. The energy she used to feel had gone from hurricane winds to a cool winter breeze.

She grimaced. Would John tell her she could stay? Or would she be fired for misconduct? And if he kept her as CEO, would she be able to face her colleagues, talent, and employees?

She sat at her desk and gazed beyond the farthest building, the road to saving her reputation so far in the distance, she couldn't fathom the strength needed to travel it.

Spinning her chair slowly around, Shane absorbed every nook, cranny, and accomplishment displayed. Was there enough to keep her here? Was it time to let it go? She blew a breath from her nose. Either way, she'd be starting again from nothing, but which path led to the better outcome?

A knock on the door jarred her. She turned. Gavin stood, defeated and worn.

"Why are you here?" She faced the windows again. Anger percolated, and she steadied her breathing to keep her composure.

His footfalls made their way to the visitors' chairs, and he sat. "I was hoping we could talk."

"There's nothing to talk about. Did you meet with the board? Guess you got what you wanted. I'm sure John is happy to have you at the helm of the label." Her chest tightened.

"Shane, please let me explain."

She spun her chair. His eyes were sunken and red, hair slightly disheveled even though his outward appearance remained sharp and professional. Clean cut and dressed in a fine three-piece suit, he rubbed his hands together as he leaned forward. She only stared, wondering why she decided to play the game. Things would be different.

"The video wasn't supposed to be released."

"Whatever the intent was, it doesn't matter now."

His lips thinned. "You're right. But you need to know what happened." He paused. "In the beginning, I needed you to fall for me."

"For my job. Right. We've covered this."

"Yes, for your position. But when you said my motives ran deeper, I believed it. You flipped it on its side, and suddenly, it all made sense. Your submission. My dominance over you. The place where we intersect and unify." She flinched, bile threatening to rise from her stomach. "When I found out you were a member of the club, things were easy for me. I was able to get you in a place where I could use you. But I didn't think I would fall for you," he said in a rush, running his hand through his hair.

"And that makes this okay? If you hadn't fallen for me, this would have been okay?" Her voice rose as her neck flushed.

"No," he responded quickly. "It wouldn't have. But showing me your submission was the piece I was missing; it released me, helped me understand there's more to life than being alone."

"Then why release the video?" She smacked a hand on the desk.

"Blair did. It happened so fast, I couldn't stop her."

The burning behind her eyes threatened tears. "What about the thirty days?"

"Not happening. It's what sent her over the edge. By admitting I loved you, I thought she would see I wasn't the one for her. I'm so sorry, Shane. Even when I'm honest, I fuck shit up."

A small part of her wanted to forgive him. His pleading eyes and solemn voice threatened her resolve. But he'd pushed too far. Even if the video release wasn't his fault, it was his responsibility to protect it. To protect her. She'd trusted him. Would it ever stop? Would he really change? With too many questions and zero answers, she had to walk away even though it pained her.

"Honesty should happen in the beginning, not the middle or the end. You were careless and manipulative. None of it can be repaired. Even your apology will never right what happened."

She was careless, allowing the domination of other people to write her story. To choose her path.

She walked to the front of her desk, each step laying a new path to the life she was meant to lead. A life she could build on her own. She had the power. She leaned on the edge of the desk. He craned his face upward. They'd come full circle, back to the place where it all began. The only difference? She was calm, and he was cowering.

"I'm sorry, Shane."

The pain he apparently harbored from his own actions dulled his otherwise beautiful irises. Her heart stung for a moment and she softened.

"Whatever it is you're fighting against, let it go. It will only continue to hold you back." She breathed out allowing her own regrets to fall to the floor. She felt for him and hoped he would find his way. "Besides, you'll need the energy in order to run this company." She made her way to the door.

"I didn't take the job," he called after her. She halted. "I came to tender my resignation."

She whipped her head around.

"It wasn't offered, either."

Wasn't offered? "I don't understand."

"I came clean. John and the board are aware it was me in that video, and I'm the reason it was released."

The shock created a track of tears down her cheeks without sobs. She clutched her purse to her chest as her heart released the final tension she held.

"And the side deal?" she blurted. He didn't appear stunned by her question.

"Yes, they know I approached Jacob about the side deal months before he agreed to it."

"Wait...*you* approached Jacob?"

His head tilted to the side. "Yes. I approached him. He hesitated for a while before agreeing to it. Not sure what changed his mind but he did, eventually."

"I thought he came to you."

"Is that what he told you?" She nodded. "He was wrong. I'm the reason all this started in the first place."

"Yeah..." her voice faded as her heart clenched.

A cleansing breath escaped, and she exhaled the anger. She wouldn't carry the disdain she felt for Gavin or Jacob into her future. She turned toward the door and whispered over her shoulder, "Thank you."

"MR. TALBOT." Shane held out her hand and shook the hand of the chairman from across the table.

"Shane." He looked at the other board members. "Gentleman, would you mind if I had a few minutes with Ms. Vaughn?" The members nodded and left them alone.

"Sir?"

He steepled his fingers, leaning his elbows on the glossy conference table. "I can't imagine what you have gone through these last few days."

Shame washed over her as she sank into the chair. "I'm so sorry, sir. I've embarrassed your company and myself."

"It's been a tough decision to make, Shane. You know how I feel about office relations and media on personal scandal."

"Yes, sir, I do. And I understand if your decision is to let me go."

The chair squeaked as John walked to meet her on the other side. He rolled the chair out, sat down, and leaned back in the leather high back. His relaxed state alarmed her.

"Going over the decision, I tried to imagine what my daughter would feel going through this. The embarrassment and shame she might have felt and what would happen if I turned my back on her."

John never shared personal insight when it came to business

matters. She swallowed and cleared her throat. "What are you saying?"

"I would like you to stay on as CEO of Omega Records. Our PR team is working diligently to lessen this monstrosity in order to help you push forward. You made us what we are, Shane, and if I turned my back on you now, I would be no better than the men who led you here."

A tear slipped from her eye, and she swiped it. Never had she shown her weak side to this man, and his kindness overwhelmed her.

"Wait, you said *men*."

His smile warmed her. "I had an interesting conversation with Jacob Andrews. He told me about your...relationship and the Icarus Descending deal."

Warmth spread to her face as her mouth opened. "I—"

His hand went up. "I understand you have reignited a past relationship, and I don't agree with it. But his sacrifice made me think differently. It was refreshing to see him put you first."

"But we aren't...I mean we were, but it ended." Her words stuttered over her admission. A wave of understanding hit her in the gut. She raised her head from her twisted hands. "Did he step down at AMG for me?"

His smile widened, and the wrinkles around his brown eyes creased. "I'll let him tell you." He stood and walked to the door. Shane followed on boneless legs. "Welcome back, Shane."

She shook his outstretched hand. "Thank you, sir." Confusion swept over her. Everything was happening so fast. Why had Jacob done this? Whatever the reason, she was grateful. But staying at Omega would only hold her back. Confidence flowed through her blood, and she straightened. As John's hand hit the knob, she said, "Mr. Talbot?"

"Yes?"

"I want to tell you how honored I am. I truly am." She stepped forward. "But I'm going to decline."

SHANE HOPPED into a cab toward home. She snatched her phone from her purse and dialed.

"Shane?" Jacob's voice sounded anxious, yet his timbre still rumbled her stomach.

"What have you done?"

A deep exhale floated through the line. "How did your meeting go?"

"It went...fine. It was fine. You left AMG for me, didn't you?"

"Are you staying with Omega?"

"Answer the question." Her stomach fluttered as the cab floated through evening traffic.

"Yes, I did. But are you staying with Omega?"

She leaned back in the cab's seat. Her heart hammered in her chest as her skin burned hot. Jacob had sacrificed his life's work for her.

"I'm not staying, Jacob. I can't. There's too much to rebuild. I need to..." Tears flowed from her eyes. "I need to find myself, even though I feel guilty because you have nothing now."

"I have more now than I ever have. Don't worry about me. Does your choice feel right?"

"Yes." Her lip quivered.

"Then nothing else matters, Lovely." His pet name zinged from her head to her toes and filled her with gratitude. "Whatever the reason I had for stepping down from AMG is in the past now. Besides, I bet you had your decision made before you walked into the boardroom."

Shane played with the hem of her red cape as a smile appeared on her face. He knew her so well. "I did."

The silence seemed to pull her in. It was comfortable and assuring.

"Congratulations, Shane."

"Thank you. You were right; I need to find myself. She's in here."

His breath hitched. It must have registered that she'd heard his final words the night before. A few long moments passed before he continued. "Where will you go?"

"I don't know."

"Wherever it is, you will do well. I'm proud of you."

"Jacob?"

"Yes?"

"Will you think of me?" Would he be there if she needed him?

His voice came through soft and anxious. "Live your life, Shane. For you. Trust your decisions and..." He breathed out. "Everything else will fall into place."

DING.

Shane shuffled down the hallway, pulling her keys along with her phone from her purse. She stopped in front of her door and clicked the link embedded in a message from David. A celebrity gossip site opened with a picture of Gavin. His hands blocked the cameras as he left the Omega Records building. A red banner flashed "Breaking News".

Gavin Mayne Leaving Omega Records. Source Claims He Is The Man Behind The Mask! Shane Vaughn Is One Lucky Lady! Who Wouldn't Want To Be Manhandled By Him?

She dialed David's number as she jammed her key into the lock and opened the door.

"Doll face!" he yelled.

"Nice job on the press release." She rolled her eyes.

"Thanks. The source was heard to be fabulous."

"Very true. But I said to out him, not revere him."

"Celeb Deb does believe in keeping it light and upbeat with a side of sex appeal," he laughed.

"And now he's officially the most sought-after male in New York," she groaned.

"Eh, what does it matter now anyway? Even though he's a scumbag, he did rock your world."

She cringed. "Ick. I'll never live down that you've seen me having sex."

"If it's any consolation, straight sex doesn't do it for me. But you, my doll…" He whistled.

"Ew, please, stop."

"It's true. So you sound good, all things considered. How did it go? Do we get to make an appearance at work next week?"

She closed the door. "Not exactly."

"What do you mean?"

"Pack a bag for somewhere warm. We're leaving in the morning."

"Really? Where?"

"It's a surprise. Tell Sean to come too. He should be off tour for the holidays, right?"

"Yes." She could hear him opening and closing drawers. "What do you think about those new Bermuda shorts I bought?" he asked absent-mindedly as if he held them in front of him.

"I think those will work." She tossed her purse on the island.

"How long will we be gone?"

She removed two sets of round trip airline tickets along with a third one-way ticket. She breathed out. "A while."

Her phone beeped.

"Hey, I gotta take this, I will fill you in when I pick you up tomorrow."

"Sure thing, doll!"

She sauntered over to the massive windows overlooking her city. The light of the moon peeked through a thin layer of clouds, presenting optimism and promise for what lay ahead. She tapped the screen switching the call to incoming.

"Anna Marie? Hi! I'm coming for you, girl."

28

ONE YEAR LATER

JACOB LEANED on the brass rails of the elevator, and as it ascended, his thumb flicked through his texts.

S: Can you believe this!?

A picture message displayed of Shane and Anna Marie on an empty stage making duck faces at the camera, the O2 arena behind them. Shane had taken Anna Marie to global status in no time. He and Shane had talked occasionally over the last year, and his heart swelled, watching her take a leap of faith and follow her own dreams.

Their discussions never revolved around their past relationship or her asking him for advice. She was free, and they only shared the wonderful things they'd experienced as two single people. He was so proud of her.

J: Yes, I can. Looks amazing!

"Liza, did you get the packages that came today?" Jacob asked, exiting the elevator. Boxes were stacked three high on her new desk, and the reception area remained covered with furniture still spun in plastic. He'd moved his new promotions company from his apartment to a small office space in downtown Austin, Texas.

"Yep." The plastic bubble wrap squeaked as she unwrapped its contents. "Do you miss this?" She held his *Achievement in Rock* award from some music foundation. He grabbed it and smoothed a thumb over the glass award.

"No. It was never the same after."

Jacob couldn't pretend to be an award-winning CEO after paying off Gavin. However, leaving AMG was the best decision he'd ever made.

"Get rid of this." The glass award thudded on the desktop as he set it down. Success did not exist in a cold shelf ornament. He only strived for happiness, and with the Austin sunshine and new space, he was off to a good start. "Do you miss it?"

She busied herself. "Not really. I mean Austin isn't a place I would have chosen to live, but my husband and the kids seem to like it.

"I appreciate you coming along."

A smile widened on her face. "You were the best boss I ever had, and making an offer I couldn't refuse helped."

Having Liza around made the move to Austin a bit more bearable. He looked out of the small window. It wasn't much. No views and no visible sunsets, like at AMG. Just another building across the street where he could see the people of Austin working hard. It kept him going and distracted him from the hole in his heart. Even with every conversation with Shane, his heart ached to tell her he still loved her, even though he was sure she knew. But it was for the best.

He touched the silver knob on the door to his office. "Oh, wait." He spun to find Liza's hands in the air, searching her desk excitedly. "There's one more thing."

Her blue eyes twinkled when she handed him a white plastic mailer from her bottom drawer. He took the package from her outstretched arms. No address or shipping label.

"What is it?"

She handed him a pair of scissors from her pencil holder. "Here."

The scissors sliced the plastic easily. He slid out a worn and rumpled t-shirt with a faded silkscreen image of his favorite band, The Ramones. The scent of wildflowers hit his nose, and a ripple of pleasure ran from head to toe. Warmth flooded his chest, and his heart skipped a few beats.

Shane.

"Is she...?" Liza grinned while motioning to the door. "Thanks."

Shane was just beyond his door. He exhaled as he stepped through the threshold, gripping the t-shirt in his hand.

"Some office, Andrews. A little small don't you think?" Sitting in his office chair, Shane spun around behind his corner desk. "And what a terrible view."

Lovely.

Her hair was darker and off her shoulders, chopped at an angle. Her blunt bangs framed her face, and a deep blue shift dress allowed her bright blue eyes to shine. She stood tall from her seated position, her full, red lips pursed in a hidden smile.

"Hi. Thanks for this." He held up his hand.

"It was your favorite." She took it. "I can see the appeal."

"You did have it all this time."

"Yeah, well...it was time it found its rightful owner." She set it on the desk and stared at it. "I thought you could use a foundation for where you're headed. You were happiest in this shirt," she joked.

"I-I thought you were in London."

She shrugged coyly. "Anna Marie's tour wrapped up last night. I jumped the red eye."

"Why?"

"I couldn't miss the grand opening of your new promotions

company. Without your help, Anna Marie wouldn't be a house-hold name."

He chuckled. She'd asked for his services to help propel Anna Marie's career and her decisions to call the shots turned him on. She'd been a ball buster, never giving him an inch.

"Anything for my best customer." They stared at each other, the heat growing between them. Somehow, after everything they'd been through, it never faded. "Can I get you something to drink?" He needed to do something or he would lose himself in front of her. He strode to the mini fridge.

"No. I'm good."

He closed the fridge and rejoined her. "Here, please sit." He motioned to the couch still wrapped in plastic covers.

"Jacob. Stop. Can we talk?"

"Yeah. I'm sorry. So how was the tour?" As his knees weakened, he sat in a visitor's chair.

"Good. But I couldn't stay away any longer."

What did she mean? His brain went into a tailspin. His hands shook as he ran his fingers through his hair.

She sat next to him. "Jacob."

"Huh," he muttered. *Pathetic*.

"Look at me." He could hear the smile in her voice at his anxious state. "Thank you for everything. I've never been this happy."

He swallowed. "Don't thank me. It was your doing."

She glanced at the floor and blushed. "Perhaps. But there is still something missing."

"What?"

Her blue eyes glistened when she met his gaze. "You."

A flutter took over his heart. "Oh, Shane. I didn't do all this so you would come back. I meant what I said about you living your life."

"I know. And I am. But I've made another decision. One

based on trusting myself and, therefore, allowing myself to trust someone else."

His shirt suddenly felt too tight as his chest expanded. Was this right to pursue? She looked different. Sounded different. Hell, she *was* different. And what he wouldn't give to taste her "different" and be with her as the strong woman before him. She was still Shane to the core, except now…she owned it. Believed it.

"When you left your job, I thought, *What a stupid ass! Jacob has everything he's ever wanted; why leave it behind?* And you did it for me." She pointed to her chest. "*For me.* And no one has *ever* done something like that. All this time, I've tried to let the thought go. Clarity and pursuing something different was my focus. But it kept coming back. And I couldn't wait to share all my accomplishments with you. Does that make sense?"

His mouth opened, but no words escaped.

"Tell me why you did it."

His body shook as a compulsion to be honest took over. He knelt in front of her and cupped her hands. A quivering lip and gasp escaped her. "Because, Lovely, I had to submit my world to you and lay it at your feet. The life your beautiful, selfless heart created for us. Our entire relationship, you always put me first." He wiped her tears and his throat constricted. "My God, Shane, I really fucked us up. I'm so sorry."

She touched his face, fingers stroking his beard. A calm tide rippled through his body, all apprehension leaving him. Their eyes flicked back and forth, conveying an understanding of the lifetime their love had spanned.

"Thank you."

She leaned forward and kissed him. The kiss leveled him. Her warm lips and tongue flew his heart to the heavens.

He broke away. "Shane, stop. This isn't right. It's not what I—"

"Do you still love me, Jake?" Her speaking his name rippled over his skin. Her fingertips ran aimlessly through his hair.

"I never stopped. No matter how hard I try."

"I can't either."

His forehead met hers as he gripped her nape. Tears tracked his cheeks. "Is this what you want, Shane? Are you deciding to be with me without influence?" Regret filled his heavy chest. "I didn't mean to sway you by keeping in touch…"

"Hey, you did nothing wrong. I'm the one always calling you." She smiled. "And you listened, cheered me on, and never once told me how to run my business. Instead you took orders from me."

He pulled back and smirked. "I did, didn't I?"

"Yep. It was an interesting role reversal."

"Perhaps." He trailed his fingertips along the outline of her face. His heart tugged in two different directions. Desire pushed him forward, yet concern stopped him in his tracks. Starting over meant doing it different this time. "Maybe we can talk about things over dinner."

"Are you asking me on a date?" Her smile crooked up on the side.

"You could call it that. I've never taken you on a real date before."

Their fingers linked as the flame simmered between them. "Sure you did, at Billy's restaurant."

"The way I remember it, we did a shot of tequila and screwed in the bathroom. We rushed it the first time. Let's take it slow, Shane." He kissed her lips and moved down her jaw.

She swallowed. "Yeah, slow. That sounds…good."

His erection pushed on his slacks when she shivered as his lips met the spot where her neck met shoulder. They'd never start over the right way if he kept this up. "Where are you staying?"

"The hotel down the street."

He reluctantly rose and helped her stand. "Seven o'clock, my Lovely. I will come by to get you."

SHANE TUGGED AT HER BLACK, form-fitting wrap dress as she stepped into the hotel lobby. A tingle swept her skin, curling her toes in her black pumps. A first date and it felt right.

When she rounded the corner, there he stood. Her Jacob. One hand in his black suit pocket, white shirt, opened at the collar, and long trench. His smile widened as she approached. Taking the wrap from her arm, he covered her.

"You look beautiful, Shane."

She blushed. "Not too bad yourself."

He ushered her outside, and the slight winter chill couldn't extinguish the heat on her skin. A year made such a difference. She'd never thought she would be here with him. What he'd done would have been deemed unforgiveable, but what he'd sacrificed forced her to consider it.

She'd hired him to manage the promotional campaign in hopes she could rebuild their relationship. But he never made an advance. Only helped on her terms. It spoke volumes.

As they strolled down the block, she curled a hand in the crook of his elbow. "Where are we headed?"

"You'll see." His warm hand covered hers.

A few blocks and he guided her into a hotel restaurant.

"Jacob Andrews. Long time no see." The man greeted him with a handshake. Tall with a buzz cut and kind brown eyes. A t-shirt with the hotel logo of a "G" under a sport coat.

"Billy, you remember Shane."

"Of course."

Her eyes widened, and she smiled, giving him a hug. "Wow, it's been forever. What are you doing here?"

"I own this joint. Come on."

"What are you up to?" she mouthed to Jacob as they followed Billy.

"You'll see."

She approached the empty wooden bar top and sat on the stool.

"Is this place even open?" Glassware still in boxes was stacked behind the wooden bar. The dining room was empty, except for a few people setting tables.

Billy went behind the bar and poured two shots of Patrón. Setting them on a napkin, he pushed them forward. "Not yet. But Andrews has a way, as I'm sure you know."

"That he does." If her heart swelled any larger, it would burst. She crooked a thumb in Billy's direction as he disappeared into the kitchen. "Billy?"

Jacob sat next to her and raised a shot. "It was an opportunity to recreate our first "non-date" date."

She clinked her glass. "You said, slow."

They swallowed the alcohol, and it warmed her. "And I plan to, even though you are making it incredibly hard in that dress." His green eyes raked over her. Butterflies danced in her belly.

Billy returned with smoking fajitas. The spicy scent filled the space.

"Even our first meal?"

"This time, we should try it."

A bottle of wine and several hours later, Jacob walked her back to her hotel. A sense of wholeness overcame her. She had missed his conversation and company as they walked a new path together. Hand-in-hand, she felt as though they would always walk beside one another, through whatever life handed them.

"Much different than the first time."

He kissed her hand. "Everything will be different this time, Shane."

Once outside her hotel room, she said, "This is me."

She turned and leaned on the door. He stood with his hands in his pockets. "Want to come in?"

"Badly. But not tonight."

"Maybe just a kiss?"

"Thought you'd never ask." His warm hand cupped her jaw as his thumb stroked her cheek. The air thickened around them. His lips slanted over hers slowly. Gently. Her toes curled in her pumps as her sex clenched with desire. She gripped his biceps and opened fully. He took his time, feeling it all. Licking every corner of her mouth. Just like she remembered the first time he kissed her all those years ago.

She lifted her leg around his hip and he held it, rubbing his pant-clad erection along her cleft. They panted in unison as the kiss came to life, desire and love filling them.

He broke away. "Slow, Lovely."

She whimpered, setting her foot on the floor. "Right, slow." His eyes raked over her face. "Good night."

He kissed her again. "Good night."

She fumbled with the keycard against the lock until it snapped open. After entering the room, she clicked the door behind her. It cooled her back as she supported herself on shaking legs. A thud sounded on the other side. "You okay?"

"Yep. Just catching myself." He chuckled, the deep timbre muffled through the door. *Couldn't agree more.*

29

SEVERAL DATES and a few months later, and Jacob was kissing her on the couch of his apartment. She felt alive and fucking hot all over. They hadn't done anything more, and every time they went out, a heavy make-out session ensued, leaving her feeling bereft and wanting more.

Had she ever made out with him like this? And he never took them further, even though she wanted him to. He'd simply whisper, *"Until next time,"* leaving them both panting and yearning to take the leap.

But she loved it. Each time they were together, their trust grew to depths she didn't know existed. Learning things about each other they'd previously missed. A deeper appreciation, respect, and love bloomed stronger.

She kissed him madly, straddling his hips. His taste, his fingers in her hair, his lips on her neck. She gyrated on his erection. Wetness soaked her panties. She couldn't wait anymore.

"Jacob, it's time. Please."

"Not yet, Lovely. I've thoroughly enjoyed making out with you." He plumped her breast in his hand, her nipples pushing against the silk shirt.

"And it's wonderful, but I need you."

"Me too, but I want to make sure this is right."

She backed away. "You don't think it is yet?"

A deep rumble came from him and clenched her pussy. A boyish smile crooked his mouth. "I do. But I want to make sure you do."

Her hands went to her hips. "Can't you tell?"

"I can, but can you?" His fingers traced the curve of her breast over her shirt in torturous glides. The smirk on his face wicked with the promise of anything she asked.

Her nimble fingers slowly pushed the buttons through the holes of his green shirt, her favorite one with his chocolate brown suit. "No decision I've ever made felt so right." She split the panels of the shirt open and smoothed her fingers along his chest and each curve of his abs. His abdomen flexed, and he breathed harder.

"Tell me what's going on in your pretty head. Tell me what you want."

"I love that we waited this long. But I'm ready close on this deal." The buckle of his belt jingled as she opened it. His green eyes held lust and love. He didn't stop her.

"Oh, yeah? What are the terms?"

She stood and shimmied out of her skirt and panties. "Well, Mr. Andrews…" She tugged his pants from his tight ass, and he kicked them off. His dick was hard and ready. He spread his arms lengthwise on the seat back. All sprawled and gorgeous with his green shirt opened and his bare chest rising and falling with need.

"You promise to never lie to me."

She straddled him, removing her shirt and bra. His eyes never left hers. "I promise."

"You promise to always put me first as I will do for you."

"Always." He rolled a nipple between his fingers. She nearly went over.

"You...promise to love me every day...forever." She lifted over him and positioned his cock at her wet opening.

"I promise. Every single day."

She slid down his length, and they both hissed at the sensation. "My Shane. So fucking amazing. Deeper. Take all of me. I want to feel all of you."

"I love you, Jake." She slid up and down until she hit the base of his cock. Then again. His hips moved with her as they rolled into each thrust. Slow and deliberate. She wanted to feel each part of him inside her. His green eyes glowed like fire. Hands gripped her hips, guiding her.

"I love you. Kiss me." Leaning forward, she took his mouth and licked the inside, touching every single part.

A moan sent shivers through her. It was perfect. This was perfect. She leaned back and braced herself with her hands on his knees. Pushing forward and back, a tidal wave of heat swept them to another place.

His hands soothed from her face to her chest and then her abdomen. His thumb landed on her clit, swirling gently.

"Shane, I've missed this. You...so beautiful..." His head went back on the couch, his eyes rolling back in pleasure. A prominent vein protruded from his neck. He hung by a thread. She controlled it. She owned him. He was hers. She increased speed, groaning with each circle of his thumb.

"Jake. Tell me this is forever, please."

"Until the day I die, Shane. It will always be us. God, when you ride me...*fuck*."

His cock swelled inside her and the light behind her eyes brightened. Her heart hammered in her chest as her breathing quickened. Spicy cologne and arousal filled her with want. She was taking them to the top. The room blurred. The universe spun. And they were the only two people in existence.

"I coming…" She grunted. Muscles contracted and her breathing ceased.

In one quick move, she was on her back. "Hold on."

She gripped his back and felt his muscles tense. His hips moved swiftly as wave after wave carried her into the clouds.

He looked into her eyes. "You're mine, forever."

"Always, Jake."

He jerked forward and hot semen filled her. His mouth found hers, and they kissed until her lips were swollen and sore. She didn't want him to stop, but he pulled away and brushed the hair from her eyes.

"Thank you for giving me another chance to love you."

"Thank you for letting me find myself to know I should."

EPILOGUE

SIX MONTHS LATER...

Jacob's warm body spooned behind Shane. His hand stroked down her side as he kissed her neck. She blinked, adjusting to the darkness of their bedroom. They'd spent the weekend combining their things and unpacking in a small, quaint apartment in the heart of Austin. She was finally home.

"Good morning." She smiled.

"Like every morning with you."

She turned, and her lips met his inviting mouth. Dawn was barely breaking through the curtained windows "What time is it?"

"Almost time to get up."

"*Almost* time?" She glanced at the clock on the nightstand. "I still have an hour."

"A much needed hour with me." His lips skirted down her neck to the spot holding all her desire. He nibbled it, and the warmth in her blood surged.

"I'm so tired..."

"Then lie still. I'll take care of you." He bit her nipple over her thin tank top.

"God...you are insatiable..."

"Making up for lost time." He raised his head and smiled. She stroked his face, running through the soft whiskers of his beard as he leaned into her hand.

Since reuniting with the love of her life, Shane welcomed any moment they had to 'make up for lost time.' But she saw it differently. A chance at creating a relationship filled with respect and unconditional love. Jacob had proven he was worth it, just as she believed in herself. They had trust as a solid foundation for a better life together.

"I have an idea. Let's cancel our meeting and tell Purple… whatever…they're in." His lips brushed her neck, and his smile against her skin rippled through her.

They had a meeting to vet a new rock band for their blossoming music company. They'd mutually decided to combine their efforts to make a powerhouse one-stop-shop for musicians. Promotions and management. Shane as CEO and Jacob as Vice President. He'd insisted, of course, that she run the business, even though labels no longer held importance. They attacked every meeting, prospect, and operational matter together. As a team. It was pure magic.

"Purple Kilts, and can you convince them to change their name to something more appealing?" He laughed.

"That's your department."

"I'll have marketing gather some ideas."

Her body went limp. Work flooding her mind. "We should go in," she groaned.

Warm lips slithered down her flesh to her hips. "Whatever you want, Shane. If we don't, David will be upset. He's been dying to meet the drummer."

She laughed. "Yeah, he would be. What does he say…? Something about browsing the menu but not ordering?"

"Something like that."

She scrunched her lips to the side. "We are king and queen of the industry now, and we can take the day, right?"

He positioned his body between her thighs, his chin on her abdomen. "We've been non-stop for a while. Couldn't hurt."

"You sound pretty confident."

He kissed her belly, and flickers of delicious tension rolled through her. He moved the waistband of her panties down and kissed lower. "If the boss says it's a hooky day…" *Kiss.* "I'm sure I can find something to fill the time." He shifted the crotch of her panties aside and licked her folds. The friction of his tongue rumbled her desire senseless.

"Consider it…*right there, Jake*…a reward for all your hard work…" She moaned and tilted her head to the ceiling.

He popped his head up from her thighs. "A reward for me? No, Lovely. I run the bedroom. It was in our gentleman's handshake, remember? This is *your* reward for how proud I am of you." The heat and wetness from his mouth closed over her pussy. Goosebumps ran along her skin. His accolades for her success—their success—were a major turn on.

"Oh…right…shit, I'm coming." She bit her lip as he brought her to orgasm in no time. Muscles clenched as she rode the wave. Shoptalk mixed with pleasure always did it for her. "God, I love you so much."

A quick kiss on her swollen tissues and then he climbed her body. "I love you too." A sheen of arousal coated his lips, and her mouth captured them. A tangy taste followed by his tongue awakened her fully. His warm embrace enveloped her body.

"We'll never get out of bed if you keep this up."

Her sex cradled his erection separated by thin layers of fabric. "I thought you said it was a team building day to strategize our next conquest while making sweet love." He grinned a white smile.

"We should go. At least until we meet this new band." She let her head hit the pillow. Work life slowly crept in, dampening her pleasure from moments ago.

His forehead hit her chest. "Fine."

She chuckled, rubbing his back. "I promise, I'm all yours after that."

"Or we could blend the two. Make the day more interesting." Eyebrows waggled, sending another jolt to her sex.

"Oh, no. I can't have you dominating my thoughts."

Green eyes flashed mischief. "We'll see…"

She ran her fingers through his hair. Even though she led the business, he still owned her in the bedroom. A true balance of power. His eyes softened as he pierced through the veil of corporate domination. It melted her to the core, her heart filling to capacity.

"But there is one thing, though," he said.

"What?"

"The king and queen thing needs to be addressed."

She snorted. "Don't tell me you're trying to take over at the office."

"I wouldn't think of it. You're too damn sexy when you order your staff. Including me." The morning chill ran rapidly over her flesh when he leaned over the edge of the bed. The nightstand drawer sounded with an easy slide, and when he returned, a black velvet box was in his hand. He knelt above her.

"Wh-wh—" She scooted to rest along the headboard, her heart lurching in her throat.

"A queen needs a ring, right?" The box creaked open and a large Asscher cut diamond glimmered in the fresh dawn of morning. The solitaire sat high in filigree swirls around the shoulder of the ring.

She cupped her mouth. "Jake. What is that?"

"Something I should have given you a long time ago." He removed the ring. "Shane, will you be my queen in the boardroom and my wife outside of it?"

Her eyes flooded with tears. It was hard to breathe through the elation filling her chest. Never had a decision to get her to this place been this perfect. "Yes. Yes."

He slipped the ring on her finger, and she leapt on top of him. They crashed to the mattress, and she showered him with kisses. His warm laughter filled the room and her bones with love.

"Jesus, Jacob!" Her shaking hand went out to view the ring. "How long have you had this?"

He kissed it. "Forever. But this is the right time to give it to you." He kissed her smiling lips. "Everything's changed. All of it, Shane. This is our time. This is our future. I wouldn't change a thing about where we are. What got us here. What you've become. I love you so much, and I will never let you get away again."

Her hands wrapped around his neck. "It's perfect, Jake. Thank you. I love it and you."

"I love you, Shane. Forever."

She pulled away. "Promise?"

"I promise." A smoldering kiss landed on her mouth and took them into another realm of love, respect, and desire.

Screw work. It could wait.

ACKNOWLEDGMENTS

Writing a book takes an army and there is no one person that can make it a success. A book's success lies within all the people an author interacts with. Putting words on the page is only the first step. I am honored to be surrounded by people who brighten my day, help me through the stress, and the ones who put the time into making this book sing.

Laura: Your support goes well beyond these pages. You are my rock and my cheerleader. I love you!

Rachael: Your kindness, love, and tenacity are in these characters.

Brielle: We shall forever live on smutty island drinking bourbon and reading about hot book boyfriends. And Gavin would not have a name without your suggestion. Yum!

Rob: The "real life David". How in the world did I find you? You are "David", my sidekick, my boo. Thank you for being you all the way to the core. Your honesty, friendship, and laughter make life worth living.

Sara: Your excitement for a rough draft exceed the bounds of my creativity, pushing me to raise the bar!

Amanda: Your support from day one until infinity will never be matched. You were the first, my love. I will never forget it.

Piper: I would have never found the HEA with Shane and Jacob if not for our awesome brain storming sessions! They are thrilled you helped me cut through the stress and just allow them to find each other...again. Forever this time. <3

Tina: Your enthusiasm and support on an unknown chick (at the time we met) summoned the words every time you emailed me: "More chapters!"

Saya: I don't have enough white pages to write what you mean to me. This story bloomed because of your artful editing, your tough criticism, and your wise follow through. Shane, Jacob, and Gavin are grateful.

Mom: Thank you for teaching me the value and importance of being a *strong* woman that can land on her feet no matter the obstacle. Shane lives within you and ALL women.

Annette: Without you and the guidance from my mom, I would have never been able to feel the true meaning of success and cherish the bond of womanly love.

Maryann (MIL): Your enthusiasm, support, and unconditional love made this book possible. And, of course, your amazing chocolate chip cookies that comforted me through the hard times and your wonderful voice of encouragement to help me overcome the fears of putting this book out. Love you!

My family and friends: Thank you for putting up with my disappearing act and angst over this book. Your patience and long talks on the phone made me never give up!

Emma, Robin, and MPP: Whoa. I have no words. You opened your hearts and wisdom to someone who fell in love with your books (and art...and hysterical online commentary) and took me in with no question. Without the 'entourage' (and Jonah *swoon*), I would still be lost. Thank you for sharing your universe. <3

The ladies of the TRRW: This is only the beginning and through your advice, business smarts, and intellect, I shall one day soar with you.

And to my fellow authors, bloggers, readers, and online friends: You changed my world and helped me see the big picture to happiness and life. Your encouragement, your laughs, and your support mean everything to a gal just starting out. Cheers to your successes and always remember: Love is Power.

ABOUT THE AUTHOR

Nicky's emotionally rich, vibrant stories are set in cities that thrum with energy. Her heroines come up against personal and professional challenges, and are pushed to break new ground and become better versions of themselves. Nicky gives her characters just the right amount of conflict to create a satisfying push and pull, one that keeps her readers up late at night, wanting to know what happens next.

As a writer, Nicky imbues each of her stories with equal parts love and lust, which she believes are among the strongest emotions we can experience. By immersing her readers into worlds of power and erotic passion, she invites them to explore their own unspoken desires. Her hope is that her stories embolden her readers to realize their fullest potential — be it in the boardroom, the bedroom, or anywhere in between.

facebook.com/nickyfgrant

twitter.com/nickyfgrant

instagram.com/nickyfgrant

27541230R00207

Made in the USA
Columbia, SC
29 September 2018